A Tale Twice Told

A Tale Twice Told

Mark Warren

SPEAKING VOLUMES, LLC
NAPLES, FLORIDA
2022

A Tale Twice Told

ISBN 978-1-64540-836-9

In memory of Robert Henshaw, of Nottinghamshire, England, who graciously guided me to the little-known secrets of Sherwood Forest.

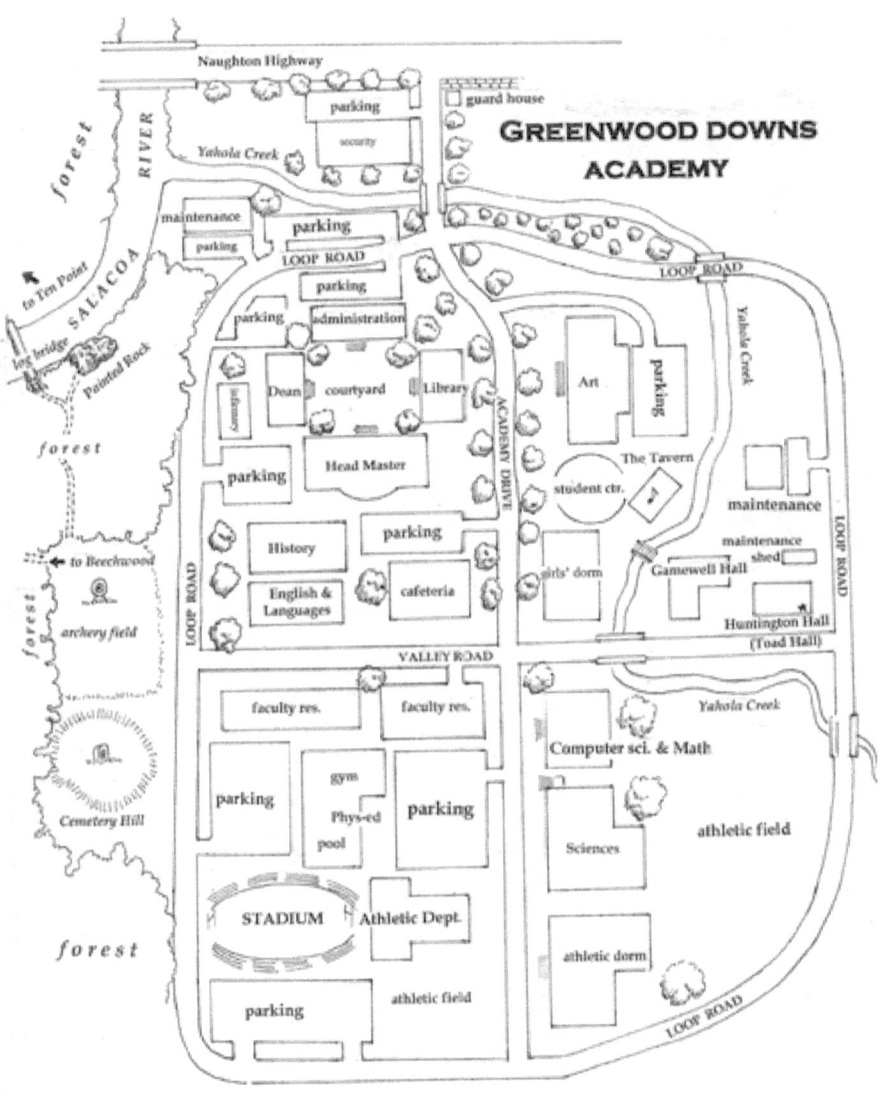

PART ONE

The Archer

Chapter One

They were the only things standing in the open field—the archer and the target—each unmoving, legs spread, facing the other as if something of consequence might be decided here on the outskirts of the high school campus. Cool air poured into the field from the dark woods. The first colors of autumn had arrived. Near the forest's edge the nodding golden-rods bobbed and burned butter-yellow. When the wind died they stilled like candles in an empty room.

Loading his last arrow, Robert Asherwood looked behind him at Cemetery Hill and its giant oaks. He did not know what made him turn, but it surprised him when he saw someone standing on the hill, looking back at him.

Trying to purge the onlooker from his mind, Ash took in a deep breath and pushed it out in a rush. Turning back to the target, he tried to concentrate on the shot, but his mind swirled with the distraction of an unwanted audience.

After a day of classes at Greenwood Downs Academy, this aban-doned field was a haven where he could step into himself, like a spirit reoccupying its dormant body to revive what he was at his center—an archer. Above all else, this was the one thing that he understood about himself, and so he held it private and dear. Now with these unexpected eyes imposing on his territory, he felt off-balance and exposed, as if a giant bell jar had been lowered over him and set down on the grass.

He closed his eyes. The quiet here was like the bottom of a lake, and it was quieter still for the sounds that came to him from a distance. A grounds-maintenance lawnmower purred from somewhere on campus.

From the football practice field a sudden husky cheer of male voices erupted and floated up to him, riding upon its own echo.

Focus, he told himself. From twenty yards he had sunk six arrows into the saucer-sized gold center, and only one arrow remained to complete a perfect round.

Rocking from leg to leg, he took his stance. *Relax . . . breathe . . . focus*. Using this mantra he glared at the target and tried to will the rest of the world into a blur. But it was hopeless. Though he fought the urge, he turned to check the hill again. The silhouette was still there, unchanged under the oaks, standing in relief against the same trapezoidal background of milk-gray sky.

But now he was not so certain. Was it someone? Or a fallen limb? Or one of the taller gravestones? When he turned back to the target, he felt those eyes press into the back of his skull like two stiff fingers.

Relax . . . breathe . . . focus. He raised the bow, pushing gracefully into the handle with the heel of his left hand, drawing the string with his right, listening to the slow slide of the arrow against wood as if the bow were inhaling for its task.

The process of aiming was like a swirling of stars in his mind's eye, an abstraction that suddenly locked into place by some unnamed law of universal alignment. The one true trajectory. When the stars fell into place, his fingers relaxed on the string with the feathery abandon he had somehow learned by himself. The whip of the bow was sudden, but his part in the release was delicate . . . like wet newspaper tearing silently along the crease of its fold.

The arrow sailed the one perfect path, seeming to set a course by its own volition. A predatory bird certain of its kill. Then came the sweet dull *thump* from the target's gold center, so many times riddled with holes that the target face no longer "smacked" a report. Still staring at the target, Ash held the pose for a few seconds, lowered the bow, and nodded once, as if confirming his place in the world.

Seven arrows jutted from the gold, their bright red feathers clustered like roses squeezed into a slender vase. A warm mercury of completeness rose up his spine. He stood very still, letting the tight group of arrows define him, transcend him . . . perhaps the way an artist steps back to see a final stroke that breathes life into his painting.

He walked to the target and pulled out his arrows, keeping his back to the hill as he looked west toward the vast forest that had beckoned him all day. Without this woodland, Ash could not have lasted two days here—let alone two years. And now a third—his last and senior year. Greenwood Downs Academy's class of 2000.

He looked for the glow of the sun to approximate the time, but the overcast sky was darkening to a portentous black. A blue cast fell over the field, and the smell of rain was in the air. No sooner had he lifted the plastic cover over the target and weighted its corners with four rocks, than a raindrop spattered off the tarp.

Pulling up the hood of his sweatshirt he frowned at the old woven-hay target. For two consecutive days he had found it uncovered upon arriving on the field. If he had not come here this afternoon, the target would have become sodden and on its way to ruin. The wind had not been the culprit. The wind did not fold a tarpaulin into a neat square and stack rocks upon it.

Thunder rumbled across the sky, heavy and resonant, like boulders rolling down a wooden hallway. Now raindrops tapped the plastic steadily and kissed his upturned face. Behind Cemetery Hill the sky brightened to an eerie bone-yellow, sharpening the dome of trees like a scene snipped out of black tin. When the wind roared in above him, the giant oaks on the hill came alive, thrashing their limbs. Then the rain came in curtains. That was when he thought he saw the figure push away

4

from the tree. He squinted but the rain surged and blurred everything to gray.

Hunch-shouldered against the downpour, Ash jogged toward Valley Road, stopping just inside the strip of pine saplings that separated his field from the campus proper. Rain hammered the ground around him. From where he stood it was impossible to see the graveyard. As he stared at the trail that led up the hill, a cold rivulet of water snaked between his shoulder blades, making him shiver. The reflex was like a kick-start. Before he knew he would do it, he bolted up the path for the crest of the hill.

Standing among the oaks and headstones, he found nothing to explain what he had seen from below. There was only the permanence of the cemetery and the rain rattling down through the leaves. He walked to the place where he thought he had seen someone standing, but the rain had matted the ground cover. There was no sign to convince him that anyone had stood there. He leaned, tilting his head, trying to substitute some surrogate figure that might have tricked his eye. There was none. The rain came on harder, hitting the leaves above him with a shattering sound.

He walked back down the trail and stood looking out at the field from the pines. The rain laid siege to the land, and he was soaked to the skin. Slogging out to the place where he had shot, he peered back at the hill between the sheets of rain and studied the spaces between the trees. Then he found it. The trapezoid was barely backlit for any contrast, but he could see that it was empty.

Lightning split the sky, quickly followed by an angry rumble of thunder. He sloshed off the field and walked down the darkly glistening road toward his dorm.

Chapter Two

On the following morning Ash ate breakfast by the cafeteria's ceiling-high windows. Alone at a table he ran through his biology notes, gazing frequently through the glass at the colors sweeping across the mountains like a wildfire spreading out of control. Overnight the change had been dramatic. The black gums and sourwoods had gone blood scarlet. The maples lent softer splashes of pastels. Already he planned to return to his forest after classes today.

When he left for first period, the dawn chill still clung to the morning, and this turning of the season was like an elixir to his soul. He could swallow whatever the school threw at him, he believed, with the autumn woods waiting for him in the afternoon.

Entering the biology auditorium, his lifted spirit evaporated. Hesitating just inside the door, he watched his teacher sort through notes at the podium. From that distance, Dr. Leonhardt might pass for the quintessential quirky professor with his unkempt white hair and the crooked knot of his necktie, but when Ash passed beneath the stage, the illusion dissolved. Beneath the old man's bushy eyebrows burned the brooding glare that meant he was marshaling tolerance for the hour's lecture. Then when the second-bell rang, Dr. Leonhardt cast cold eyes on his audience. He was set for battle.

Leonhardt launched into a hit-the-ground-running continuation of his lectures on chromosomal duplication. Like everyone else, Ash was ready this time, and the cavernous room filled with the scratching of forty pens trying to keep up. Leonhardt showed no mercy.

Halfway into the hour something changed. It was subtle, but Ash paused in his writing to watch the old man's movements at the drawing board. Absorbed in his work, the aging professor dropped his crusty demeanor and slipped into what seemed academic rapture. A hint of affection crept into his voice. Ash noted the old man's head swaying with the rhythm of his writing, like a grandfather relating a tale from his youth. Then, turning back to the class, Dr. Leonhardt seemed to awaken to the reality of his audience. His eyebrows lowered and shadowed his eyes, and he resumed the lesson in a monotone that could numb the sharpest of nerve endings.

It did not matter how convoluted the lecture might be delivered, Ash knew that no hands would be raised. In those first days when questions had been asked—and few students had dared them—Leonhardt had chosen from one of three responses that comprised his repertoire. One: He ignored what he considered an inane query. Two: If a question touched on some point previously explained in his lecture, he offered a dispassionate referral: "Why don't you consult—" Then he would point to anyone hunched over a desk still writing. Three: When he deemed a rare question worthy of his time, he threw out a challenge: "Ah, yes! Research that and share with us tomorrow."

Ash had once posed such an "ah-yes" question. The next day when Leonhardt called on him to report, Ash did and felt his research had been a contribution. Leonhardt did not acknowledge it. This rudeness and the snide glances from the students prompted Ash to continue his researches but to keep his questions and answers to himself. In two weeks' time Dr. Leonhardt had achieved a vocal paralysis of the entire class.

The hour came to its typical end. Before the bell could unleash its Pavlovian effect of books slapping shut and shoes scuffing the floor, Leonhardt, with precision timing, glanced at his watch, picked up his notebook, and walked offstage. After the door closed, before any student dared to escape, a voice boomed from the back of the auditorium.

"Tune in tomorrow for the exciting conclusion of . . . *chromosomes gettin' it on!*"

A sea of smiling faces turned to the jock section in back, but before anyone could laugh, a deep counter-challenge rang out from the other side of the room. "Hey! The man can't help it!" It was yelled so forcefully that everyone froze.

Ash leaned in his seat to see who would want to defend Leonhardt. With the class poised to see where this would go, the second speaker continued in an edifying tone.

"Man, when those stewed prunes kick in, a man's gotta do what a—"

The roar of laughter drowned out the last words and made the clatter of the bell barely audible. Everyone left laughing, claiming a piece of the small revolution that had just been born. As Ash joined the crowd drifting toward the door, a thin voice at his shoulder cut through the din.

"I don't buy the prunes theory."

Ash turned. The boy speaking to him slouched as he shuffled along. Ash had noticed him before—a junior, thin and gangly in a school blazer so rumpled it hung on him like crepe. A stiff cowlick arched from the back of his blond hair like a pale antenna.

His eyes slid to Ash. "Know what I think," the boy murmured without any inflection of a question. "Old *Lee-on-hard* is only a biology teacher on the side. That's not his real job." He pushed his lower lip forward and shook his head. "Here's what I think: Old *Lee-on-hard* is the school's bell ringer." He broke out of his shuffle and pantomimed the lurching step of a hunchback tugging on a rope. "He's up there in his bell tower right now, waiting on second period bell."

Ash said nothing and turned his attention to the door.

"Test tomorrow's gonna rattle some heads," the boy prophesied.

Ash looked back and gave him a sober look.

The boy shrugged. "I had him before. He likes to hit you hard at the start." He scanned the crowd with a smug smile. "These preppies won't know what hit 'em. Next week they'll be changing their pre-majors from biology to tennis." He sniggered. "Gonna be a lot of disappointed daddy-doctors counting on junior to take over the practice."

Together they passed through the door into the still-crisp morning, and Ash picked up his pace. "Hey, you a biology pre-major?" the boy called to his back.

Speeding up, Ash shook his head as a parting gesture. "Nope."

"Well, *there's* some irony. You'll ace the test, man. What are you . . . zoology?"

When the boy matched his speed, Ash shook his head again. "Nope."

"One of the sciences though, right?"

"Nope."

The boy was breathing heavier now, working up a surly glare as he came alongside Ash. "Wow," he deadpanned. "Three 'nopes' in a row." He assumed a studious expression, snapped his fingers twice and bobbed a finger at Ash's face. "Lemme guess. You're in drama and you're doing . . . what . . . Gary Cooper? James Dean?"

Ash kept his face neutral and continued walking. It wasn't the first time someone had approached him about getting some "help" on a test. The boy stayed with him.

"So, how come you voluntarily walk into *Lee-on-hard's* torture chamber if you're not a science pre-major?"

Almost certain where all this was headed, Ash looked him in the eye for a few paces. It was like waiting for the obvious punch line to a bad joke.

"What makes you think I'll ace the test?" Ash said.

The boy cracked a crooked smile. "You'll ace it, man." There was a wry certainty in his voice. He stretched his chin toward Ash. "See you around, man." He quit the pace Ash had set and, with jaded eyes back in place, angled away in his preferred shuffle.

As Ash strode across campus, the conversation stayed with him. He considered it an improvement if the class were to be culled of its do-nothings. Like the jocks in the back rows. In the quieter moments of a lecture, whenever Ash looked back at the top tiers of seats, he was sure to see several athletes heads-down on their desks, each using a forearm as a pillow. If the exam was as bad as the boy predicted, there was no way they could survive it. Maybe then Leonhardt would relax and shed his cold armor—even show some respect to the serious students.

After a tedious hour of Chaucer, a probe into the causes of World War II, an institutional lunch, the mind-numbing blue glow of a computer class, then an hour of charcoal sketching, Ash nestled into the basement of the library with his notebook to re-read every word spoken from Dr. Leonhardt's mouth these past weeks. He redrew all the chromosomal arrangements taken from the board until his mind became an arsenal of genetic information. By the time he left the library, he was looking forward to the test.

With the sun still an hour high over the trees, he stepped onto the field with his bow and was relieved to see Cemetery Hill vacant. The cover was draped neatly over the target. Chromosomes and Dr. Leonhardt drifted to the back of his mind as he prepared for the ritual of the first shot.

On any given day the initial shot was, in Ash's estimation, the true measure of an archer. Anyone could stand at a fixed distance and, with a quiver-full of arrows, eventually work out the problem of trajectory. But centuries ago, he knew, this shot had meant food or clothing or killing an enemy. An impromptu first shot—without benefit of practice—was the one that counted. It determined life or death. Today, he decided, it would symbolize acing tomorrow's biology test.

After uncovering the target, he walked away an arbitrary distance, and drew a shaft from his quiver. "First arrow," he said aloud. He preened each feather with care, then loaded, and drew. Settling his eye over the shaft, he brought the gold circle into crisp focus. The string twanged and the whisper of the arrow had hardly begun, but already he knew the flight to be true. The arrow arced neatly into the gold with a dull *thut!* Lowering the bow he stood very still, feeling the thread of validation pull tight at the center of him. It was enough. This arrow had earned his way into the woods.

Once inside the trees he found the forest dark and cleansing. Cool air lifted from the river, spreading the sharp ferment of decaying wood over the floodplain. He passed Painted Rock—the vandalized slab of sandstone that over the years had been spray-painted into a rainbow of graffiti. Beer cans littered the ground around it.

Last year the school had declared this place off-limits to students, and a new rendezvous point for partyers had emerged on the ridge across the river. It was the old cabin called "Ten Point." Because it was accessed by road, it kept trespassers from his side of the river. For this, he was grateful.

Through the fern beds he followed the river deeper into the forest. Here the Salacoa River was forty feet wide, flanked by tall lacy hemlocks that leaned inward, shading the river inside a tunnel of dark evergreen boughs. The current moved quietly, and he set his feet softly to earth to match this quietness.

Tracks crisscrossed the sand: deer, raccoon, fox, and heron. This invisible company sharpened his vigil, until fifty yards later he was rewarded with the sudden flash of an otter running along a beach, plunging like a thick black spear into the green water. He watched isolated bursts of bubbles mark the animal's progress downstream.

He had seen their tracks and sniffed their musky territorial mounds of leaves dragged from the river bottom, but this was his first sighting of an otter. It pleased him to finally see this phantom, living out its life in the woods, secure in its rightful place in the order of things.

Half a mile upriver he reached his destination—a small grassy plateau that overlooked a sharp bend in the river. The hushed roar of shoals upstream gave this place a heightened sense of being alive. It was like hearing the forest breathe. The water seemed purer there, churning brilliant-white in the deep shadow of evergreens.

Standing sentinel on the raised ground was an aged beech tree of uncommon symmetry. The long-reaching branches spread skyward in a resplendent sunburst of coppery leaves. The tree gathered more light than seemed plausible—like a curved lens—and light rained down through it jewel-like and blinking. Each time he stood beneath it, Ash felt a part of something holy—a baptism of light and the whisper of the river.

He climbed to the terrace and found his old fire ring. In his sophomore and junior years he had camped here a number of times, but now he was ready for a grander plan. His eyes scoured the slope above the plateau. Among the laurel and deerberry his eye composed a forest dwelling and the way he would construct it. Already he knew its name and he tested the sound of it now, offering up the word to the ears of the wild.

"Beechwood," he whispered and felt the project take root in him. This was the year, his last at the school. He would begin construction on the coming weekend, and the prospect of a remote home in the forest set his soul on fire.

Chapter Three

"So how'd you do, man?"

Ash was halfway down the steps from the science building. Without slowing he turned to see the scruffy prophet of biology class wearing his trademark smirk. As though he'd been waiting for Ash, the boy slid off the wall and hurried to catch up.

"I did all right," Ash said.

The boy's mouth curled into an impish grin. "You aced it."

Ash eyed the boy. "You finished before I did. You must have done all right."

"I did okay, I guess. I just don't stick around and waste time on what I don't know . . . 'cause one thing I do know about old *Lee-on-hard*—"

Ash kept walking but then abruptly stopped. "Okay," he sighed. "What one thing do you know?"

The boy laughed quietly. "Well, besides keeping snakes in cages in his basement—" His grin widened, and he waited for a reaction. Ash gave him nothing. "Well, besides that, he doesn't like any bullshit on his tests, so I just answer what I know and pray for leniency."

" 'Leniency!' " Ash said, his voice edged with doubt. "Good luck with that." He turned to go.

"Well, he used to be pretty reasonable," the boy said, hurrying to keep up.

Ash kept his eyes on the intersection ahead. It was the second time the boy had mentioned having Leonhardt as a teacher before.

"Yeah, I got an A under him. That was at a different school. But here at GDA, he's changed, man. He's out for blood."

"I thought Leonhardt had taught here for decades," Ash said.

"Yeah," the rumpled boy agreed. "But he taught overseas one year. That's where I had 'im."

Ash eyed the boy. "So why'd you follow him here to Greenwood Downs?"

"Total irony, man. I got financial aid to come here to preppy-ville."

"So . . . why are you repeating the course?"

The boy winced. "I'm not repeating anything, man. Different course. Need one more biology credit." He shrugged. "I'm pre-majoring in food management."

Ash sensed what was coming—the bonding handshake, the shared complaints, the camaraderie of their common miserable ground under Leonhardt's rule. Next would come the compliments on Ash's questions in that first week of class, then finally the plea for help . . . like a clear view over Ash's shoulder during the next test.

They stopped at the intersection and waited for a security car to cruise past. The boy pushed out his lower lip, and his eyes glazed over as he stared off into the void.

"It ain't over yet, man. I'll study my ass off just to spite him." The boy squinted. "Name's Mick. It's Michael, but everybody calls me 'Mick'." Ash waited for the handshake, but Mick's hands remained buried in the pockets of his wrinkled blazer. "Gotta class to get to." He cracked a grin, and shuffled diagonally across the intersection.

After classes Ash dropped off his books at his room and began gathering supplies from the mental list he had been working on all day. Into his father's Navy duffel he packed his hatchet, a coil of nylon rope, a plastic tarp, matches, and two oranges he had pocketed at the cafeteria.

From the maintenance shed behind his dorm he borrowed a shovel and bow-saw. Adrenaline was coursing through his veins as he started for the woods. He was ready for an afternoon of dedicated labor.

It was Friday. Up and down Valley Road, traffic was bumper-to-bumper. Just as cell phones were taboo, cars were a forbidden fruit for Greenwood's students, but friends and relatives had come to rescue the Academy's prisoners for the weekend. Music throbbed from every vehicle and from the dormitory windows, and above all this could be heard whoops of revelry. It was all a prelude for the next weekend when god-football would arrive here to dominate the lives of the student body for two and a half months. Ash squinted through the haze of exhaust hovering in the valley, but he smiled at the silver lining in this cloud. In a few hours the school would be virtually deserted.

As soon as he stepped onto the west field, his eyes riveted to the target. For the third time this week the cover lay folded on the ground, the four rocks squared neatly on top. Irritated, he scanned the empty field and then covered the target. When he hoisted the duffel to his shoulder, his eyes locked on two figures atop Cemetery Hill. They stood side by side, still and attentive. Resentment buzzed through him like an electric current. For five heartbeats he stared back, then, breaking the standoff, he marched off to the forest.

It took the river to calm him. The emerald water slid between its ferny banks like the one constant the world had to offer. By the time he reached the beech tree on the plateau his mind was clear and focused on the work ahead of him. Dropping the duffle on the tree's roots, he hefted the shovel and climbed to the work site.

With the shoals whispering to his back, he labored for hours excavating a six-foot by eight-foot cavity from the side of the mountain. Each shovel-load of dirt was piled on a tarp and hauled from the worksite. When he had reached a depth of five feet on the uphill side, he got to work with the saw and shored up the walls with logs cut to length.

At twilight he laid the first rafters across the uprights, running the stout beams downhill to match the slope of the mountain. When the last rafter went up, the shelter began to look like the secret home he had envisioned.

Sitting with his back to the beech tree, he ate both oranges and watched darkness begin to tint the valley. Across the river a barred owl piped a single, liquid note, then followed with its familiar mellow phrase. Standing, he stretched his back and took a last look at the recessed lair. Already looking forward to tomorrow's work, he started back for his dorm.

*****

On Saturday he hauled leaves in the tarp and carpeted the floor to a soft six-inch loft. Then he hiked upriver to retrieve two sheets of roofing metal he had found last year after a tornado had ripped through the farmlands of Nacoochee County. Folding each in half until it broke, he laid three halves over the rafters. The fourth he hammered into a three-sided column for a chimney.

After constructing a hearth of river stones at the uphill side of the room he lowered the angular flue through an opening in the roof and propped it on the rock hearth. Crawling back inside he pried open the bottom of the flue to flare over the stones.

By late afternoon he had covered the roof with the plastic tarp and added several inches of dirt and a layer of sticks and leaves. For the final touch he transplanted galax and Christmas ferns to break up the bare rectangle he had created. Finally he chopped and wrestled a hollow sycamore stump from the flood plain and sleeved it over the chimney, hiding the metal from anyone who might pass by on the lower ground.

Standing on the level terrace under the beech, he studied the hillside. The construction was barely detectable. After collecting driftwood along the beaches, he crawled inside the dark room and carefully arranged sticks for the inaugural fire.

The scratch of the match seemed to fill the quiet room with reverence and expectation. The flame took and licked upward, crackling through the dry wood, and the cubicle began to undulate with shadows. A thin stratum of smoke collected at the ceiling, but, as the flame grew, the smoke began to purl like water in a funnel. It channeled upward through the flue as if it had suddenly recognized its outlet.

When he lay back to pocket the matches, the day of non-stop labor caught up to him. His body gave in to the soft cushion beneath. Staring at the ceiling he listened to the shoals upriver, as his eye moved lovingly over the glowing beams, the grains of the timber, the amber colors reflecting from the fire. He had gone feral. Like the otter, he had his place in the order of things. He added a log to the fire, closed his eyes, and slept.

*****

It was late Sunday when Ash returned to his dorm. Now that he had constructed an abode of his own from scratch, he paused on the lawn and studied the building with new appreciation. Huntington Hall was one of the last relics of the school's founding year. Its three stories of rust-colored brick, weathered stone, and creaking timbers crouched in the shadow of newly built Gamewell Hall—six levels of immaculate architectural conception that stood as the beacon of things to come.

Huntington was scheduled for demolition in summer. Once razed, in its place would rise a mirror image of Gamewell thirty yards away. The two buildings would share a common courtyard.

Ash could not deny that Huntington had deteriorated, but it did have charm. Ornate stonework under forest green gables gave the street-side facade a European look. But one nuance of the building's design had doomed it to a less than stately moniker. Two round windows were tucked under the end gables and gave the appearance of gawking, wide-set eyes that gazed unblinking across the valley. For this, Huntington had long ago been dubbed "Toad Hall" by the students. The name had stuck.

With the maintenance shed locked, he carried the borrowed tools up the stairs. Upon opening the stairwell door on the third floor, he heard the soft pluck of guitar strings coming from inside his room. He eased the hall door shut and listened for a time, head down, smiling. When the music ended he opened his door to the scene he expected.

Alan Odell sat on the desk, his stockinged feet crossed in the chair, and Ash's guitar cradled in his lap. Alan's wide smile flashed across his narrow face, as he swept from his eyes the long blond hair that always pushed the limits of the school's dress code.

"Enter ye of impeccable taste and generous largesse for endowment of the arts," Alan greeted.

" 'Largesse'?" Ash said.

Alan spun the guitar in his hands, and his smile widened. "My guitar's in for a tune-up. I need to borrow yours." He drummed a smart paradiddle on the body of the guitar. " 'Tune-up' . . . get it?"

"I was beginning to wonder if you were back at school," Ash said and tossed the duffel into the closet. He laid the bow-saw and shovel next to the door and took Alan's strong handshake over the guitar. As they clasped hands, each looked the other in the eye.

"Young Asher, if not I, who would chronicle your heroic deeds?" Alan's voice carried its typical undercurrent of parody. He frowned as he studied Ash's mud-stained clothes. "Are we cleaning the Aegean stables today?"

Ash nodded at the guitar. "What was that you were playing?"

Alan bent over the guitar and rendered the opening phrase again, his fingers walking effortlessly over the frets like a spider traversing its web. "Something new. I'm still working on it." He muted the strings with the flat of his hand and frowned at the tools stacked by the door. *GDA* was stenciled on the hafts in bright red paint. "Whatever you've been doing, don't you think you should hide those? What if your hall proctor should happen by?"

Ash shook his head. "He never checks on me. He's got problems at the other end of the hall." Ash sat on his bed and removed his shoes. "Have you been waiting long?"

Alan cocked his wrist, a gesture Ash had witnessed countless times when Alan played sets at The Tavern. "Oh, three hours, give or take." He smiled at the look Ash gave him. "Hey, if *I* don't visit you up here inside the crumbling walls of Toad Hall, who will? You *are* a little off the beaten path." Alan smiled at the state of Ash's clothes. "Or maybe you *are* the beaten path." He narrowed his eyes. "You need some social life, Young Asher. To prepare you for the big bad world of college waiting out there for you. Correct me if I'm wrong, but every friend you have at this school is in this room as we speak."

Ash offered a tolerant smile. "Do you know a junior? Looks like he sleeps in his clothes, kind of off-beat. 'Michael' something?"

A mischievous light flickered in Alan's eyes. "I know a senior, looks like he sleeps in his clothes, off-beat . . . name of 'Robert' something. Why?"

Shaking his head, Ash took off his socks and tossed them into the closet. "Not important." When he began pulling out of his dirty clothes, Alan leaned over the guitar and started the new melody again from the beginning.

"So, how was the summer of O-nineteen, Young Asher? Any epiphanies? Figure out a pre-major yet? Or a college that meets your standards? Or meet the girl of your dreams?" Alan waggled his eyebrows.

"Summer was okay." Ash wrapped a towel around his waist. "No revelations."

Alan stilled the strings and gave Ash his exasperated look. "You know, just because these girls at the Academy are rich doesn't mean you won't like any of them." He watched Ash gather up shampoo and soap. "Remember that girl I introduced you to? Shyla? Long black hair, almost as black as yours? She's going into forestry at Auburn. So, what was wrong with her?"

Ash hesitated at the door. "Nothing."

"And so?"

" 'And so' what?" Ash said.

Alan closed his eyes, letting his head hang forward as he shook it. "You know, Young Asher, I think you have mastered the three-words-or-less sentence. Maybe you can pre-major in laconics."

Ash leaned against the doorframe. "Next to you a whippoorwill would seem laconic." He rolled off the doorframe and started for the showers.

"But Young Asher!" Alan called after him. "How can I complete *The Ballad* if all I have to work with are these three-word jewels of input from you?"

Looking ill, Ash leaned back inside. "Don't tell me *The Ballad's* not complete?"

Alan hunched over the guitar and delivered the introduction to his magnum opus: *The Ballad of Young Asher of Greenwood.* The familiar chords suspended on a final dramatic strum, and Alan added his deep melodic voice to the fading acoustics.

"In the final three seconds . . . for a field goal so late
Their kicker was beckoned . . . to seal Greenwood's fate"

Ash groaned. "Is this the one where I shoot the ball out of the air before it sails through the uprights? Save the game for GDA?"

Alan smiled and continued the song.

"And the ball fell deflated . . . as the clock ticked to zero
So they couldn't replay it . . . as Young Asher, our hero
Without even a wave . . . to the praises they called
Slipped quietly away . . . to his room in Toad Hall."

Alan up-stroked the last chord and raised his arm like a matador.

Ash winced. "Isn't hyperbole frowned upon in songwriter circles?"

Alan smiled. "Hyperbole forces our heads out of the box. And speaking of 'the box,' what nice hypocritical pre-major have you conjured up for yourself here in the eleventh hour? They're gonna demand it this year, you know."

Ash offered his usual scowl for the concept of a pre-major. "It's ludicrous. This is a high school. We're supposed to be getting a taste of everything so we can decide later in college . . . if we're lucky."

"It *is* ludicrous," Alan agreed, "but it's not going to change. The way it's set up, you might not be able to graduate without it." He perked up and raised his forefinger. "Hey, maybe that'll be my Pulitzer newspaper article." He swept a hand across the air, typesetting an imaginary headline. "*Cutting Edge Academy's Top Scholastic Student Fails to Graduate Over Pre-Major Issue!*" He laid the guitar flat on his thighs. "Listen, my friend, Greenwood Downs is the golden child of academia, so sayeth the *Journal of Southern Educators*, remember?" Alan angled his eyes to the ceiling as he recalled the article. " 'Crackling with innovative ideas for creating ambitious students and college successes.' Quote, unquote." He coughed up a laugh. "This school tucked away up here in the hills is not about to surrender its budding reputation by bending a rule for you."

Ash waited to see if Alan was through quoting magazines. "It's still ludicrous."

Alan sagged. "True, but you know as well as I do that your name is gonna surface on some administrative watchdog's list, and you're gonna find yourself standing on the dean's carpet for some explaining. You might want to try to skip all that and just put your checkmark on a pre-major. You think?"

"I think," Ash said, "that I'm going to take a shower."

"Hey!" Alan called, stopping him again. "I didn't just come by to borrow your guitar. Come by The Tavern tonight. Something I want to talk to you about."

Ash's head bobbed back into the open doorway. "Take the guitar but tell me now. I've got some reading I need to do tonight."

Alan slid off the desk and laid the instrument in its open case. Slowly he closed the latches on the lid and then idly wiped at the dust on the top cover.

"There's this girl in my English composition class. She writes poetry, and—" He kept pushing around the dust. "She's—"

Ash cringed. "You're not trying to fix me up with somebody again, are you?"

"No, no," Alan said quickly and brushed his hands together briskly.

Ash crossed his arms. "You're trying to fix *you* up with somebody."

"Okay," Alan sighed. "Now you know. I've met somebody who makes me jabber with incomplete sentences." He sat on the desk again, inflated his cheeks, and exhaled a long stream of air. "Her name's Elaine. She's—" He held his breath as he struggled for the right word.

"She's coming to The Tavern this week. You want to stop by? Meet her?"

Ash kept smiling but said nothing.

Alan managed a defensive look. "What!?"

Ash waved as he turned. "Just let me know which night. I'll be there."

Chapter Four

It was an odd way to hand out tests, but no one was going to question Dr. Leonhardt's methods. He stood at the edge of the stage and called another name. A tall girl clopped down the aisle steps, and Leonhardt stared at her as if committing her face to memory. When she reached the foot of the stage and waited, he ceremoniously handed down her graded test and watched her walk back to her desk before calling the next name.

A full ten minutes later, Ash heard his name. His part in the ritual was no different than the others. He received his test from the cold statue that towered above him on stage. He noted the red *96* scrawled below his name, then returned to his seat.

Leonhardt checked his watch. "You have fifteen minutes to go over your tests. There will be no talking." Already, voices began whispering. "I repeat!" Leonhardt called out, and the room silenced again. "No! . . . Talking!"

The auditorium became a tomb. Pages turned intermittently. Shoes scuffed the floor. From midway up the tiered room someone exhaled a long sigh. All the while Dr. Richard Leonhardt kept watch over the mute and suffering.

Ash sat quietly victorious, his hands folded over his grade. It was, as Mick had warned, a test for the serious student, and Ash had proved himself as such and now took satisfaction in stinging Leonhardt's ego. At the very least he had altered the old man's stereotype of his students, if only by a margin of one student.

In this dead time, he flipped the test face-down on his desk, sat back, and folded his arms across his chest. The movement caught Dr. Leonhardt's attention, and for the briefest of moments they locked eyes. Ash felt a chill run up his spine.

"Dr. Leonhardt?" came a female voice from high up in the stair-step rows of seats. The words broke the silence in the room like a glass jar dropping onto a concrete floor. Every head came up and turned to see who had dared to speak.

Leonhardt thrust both palms toward the girl. "No talking!" he repeated.

"But, sir, I have—"

Leonhardt stiffened his arms and raised his voice. "No! . . . Talking!"

Incredibly, she persisted. Leonhardt bellowed something that no one understood, stormed down from the stage, and climbed the aisle stairs. She waited, her jaw set, determined to have her say. Ash felt a nudge on his shoulder, and Mick leaned forward from the row behind him.

"Flip to page three," Mick whispered.

Ash checked on his teacher and then opened his test to page three. Mick began reciting one of Ash's answers under his breath. Abruptly his voice stopped, then repeated a line. Mick sat back and hissed air through his teeth. The conflict across the room had subsided to a less public but stern dictum from Dr. Leonhardt. After the old man returned to his podium, the only sound in the room was the rustle of turning pages.

Twenty minutes before the class was to be over, Dr. Leonhardt opened his roll book. "When I call your name, return your test to me, then you may leave one at a time."

When the class went dead quiet, Ash turned to see a consensus of bewildered faces scattered across the room. Mick's smirk was etched into his face like a checkmark.

"Arnette!" Leonhardt called out and waited for the student to approach. A slender girl with curly hair came down the stairs, surrendered her test, and exited. "Asherwood!" Leonhardt continued. Ash collected his books, approached the stage, and held out his test. "Mr. Asherwood," Leonhardt mumbled like a greeting. Ash waited, curious as to why the man had spoken his name again, but Leonhardt's eyes lowered to his list. "Barlow!"

Ash moved on but hesitated at the door, waiting to see if Leonhardt addressed the next student quietly by name. It was the tall girl who had argued with Leonhardt.

"Dr. Leonhardt, I don't—"

"Not now!" he snapped and read the next name. "Baxter!"

Barlow's face reddened, and she slapped her paper on the edge of the stage. As she marched toward the exit, her heels stabbed the concrete floor in angry clicks. Ash reached to open the door for her, but she slammed into the door bar, knocking his books from his hands. She never looked back. Ash knelt to collect his books, and his teacher returned to the roll call. Another student filed out before Ash could gather his belongings and escape.

Mick, disheveled and winded, caught him at the intersection. "Ninety-six, huh?" He was smiling and nodding. "Hey, did you get that Amazon's tag number?" He snickered. "That was a hit-and-run, no question."

As Ash started across the street, Mick tugged at his sleeve. "Hey, wait up. I gotta question for you." He stepped around Ash to face him. "Man, was that the weirdest hour you ever spent or what?"

"That's your question?"

Mick's eyes went cold. "No, that's not my question, *Mr. Asherwood*," he said, mimicking Leonhardt's gruff voice. They started across the street at Mick-speed. "Okay, look . . . I left question nine blank. So today I look next to me—you know, the girl with the jingly bracelets? She's got number nine neatly answered. Not a red mark on it."

"So?" Ash said looking straight ahead.

"So," Mick retorted, "I read her answer, and it makes no sense." Mick sped up when Ash picked up the pace. "So, I read your answer, which also has no red mark." Mick's gaze was intense now. "So here's the thing. Your answer was completely opposite from hers. I'm talking *diametric*, man . . . a hundred and eighty degrees." He raised his arms just high enough to slap them back to his sides. "Explain *that* to me?"

Ash kept his expression blank. "Are you sure you know enough about it to tell?"

Mick stopped, his face frozen with insult. "Thanks a lot, Einstein. I'm not stupid!"

Ash slowed to a stop and exhaled heavily. "Okay. Which question did you say?"

Pouting, Mick stared across the valley. "Number nine . . . the mutation question."

Ash thought about it and began to nod. "That one needed a subjective and an objective answer. I could see getting confused on it."

Mick's frosted eyes came up. "Zzzhheeee." He glared at Ash. "Do you think you could be any more patronizing? Look, man, I made an eighty-three, okay?"

Ash did the math. "So, you just missed the one you left blank and—"

"And I misspelled a word!" Mick said. "Big friggin' deal!"

Ash felt himself reappraising Mick, who must have known the complete answer to number five—the one which had cost Ash four points. And besides that, Dr. Leonhardt had not prepared the class for question nine. Outside research had saved Ash on that one.

"Maybe Dr. Leonhardt just screwed up," Ash said. "He's old and he's angry."

"Maybe," Mick said, "but I've never seen him screw up grading before."

Ash gazed back toward the science building. "Did you ever see him pull that before? Handing out the tests and then taking them up that way?"

Mick shook his head. "Not in my classes." Together they started up the hill. "Hey, what did Leonhardt say to you, anyway? Just before the Amazon ran over you."

Ash shrugged. "Just my name . . . which is 'Ash,' by the way."

In this belated second half of their introductions, Mick just nodded and then looked away.

"If you want," Ash offered, "I can write out that answer to number nine for you."

Mick chewed on his lower lip and shrugged. "Yeah, okay. Whatever."

When a girl in Ash's art class hurried by, his attention was grabbed by the poster board in her hand. It showed a grid of squares with myriad shades of deepening blues.

Ash started walking backward down the hill. "Sorry, I forgot something. Gotta go to my dorm." Breaking into a run he hurried to Huntington. Rushing through the lobby he glanced at his mailbox and spotted a white envelope slanted across its glass pane. As he raced upstairs, the letter nagged at him. Mail should not have arrived so early.

In his room he grabbed his color chart, tapped back down the stairs to the lobby, and spun the mailbox dial through its combination. The envelope was crisp and white, with no stamp, postmark, or return address. Apparently, it had been hand-delivered. *Robert Asherwood, 322 Huntington Hall* was typed on the front. A quick inspection showed no similar envelopes in any of the other boxes.

Ash groaned. His days of anonymity were over. This would be his ultimatum to commit to a pre-major. When the second bell rang he bolted out the door.

Arriving late for English, he settled into a desk at the back as the teacher read from Chaucer. Ash quietly unfolded the letter and read two typed lines.

> *Mr. Asherwood,*
> *Kindly come by my office today before 3 p.m. or between 5-*
> *6 p.m. Your prompt attention will be appreciated.*
> *~ Richard Oberleigh, Dean of Students*

Three hours later, when he arrived at the art studio, Ash saw a sheet of newsprint pinned to the curtain of the modeling stage, and on it was a message hurriedly written in his teacher's familiar hand: *Charts due when I return at 3!* As the other students were putting final touches to their color charts, Ash decided to go to the dean now. In case he could not get back within the hour, he needed someone to turn in his color chart.

Because he was the lone senior in a course that normally fell in an art pre-major's sophomore year, Ash shared no history with his classmates. Friendships and cliques had already been established, and he belonged to none of them.

However, one common emissary moved easily through the various cliques of artists and spoke their languages fluently. Anne Metter was the butterfly of art class, flitting from flower to flower, insinuating herself into each enclave—ooh-ing and ah-ing over sketchbooks.

When she laughed, Anne Metter's silky blonde hair tossed from side to side and recomposed into perfect order. Her clean and flawless features rated covert glances from the other girls and routine approaches by the boys. She was lean and fit from sheer bounce and energy. Ash thought her pretty, in a generic sort of way, but his appraisal of her had suffered with her transparency. She was harmless and sweet, but Ash had watched her mirror every person she stood before. Not once had she countered another person's opinion during critique. She had contributed no original thoughts—only supportive reiterations designed to please.

He decided to leave his chart where Mr. Lowery would find it. The problem was: where? His teacher had no desk. The front table was a mountain of drawings and papers where Ash's chart could easily be swallowed up in an avalanche. But there *was* the stool at the corner of the stage where Mr. Lowery perched. The teacher was sure to notice a chart left there. Ash skirted the rows of drawing tables and propped his assignment against the legs of the stool, angling the chart so as not to be on display.

Hurrying down the marbled hallway, he was charged with nervous energy over the coming confrontation with the dean. When he shouldered into the heavy glass door, the impact jarred his books, and they tumbled to the floor. When he knelt to pick them up, his signature inside an open book cover triggered a thought: He had not signed his name to his color chart. He gathered his books and hurried back to the studio.

Stepping into the classroom he saw a group of students bunched around the stool, as a lone singsong voice delivered a Lowery-esque monologue. The group exploded with laughter but quickly hushed to hear the narration continue. Covering the distance silently, Ash took a place in back of the crowd. Through a gap between the heads and shoulders, he spied his color chart rotated into full view. Next to it was another chart, stunning in its precision and subtly darkening spectrum of blues.

The comic critic gestured with Mr. Lowery's flamboyant sweep of an arm toward Ash's work. "Where is the continuity?" The speaker, a hyperactive class clown, propped a fist under his chin, capturing another Lowery pose. "Even a graveyard has continuity!" Another Lowery-ism, another burst of laughter. "Alas," he sighed. "The death of color."

30

"Maybe you don't know everything you think you do about color." It was Anne Metter's voice, striving for lightheartedness but at the same time challenging.

The critic leaned in. "Would madam consent to a free eye exam at the infirmary?"

Anne made the obligatory laugh. "No, really. I don't think you should compare two works inside our class . . . not without consent anyway." She swallowed and looked around, trying for a diplomatic smile. The smile snapped off when she saw Ash. From the startled look in her eyes he knew that she knew the chart on display belonged to him. He assumed they all knew. Without speaking he turned and walked out of the studio.

She caught up to him in the hallway and slowed to a walk beside him. When he looked at her, she smiled the way people do at funerals.

"I'm sorry," she said.

Ash's voice came out as a tired whisper. "Do me a favor? Would you write my name on my masterpiece for me? It's 'Asherwood'." He spelled it for her.

"Sure," she said and pressed her lips into a thin line, as though locking her mouth shut while she thought of the right thing to say. "Mine's 'Anne'."

Ash nodded and backed through the door. "Thanks," he said in a lifeless monotone. He turned and made his way across the street toward the administration buildings.

Chapter Five

He stood before the door marked *Dean of Students* and listened to the staccato typing inside the room. After combing his fingers through his hair, he went inside.

Three students sat on a bench against the wall and turned their heads in unison. The typist, a middle-aged woman conveying a look of strained tolerance, ignored him. When Ash approached, she spoke to the computer screen in a bloodless voice.

"Have a seat. Dean Oberleigh will see you in your turn."

A sign on her desk read *Sara Birmingham*. Her thin fingers punched the keys in a cold virtuosity as her unblinking eyes fixed on dictation notes.

"I have an appointment with the dean. My name is Asherwood."

The typing stopped, and Sara Birmingham looked directly at him. "Asherwood?" She checked a sheet of paper on her desk, stood, walked to the heavy oak door, and knocked. When she slipped into the dean's inner sanctum, Ash cut his eyes to the bench. The three students stared at him with expressions ranging from resentment to pity. The dean's door swung open, and a grim-faced student wasted no time in exiting. When the hallway door slammed, the rattle of glass did nothing for the sinking morale in the room.

"Mr. Asherwood," Sara Birmingham intoned as she returned to her desk, "Dean Oberleigh will see you."

When the typing resumed, Ash stacked his books on a chair and entered the dean's office.

Richard Oberleigh was six feet two inches of authority. His physique seemed not so much the sculpting of muscle as a naturally inherited frame of wide shoulders and narrow hips. He was a walking wedge. His mass seemed to burden him as he lumbered around his desk. When they shook, his hand swallowed Ash's.

The dean gestured to a wooden chair. "Have a seat," he said, his voice deep and businesslike. When Ash sat, the dean sank into the cushions of his armchair. The man looked Ash over as if sizing him up for a position on the football team. Then he removed his glasses and cleaned them with a white handkerchief. The puffy tissue around his eyes gave him a vulnerable look, like a child just awakened. The countenance of authority returned when the glasses slid back into place.

"I appreciate your coming by. I am very pressed for time today. I'm going to ask you some very direct questions. Please be equally forthcoming with your answers." To show he wanted a response, he let his eyebrows float up.

"Yes, sir," Ash said.

A stillness gathered in the room. The typing outside was like the drum roll before an execution. The dean's eyes hardened with the stare of a prosecutor.

"Have you ever cheated on a test here at GDA?"

The room seemed to drop out of time. Ash had to catch the dean's words and run them through his head again like a rewound tape. They both waited as if his answer would set the clocks of the world back into motion.

"No, sir." His voice sounded distant, as if an air bubble was trapped in his ear.

"Have you ever helped anyone cheat?"

Ash frowned. "No, sir."

"If you saw someone cheat, would you report it?"

Ash opened his mouth, closed it, and looked out the window. "I don't know."

The dean waited for Ash to meet his eyes again. "Do you think cheating goes on, say, in your first period biology class?"

This took Ash off guard—that this man knew his schedule from memory. He glanced at a pile of papers on the dean's desk, and wondered if his records lay there.

"I wouldn't know. I don't really know anybody in my class."

The dean spread his hands as though opening up a possibility. "What if you saw it happen? Say, the fellow next to you. Would you report it?"

Ash erased the image of Mick's face as soon as it materialized. "I doubt I would."

Dean Oberleigh sat forward, more curious than disappointed. "But it *is* wrong, isn't it? It hurts you and—" He sat back and shook his head. Turning to the window, he tapped an index finger on the arm of the chair. To hike up his sleeve, he punched the air with his left arm and read his watch. "Can you come to my house for supper tonight?"

Without waiting for an answer, Dean Oberleigh pushed up from the chair and leaned over his desk to scratch on a notepad. He peeled off the page and held it out.

"Seven o'clock?" the dean said. "Do you know where Maple Street is?"

Ash took the paper and read the address. "Yes, sir."

When the big man strode to the door and opened it an inch, Ash took the cue and stood. "Sir . . . if you think I am cheating . . . then why—"

The dean signaled for quiet and peered through the crack in the door before easing it shut. "Robert," he said in a low whisper. "I don't want you talking about this meeting to anyone." He nodded to the note in Ash's hand. "Or about tonight." When Ash frowned and started to talk, the dean added, "We just need to talk."

Then they were shaking hands, and suddenly it was all over.

Ash stood in the waiting room where the rapid tap of the typewriter still dominated. Facing the death's row trio, Ash realized that their confused expressions were mirroring his own. He had to wonder: How often were supper invitations tendered to students who were summoned here?

The riddle of the interview stayed with him on his walk to the field, but as he slid through the border of sapling pines he shed all thoughts of the Academy. One arrow would be enough today. He was anxious to crawl into the womb of Beechwood, to work on the finishing touches of his new home. Yoked around his neck was a rolled wool blanket he would install as a door flap. In his pocket were candles his hall proctor had dispensed during last year's power blackout.

Above the field the sun was a bright jewel stamped into the cloudless blue. The air was pleasantly cool, and the only sound to be heard was the lazy chirr of a squirrel at the edge of the forest. Not until he was halfway across the field did he notice that the target was once again uncovered. A lone, gray-fletched arrow jutted from the red ring.

Ash stopped to survey the field. The plain of yellow grass was empty. He walked to the front of the target and glared at the arrow, wanting to jerk it free so he could cover the target. Then a better idea occurred to him. He would destroy it with a shot of his own.

After stringing his bow he stepped away on an angle that would offer a side-view of the gray arrow. There he loaded, drew, and funneled his vision down to the unwanted shaft. When he released, the red arrow smacked the target and rattled against the gray arrow like the chiseling of a woodpecker. Now he could see that the gray arrow had descended from a much higher arc. Gazing up-field he began to estimate the flight the trespassing arrow must have taken, and the calculation pulled his eyes all the way to Cemetery Hill. A movement on top snapped him alert. Someone was there . . . waving. Ash averted his eyes and loaded a new arrow, but the trespasser was like a buzzing bee trapped in his head. He looked back to see the distant arm wave again.

"Go away," he breathed.

He set up for another shot, but his concentration had been hijacked. Clenching his teeth, Ash tried to force discipline into his draw, but his second shot flew wide, deflecting off the edge of the target and skittering along the grass. His face flushed and hardened. He shot four more times, but still the gray arrow silently mocked him. Breathing in deeply he slipped the last arrow from his quiver and faced the hill, directing all blame for his ineptness there. Another wave. Reluctantly he raised his hand.

"Okay, I see you," he hissed under his breath. "Now go away."

Settling in for the last shot, he drew and began to visualize the perfect flight. Into this silence came a long, searing whisper that streaked overhead and stopped when the target face spat out a report. Staring stupidly at the second gray arrow in the target, Ash lowered his bow and felt ice water surge through his veins.

Turning stiffly, he faced the hill, now realizing that both gray arrows had been launched from the top of the rise. As he stared at the interloper, he saw the wave again—this time its message clear: *Move out of the way!*

Working up indignation over a breach of safety, Ash walked to the pines in long angry strides and climbed the trail that led to the old graveyard. Twice during his ascent his head turned involuntarily when the target spat out reports of accurate shots.

At the top of the trail he stopped under the giant oaks and looked at the serenity of the gravestones. His fevered temper seemed out of place here, and he felt his resolve weaken. From behind a thick oak trunk a bowstring twanged, and he could not help but follow the arrow's long arcing flight with his eyes. The missile flew across the vast openness and dropped perfectly into the target. Seconds after the arrow had claimed its mark, the faint tap of impact traveled back to him, and he could not hold down the question trying to rise inside him. *Could he make such a shot?*

Reviving his anger, he marched toward the tree that shielded the archer from view. When he rounded the oak, the protest he had bottled up in his throat dropped to the pit of his stomach.

She appeared to be waiting for him, her smile neither mocking nor contrite but seeming to match her ingenuous pearl-gray eyes. She wore black jeans and a man's gray and black plaid flannel shirt. Her bearing was lithe and youthful, but the delicate lines etched around her mouth and eyes recorded a longer history. A leather quiver showed over her shoulder where her tawny brown hair was swept back and tucked under her collar. The elegant wooden bow in her hand showed a russet belly and a pale back. When she propped it upon her shoe, it reached well above her head. The tapered limbs were capped by carvings of bone for the string notches. Ash recognized the weapon. It was an English long-bow.

"We meet again," she said.

These three hushed words were delivered with an unexpected British lilt. The whispery timbre of her voice made him think of summer leaves stirring in a breeze. He stared at her, mesmerized by a sound that seemed so alien to this place. Then the content of her words registered, and he frowned.

" 'Again'?" he echoed.

"Last Friday," she explained. "I was here when you walked onto the field." Her accent disarmed him in some way, and he realized he was hearing less of *what* she said than *how* she said it. She cocked her head as though unsure he was following her words. "And then you covered the target?"

Friday. He had seen two people here. Now he had to reverse his entire train of thought to see himself in the role of trespasser. When he felt his face redden, he attempted to resurrect the anger that had propelled him up the hill.

"That was dangerous," he said and pointed to the field where he had stood as she shot. "You could have hit me."

Her eyes softened. "I am sorry if I upset you,' she said. "When you walked off to one side, well . . . I thought you were waving me on to shoot."

She seemed comfortable with her part in the conversation—neither hurried nor argumentative—as if she were patiently waiting for him to come around to the obvious. He looked at the field, picturing himself down there walking off to the side for a better angle to splinter her arrow. And then waving to her. He closed his eyes and exhaled.

"You were here the day of the storm, weren't you?" Ash said.

She smiled at the ground. Now she looked older. Streaks of silver ribboned through the honey-gold of her hair. She stood relaxed, content in the wordless moment. Then she looked up, and the way the light caught her face erased the years he had just assumed for her.

"Yes. I was told it was all right to shoot here. I checked with the physical education director."

"Of course," Ash heard himself say, now defending her. "It's the only target set up on campus." Words were tripping off his tongue before he could choose them.

"It's quite a lovely flight from up here. I'll just finish up."

As a prelude to shooting, she took a poised stance, and her face hardened with concentration. He watched, fascinated, as she drew the bow and steadied her aim. The angle of the arrow's elevation looked as though she intended it to fly to Naughton. Her focus was absolute.

The sudden release and whip of the longbow was powerful. The arrow carved another long suspended arc through the air, and finally the target face shuddered. When the report reached them, she straightened, and the intensity in her face drained away.

"Well," she said, "I'm going down to retrieve arrows." But she hesitated, and her eyes warmed with an earnest invitation. "Unless you would like a turn?"

He shook his head. As her footsteps faded down the trail, he moved to the spot where she had stood, looked down on the field, and considered the skill needed to hit the target from there. He whistled a sliding note of awe and then hurried to catch her.

When they were walking side by side on the field, he asked, "Are you a teacher?"

"Yes. I've been here only a few weeks. And what about you?"

"I'm a senior," he said as they reached the target. He watched her pull her arrows. "Phys-ed gave up archery back in the seventies. This is one of their old targets."

"But *your* field," she said. He started to agree but instead pulled his arrows and watched her survey the boundaries of the field. She turned as if she had reached some conclusion. "I suppose that makes me the foreign invader. Like William at Hastings?" When he made no reply, she added, "I fear I have insinuated into your private place." Her eyes began to shine with good humor. "Then let me earn my place. What do you say to trial by arrow?"

Ash stared blankly at her, fascinated at her change of mood.

"You've just been challenged, sir," she advised with a conspiratorial wink.

She handed him an arrow from her quiver and pointed out into the field. "Throw it as far as you can. Make it good," she teased, "or you might come to regret it."

He stared at the arrow as though all this were some kind of trick. But when he saw that she was waiting, he faced up-field, took the arrow on his fingertips, and balanced it above his shoulder javelin-style. Skipping forward he drew back his arm and hurled the shaft with a grunt. The arrow covered about twenty-five yards, came down into the dry grasses, and lightly pinned at an angle into the earth.

"I shall shoot from there," she explained. "Now, if I may have one of yours?"

He offered an arrow and watched her place it in the flat of her hand with the feathers nestled just above her wrist. It was held in place by the press of her thumb. Rotating at the waist, she made two warm-up arcs with her arm and then spun in a semi-circle like a discus thrower. Whipping her arm and extending her body, she slung the arrow side-arm. It flew twice the distance of the other arrow.

"One shot," she said. "The better archer rules the field." She winked again and walked to her arrow.

He could see that it was all in fun, but in his soul he craved revenge. He walked past her and set his arrow to string. At her invitation, he shot first, striking the gold just half an inch below dead center. She made a slight bow to him, then readied for her shot, and at that moment he realized how the tables had been turned. Because of their different angles from the target, she now had an opportunity to splinter his arrow from the side.

When she shot, her arrow slipped into the top of the gold, pinning the bull's eye just inside its edge. Ash stared at its placement, wondering if she had opted for this more difficult challenge—half a bull's eye—to spare him a broken shaft.

They approached the target in silence. Though his arrow was closer to the center, by the conventional rules of archery competition they had scored equally. But if she had been trying for the upper half of the gold to avoid damaging his arrow, her bull's eye had been half the size of his.

"The field is yours," she said, bowing. "I hope that I might I share it on occasion."

"Sure," he heard himself say.

He pulled his arrow from the tightly woven hay and watched her do the same. In the dying twilight, her age seemed transformed. She might have been a student.

"Hold out your hand," she whispered. The sudden crack surprised him. She had broken her arrow and laid the two halves in his palm. "Peace offering," she explained.

It was her apology, he knew, for the arrow shot past him from the hill. He strained to see her face, but now she was little more than a black silhouette against the faint luminescence of the field.

Realizing that darkness set in by seven, Ash remembered the dean's invitation. "I forgot!" he said and began backing away. "I've got to go!" He broke into a run. At the pines he stopped and turned. "Thanks!" he yelled and as soon as he had said it, he wanted to catch the word and drag it back. *Thanks for what?*

"And thank you," she called back. And then he was glad he had said it.

*****

After he had disappeared through the pines, she found the arrow he had shot into the grass and propped it against the tripod. Then over the target she draped the rolled blanket he had forgotten in his haste. She covered it all with the tarp, squared the stones on the corners, and walked north toward the edge of the dark woods. A small light flicked on there, giving her a beacon to follow.

41

"The night air is not good for you," she said. "We agreed you would not stay out in the dark."

"I know . . . I know," he said and flipped the cover of his lighter to snuff the flame. "Did you bring a torch? The wood is black as tar."

She took a small flashlight from her pocket and then cradled his bony elbow in her hand to turn him. He resisted. She could hear his labored breath, and more than that she could feel the questions burning inside him.

"He is quite good, isn't he?" he said, gloating. "I told you, didn't I?"

"Yes, you've told me many times. Now let's get you back home."

She got him moving in his plodding gait and led the way toward the river. Following the thin beam of her light angled down on the trail, they did not speak. By the time they reached the log bridge he was coughing, a hacking rhythm that shook him to the core. They rested for a time as the dark river slid past them.

"When will you approach him?" she asked. "Shouldn't you begin explaining things?"

He patted the back of her hand. "Give it time . . . give it time. Let's not frighten the poor boy from the get-go."

Chapter Six

Outside the cone of light cast by the streetlamp, Ash knelt in the Oberleigh's front yard in the dappled shadow of a maple. His heart hammered in his ears, as he sucked in cold doses of air. After stripping off his sweatshirt and damp tee shirt, he mopped the sweat from his face with the tee shirt and fanned himself with it. After hanging the shirt over a limb, he slipped back into the sweatshirt and stashed his archery gear in the tree.

Inside the house he could hear the clink of plates and silverware and the occasional melody of a woman's voice—all of it carrying the memories of his childhood, of coming home after playing hard, his mother working in the kitchen. Then came the chiming of a clock, four notes that marked a quarter after the hour.

Climbing up onto the porch, he stopped, combed his fingers through his hair, took a last deep breath, and knocked on the door. When it opened, Dean Oberleigh filled the doorframe and ushered Ash inside with a smothering handshake. In the entrance hall a full-length mirror presented Ash with an unexpected look at himself. It reflected less of the mile run that had disheveled him than the distance he had yet to go this night.

The dean's white shirt was wrinkled from the day and open at the collar with no tie. He led the way to a dining room, where three place settings were spaced on a white tablecloth. Steaming bowls of food crowded around a lighted candle. The kitchen door swung open, and the candle flame flickered. A woman backed into the room carrying a tray. When she saw Ash, her smile outshone the candle.

"Well, *there* he is!" Mrs. Oberleigh's voice sang with the same Southern timbre that had nurtured Ash as a fatherless boy among a devoted mother, doting aunts, and a loving grandmother. She was lean and sprightly in her mid-thirties, as fit as a cross-country runner. Her hair was pulled back into a ponytail that bounced when she walked.

"Dory, this is Robert Asherwood." The dean now sounded nothing like a dean. "Dory is the creator of all things delicious that will shortly pass through our lips."

"Delicious *and* nutritious," she amended with a wink to Ash. "I'm so glad you could come, Robert. Please call me 'Dory.' " There was in the dean's wife a no-nonsense promise of directness that appealed to Ash. Stepping back she propped her fists on her hips and appraised the table. "All right, I think we're ready." She sat and waved Ash to a seat. "Richard tells me you've got Dr. Leonhardt this quarter."

"Yes, ma'am." He took a seat and cleared his throat. "I apologize for being late. I didn't have time to change clothes."

She made a dismissive flutter of the hand. "Well, you hang in there with him. He wasn't always so grumpy." The dean gave her a look, which she ignored, suggesting that the Dean of Students' jurisdiction did not extend inside these walls. "We hope to get him back the way he was. Before he went overseas." She dipped her head to one side. "Still he does have his redeeming moments. The new chapel. That's his baby, you know."

"New chapel?" Ash said.

"It's been a crusade of his. He spearheads all the fund-raising. He's a tough one to say 'no' to." She flashed a bright smile for her husband. "Richard? Grace?"

Watching the couple bow their heads, Ash was curious to see how the Dean of Students conversed with a higher power. It was a brief and rote ritual, but Dory Oberleigh seemed satisfied.

Dory spooned vegetables onto her husband's plate. "Where is family, Robert?"

"We live in Locksfield . . . down in Lincoln County. It's a small town."

"Any brothers or sisters?"

"No, ma'am. It's just my mother and me."

She doled out a single egg-sized potato on the dean's plate. She had taken such control over the conversation that Ash wondered if she would be the one to bring up the subject of a pre-major.

"You help yourself, Robert. As much as you want."

"Dory," the dean complained, "a little more than that!" He tried for the spoon in her hand, but she was too quick. Smiling, she moved the bowl out of his reach. When she pushed the gravy boat to Ash, he felt the dean's eyes on him. Ash dribbled the brown droplets sparingly over his potatoes.

For the first ten minutes of the meal, Ash listened to Dory prattle on about life as a dean's wife. Unasked, she served him more from each of the bowls as the dean watched helplessly from a quiet place of enforced moderation.

"Maybe you'll become Dean of Students at Greenwood, Robert, and you can eat like this every night. Provided, of course, you find an extraordinary catch like me who can cook the pants off a French chef. So what are your plans? Have you signed away your life to a pre-major?"

Ash stopped chewing. He could see no guile in her face. The dean seemed more interested in the distant bowl of gravy than the question.

"I haven't decided," Ash said and watched for their reactions.

Dory wrinkled her nose. "Well, good for you. It's a silly rule. There's plenty of time for that in college. That's what college is for, for goodness sakes!" Ash looked at the dean for confirmation, but he was busy scraping his spoon in parallel streaks across the thin film that remained on his plate.

"This is a nice change from the cafeteria," Ash said. "I appreciate it."

"Well, you eat all you want. More peas, Richard?"

"Peas, yes." He cleared his throat. "What about a little gravy on them?"

She served his peas—gravy-less—and offered more to Ash.

Ash clapped a hand to his belly. "No, ma'am. Thank you."

"I'll clear the table while you two talk." She lifted the potato bowl as she stood.

The dean watched as she backed through the kitchen door, and when it swung shut he pointed. "Just hand me one of those rolls," he mumbled. "And the gravy."

Unceremoniously the dean plunged the pilfered roll into the gravy and stuffed the whole thing into his mouth. The maneuver was complete before Dory returned from the kitchen. The dean stood and lumbered from the table, his jaws working steadily.

"Let's go back into my study," he suggested, his voice enunciative and clear. Ash wondered how he managed that with a mouthful of dinner roll sopped in gravy.

The study walls were shelved with books, framed documents, and photographs, giving the room the warmth of a private retreat. Dean Oberleigh sank heavily into an armchair and stretched his long legs before him as if dropping anchor for a long stay. Ash eased down onto the short sofa and waited.

"We have a dilemma," the dean began, his voice formal now, resurrecting the weight of his office. "This cheating." He frowned and shook his head. "It's a damned sorry mess, and it looks like it involves a great many of our students."

"Sir, I don't know why you think I'm connected to any of—"

The dean raised a palm to interrupt. "I know you're not connected to it."

Ash laughed softly. "Well, I don't know how you can know that either."

The dean offered a bland stare. "Dr. Leonhardt told me."

Ash tried to imagine his crusty teacher confiding such information. He heard Leonhardt's voice echo from memory, speaking Ash's name when collecting his test. The dean sat forward and wrapped one big fist inside the other hand.

"Robert, I'm going to ask you if you would be willing to do something for me. And no matter what your answer, I need your assurance that this discussion does not leave this room. You tell no one. Understood?"

Ash pushed back deeper into the sofa. "Okay."

The big man's face took on a pained expression. "We think it started last winter. We weren't sure then, but now we know."

"And this is in my biology class?"

"Yes . . . among others." The dean raised a finger for each department that he named. When he began smoothing a wrinkle on his pants, Ash began to suspect where this was going and what he might be asked to do.

"But how can you know all this for sure?" Ash said, delaying the inevitable.

The dean took in a long breath and then exhaled in a rush. "All right, here it is," he said, as though he had reached some decision. "Leonhardt came up with a method to detect if a student was cheating, but—" He spread his hands. "The board didn't approve it. So he went ahead and put it into practice anyway. He calls it a 'hidden-reversal.' "

Ash sat forward and propped his forearms on his knees. "What's a 'hidden-reversal'?"

Dean Oberleigh's voice dropped to a confiding tone. "First, Leonhardt positioned test monitors around the room, but no matter how innocent the classroom appeared, the test answers clearly indicated collaboration between students. Too many perfect answers. Too many identical phrases. He started introducing questions beyond the scope of the textbook and lectures. Same results. Because these students were scattered all over the room, he concluded that his tests were somehow being made public before the exam."

"Leonhardt made out each of his tests in longhand, then his secretary typed and copied it. So there were two possibilities: One, someone was getting into his office. Two, the secretary was the leak. At the next test time, he took all the copies home with him. Same results. He had no choice but to suspect his secretary. On the next test, he kept her out of the loop, typing and copying the tests himself. Same results."

"So maybe there's not any cheating going on after all," Ash said.

The dean held up an index finger. "Just wait. One morning before a test, he used a bottle of *White-Out* and removed one word from a question. The word was at the end of a line, and so there was no noticeable gap. The word he removed was 'not.' So, you see, he completely turned around the meaning of the question. A diametric change."

Diametric. The word welled up from Ash's memory in Mick's whining voice. Ash began to connect the dots from Mick's complaint to the hidden-reversal.

The dean continued. "Leonhardt applied the blot to as many tests as he could before class, altering less than half, but he decided to hand them out as they were. When he graded the tests, every altered question—except in two cases, I think—had been answered as if the word 'not' had remained in the question."

"Which means," Ash said, "they weren't reading the question carefully, because they thought they already knew what it said."

"Exactly," the dean whispered, pointing both index fingers at Ash. "They jumped right in with their prepared answers."

Ash was fascinated by this revelation of Dr. Leonhardt's methods. These secret doings explained a lot about Leonhardt's blatant disdain of the students and his reasons for retrieving the tests after handing them out. He could not have the students discovering the variations in the questions.

"So," the dean went on, "he brought his findings to the board and proposed to ferret out every guilty party. But the board reprimanded him. You can't give different tests in a class. That's standard policy. If that ever got out, the newspapers would crucify us. It would look like cheating, all right . . . by the teacher. And since Leonhardt couldn't mark the answers wrong without alerting the guilty ones that something was amiss, he was, in effect, showing favoritism." Dean Oberleigh shook his head and shrugged. "And there's no solid proof how the cheating is done. Or for that matter, that it's *being* done. And without proof—" He spread his hands and slapped them on the arms of the chair.

Ash thought about the hidden-reversal. "Eventually, even if the board approves its use, someone's bound to notice the word omission, aren't they?"

The dean shrugged. "He thought of that. He had his secretary type the word back in before the tests were returned."

Ash realized that he himself must have received a test *with* the hidden-reversal, because by answering the question as phrased he had shown Dr. Leonhardt that he did not have a predisposed answer. The girl with the bracelets had either received a test without the reversal or she was cheating and hastily gave a right answer to the wrong question.

"But what if I *had* gotten hold of a test," Ash challenged, "memorized the answers and spotted the reversal? Couldn't I have adapted my answer accordingly?"

"It's possible." Dean Oberleigh agreed. "But you didn't. Your approach to the answer didn't follow the formulaic nature of the other students' answers."

"But if I were creative enough to disguise that . . . word it in my own way—"

The dean was shaking his head throughout Ash's argument. "You didn't. On the test you took Friday, a particular question was reversed in such a way that you could not just flip over your answer to satisfy the new intent of the question. You had to have a grasp of the material. It took a subjective analysis."

Ash heard Dory set something down on the dining table. The dean heard it, too. When her knock sounded at the open door, the dean dropped his administrator's demeanor and pushed out of his chair.

"Dessert?" he said hopefully.

"Come and get it," she announced. "I hope you like apple pie, Robert."

Dean Oberleigh's face went slack. "We have apple pie?" Now a changed man, he followed his wife in a spirited gait, as Ash trailed behind.

A generous wedge of pie and a glass of milk waited at Ash's place. A smaller slice sat at Dory's. The dean's place was empty.

"Decaf or skimmed milk, honey?" Dory said.

The dean's eyes were fixed on Ash's pie. "Decaf," he said in a lackluster mumble. He lowered himself into his chair like a blind man. Ash sat and busied himself with his napkin in his lap until Dory returned and set down coffee and a bowl before the dean.

"Apple sauce?" he said and looked up at her, but she only sat and smiled at Ash.

"Do you play a sport, Robert?"

"No, ma'am."

She cocked her head as she cut into her pie. "Don't the coaches come after you with those shoulders? Football or something?"

Ash took a forkful of pie and shook his head.

"Well." She raised her cup. "Here's to your knees. Some mornings Richard's knees sound like popcorn cooking. Relics of his football days."

The dean pushed up from the table. "I think I'll try out those knees right now," he announced and carried his bowl into the kitchen.

"Honey?" Dory called, looking into her coffee. "You have your appointment on Wednesday." She cut her eyes to Ash. "Cholesterol," she whispered.

A cabinet door banged in the kitchen. Waxed paper crackled. In the silence that followed, a spoon tapped repeatedly on porcelain.

Dean Oberleigh returned with a triumphant smile and set his bowl on the table. "Poor man's apple pie," he announced. Amid the applesauce were broken sections of a graham cracker. He sat and spooned up a mouthful.

Dory watched him chew. "Have you and Robert come to any decision, honey?"

The dean's mouthful of pseudo-pie kept him busy. Filling the gap Ash said, "Nobody really calls me 'Robert.' I go by 'Ash.' "

The dean wiped his mouth with his napkin. "We haven't finished talking."

Dory's eyes widened, and her mouth formed an apologetic O. Each focused on eating in the awkward silence that followed. Finally, Dory finished her coffee and rose.

"More pie, Ash?"

"No, ma'am. Thank you."

She took Ash's plate and glass and turned to her husband. "Finished, honey?" His spontaneous concoction lay in ruins, cold and only half-eaten.

He wiped his mouth and dropped his napkin. "Let's go in the study, Robert."

As he passed through the main room, Dean Oberleigh selected a pipe from a stand before moving back into the study. While he tamped tobacco, Ash browsed the books and framed photos on the wall.

"Is this you?" Ash asked with more surprise than he intended. The photo captured the pose of a square-jawed teen with a crewcut, his muscular body filling out a dark football uniform. Number 77. From ox-yoke shoulders his jersey tapered in a ruler-straight V to the waistline of a greyhound.

The dean nodded with the pipe in his mouth. "Mm-hmm." A match spurted and the sweet scent of tobacco hung in the room. "Robert, I'm going to ask for your help."

Still studying the photo with his back to the dean, Ash closed his eyes to hold onto a mental picture of Beechwood. With this image intact, he felt prepared to reject any proposal that might be offered.

"Do you have a reputation in your biology class?" the dean asked.

Ash turned. "A reputation? What do you mean?"

"Well, do you participate in class? Do you ask questions . . . or answer them?"

Ash huffed a quiet laugh. "Not anymore. No one does."

The dean nodded and checked the smolder of his pipe. "Would you be willing to buy a test for us? You know, ask around so we can see how it's done?" They looked at one another through the cloud of smoke spreading across the room. "You would need to flunk a test—in appearance only, of course. They—the people stealing these tests—would need to believe that you need some help."

Ash frowned. "Grades aren't posted. And no one's going to ask what I made."

Pursing his lips, the dean thought about that and then pointed the pipe at Ash. "What if the grades *were* made public? What if Dr. Leonhardt announced that he was going to hand out the tests by ascending grades—beginning with the lowest?"

That would be like Leonhardt, Ash knew. He scrambled for another argument but could think of nothing.

"Now imagine the class," the dean continued, "holding its breath to see who would first be called to walk to the front of the room for his graded test . . . and it's *you*."

The scene rolled through Ash's mind like a filmstrip. He sat, leaned forward with his elbows on his knees, and pressed the heels of his palms into his eyes. He thought of the people with whom he would have to associate if he agreed to help. Looking down at his hands he said the words he knew he had to say.

"Sir, I'm not inclined to do this."

The dean stared at him through a blue haze of smoke. "May I ask why?"

Ash settled back in the sofa, and the words seemed to spill out of nowhere. "I'm an A student senior with no pre-major. I haven't fit in too well here, and I'm not sure I'm ready for college. I've got things to figure out for myself. I can't see putting my energy into this." He shook his head and sat back into the cushions. "It's probably the jocks anyway. They—" Ash held his tongue as he thought of the photograph on the wall behind him—a younger Richard Oberleigh in football pads. He shrugged. "I just don't want to step into that world of thieves, you know?"

Through the wall they heard Dory's light ascent up the stairs to the upper level. Soon her muted footsteps began to crisscross the floor above them.

"Well," the dean finally said and tapped his pipe against a glass ashtray. "I won't push it if you feel strongly about it."

There it was: the *out*. But the surge of relief Ash had anticipated did not come.

The dean stood. "Well, it's late. You've probably got some studying to do." He laid the pipe on his desk, and the simple act seemed to carry the weight of all his disappointments. In a strained silence they walked to the front hall where Ash had to face the mirror again. They exchanged perfunctory lines of parting, and then Ash was on the porch, and the door closed behind him. It was over.

He tried to inhale the freedom of the cool night air and wrap himself in the solitude he had left waiting outside this door. But the night had somehow rearranged itself in his absence. He felt alien, as if he had stepped off a bus in the wrong town. The sound of his feet on the steps was hollow and somehow shameful. He turned and looked at the house just in time to see the porch light click off. Then he heard the dean's heavy footsteps move deeper into the house.

Head down, Ash crossed the lawn and retrieved his tee shirt and archery gear. As he stood looking at the house, a window lit up and threw a rectangle of yellow light across the driveway. Across this a shadow moved. Ash pictured Dean Oberleigh sitting with a cup of coffee before a pile of papers, digging into his night's work. Moving toward the window, Ash imagined the man's expression if he were to tap on the glass and say, *I'll do it!* The notion spread through him like a reprieve that would set something back into balance. He picked up his pace and strode to the window.

Spanning the open refrigerator, Dean Oberleigh's broad back was in dark silhouette against the light coming from the interior bulb. His elbows rose and fell as he spooned from the pie-tin like a man who had not eaten for a week. Ash turned away and began the walk back to Huntington Hall.

Chapter Seven

The Tavern was the last place Ash would have chosen to be were it not for his promise to meet Elaine. It was early on Friday night, and the crowd was working itself up to the rowdiness needed for the coming football game on Saturday. One table of boys had painted their faces green, and they were making the most of their moment of celebrity.

Perched on the small stage, Alan closed his eyes and draped his lanky body over Ash's guitar, his eyes hidden by the long blond hair that hung over his face. His long fingers walked over the frets, and the amplified notes cascaded out of the speakers. It was hard to know when he was opening up a serious tune or one of his parodies. Tonight it didn't matter. With the game less than twenty-four hours away, every table was full of talk. And all the talk was football.

"Once upon a modern time . . . at a prep school for the elite
There lived an arcane archer man . . . whom you'll not likely meet."

And so began *The Ballad of Young Asher of Greenwood.* Alan played for Ash and a few front-row loyalists. The room had grown louder, and a brown paper sack pressed into the shape of a bottle was passed around from table to table like a communal ritual. When the song ended, the crowd was so boisterous that only a few knew to applaud.

Right away Alan lowered his head and began a new composition, coaxing a haunting melody from the bass strings while the higher strings rained down a minor key accompaniment. Ash remembered it from his room. The song written for Elaine.

When the words began, soulful and questioning, some of the girls in the room visibly disengaged from their dates and listened, staring from the dark like voyeurs. The song carved its own quiet place out of the din in the room, and when it was done, Alan accepted the minority applause with a minimal smile. After slipping the guitar strap off his head, he weaved his way to Ash's booth, where he sat and shrugged.

"I don't know what happened. She was supposed to be here." Alan shook his head. "If the school won't let us have a cell phone, you'd think they could provide pay phones that work." He pointed to the back. "That one eats your money half the time." He stood and looked around the room. "Let me go try her dorm once more."

Ash watched him drop coins into the wall phone. Alan pressed the receiver to one ear and flattened a hand over the other. After a minute of waiting, he hung up.

Ash stood and tried to catch Alan's eye to wave goodbye, but a head of pale blonde hair came between them, and Alan turned to it as if called by name. For a moment Ash thought the elusive Elaine had arrived, but then he remembered that, according to her song, her hair was "the rich brown of a sylvan doe." Alan had never lacked for female admirers, Ash knew, so he took the opportunity to leave the noisy cafe.

*****

Greenwood Downs was the only school in the state to hold its football games on Saturdays—a concession strong-armed on the state high school commission by powerful alumni-businessmen who found Fridays inconvenient. On each Saturday game day, they flew in on private jets from all parts of the country, bringing with them an entourage of associates and clients who needed impressing. And so it was on this day.

As the campus became an anthill of activity, Ash packed up the few things he needed and headed west. At the archery field he found the rolled up blanket snug under the target cover with one of his arrows. Adding these to his load, he trekked the half mile upriver.

Once inside his retreat he attached the blanket as a door flap, built a fire, and unpacked canned foods, candles, batteries, sleeping bag, and canteen. Using his father's duffel, he collected new leaves for a fresh mattress and piled firewood for the night. Then using needle and thread he camouflaged the door flap by attaching leaves and ferns in random patterns. When he finished, darkness had begun to creep into the valley.

He prepared a meal of soup and crackers and ate by the fire. As he cleaned up at the water's edge, a roar of voices carried up the river from the stadium. When the cheer faded, the soundtrack of the forest seemed to return with an enhanced intimacy—the riffle of the current, the wind sieving through the hemlock boughs, the hiss of the shoals upstream—all of it confirming his defection to a place of his own.

Inside the shelter he lighted a candle and lay down to study his biology notes, but within minutes his eyes grew heavy. He blew out the candle and fell asleep to the sound of the crackling fire.

*****

On Sunday afternoon he gathered up bow and quiver and headed back toward campus. As he neared the archery field, it surprised him that all his senses were focused ahead of him, toward the possibility of seeing the woman archer again. And then, as if conjured up from nothing but wishful thinking, she was there, shooting from twenty yards out. He watched her empty her quiver before he stepped out onto the field.

"Hello!" she called out, her accent adorning the single word with British charm.

As he got closer he saw that she had gathered her hair into a single plait that hung over one shoulder, streaks of silver and gold interweaving in a pleasing contrast. The chill in the air had brought out a rose blush in her cheeks. The spider web lines that radiated from her eyes showed that she was as pleased to see him as he to see her.

"Would you like to join me?" she asked, her invitation delivered with the comfortable familiarity of a longstanding friend.

"Sure." His voice cracked, and he realized he had not spoken for more than a day.

She nodded toward the woods. "Have you been shooting in the forest today?"

He shook his head. "I haven't shot for a couple of days."

She beamed. "Oh, splendid, I'll get to see your 'reckoning arrow.' "

"My what?" he said and followed as she led the way.

Stopping at her shooting spot, she turned. "It's an old Saxon term for a first shot of the day. Without benefit of warm-up, you see. It was thought to be the true test of an archer's mettle. Have you heard of it?"

"Not by that name."

She swept her arm toward the target. "After you then, if you please."

After stringing his bow, Ash loaded an arrow and settled into his stance. He was surprised how comfortable he felt in her presence. When he drew and sighted down his shaft, he felt her moral support like a palpable presence steadying his aim. The arrow flew true, impaling the gold circle within an inch of its center.

When he turned to her, she bowed just as she had before. Then she stepped beside him, and they fell into a rhythm of alternating shots, filling the bull's eye with an island of red and gray feathers. When their quivers were empty they walked together to the target. While pulling his arrows, Ash was surprised to see a lone figure on the hill.

"Looks like somebody has your place today," he said, nodding at the cemetery.

Without bothering to look, she smiled as if she already knew. "Another round?"

This time she led the way to a different spot. As he followed, he stole another glimpse at the distant observer. Something in the stoop of the shoulders and the style of the hat suggested an elderly person . . . a man, he thought.

"I don't know your name," he said to her back.

She stopped and loaded. "Marin," she answered softly and turned to face him. Her gray irises contained their own light. Looking into them was like gazing up through cold clear springwater at the wavering sun.

"My name is Robert. But my friends call me 'Ash.' "

"Yes," she said simply. Her eyes remained on him, waiting for more.

"What should I call you?" he asked, embarrassed. "Is it 'Dr. Marin' or—?"

"Marin," she said again, exactly as she had before.

He squinted at the hill. The onlooker had not moved. When Ash turned back to Marin, she too was staring at the cemetery.

"It will be dark soon," she said, backing away toward the pines. "I should go."

When she began walking for the campus, Ash called out, "Thank you for covering my blanket the other day. And my arrow." When she had almost reached the pines, he cupped his hands to his mouth to ask when she might be shooting again. But he said nothing as she disappeared through the pines. After covering the target he ran to catch her. From the curb he looked in every direction. She was gone.

*****

Marin heard the hacking cough as she topped the trail at the cemetery. He was waiting with an embarrassed smile, his eyes watery over the closed fist pressed to his mouth.

"I should not have stayed so long," she said.

He waved away her apology. "This takes time," he assured her. When another coughing spasm seized him, she layered the lapels of his wool coat over his chest and secured the button at his throat. He chuckled. "T'would be ironic to kick off in a graveyard, wouldn't it now?"

She felt his forehead with the back of her hand. "Let's go back. The night air is coming in."

She braced her forearm against his and eased him down the trail, stopping each time the coughing seized him. In a slow march they crossed the field toward the trail near Painted Rock.

"Has he talked about how he learned his shooting form?" he said.

She shook her head. "I have not asked. Like you said . . . 'this takes time.' "

They moved steadily on toward the log bridge, and his breathing became more labored. "Next time," she said, "I shall ask him."

Chapter Eight

On Monday morning Ash tapped down the stairwell into Huntington's lobby, where a dozen students huddled around someone reading aloud from the *Clarion*. When he heard Dr. Leonhardt's name, he stopped cold. Walking to the crowd he saw the newspaper headline: *GDA Grading Scandal Exposed—Department Head Leonhardt Suspended.*

Ash's body went as light as smoke.

" 'Dr. Johns brought formal charges against Leonhardt late yesterday,' " the reader continued, " 'after an unnamed student proved that an unethical manipulation of test scoring favored some students while it penalized others.' "

"I bet I know that guy," a thin boy said. "Always bellyachin' about Leonhardt."

Ash sidled through the crowd to face this boy. "Who was it?"

The boy shrugged. "He's in my biz-econ class . . . 'Michael' something."

Ash made his way out the door and started running. Up at the intersection ahead of him, a TV van with a satellite dish slowed at the stop sign and then climbed the hill toward the science building. Looking south on Academy Drive, Ash saw other vans, each showing the call letters of radio stations. He ran for the cafeteria.

Calling from the pay phone, he listened to the dean's office phone ring twenty times. He tried to eat some breakfast, but he kept getting up to drop the same coin into the telephone. When, finally, Sara Birmingham picked up, he was told the dean would not be in until afternoon. Stepping outside, Ash stared up at the sky. The clouds looked as heavy as slate. The first bell rang, and he started for his class.

The clamor of conversations in the auditorium was like the sustained roar of a seashore. A camera crew was setting up in one of the tiered aisles, blocking students who needed to gain the upper rows. Some of the more agile students detoured, using desktops as steppingstones. There was a certain urgency sparking through the room, but the prevailing mood among the students in the top rows was festive.

Mick slouched forward on his desk, his chin hooked over his forearms, his eyes open but fixed on nothing. When the second-bell clanged, out of reflex the crowd made a feint toward quietness, but their excited voices surged again right away.

The stage door opened, and Princeton Johns marched to the podium. He was thin with straight mousy brown hair fringed over the back of his shirt collar. A neatly trimmed mustache added a thin arching line to his narrow face but did nothing to detract from the slit of his mouth. Not quite a smirk, his subtle smile seemed designed to boast of a secret advantage he held over others.

Slapping a notebook down on the podium he glared out at the chaos reigning over the room. Without speaking, he spun around, returned the way he had come, opened the door, and slammed it with a dramatic rotation of his body. The sound hushed the room to remarkable effect.

Now the sharp taps of his heels on the wooden floor sent a message to the class: *Things are about to change!* Satisfaction glowed in his cadaverous face. He gripped the sides of the podium and stood erect, staring at the camera crew in the center aisle.

"On whose authority are you here?"

A cameraman's head bobbed up from behind his lens. Johns stretched a long finger toward the door.

"You may leave!"

A familiar newsman in a dark suit ventured forward a step. "Dr. Johns, we're from Atlanta's Nine Nightly News and we—"

"As of today," Johns interrupted, "*this* is a classroom! It is *not* a TV studio!"

There was a moment of suspended uncertainty. Then without protest the television crew began to break camp, every *click* and *snap* in the dismantling of gear like an utterance of deference and defeat. Johns adopted a business-as-usual air, not deigning to recognize the media's presence again. He was several sentences into his lecture before anyone realized that the class had begun. A chain reaction of opening notebooks rattled around the room. Johns never broke stride.

When the TV crew was clustered at the door, he threw them a morsel. "Perhaps I will meet with you outside on the steps . . . say a few minutes after nine o'clock." He then picked up where he had left off in his lecture.

Ash had heard of Princeton Johns's talent for drawing blood in a classroom. His ego was equally notorious. Now his face would be all over the evening news. Ousting the press from his class had only been a show of power.

It was a long hour of nonstop note-taking. When Ash exited the building he found the camera crew set up beside the steps. Lingering on the sidewalk, Ash watched, and soon Mick scuffed down the steps to join him.

When Johns appeared, his hair was freshly combed. A crook-necked pipe was clamped in his teeth, and he wore a tweed jacket. An interviewer jockeyed for position, thrusting a microphone at him. Johns ignored the man and struck a pose on the steps.

"You gotta be kidding me," Mick mumbled. "What a showboat."

"Dr. Johns!" the interviewer began, "did you bring charges against Leonhardt?"

Johns raised his chin and spoke around the pipe. "Correct . . . with the direct testimony of a student to validate the charge."

The TV man bombarded him with questions, but Johns kept his composure and answered whatever query he deemed relevant. He spoke at length on the unethical nature of what his predecessor had done.

"Who came forward, Dr. Johns?" the man finally asked. "Who was the student?"

Johns sniffed. "The student's name cannot be released at this time."

"Exactly how was the favoritism dealt out? Was it in the grading?"

"Yes," Johns said, "simply by not marking off points on incorrect answers."

"But how can you prove it was not simply an oversight on Dr. Leonhardt's part?"

Johns removed the pipe to affect a dry laugh. "Because in this class alone," he pointed back at the auditorium with his pipe stem, "it happened thirty-six times."

Ash closed his eyes and shook his head. "That's ridiculous!" he hissed. The hidden-reversal sat on his tongue like a hot coal.

Mick snorted a laugh. "It's not ridiculous to me!"

Ash turned angrily to Mick but said nothing. Shaking his head, he started down the hill in a purposeful stride.

At the student center Ash telephoned the dean's home, letting the phone ring a dozen times before leaving for English class. He tried the call after each of his next two classes. In the art studio he buried his thoughts in the day's sketching assignment, but twenty minutes before the class was to be over, he walked to the front of the room and dropped his work on Mr. Lowery's stool.

When he walked past Anne Metter, something pulled his eyes back to her drawing table. Over her shoulder he saw a book cover showing a medieval archer poised at full draw. The title read *Archery Yesterday and Today.* Frowning, Ash returned to his drawing table, picked up his books, and left.

Inside the library he descended into the perpetual twilight of the basement. Dropping his books on the table he looked around the dusky room at the rows of reference books that lined the walls. This space had been a retreat for him these years. Now it felt like a dungeon.

Leaning on the table he let his head sag between his shoulders. He now felt an unexpected bond with Dr. Leonhardt. When he imagined going to the dean and accepting the offer to get involved, right away the hole inside him filled with purpose.

Studying with a new ferocity, he slapped the pages over as he devoured their contents. He did this without let-up for two hours. Then with two hours of light left in the day, he ran to Huntington to pick up his archery gear, and now all his thoughts turned to Marin, wondering if she might be at the west field.

Inside his room, he found his guitar lying on his bed with a folded note on top.

> *Young Asher, the friend who repaired my guitar last week lives in Gamewell. He is a master woodworker. He makes bows! He's coming by The Tavern tonight. Can you drop by?*
> *~ Alan*
> *P.S. Any new women in your life?*

After jogging up Valley Road with his bow and quiver, he stopped inside the pines that bordered the field and tried to make sense of the scene before him. Four people were grouped at the covered target. None was Marin. A female holding a bow was the focus amid three males. One insistent voice rose above the rest, followed by a chorus of laughter—a part of that being Anne Metter's familiar warble.

Ash recognized the loud performer. He was a wrestler—'Guy' something—whose picture often made the school paper. Thick-chested, hairy, and muscular, he dominated the gathering, bursting with a bawdy laugh, which the other boys tried to mimic.

"Aw, come on, Anne!" Guy pleaded. "Shoot it! We wanna watch!"

When she shook her head, he took from her the bow and one of her yellow arrows. "Well, hell, if you won't . . . then let me!" He strutted ten yards from the draped target and turned to shoot. His two buddies backed away in mock panic, dragging Anne with them. "Hey, Trout!" Guy yelled. "Put a apple on Jeep's head, why don'cha!" He laughed and drew the bow string and arrow back to his ear.

"That's a rain cover!" Ash called out as he stepped from the pines. Every head turned his way and watched his approach. "It works better if there are no holes in it."

Anne's face flushed with color, but Ash did not acknowledge her. Stopping in front of the target with his back turned to Guy, Ash removed and folded the plastic tarp and then weighted it with the stones. Then he turned to face the wrestler.

"When you finish," Ash said, "be sure to cover it again." He hitched his head toward the target. "It's just hay. It'll rot if it gets wet."

One of the boys standing with Anne made a snorting sound. "You rich preppies ought'a be able to buy somethin' a little fancier than hay."

Ash looked at him, seeing now that this one was too old to be a student at Greenwood. He wore a gray uniform with the name *Troutman* embroidered over the breast pocket. Troutman was wiry, standing with his head cocked, arms slightly arced from his torso, and a smirk skewing his mouth. His cheekbones sharpened around his hook nose, giving his face the taper of an axe blade. Something quick and mean flickered in his eyes.

The stocky wrestler approached Ash with a tight smile. Guy lacked two inches to match Ash's six feet, but his neck was a tree stump rooted in the boulder-field of his shoulders. His simian jaw branded him with a look of perpetual aggression. He wore sweats cut off at the armpits and thighs, exposing tufts of black curly hair. The rancid scent of sweat and salt emanated from him.

"We'll cover it up," said the third boy.

Ash turned to this earnest voice and recognized the third member of the trio from his biology class. He was muscular but without the bulk of Guy or the menace of the one named Troutman. His face seemed trapped in childish surprise.

"So," Guy said, "you and Anne getting ready for deer season?" He kept a straight face and poked a thumb over his shoulder. "Ol' Trout there is our local Dan'l Boone. Eats so much venison, he's half-deer." Guy grinned at Troutman. "Half-deer, half-beer." When Troutman didn't smile, Guy laughed. "How many deer you kill last year, Trout?"

Troutman clamped a stem of grass in his teeth and glared at Ash. "Six," he claimed. Ash knew the legal limit for deer was two. Troutman was either lying or admitting to a federal crime.

Guy swept an arm toward the target. "Aw-right, boys and girls! Let's see some shootin'!" He looked from Ash to Anne then turned to give his buddies a wink.

"Have fun," Ash said quietly and walked past them toward the woods.

Anne caught him by his sleeve. "Ash, please don't leave me here with them!"

He looked past her at Guy clowning with the bow. "Why did you bring them?"

"I didn't! I mean, I didn't mean to. One of the coaches told me I could shoot in the west field, but I wasn't sure where it was, and Guy said he would show me."

Ash started to ask why she had come at all, but instead he said, "That your bow?"

"It's on loan from phys-ed."

Ash nodded and watched the big wrestler carry the bow back to a shooting distance of ten yards. "Go get your bow, Anne. Tell them you're coming with me."

She looked lost, as though she needed him to say more, but finally she turned and approached Guy. Ash watched the conference, Guy smiling throughout as he took a silly shooting stance. Exasperated, Anne looked back at Ash and let her arms rise and then fall to her sides. Ash clenched his teeth and walked back to them.

Both the bow and the arrow were too small for Guy's long arms. When he drew the string, the arrow tip came off the rest a full inch behind the handle and wavered there.

"Ease up!" Ash called, but he could see by the gleam in Guy's eye that he would shoot. Ash pulled Anne behind him as the string twanged with a strange, clunky sound.

Guy rocked with laughter at the bizarre predicament in his hands. He had let go the string, but the arrow was still fully drawn, wedged between string and bow.

"Hey!" Guy crowed. "Who hit the pause button?" He turned in a mindless full-circle parade, brandishing the cocked bow with one hand. Troutman's composure left him as he dodged to one side. When the metal tip of the arrow slipped, the bow shuddered in Guy's loose grip and dropped to the grass. Against all odds the arrow smacked into the target.

The trio howled in disbelief. Ash picked up the bow and remaining arrows, handed them to Anne, and walked past her toward the woods.

"If you're coming, this would be the time," he said over his shoulder.

He heard her footsteps come up behind him as he moved toward the forest. Behind him the squeals of laughter on the field grated in his ear.

They stood on Painted Rock with its garish splash of colors, Ash looking upriver and Anne thinking what to say. "So now you're an archer?" he asked, turning to her.

She cleared her throat with a nervous laugh. "No, not really." She lowered her eyes. "But I'd like to learn." Then the apology in her voice was replaced by something brave. "I wanted to get to know you," she admitted.

Her honesty surprised him. They stood for a time listening to the water riffle past them. When he heard the languid caw of a crow near the field, he nodded that way.

"They'll be gone now. You should be able to shoot in peace."

Her face tightened with curiosity, but before she could speak, he started back up the trail. Following him, she tried to match his walk by finding the quieter spots for her feet. When they stepped onto the empty field, a crow barked three quick notes, flapped from its perch, and flew low into the woods like a thief dodging into cover.

"How did you know I was an archer?" Ash said as they walked toward the target.

She swished her hair and smiled. "I met your friend Alan at The Tavern. A song of his was about someone whose name was similar to yours. So I asked him."

Ash nodded, now remembering the head of blonde hair he had seen with Alan at the Tavern's pay phone. He stopped and stared at the arrow jutting from the target.

"Was that dangerous?" Anne asked, pointing at the arrow.

"Like a loaded gun, cocked, and spinning on a table."

Two vertical lines creased above the bridge of her nose. "The idiot," she hissed.

"And the brothers Karamazov," Ash added. He looked at her so intently that she swallowed. "You don't have to get to know me this way, Anne."

"But I do want to learn about it." She slid a finger along the curve of the bow. "Actually, I *need* to learn about it. Would you be willing to teach me? I could pay you."

He could see that she was struggling with her courage and decided to put her to the one test she was sure to fail. "What about Saturday at two?"

Her face lit up. "That would be great!"

Ash hid his surprise. "During the football game?" he reminded.

Her smile relaxed. "Oh, that's right. It's an afternoon game, isn't it?"

He kept his face expressionless as he studied her troubled eyes. He could almost see her recalculating her weekend agenda.

"Should we meet here?" she asked, her joy quickly resurrected.

He nodded. "Will phys-ed let you hang on to this gear for a while?"

When she nodded with enthusiasm, he pulled the yellow arrow from the target and handed it to her. "Okay, Saturday, two o'clock."

Buoyed by the happily-ever-after ways of the world, Anne Metter waved and made a little bounce with her body. "See you tomorrow in the studio?" She bobbed her head in the familiar way that made her hair swish around and somehow return to its original order. She walked off the field, turning one last time to wave from the pines.

Chapter Nine

It was twilight when Ash jogged into the Oberleigh's driveway. As he approached the house, the dean's Pontiac fired up and spewed a plume of white exhaust into the cool air. Through the back window, Ash could make out two heads in the front seats. When he gained the driver's window, Dean Oberleigh turned, surprised, then looked at him through the glass with dead eyes. When the window powered down, Dory leaned over her husband to offer a strained smile.

"We're on our way to see the headmaster," she began. "They're talking about firing Dr. Leonhardt."

Ash stared at the dean's stoic profile. "To tell him about the hidden-reversal?"

The dean's voice matched his grim face. "He already knows about that."

"Then how can they fire him?"

"Because," the dean shot back, "the board had vetoed it, remember?"

Dory patted her husband's leg. "Ash," she said, "they know all that, but—"

"But," the dean interrupted, "*one of them* won't let it go that Leonhardt went against their ruling." He shut off the engine. "*One of them* stands to gain from his dismissal." He inhaled deeply through his nose and stared through the windshield.

"Dr. Johns," Ash said, putting a name to the problem.

"The chapel project has been canned, too, Ash," Dory said.

Ash ducked lower to see her. "But there was already money raised for that."

"There's a move to redirect those funds," Dory said. "For faculty housing."

"Princeton Johns," the dean said under his breath. "*His* housing."

For a time they did not speak. Somewhere down the street a dog began barking in an incessant rhythm. A man yelled an angry command, and the barking stopped.

"What can I do, Dean Oberleigh?" Ash said, but the dean was already shaking his head. Ash leaned on the car. "If you need somebody to buy those tests—"

The dean removed his glasses and pinched the bridge of his nose. "There's nothing to do now." His voice was cold and final.

"I want to help," Ash said. "Just tell me what to do."

The dean slid his glasses back in place and looked squarely at Ash. "I've got someone else to help . . . a student. You turned me down, remember?"

Ash felt himself wither inside. He straightened and stepped back.

"It's still important that you not mention our meeting to anyone," the dean reminded. He reached for the ignition. "We're going to be late."

"Richard," Dory said, touching his arm. "Maybe there is a way Ash can help. Remember what your new helper's main concerns were?"

The dean turned toward her, and she tapped a finger twice to her ear. He took his hand off the key and stared through the windshield again.

"Do you really want to contribute in this?" he said, facing Ash.

"Yes, sir. I do."

The dean continued to stare at Ash. "Then I want you to tutor someone."

* * * * *

At the Tavern, Ash sipped hot cocoa as Alan finished his set. When enthusiastic applause filled the room, Alan set his guitar aside and sidled through the tables to Ash's booth.

"They love you," Ash said as Alan slid into the seat opposite him.

"All part of the formula, Young Asher." He counted off on his fingers. "You sing to cowboys, you sing about a horse—preferably a favorite one that died. Sing to rednecks . . . it's whiskey, your mama, and being sorry for the way you treated your woman . . . or man . . . or dog . . . especially one that died. Play for yuppies . . . it's relationships that screw up. And play for GDA students?" Alan smiled. "Anarchy." He breathed the word with conspiratorial satisfaction.

When a lithe student with a head of bronze-red hair appeared at the end of the table, Alan slid over. The newcomer glided into the booth with the grace of a gymnast.

"Sorry I'm late," he said with a shy smile. He nodded to Ash. "I've heard a lot about you." His voice registered low in decibels, high in courtesy. He offered his hand.

"Ash," Alan said, taking over introductions. "Will Scathlock is, pound for pound, our best wrestler. He's the woodworker I was telling you about."

"Call me 'Cat.' Everyone else does."

"So you're a bowyer," Ash said and clasped the boy's hand. They shook.

Cat cracked a modest grin and nodded. "And I hear you are quite the archer."

Ash sat back and pinned Alan with a stare. "You made him sit through *The Ballad,* didn't you?"

Holding a poker face, Alan held up both palms.

"The fact is," Ash said to Cat, "Alan has never seen me shoot a single arrow."

Cat shrugged. "Maybe he doesn't need to."

Ash smiled at this unexpected jewel of philosophy. "Are you an archer?"

"Just enough to know if a bow I've made is good or mediocre."

"Then how did you get into making them?"

"If it's made from trees," Alan said, "he da man! He did a great job on my guitar."

Cat flashed another grin. "I started in England. I was there with Alan. You know about the Fitzwalter scholarship? Mr. Fitzhugh apprenticed me. You'd'a loved it there."

Ash settled his gaze on Alan. "So I've been told . . . a number of times."

The three sat without speaking for a time until Alan checked his watch and patted both hands down on the tabletop. "Well, I'd better make some music. My retinue calls."

Cat glided off the seat to let Alan out.

"I just thought you two should meet," Alan said. "Enjoy the show, gentlemen." He made his way through the tables back to the stage.

Cat, still standing, slipped his hands in his pockets. "Did I say something wrong?"

Ash shook his head and pushed his cup aside. "I was offered the Fitzwalter. I turned it down." He gestured for Cat to sit. "Alan thinks I was crazy. I made him promise to stop bringing it up."

When Alan's guitar notes rose from the speakers, Cat sat again.

"Where were you in school before?" Ash asked.

"Before England?" Cat said. "Oregon."

"Small world that you and Alan would end up here."

"Well, this is where they sent all of us."

Ash frowned. "All of who?"

"The students at the Fitzwalter School. And a few teachers."

Ash frowned. "Why here?"

Cat shrugged. "They just told us the program was transferred here."

Ash glanced briefly at Alan on stage and then leaned toward Cat. "Do you mean you and Alan are still on scholarship? Here at GDA? Alan never told me that."

Cat sat forward. "We can drop the subject, if you want to."

Ash shook his head. "Why Greenwood Downs?"

Cat shrugged again. "Don't know. GDA is nothing like the Fitzwalter School. It was like a castle. And it backs up to some historic grounds. It's really something."

Listening to the music, Ash realized how true Alan had been to his promise not to mention the scholarship. "So who else came here to the Academy with this program?"

Cat squinted into the middle distance and began a count. "Well, there's another wrestler and the trainer. One fellow I never really got to know. Kind of a misfit. And there was Dr. Leonhardt, the one who just got fired, and—"

"Wait a minute," Ash said. "Leonhardt was at the Fitzwalter School in England?"

"Yeah, he'd been here at Greenwood forever, but GDA loaned him out, I think. He lasted there only a year. Not sure what happened." He thought for a few seconds. "Hey, I wonder if they caught him altering grades over there?"

"He wasn't altering anything!" Ash said, his voice sharper than intended.

Cat squared the salt and pepper shakers side by side and said nothing.

"Sorry," Ash whispered. "I guess I'm a little touchy. I know Dr. Leonhardt well enough to say he didn't do any of these things he's accused of."

Cat shook his head. "I shouldn't have said anything. I hardly know him. Never had him for a course. He probably left England just to get away from Dr. Johns."

Ash felt a shower of cool sparks climb up his spine. "Princeton Johns?"

"The one and only," Cat said and tilted his head. "If you don't mind my asking, why'd *you* come here if not for the Fitzwalter? Alan says you're not too fond of GDA."

"My mom," Ash said. "She wanted me to try it."

"But why'd you stay if you hate it so much?"

A scrapbook of forest images leafed through Ash's mind, but when he spoke, he gave a simpler answer. "My dad was in the Navy. When he died, my mom found out there were government funds available for me to go to GDA. So I just stuck it out."

Cat aligned the salt and pepper shakers again. "Sorry about your father."

"He died before I was born," Ash allowed.

When the crowd applauded Alan's song, Cat checked his watch. "Well," he said, "I just dropped by to meet you. I need to get back and study." He eased out of his seat. "If you'd like to try out my bows, come by my room. I'm in six-O-one Gamewell."

"I'll do that," Ash replied. "It was good to meet you."

Cat buttoned his blazer and stood watching Alan fine-tune his guitar. "Hey, listen," he said and sat back on the edge of the seat. "I know it's none of my business, but does your financial aid cover everything? Is it a hundred per cent?"

Ash pursed his lips. "I'm not sure. Why?"

"You ought to check. If it's not, maybe you could get the Fitzwalter to take up the slack. They're both here at GDA, you know."

" 'Both' who?"

"Mr. Fitzhugh and Mrs. Fitzwalter." When Ash's face compressed into a question, Cat smiled encouragingly. "Yeah, maybe they could even pick up the tab for the years you've already been here." Cat stood. "It's just a thought. Anyway, great to finally meet you."

After Cat had walked away, Ash watched Alan lower his head away from the microphone to indulge in an instrumental verse of the song he was singing. Alan's blond hair fell over his face like a shield to hide his emotions, as his fingers worked blindly to awe the crowd. When he plucked the final note, the sound from the amplifier faded into perfect silence in the room. Even the sounds from the kitchen seemed to abate.

Then the students erupted with applause and whistles and a roar of voices. Ash took the moment as his own shield to slip unnoticed out of the room and head for Huntington Hall, where he would shower, slip into bed, and reread his notes from biology class before drifting off to sleep.

Chapter Ten

"Test!" Princeton Johns delivered the single word like a slap in the face. The room became so still that the hollow bounce of a basketball could be heard across the street from the gym. "On Friday," Johns added as he closed his book. His quick smile caused his mustache to twitch. Seeming to draw strength from the dread gripping his students' faces, he strode off the stage with swagger. The bell rang just as he closed the door.

"Friday!" Mick moaned and slammed his books into a stack.

On the sidewalk Ash set a brisk pace to avoid hearing Mick expand on his complaint. But halfway down the hill, Ash looked back to see Mick fast-walking across the parking lot toward the gym.

The hour with Princeton Johns had been grueling. His body language had all the markings of a spider weaving its web, which led Ash to predict a test designed to punish. It was not hard to imagine Johns leading the effort to drive Leonhardt from his department head chair, then slipping into that seat while it was still warm. Ash wondered if Johns and Leonhardt had had some kind of falling out when they were in England.

Ash recalled that first letter from the Fitzwalter four years ago. The invitation had been appealing. Among the courses offered was a series on English archery. By accepting the grant, he would have attended school without paying a dime. In fact, he would have received an allowance for spending money. And he could have seen where his father had spent his last years at the U.S. Navy base on the North Sea.

But Ash had turned it down for his mother's sake. He could not put an ocean between them. She had lost one man to that far off place. He would stay close.

After his freshman year at Lincoln County High, it had come as a surprise to him when his mother had nudged him toward Greenwood Downs Academy. GDA was known as a place for the sons of governors and even the daughter of a President. GDA was a hive of connections that took the progeny of the elite by the hand and led them into prestigious colleges which, in turn, opened the doors to lofty vocations. On this campus Ash had always felt like the hired help mingling with the rich at an expensive country club.

His father's military pension had kept them afloat, but just barely. When his mother had learned there were special funds available for GDA, he agreed to try it simply because of the money . . . and because she so fervently wanted it for him.

After that first year at Greenwood, Ash had every intention of returning to Lincoln High, but in taking the steps of self-imposed exile from the other GDA students, he had found the wildness along the Salacoa and fallen in love with the montane forest.

At his lunch hour Ash called Dean Oberleigh from the cafeteria phone. Sara Birmingham connected him right away.

"Do you still want to help?" the dean asked.

"Yes, sir, I do."

"Okay," the dean sighed. "Are you free tonight? Around eight o'clock?"

"Yes, sir. Meet at your house?"

"No, this is not with me. You'll be meeting with the student you're to tutor. He'll meet you at the backdoor to the natatorium at eight sharp."

"Who is it I'm supposed to meet?"

The dean lowered his voice. "John Naylor."

Ash sat down. "The football player?"

"I assume you'll know him when you see him?" It was a rhetorical question. "See what you two can work out. I'll be talking to him later tonight."

"Wait . . . what will I be helping him with?"

"Biology," the dean said. "He's in your first period biology."

Ash frowned. How could he have missed seeing Greenwood Downs's most celebrated football player—the tallest black athlete in the state—sitting in his class?

"Eight o'clock," the dean reminded. "And remember . . . you asked to help."

When he turned from the phone, the first thing Ash saw was the sports section from the *Clarion* spread out on an unoccupied table. There on the front page was a large close-up picture of John Naylor. Ash leaned on stiffened arms and faced his new tutoring pupil. In the post-game photo, the whites of Naylor's piercing eyes appeared to rise off the page. His skin was as black as the night behind him. Beads of sweat glistened on his brow, each droplet highlighted by a tiny quarter-moon reflection.

Warriors Maul Cherokee County 30-0, read the headline. Beneath Naylor's picture was the caption: *John "the Hammer" Naylor's sixteen tackles holds Indians' offense to 23 yards.*

In another photo the dark giant wearing number seventy crashed into a jack-knifed body that had been lifted high off the ground. The football had squirted free and was frozen in the air. *The Hammer nails his man*, it read. Ash sighed and let his head slump from his shoulders.

Ash had just started to uncover the target when he heard Marin's "hello" call out. Raising his hand in greeting, he stood perplexed. He had been expecting her to arrive from the direction of the academic buildings . . . not from the woods.

"Ready to shoot rovers?" she asked with a smile.

Ash narrowed his eyes. "I guess that depends on what a rover is."

She led the way to a spreading post oak at the edge of the field, where she knelt to gather acorns scattered in the grass. "Keep these in a pocket," she instructed and counted out seven into his hand. Then she counted out seven more for herself. "Now we rove."

It was warm for October and the cool of the forest was welcome. He followed her in silence, watching her search until she stopped and pointed toward a small rise of land.

"See the red leaf on the ground? There."

Black gum, he almost said and smiled at his urge to impress her.

"Hit the leaf and you discard an acorn," she explained. "If you miss by no more than a hand-span, you stand pat." She extended her thumb and little finger in a measuring gesture. "Hit outside that distance, you pick up a new acorn to add to your collection. We'll take turns roving for a target. First to empty a pocket is champion of the day."

Ash liked it, and told her so with his smile.

"Whoever names a target always shoots first," she said as she loaded.

He watched her face harden with concentration. *The reckoning arrow,* he thought.

When she released, the leaf jumped like a red frog. When it came to rest, a tear was visible at its edge. He loaded an arrow and stared at the leaf as if it were already his prize. When he released, the leaf closed like a book on his shaft and buried in the dirt. After they pulled their arrows, she dug a small hole in the soil and planted an acorn. He did the same.

For the remainder of the afternoon their shooting was less a duel than a duet. Between shots she told him of her English forests—the similarities and differences to his Georgia woodlands. She asked many questions about the plants, and when he answered she seemed to soak up his words through the attentiveness of her lucid gray eyes.

He found the last green leaf of jewelweed and took it to the river so she could see the spectacle of its silvery shimmer when submerged. He picked up a spirobolida millipede that smelled like adhesive tape and held it before her nose to see if she could name the scent. She couldn't but laughed and nodded when he told her. Often she stopped to smell a leaf or touch a tuft of moss or listen to a bird's song. He watched her much the way he watched himself in his mind's eye whenever he was alone in the woods.

The long shadows at last turned them back toward the field, and they walked quietly, listening to the new sounds ushered in by twilight. Their acorns had long-since been planted without a word of who had won. In the field they heard the school band inside the gymnasium, flooded into a blur by its own echo.

"How did you come to use a bow, Ash?"

Feeling the nostalgic glow of his childhood, he smiled. "I was eight. I had this dream about shooting a bow. Next morning I broke my piggy bank and bought my first bow. It had been on a shelf of our hardware store for as long as I could remember."

"Tell me about the dream?" she asked.

They had been walking slowly and now they stopped near the target in the field. "Someone was with me. I have no idea who it was. Someone helping me bend the bow. An old person, I think." He let the smile of remembering fade. "What about you?"

"I, too, was very young. But I had a flesh-and-blood teacher."

"How long did you take lessons?"

A subtle smile played at her mouth. "To this day," she said.

He was hardly listening to her words, because once again the waning light was transforming her face—the years melting into shadow. A bell rang out, and he turned to face the sound—incongruous and baffling by

83

its point of origin across the river. It seemed to come from high on the ridge. Marin was already moving toward it.

"I must go," she said.

"What's wrong?" He stepped toward her. The bell kept ringing. "What is that?"

She walked faster and half-turned without slowing. "Ash, I have to go home."

The monotony of the bell invoked its own rhythm against the marching band's music from the gym. When she disappeared down the trail to Painted Rock, questions churned inside him like currents swirling beneath a waterfall.

"Home?" he whispered aloud.

Ash was ten minutes early for the rendezvous with John Naylor. The temperature had dropped fifteen degrees in the last hour. The light behind the glassed double doors of the pool building made two milky rectangles, dulled by condensation. Approaching the rear entrance, Ash heard the hollow echoes of activity inside. He took up a post just outside the spread of light that spilled over the concrete porch, and there he waited.

At ten minutes after eight, he had begun to wonder on which side of these doors he should be waiting, inside or out. Cupping his hands to the glass he tried to peer through. He tugged at the handle and again made the tunnel with his hands. When a dark blur filled his vision, he stepped back. The latch tripped, and a girl with dripping hair pushed open the door and stepped back from the cold air. He thanked her and entered the warm chlorine-scented air of the natatorium.

The surface of the Olympic-size pool was cluttered with red, blue, and yellow kayaks. The students sitting in them were decked out in bright nylon pullovers, life vests, and helmets as they listened attentively to a bare-chested instructor. It was Greenwood's *Touch the Earth* program in full swing.

On the far side of the pool someone in dark green trousers sat alone in the bleachers behind a newspaper. The hands holding the paper were black. Ash walked the corners of the pool and started up the bleachers until he recognized the man's GDA maintenance uniform. Scanning the room, he could see no one else who might be Naylor.

A large audience had crowded around the smaller pool that was separated from the larger by a low retaining wall. Deciding to check there, Ash came up on a phalanx of bare backs—spectators yelling encouragement to someone in the water. No one in the crowd was tall enough to be Naylor. Ash decided to circle the big pool before checking outside again. To do this he had to either thread his way through this maze of wet bodies or cross the shortcut offered by the low blue-tiled divider. He had crossed deadfalls narrower than this over the Salacoa. With everyone laughing at something, he stepped onto the wall to test its traction; then, just to be done with it, he started across quickly, his focus riveted to the four-inch-wide bridge of tile.

In his peripheral vision Ash saw a long, dark arm stretch from a kayak to the wall. A body rose up, squirming out of the boat. Right away the single note of a gong struck a heavy note inside Ash's skull. A meteor shower burst across the black screen that dropped behind his eyes. He had only the vaguest sensation of hitting the water.

When he opened his eyes he felt concrete pressing into his back. He was wet from head to toe. A dozen blurred faces hovered above him, and one was a black bear. The bear had its paw under Ash's head and kept asking a question that Ash could not grasp.

"Let's get him in the office," someone said.

Then he was floating, gently bobbing to the rhythm of the bear's long stride. Soon he was laid onto soft cushions. Then a door closed, muting the echoes from the pool.

"What hit me?" Ash asked in a dry voice. He raised his head, and when his vision cleared he saw that the bear was John Naylor.

"Paddle," Naylor said in a deep voice. "I was trying to get outta that damn kayak before I drowned, and I was in a hurry. I should'a let go o' the paddle."

"What were you doing in a kayak? We were supposed to meet at the backdoor."

Naylor's dark forehead furrowed with three deep creases. "Asherwood?"

Ash propped up on his elbows. Through the glass of the adjoining office he saw a lifeguard—his blond hair loose and dry—talking on a telephone, staring back at him.

"How'd I get out of the water?"

Naylor shrugged. "I knocked you in. Figured I oughta pull you out." He made a self-deprecatory shrug and looked away. "Guess I panicked in that little boat. Damn thing's hardly bigger than one o' my shoes. That damn Jerome talked me into it."

"I waited a half-hour at the backdoor," Ash said, pointing through the glass.

Naylor gave him a doubtful look. "*I* waited a half-hour. Opened the door twice to check." He raised his arm to point, and they saw that their extended arms were aimed in different directions. John Naylor's door was at the true back of the building. *Emergency Exit Only* was stenciled in yellow across its gray metal finish. Ash's double-doors were toward the back end of the natatorium but situated on the right-hand wall.

"We were supposed to meet there," Ash said, still pointing.

Naylor shook his head. "We s'posed to meet at the back," he said and pointed again to the rear wall. "That's the back."

"But nobody uses that door," Ash argued.

Naylor raised both eyebrows. "Still the back," he countered.

Through the glass they saw two EMTs hurrying toward them. Both were dressed in blue jumpsuits. One was a heavy, mustachioed man and the other a short lean woman with hair sculpted like a helmet. They bustled into the room and leaned over Ash.

"How we doin'?" the man said. "We swaller some water?"

Ash ran his tongue around his mouth. "I don't think so. I'm all right."

The man seemed not to hear him. "I hear you was tryin' ta cross that divider wall out there." He placed his fingertips on Ash's cheek, gently turned Ash's head, and whistled softly at the lump above Ash's ear. "You hit the wall?"

"Paddle," Naylor answered. "Got tangled in my arms and swung around hard."

The woman slid a plastic brace under Ash's neck. "We're stabilizing your head," she said. "So we don't cause any more injury."

The door opened again and a young black man entered wearing the same blue uniform as the other two. "You gonna want the stretcher or the gurney, J.T.?"

"We'll use the gurney. Pam, go roll it on in and, Leon, you can bring the ambulance around to the backdoor. We'll roll 'im out that way. It'll be closer."

Leon and Pam left, but in seconds Leon stuck his head back inside the room. "Which backdoor, J.T.? There's two of 'em."

PART TWO

The Bitter Taste

It was Thursday night, eight o'clock sharp. Ash looked up from his book to see John Naylor standing just outside the doorway of the library's basement. The oversized athlete appraised the semi-dark room and then bowed his head to clear the top of the doorframe.

"We always gonna meet in a cave?" Naylor said in his deep voice.

Ash laid down his pen. "It's private," he said and swept a hand around the room. "In the two years I've been coming down here, this is the most crowded I've seen it."

Naylor pursed his lips and nodded. "Sounds pretty private." He laid his books on the table, pulled out a chair across from Ash, and sat.

"So, you're having trouble with your grades?" Ash said, trying to get to business.

Naylor shook his head. "Just biology."

Ash nodded with understanding. "The sciences can be a little intimidating."

A subtle grin pulled at one corner of Naylor's mouth. "I'm takin' bio-chem, too. Got an A in that, but I expect to bring it up to an A-plus. In Veterinary Diseases I got an A-plus. *And*, I made a ninety-eight on Leonhardt's last test."

Ash started to speak but closed his mouth. Naylor laughed quietly.

"Got tinnitus," Naylor said and pointed at the side of his head.

Ash frowned. " 'Ten' what?"

"Tinnitus," John repeated. "It's a disease of the ear. I worked around farm machinery all my life. There's this high frequency pinging in my head that won't stop."

Ash nodded, but still he had not grasped the relevance of Naylor's story.

Naylor shrugged. "Most people I can hear okay. But some high voices blend into that frequency and get lost in the noise." He gestured toward the south end of campus. "Coach had to change the defensive play caller 'cause I couldn' hear the play when Peewee Duncan was callin' it. He's gotta voice like a vacuum cleaner."

"Aah," Ash said and pointed at Naylor. "Dr. Johns's raspy voice?"

Naylor pointed back at Ash. "Touchdown!"

Ash began to nod with relief. "So you just need someone's notes to look at. That's easy. I can make you a copy every day. Just tell me where to leave it."

Naylor was shaking his head halfway through Ash's suggestion. "If I'm readin' your notes at night in my dorm room . . . can't raise my hand to ask a question. Nobody there to answer." He shrugged. "Need my questions answered before I can proceed. You understand?"

Ash frowned. "So, I sit here while you read, and I wait for a question?"

"Depends," Naylor said and turned around Ash's notebook. Then he shook his head. "Can't read your handwriting. You'll have to play Dr. Johns and read it out loud."

The image of Beechwood floated into Ash's mind, and his frown deepened. "That means every night."

Naylor eyed Ash with a no-nonsense glare. "Dean said you wanted to help. You in or out?"

Ash looked down at the rushed cursive forced by their teacher's rapid-fire style. "Should I pencil on a thin mustache and conjure up an evil eye before I begin?"

Naylor shrugged. "Long as you answer my questions."

As they forged their way through Princeton Johns's lectures, John Naylor proved to be a quiet and determined student. Whenever he posed a question, its insightful nature was evident. By the time they had finished the session, Ash realized that he, himself, had gained a better grasp of the material.

As they walked side by side down Academy Drive, Ash took two strides for every one of Naylor's. "So, what got you headed toward veterinary medicine?"

Naylor laughed. "All those years on the ranch I prob'ly talked more to cows an' pigs an' horses than to people." He shook his head. "We just scraped by, so I didn' figure on college at all till the Greenwood offer fell in my lap. Got a full scholarship."

Ash grinned. "That's a long way to come for a high school recruitment. Guess it didn't hurt that you were the Texas terror in football."

Naylor shook his head. "Didn't play ball in Texas. Too much farm work." John chuckled. "You think Georgia is a long way. First they wanted me to leave the country."

Even before he spoke, Ash heard his own voice go small. "To where?"

Naylor snorted and shook his head. "Somewhere in England."

When Ash stopped, John took one more step and turned.

"The Fitzwalter?" Ash whispered.

Naylor nodded. "They pay everything. Playing ball is sorta my idea of payback." Naylor leaned in. "Hey, you all right?"

*****

On Friday morning Ash strode toward his biology class, feeling confident not only in himself but also in John Naylor. Both were prepared for Dr. Johns's declaration of war.

The auditorium was a morgue. Heads were bowed, everyone cramming as the clock ate up the final seconds. Ash took his seat, closed his eyes, and relaxed. When he opened his eyes he saw on his neighbor's desk a copy of the *Greenwood Leaves*. The headline read: *Johns Blasts Department Head Leonhardt in Grading Controversy*. Ash leaned in to read the interview with Princeton Johns that ran two columns.

A student in one of Dr. Richard Leonhardt's classes came forth with a complaint that Leonhardt was showing favoritism in his grading.

Ash looked up to see Mick climb the steps to the row behind him. After he heard Mick sit, Ash felt a tap on his shoulder.

"I hope you brought bandages," Mick whispered. "Gonna be a slaughter in here."

Ash turned and frowned at the papers in Mick's hand. "How do you know that?"

Mick grinned and pushed the papers on him. Ash's hand came up by reflex.

"Might wanna check number six," Mick quipped. "It's a killer."

Ash glanced at the top sheet and saw half a dozen typed questions.

"Answers are on the last two pages," Mick whispered.

When Ash turned and pushed the papers back on Mick, the boy's wicked smile suddenly snapped off. His eyes—glazed with fear—were fixed on the stage.

Ash turned to see Princeton Johns glaring at the two of them. Keeping his eyes locked on the two students, Johns crept down the steps like a cat stalking its prey. After taking two steps up the aisle he stopped and extended his arm toward Mick.

"Let me see that, Mr. Millerson!" Johns demanded. A surreal silence spread over the auditorium. Every eye in the room bore down on them. Johns's mouth tightened into a shallow V. "I believe you have something of mine."

"No, sir!" Mick insisted in his pitiful whine. "This is my stuff."

Johns raised his voice. "Those papers are mine! I recognize them!" The bell rattled its firehouse alarm but defused nothing. "Is that today's test?" Johns challenged. When Mick said nothing, Johns leveled his eyes on Ash. "Well?"

The blood in Ash's ears roared as he tried to think. He reasoned that there was no way for him to know if what Mick had was actually today's test.

"I don't know, sir."

Johns's face darkened. He strode back down the stairs, vaulted onto the stage, and whipped a test off the podium. Jumping back to the concrete floor, he held out the paper.

"Is this what you held?" he demanded of Ash.

Ash cringed at the lameness of his answer. "I didn't really look at it, sir."

Johns opened his hand to Mick. "Give it to me!"

Ash heard Mick's papers rustle, and Princeton Johns stepped back victorious. One look at the top page, and he gloated as he raised the papers above his head.

"Today's test!" he announced to the room. "Who else has one?"

No one made a sound. Johns marched back to the stage. From the podium he lifted a stack of papers and slammed them down on the edge of the stage.

"Hand out these tests!" he ordered, pointing to four girls who sat together in the front row. Then, looking directly at Mick and Ash, he made a dismissive flick of the wrist toward the door. "You two may leave."

It was like a dream. Moving on automatic pilot, Ash gathered his things and walked to the door with Mick shuffling behind him. The other students bent over their desks, absorbed in the test. Outside, Ash grabbed Mick's arm and shook him.

"Why did you hand that to me?"

Mick glared back defiantly. "I thought you'd wanna see Johns's trick question, that's all. His wording is sneakier than that stupid reversal thing that Leonhardt used."

Ash stared at Mick as if seeing the boy for the first time. "You're the one who turned in Dr. Leonhardt, aren't you? That's how Dr. Johns knew your name."

Mick tried to work up some anger. "Look, I didn't go to turn Leonhardt in. I just wanted some answers."

Ash clenched his teeth and nodded. "Looks like you got some."

"Look, man!" Mick said with uncharacteristic passion, "I'm just tryin' to survive this preppy prison! Johns is vicious! I can't let him ruin the deal I've got here."

Ash felt a pit open in his stomach. "What deal?"

"My scholarship. I—"

Ash closed his eyes. "Please don't tell me you're here on the Fitzwalter grant."

Mick frowned. "Yeah, but I won't be if I get kicked outta here!"

"You've probably gotten us both kicked out, Mick!"

Mick scuffed his feet on the pavement. "Well, what can I do about that now?"

"You can tell Dr. Johns what happened. That I wasn't looking at that test."

Mick ratcheted up his whine. "He won't believe that! He saw you holding it!"

Tightening his grip on the boy's arm, Ash hauled him up the steps and planted him by the door. "Stand here and don't talk." Mick slapped his books on top of the wall, punched his hands into his overcoat pockets, and aimed his sulk out at the world.

The remainder of the hour dragged by without a word. When the bell rang, students began to exit in a disconnected stream, each glancing warily at the pair of outcasts. When it seemed that the auditorium might be empty, Ash ventured inside with Mick in tow. Dr. Johns was on the stage collecting tests from the late finishers. He took one glance at the door and promptly ignored the two boys.

"Dr. Johns!" Ash called out. "Millerson has something to say to you."

When Johns leaned on his podium and waited, Mick looked down at his shoes and mumbled, "He didn't have anything to do with the—"

Johns interrupted loudly. "Speak up, Mr. Millerson! I can't hear you!"

Mick looked up and cleared his throat. "I said . . . he didn't have anything—"

"He held my test, Mr. Millerson!" Johns cut in. "You both did!"

Mick began to look sick. "Yeah, but he—"

"What is your name?" Johns said, his predatory gaze set on Ash.

"Asherwood."

Johns cocked his head. "Were you not holding that test paper in your hands?"

Ash raised his chin. "I held those papers for about two seconds."

Johns screwed a vindictive smile onto his face. "I will be submitting your names to the disciplinary board. We will let you know the date of your hearing."

"Dr. Johns," Ash said in a level voice, "I had only just held those papers for—"

"Save it for the hearing," Johns suggested. He waved the back of his hand at the door. "Now, both of you, go away!"

Ash stood fast. "I didn't know it was a test!" He pulled at Mick. "Tell him!"

Mick tottered in Ash's grip. "He's not gonna listen, man! I told you."

Ignoring the pair, Johns gathered his tests and marched offstage. Mick jerked his arm free, scuffed toward the exit, and pushed out through the door. Ash considered following Dr. Johns into his office, but instead he moved robotically for fresh air. On the sidewalk he followed Mick's back as it blinked through the shadows of the trees lining the road. At the intersection, Mick crossed diagonally and made for the English building.

That was the moment the reality of the debacle fell over Ash like a smothering blanket. He considered the smearing of his record that would follow. Knowing that Mick was his only chance at clearing his name, he ran for the English building.

Inside Jeffrey Hall Ash marched down one corridor and then another as he peeked into the rooms. As he neared a small classroom under the stairwell he heard the whimpering timbre of Mick's voice. Stepping to the threshold, Ash saw a dozen students seated and talking to one another. Then a thousand scattering birds took flight in the pit of his stomach. Dumbfounded, he stared at the face absorbing Mick's story. As if trying to find his way out of a dream, he looked at the card tacked to the door. It read: *Fitzwalter—English Literature*.

Backing into the hall, Ash opened his notebook and scribbled a message to Marin. Tearing the page free, he folded it and stopped a girl on her way into the classroom.

"Excuse me!" he whispered "Could you give this to your teacher?" Before she could speak, the bell rang and he stuffed the paper in her hand. Then he hurried down the hall for the main door, stepped outside, and realized there was nowhere he needed to be. He was as good as gone.

Chapter Twelve

Ash stood among the scarlet sumacs at the forest's edge. There he could keep watch on the border of pines as well as the trail to Painted Rock. In his note to Marin, he had asked to meet at five o'clock. That time had come and gone twenty minutes ago.

After five more minutes she came from the campus side and walked to the target. There she stood for a time, her head sagging, and her hands deep in her overcoat pockets. Her hair was loose, whipping across her face in the wind. She bent slowly and sat on the grass with her arms stacked across her knees and her head resting on her forearms. After a few minutes she lay back on the earth and did not move.

When he reached her, she was nestled in the yellowed grasses like a fallen scarecrow, her face relaxed, her breathing deep and steady. He studied the line of her nose, the contrasting colors of her hair. The hand that stretched nearest him lay palm up, the fingers curled unevenly. He sat down on the grass beside her and waited.

When the cold began to creep into his bones, he touched her shoulder. Stirring, she sat up and looked at the sky. The sun was well below the trees in the west.

"Where were you?" she said.

"Right here." He rose with her and watched her comb strands of hair from her face. "You're Marin Fitzwalter," he said like an accusation. "With the scholarship."

She brushed at the flecks of dried grass clinging to her coat. Then she looked away. Twilight was spreading over the field like a gray gauze, and once again her age seemed to dissolve in the fading light.

"I was offered the scholarship a few years ago," he said. "I turned it down."

She hugged herself and rubbed each hand up and down the opposite upper arm as she looked off toward the trees. "Yes," was all she said, and the ache in her voice unnerved him. She turned to look him in the eye. "It could have been so much easier."

"*What* could?" he asked.

She shook her head, then looked down at the grass. "You could have accepted," she said so quietly that if he had not watched her lips he might not have understood. She closed her eyes and let her head tilt back. "How long have you known me, Ash?"

He frowned at the irrelevance of the question. "A week or so, I guess."

She looked toward Cemetery Hill with a sad smile. "That day we met . . . did you feel like we . . . did I seem at all familiar to you?"

" 'Familiar'?" He followed her gaze to the hill, trying to see what she saw.

"Let's walk," she said. "I'm cold."

Darkness came on. There was no sound from the forest, only the far-off traffic from the highway. They'd traveled half the perimeter of the field before she spoke.

"Ash?" Her voice was close now, as if they were on the same side of a problem that faced the two of them. "What, would you say, is at the center of who you are?"

They swished through the dry grasses for a dozen steps as he thought about her question. "I don't know," he mumbled. "Maybe that I'm out of sync."

"With what?"

He shrugged. "School . . . students . . . their values. Their world is over there." He nodded toward campus and then hitched his head toward the forest. "Mine is here."

Marin stopped and he with her. "Ash, do you ever feel out of sync with time?"

He narrowed his eyes. "As in . . . born in the wrong time?" He looked up and singled out one of the few early stars. He knew from physics that he was seeing an ancient light, originated before his life, only now reaching earth centuries later. To him the concept seemed to make the past a part of the present. "I don't know. Maybe."

"Have you traced your family history?" she asked. "Have you looked into that?"

Ash shrugged. "An aunt on my father's side got into genealogy a little."

"And?"

"We go back to England. But it gets muddy. I think the line was hard to follow."

They began to walk again, and he sensed that she was choosing her words with care. "Sometimes when people are stripped of their title or land . . . or both . . . the genealogical trail fades. It can be difficult to follow."

"I think my father did a little research for her when he was in England. He was at a Navy base on the North Sea. He died in an accident over there the year I was born."

"But you weren't born in England?"

"No, my mom never lived there. She visited only once . . . to see him."

"When were they last in England together?"

"I don't know. Why?"

"It might be interesting to find out . . . and where they spent their time."

The full moon showed its burning edge over the pine saplings. They watched it top the trees and bathe the field in a cool lunar glow.

"Michael Millerson came to see you today," Ash said. "Did he mention me?"

She turned quickly. "You?"

He nodded. "There's a good chance I'll be expelled from school along with him."

Marin stopped and her hand went to her throat. "Oh, dear God," she breathed.

"I didn't do anything wrong, but Dr. Johns won't listen to—"

"Dr. Johns," she rasped and lowered her face into her hands. "Oh, Hubert." The name slipped through her fingers like a last breath. She wiped at her cheeks and looked away. "Ash," she whispered to the dark, "two days ago I lost my husband."

"Lost him?" A knot formed in his throat. "You mean—?" Now he recognized the signs of loss—her lethargy, the slump of her shoulders, her aimless walk.

"He'll never be able to talk to you now." Her words were barely audible. "I don't know how to do all of this," she said. Lowering her head, she hid her eyes with a hand.

" 'Do all of' what?"

For a long time she said nothing. Then she sniffed wetly.

"Do you know the old lodge in the woods? Up there?" She pointed across the river to the ridge. "The one called 'Ten Point'?"

Ash nodded. "It's just a place where students go to party."

She lowered her arm and faced him. "Can you come there in the morning?"

"To Ten Point?" he said. "Why?"

She turned toward the moon, and her eyes shone like pearls in the soft light. "Just come, will you?" Without waiting for an answer she turned and walked to the trail that led to Painted Rock.

He watched her grow smaller and then vanish altogether in the dark of the wood. If she was bound for Ten Point, he wondered how she would cross the river, and this made him want to go after her, to help somehow. But he felt he had no right to impose on her in this time of mourning.

Now the complete orb of the moon was above the trees, illuminating the grass as if a luminescent gas were seeping from the earth. Crossing the field he made for the pines and the Loop Road beyond. By the time he hit the street, he was running for Huntington Hall.

"Hello?" His mother's voice in the phone's earpiece filled him with the familiar warmth of home. Behind her greeting he heard the television and the way it resonated off the tiles of the kitchen walls and floor. He could almost smell the scent of her cornbread.

"Hey, Mom, it's me."

"Ash," she said, putting all the love of the world into the single word. Her voice turned away from the phone, fulfilling her standard ritual. "Archer!? It's Ash!"

The barking began on cue, its constancy always the same. The sound grew steadily louder as Archer's paws tapped across the kitchen floor.

"I heard about your teacher," she said, her voice now grave. "It's on the news."

"Mom . . . the last time you saw Dad . . . was it in England or here in the states?"

For several seconds all he heard was a game show on TV. Then she exhaled and a dish clacked in water, and he knew she was standing before the window at the sink.

"Are you all right, Ash?" she asked, her words now full of motherly compassion.

"I just need to know," he said quietly. "Do you mind talking about it?"

"Not with you," she said, and by the tone in her voice he knew she was smiling. "I last saw him in England."

"Can you tell me about that?"

She took in a lot of air. "It was March, the year you were born. I'd flown over to see him. We had a whole week together. Our last."

"What did you do over there, Mom? Where did you two go?"

He heard her settle into her chair at the table. Archer's head would be in her lap.

"Well, we toured the countryside. Sheffield and Mansfield and Edwinstowe. And some of the smaller villages. Your father loved that area. Lord but it was cold and wet, but he was set on doing it. We camped along the way."

" 'Camped'? You told me Dad got his fill of that in the Navy."

"Well, he loved those forests there. I don't know why. He just did."

Ash leaned against the wall and stared down the empty hall of his dormitory. "Mom, exactly how much does the Navy give us for my tuition?"

This time a silence drew out. He heard the familiar grunt that she made whenever she stood. Then he heard her footsteps. The *Jeopardy* theme bounced happily then shut off, and the line was quiet as she walked back from the mute TV and sat again.

"Well, I guess it's confession time," she said. "I didn't want you to feel obligated if you didn't like it there. I know you. You'd join the foreign legion if you thought it would help finances. But, honey . . . it's all paid for. Every cent. As long as it was Greenwood Downs."

"But why does the Navy care that I go to school here?"

"It's not the Navy, Ash. It's the people who offered you the scholarship. I thought if you knew that . . . since you were feeling guilty about not going to England . . . you'd stay up there at Greenwood even if you hated it . . . and I didn't want that."

He slid his back down the wall and sat on the threadbare carpet. Lowering his head into the cradle of his hand, he closed his eyes.

"While you were over there, did you meet the people offering the Fitzwalter?"

"No. I never even heard of them until that first letter came. When you turned them down and went to Lincoln High, they started writing again. I didn't show you those letters about your going to Greenwood. I didn't understand why they didn't offer that first. It's so close. Surely there were enough students in England who had lost fathers."

"Is that what they told you? That the scholarship was based on us losing Dad?"

"Well, what else would it be? I just knew it was a wonderful opportunity, and I wanted it for you so much." She hesitated a beat. "Is there some problem, honey?"

"I just wanted to know when you were last with Dad. That's all. Do you mind?"

"No," she said with a mother's absolution. "Our last memory that cold March is a precious one. I have a memento I've kept all these years."

He frowned, wondering what relic she had never shown him. "What is it?"

The miles between them hummed over the wire. "You," she whispered.

After they had hung up, he stood in the empty hallway and counted the months on his fingers, starting with March. The ninth finger opened to December, his birth month. He hurried down the hall to his room and pulled down the Atlas from the shelf. Opening it to the United Kingdom he located Sheffield. Right below it was Mansfield. Then Edwinstowe. Just outside of the village, written in an arc of light green letters, were the words: *Sherwood Forest*.

Chapter Thirteen

Saturday morning was cold and mist lifted off the Salacoa like wisps of cotton. From Painted Rock a faint trail led upstream, and he supposed it to be the path that Marin had used. Still he could not see where it could take her. Then he saw the massive white pine that spanned the river from bank to bank, its stump showing an angled cut designed to fell the tree toward the water. The branches were trimmed and its upper side leveled by a chainsaw. Three steps had been cut into the trunk for mounting the bridge. He crossed and climbed down another set of steps where a trail led up into a laurel thicket.

At the top of the ridge the smell of woodsmoke greeted him. Then he caught sight of Ten Point's sloping roof. Smoke raced from a new silver flue emerging from the old rock chimney. Under a palisade of towering white pines, the building lay in deep blue shadow, its windows noticeably clean, reflecting the grays and greens of the forest. The dirt drive was bedded with new gravel and sparkled in the sun. A woodpile was stacked high under the west eave, and the bilious odor of split red oak lent a tang to the cold air.

He knocked on the door, and soon a metal latch clicked. The door scraped open, and there was Marin dressed in jeans and a plaid shirt beneath a gray sweater.

"Good morning," she said and stepped back as an invitation to enter. Her hair was neatly gathered in back. A rose pink in her cheeks had replaced yesterday's pallor.

The cans, bottles, and trash that Ash remembered strewn about in the old cabin were an incongruous memory to the room he now beheld. The floors and walls had been scrubbed, spider webs wiped away, and the cold chill of neglect banished by a new woodstove partially set back into the stone fireplace. Two beds made a right-angle in one corner, one neatly made up with sheets and pillow and folded blankets, the other bare and whispering of loss. Above each bed hung a longbow. One was Marin's. The other was heavier, darker, and blemished by time. Even unstrung it was an imposing weapon.

After stoking the fire in the stove, she said, "I'll make tea." At the back of the room, she worked a pitcher pump and set a kettle on the woodstove. On the heavy oaken table she set two mugs and dropped a teabag into each. At one end of the table sat an oil lamp and a thick black book with worn covers. "Won't you sit?" she offered.

He sat on the bench and listened to the wood pop and crackle.

"Why do they call it 'Ten Point'?" she asked as she set down two spoons.

He pointed above the door. "There was a buck's head mounted right there. A ten-pointer." He watched her gaze at the empty spot. "How did you know about this place?"

"My husband was an avid researcher," she explained. "He studied the school's original charter. Hubert would say 'to truly understand a place you've got to dig into its roots.' Greenwood Downs was founded by a man who loved his forests. That's why much of the property is undeveloped. Do you know about Mr. Jeffrey?"

Ash shrugged. "Just what's written on the plaque outside Jeffrey Hall."

"When he donated the land for the school," Marin explained, "he stipulated that all woodlands be preserved. Ten Point was his hunting lodge. It was to be maintained for use by the family. But it appears that no one has cared enough to contest its ruin."

"Until now," Ash said.

She smiled. "The Jeffrey family gave us permission to use it. I dare say the school must have panicked. The maintenance staff was busy for weeks tidying up here."

When the kettle hissed, Marin poured water into their mugs and sat on the bench. "There was so much mold. I suspect that is what started Hubert's lungs to decline so."

Ash nodded and softened his voice. "Will the funeral be in England?"

Looking out the back window, she shook her head. "No."

Watching her trancelike expression, Ash decided to change directions. "What happens to Mick now, Marin?"

She snapped out of her reverie. "It's in the hands of the school. If he remains at Greenwood, his scholarship holds. Otherwise—"

Ash felt his heart begin to hammer inside his chest. "Marin? Why is Greenwood Downs the venue for this scholarship?"

She stirred her tea, keeping her eyes on the slow eddy swirling at its surface. "What we needed was here."

He waited, but she would not meet his eyes. "And what was that?" he pressed.

Her lambent gray eyes fixed on him. "That is what we need to talk about, Ash."

She leaned over the table and pulled the heavy, black book closer. When she opened it, Ash saw that all *verso* pages were handwritten and all *recto* were typed. She moved her fingertips over a page, like a blind person reading Braille.

"I use this in my teaching," she said. "It's a journal from the thirteenth century." Her eyes darkened like the shadow of a cloud moving across the surface of a lake.

Seated four feet from the stove, they were bathed in its radiant heat, but now her breathing trembled as though from a chill. "I'd like you to read this, Ash."

He frowned at the book. "Why?" he said, and right away he knew he had disappointed her. Picking up his mug, he sipped the hot tea and turned his attention to the dark bow on the wall. When she closed the book, a wave of relief washed through him.

"That bow," she said quietly, "was Hubert's."

He studied the stout limbs and the carved bone nocks. "It looks old."

"Yes," she affirmed. "I thought perhaps you might like to have it."

Without meaning to, he laughed. "Me? I doubt I could even string it."

She looked at him with a cold certainty. "You could," she stated.

Ash felt himself go wary. Her presence next to him was like the edge of a precipice. He wanted to leave. When she stood and walked to the bare bed, he feared she would take down the bow to push it on him. Instead, she knelt and slid from under the bed a wooden box. This she brought back to the table. Then she sat.

"I don't know how to do all of this," she admitted. The dreamy tone in her voice made him wonder if she was talking to him or to the box. It was the second time she had used this vague phraseology.

" 'Do all' what, Marin?"

She lifted the lid and began to unwrap a mass of wrinkled, yellowed paper. The quiet supple creases in the paper spoke of a thousand times that hands had folded and unfolded it. Ash pried his gaze from the box to watch her face, as if spying on her from a secretive place. With some alarm he realized he was searching her features for signs of sanity.

"Marin, what exactly did you want to talk to me about?"

Her fingers stopped fidgeting with the paper, and her hands fell limp inside the box. When she turned to him, her eyes were like those of a lost child.

"I won't know how to answer all you'll need to ask," she whispered. "I have little more understanding of it than you. Please believe that, Ash."

Closing his eyes, he propped an elbow on the table and leaned his forehead into the cradle of his hand. Taking in a deep breath, he let it seep out in a long sigh.

"It's all right," she said. She pushed the paper back into the box and lowered the lid. "We don't have to do all of this now."

The brassy blare of the Warrior band throbbed from the stadium. Cars and picnicking fans swarmed over the campus, giving the archery field a magnified sense of isolation. Ash was pulling arrows from the target when Anne Metter appeared with her fiberglass bow and handful of arrows. It was his first time seeing her wear anything other than the Academy's regulation gray skirt, white blouse, and dark green blazer. Her brown and yellow plaid outfit looked fresh out of a fall clothing catalogue.

"Hi, there," she said with her trademark toss of hair.

And so began the lesson. For a half hour he took her through the fundamentals until she was ready to begin the more difficult work of the string release. She was slow to grasp the concepts, but Ash knew that much of the fault lay with him. His mind was on Marin. Each time Anne tossed her hair and flashed eager eyes to him, looking for praise or guidance, he found himself snapping awake to the present, mentally replaying what she had said or done so he could respond.

Anne shot like every novice, but she would not be disheartened. Her occasional successes brought little bursts of celebration to the session.

Sometimes, after she had shot, in a whimsical coincidence of timing, the stadium crowd roared as if praising her efforts, but she never seemed to notice.

He thought of John Naylor and wondered how many of those cheers from the crowd were for "the Hammer." Ash was not scheduled to meet with him again until Monday night, but now he wondered if the dean might have already made arrangements to assign a new tutor to replace the one to be expelled from school for cheating.

By the second hour of the lesson, it was obvious that Anne's bare fingers suffered the abrasion of the string. When he suggested that the lesson end, her face was a mixture of disappointment and relief. They walked to the target to retrieve her arrows.

"Have you ever competed in archery, Ash?"

"No," he said and covered the target. Busying himself with the corner stones, he saw no point in explaining his preference for privacy.

"Have you heard what we're doing for homecoming next month?" she asked.

He shook his head, thinking he would likely be at another school by then.

When she tossed her hair and smiled, her teeth flashed white. "It's called 'Renaissance Days.' It's one of the reasons I wanted to learn about archery."

As she gathered stray arrows from the grass, he began composing his parting line—one that would *not* lead to more lessons. But her bright smile derailed him.

"You're a good teacher, Ash. There's a lot more to archery than I thought. I know I don't have a gift for it. It doesn't come to me like, say, sketching does. But just to see the arrow fly—no matter how good or bad the shot—it's so beautiful. It's like giving life to a feathered stick." She made a comic face. "And then on the negative side—" She held up her right hand. Her three string-fingers looked as if they had been soaked in red wine.

He held up his gloved hand. "See if Coach Torrence can find an archery glove for you. You'll need one if you stick with it."

She nodded quickly three times. "I'll stick!" When he made no reply, she added, "I'd like to buy you dinner to thank you for the lesson." She made the sideways bob of her head that made her hair swing and settle. "Tonight maybe? In town?"

He turned to the forest, still feeling her eyes on him. The picture of a fire in the hearth of Beechwood was like a siren's song calling to him from the woods.

"I can't tonight," he said. "But thank you."

"What about one night next week?" she pressed.

He imagined her reading about his expulsion in the next issue of *The Greenwood Leaves*. "I'm not too sure of my schedule next week, Anne."

Trying to cover her disappointment, she smiled. "Then I'll just say 'thank you.' "

Feeling his face warm, Ash looked away. "You're welcome."

For a time after Anne had gone, he stood in the field and watched the leaden clouds move in low over the campus from the west. Now without the distraction of teaching an archery lesson, the harsh reality of the last two days weighed heavily on him. A chain of images flashed through his mind: Mick's petulant pout; Princeton Johns's smirk of victory; and Dean Oberleigh's disappointed eyes. When he visualized his mother's look of shock when he would tell her of his dismissal, a fireball of anger rose up inside him.

Staring at the forested ridge across the river he channeled all his indignation at the vague mysteries that seemed to hover around Marin Fitzwalter. He thought of the black book and the box she had tried to impose on him, as if suggesting that he had some duty to receive them. Intent on getting solid answers, he started for the trail to Ten Point.

By the time he had crossed the bridge, his impulse had become a fevered mission. As he reached the top of the ridge, he was resigned to put an end to whatever delusions Marin seemed determined to foist upon him. He ran a speech of disengagement through his mind and willed himself to hold to its cold pragmatism.

After knocking on the heavy front door several times, he peered through the window and rapped on the glass, but the sound fell impotent on the empty room. He walked to the back where the ridge top narrowed to an overlook, and on that promontory he stood and saw a partial view of Cemetery Hill a half mile away.

Feeling the spontaneity of his purpose dissolve, he laid down his bow and quiver and sat on a bed of pine needles to wait for Marin. He slid his hands into his sweatshirt pocket and fingered his shooting glove. Feeling suddenly spent, he lay back with his head on a low dirt mound, and right away the clean smell of freshly dug earth enveloped him. Above, the branches of a dead pine stood black against the gray sky, and he studied the gnarled limbs until his eyes grew heavy. As he listened to the wind scour the ridgetop he drifted off into a fitful sleep.

*

The bow was thick in his hand, yet it drew smoothly, not by his strength alone but by the arms enfolding him from behind. One hand was clamped to his left wrist for the push of the bow, the other gripped his right, pulling the string. These were strong sinewy hands guiding the movement of his arms.

"Now don't go and lock up on me," the voice chuckled. "You're not a statue. You've come to full draw, yes? And the arrow is at rest on the

bow, yes? But you're still pushing and pulling to keep it there, just not moving! Can you feel it?"

He could. He was still exerting two forces . . . but without moving.

"Now, stay at the center of those two forces, and when you're ready . . . don't open your fingers . . . simply stop holding the string! That's the secret! You just relax and let both arms flow in the directions they are trying to go."

"Flow," the voice repeated, whispered so close to his ear that he felt the stir of the man's warm breath in his hair. The arrow flew and the two guiding hands helped his arms to glide in opposing directions, balletic and balanced, like rain parting at a watershed. "Did you feel it? Tension unleashed not with aggression, but with grace. You allow the bow to do its work by getting out of its way." A quiet laugh at his ear. "You'll get it. And when you do, you'll feel it in your bones."

*

The sky had cleared. Above him a nuthatch hopped around the trunk of the pine, loosing flakes of bark, and he supposed it was this that had awakened him. He rolled his head to check any activity at the lodge. There was none. When he looked up at the bluing sky, the memory of the dream flooded his mind, and he sat upright.

The details crystallized, and he laid them out on a mental table to inspect each one: the strong hands gripping his wrists, the fluidity of the follow-through. Especially the rusty old voice, almost musical with its accent. It was the same dream that had come to him many years ago as a boy, and now he felt the same hunger to put the lessons to work on the archery field.

Gathering his things, he rose and bolted down the trail through the laurels. After following the river trail for a short stretch, he crossed the footbridge and ran out onto the field. As he set up to shoot, he discovered his glove was missing. With this yearning to practice, he had no wish to retrace his steps, and so he began shooting bare-handed.

For an hour he revived the fine points of the dream and refined each element of form. Quiver after quiver of arrows brought him closer to the essence of the lesson, until the refresher course paid off with a consistency in accuracy that he had never before experienced.

Finally his raw fingers forced him to stop. Looking at his abraded fingertips, he laughed quietly. Anne Metter had shown more fortitude than this. He covered the target and started for his dorm.

Three maintenance trucks were parked on the lawn of Huntington, and a ladder leaned against the building beneath an end gable. In the lobby Ash walked past a group of men huddled around a fuse box, their low conversation the only sound in the building.

Upon entering his room he flipped the light switch. It was dead. Across the hall, a door opened, and Crawley, his neighbor, leaned on crutches in his doorway.

"No power," he said. "Somebody smelled smoke. They think it's the wiring."

Ash nodded to Crawley's foot. "What happened to you?"

Crawley looked down and shrugged. "Broken toe. Ultimate Frisbee." He shrugged again. "Everybody's gone over to Gamewell to find a television. They're showing some of today's game." He shook his head. "Can you believe that Naylor?"

"What about him?"

"You didn't go to the game?"

Ash shook his head. "What happened to Naylor?"

Crawley laughed. "It's not what happened to *him*. It's what happened to anybody who tried to run *against* him. He made every tackle in the game but four. Their offense chalked up negative yardage. Score was sixty-three, zip. Hey, you need any candles?"

Ash shook his head. "No, I've got what I need."

When the heavy thud of a sledgehammer started up from deep in the building, Crawley glowered down the dark hallway. "So much for gettin' some sleep." He nodded toward Ash's bow. "Hey, can I pay you to shoot whoever that is tearing down the walls?" When Ash made no reply, Crawley wheeled around on his crutches, swung into his room, and slammed the door.

Back in his room, Ash looked out his window and saw that twilight had begun to darken the woods across the street. He found his spare archery glove, packed a few items in the duffel, grabbed his archery gear, and started for Beechwood.

Chapter Fourteen

After spending the early morning hours adding fresh leaves to his shelter floor, Ash snatched up bow and quiver and started for the archery field. While still a stone's throw from the field, he heard voices. Easing forward he saw Anne Metter, the fingers of her right hand individually wrapped in bright white tape. With her was the wrestler, Guy Guisburn, dressed in dark-green GDA sweats. Troutman, in jeans and camouflage jacket, stood back with his arms folded across his stomach as he watched Guy try to coach Anne.

"Déjà vu," Ash mumbled to himself.

But this time Anne was not laughing. Guy struck a pose before the target and drew back an arrow. When he shot he whipped the bow forward like a child with a slingshot. The arrow wobbled in flight, glanced off the target, and skidded into the grass.

"That was a bum arrow!" Guy announced and loaded again. "All you gotta do is pull the arrow back beside your eye, Anne, then you let 'er go."

Troutman snorted when Guy's second shot skipped off the side of the target. Guy frowned at the bow in his hand and hissed a laugh through his teeth.

"It's the stupid bow!" Guy carped. "No wonder they dumped archery from phys-ed."

"Right," Troutman purred, shook his head, and spat to one side. Guy pulled the unloaded bow to full draw and swung on Troutman, who watched the performance with a sly grin. He pulled a cigarette from his pocket, and flipped open a lighter.

When Guy let go of the string, he yelped like a mouse caught in a trap. The string, without the burden of an arrow, had whipped forward an extra few inches and stung his bare arm. Troutman laughed so hard he spat out his cigarette.

Along with the twang of the string came the dry tick of cracking fiberglass. Ash heard it because he was listening for it. He knew what a "dry-fire" could do to a bow.

"This should be fun," he said under his breath and settled in to watch.

He had seen it happen once before. Back home, behind the farmer's co-op, two men had been shooting into a hay bale. A dry-fire like the one Guy had just performed had cracked one man's bow, but it hadn't splintered apart until his next full draw. The bow broke cleanly then, and the two halves whipped around to lash at the man, one smacking his buttocks and the other cracking a rib.

As Ash waited for the laws of probability to take their course, Guy played up his disgust for the inferior bow. When the wrestler handed it back to Anne, Ash stiffened, knowing that the danger had been passed along to her.

Guy put his hands on Anne's shoulders and walked her to a shooting position. She loaded an arrow, following the steps just as Ash had taught her. When she curled her fingers around the string, Ash had no choice but to step out onto the field.

"Anne! Wait!"

They all turned to his approach. Anne's face was a double exposure of surprise and dismay. "Your bow is broken," Ash informed her.

"See?" Guy crowed. "I told you it was a lame bow."

Anne, looking miserable, began walking toward Ash, whispering a desperate rush of apology. "They followed me, Ash. I'm stuck with them

. . . again." Her irritated expression melted to a plea. "Rescue me? Please? One more time?"

Wearing his big smile, Guy strode up to them. "You goin' huntin', Chief?" He bobbed his eyebrows and turned to flash a grin at Troutman.

Troutman picked up his cigarette and strolled toward them. "Huntin'?" His laugh was a surly bounce of his shoulders. "With *that*?" he mocked, nodding at Ash's bow. "That cain't be up to hunting weight. More like a toy, ain't it?" Troutman made a tight smile. "Got me a aught-six . . . Browning . . . semi-auto."

Ash's face showed nothing as he baited Troutman. "Scope?"

"Oh, yeah," Troutman boasted and flicked ashes from his cigarette. "Leupold, three to nine variable."

"You use a tree stand?"

Troutman squinted through the smoke. "I usually rig it about twenty feet up."

Ash let the moment inflate like a balloon. He watched Troutman draw on his cigarette and exhale through his nose before delivering his *coup de grace*.

"Sounds easy," Ash said in a flat tone. "Sit, wait, and pull a trigger."

Troutman had raised the cigarette again but paused with it an inch from his lips. Only now did he realize the path of ridicule down which Ash had led him.

Guy laughed. "Go on, Anne, see if *you* can hit anything with that spastic bow."

"Her bow is broken," Ash informed him again.

Guy shrugged. "Well, hell, go tell the phys-ed retards they gave ya a bum bow."

"It wasn't broken when she brought it out," Ash said. He pointed casually to the inside of Guy's forearm, where the raised welt looked like a small, pale balloon attached to the skin. "A dry-fire not only stings your arm . . . it can crack a bow."

Guy's mouth fell open and his eyes widened. Clapping a hand to his heart, he played out his drama like a caricature of contrition. "You're sayin' *I* broke it?"

Troutman blew a quick jet of smoke and shook his head. "Hell, prob'ly got a hunerd cracks in it. Prob'ly been dry-fired a thousand times."

"Then maybe you'd like to test it out," Ash said.

Troutman stood taller. "Or maybe I'd like to shut your smart mouth for you!"

Guy crossed his arms over his chest and smiled. "Uh-oh, Chief. Looks like you got ol' Trout's hair up."

Anne stepped forward and held the bow out to Guy. "You'll have to take it back to Coach Torrence. You're the one who broke it."

"Aw, Anne," Guy moaned. "It's just a piece of junk the school doesn't use anymore. Forget it." He began pulling Troutman away. "Come on, Trout. I think you're scarin' him to death." Fixing his hard gaze on Ash, Guy smiled, his eyes like chips of blue ice. "So long, Chief. We'll see you again sometime."

Anne and Ash watched them cross the field, Guy jogging backward in front of Troutman, taking air-jabs at him. When he connected, tapping the top of Troutman's head, Guy made a cackling laugh. Troutman never broke stride.

Anne's arms went limp by her sides. "I'm so sorry, Ash. I feel awful about this."

"You'd better take that bow back. Just tell the coach what happened. See if you can set up a target somewhere else so you won't have to deal with those two anymore."

She tried to smile. "Will you teach me more? I do need to learn it."

Ash began covering the target. "I can't promise anything right now, Anne."

She watched him weight the tarp with the four stones. "Would my bow really have broken if we'd used it again?"

"Maybe, maybe not," he said. "Eventually it will break, and when it does you don't want to be the one holding it. Be sure to tell Coach Torrence."

They left the field together and stopped at the street, where she pivoted to face him and smiled a last apology. "Thank you again," she said and started toward the gym.

Walking to his dorm, Ash felt a pang of remorse. Anne was trying to be his friend. But what would be the point? He would be gone from GDA within days.

At Huntington Hall a workman on a ladder swung a sledgehammer, breaking open the outside west wall of the third story. Two men in coveralls watched him from below.

"They're tearing it down already?" said a voice behind Ash. He turned to see Will Scathlock in sweats and running shoes. Cat propped his hands on his hips as he caught his breath. Beads of perspiration stood on his forehead.

"It's some kind of electrical problem," Ash explained.

Cat nodded and glanced at Ash's bow. "Hey, want to come up and see my bows?"

Five floors up in Gamewell Hall, Cat opened his door and led the way in. The cloying smell of varnish dominated the room. Ash began a slow tour of Cat's woodwork: a freshly sanded chest of drawers, a rocking chair, a toy wooden train that sprawled across the floor, and a series of boxes with hinged lids. All of it was quality work.

"The bows are over here," Cat said.

Ash crossed the room to a rack of longbows resting horizontally on pegs. Cat took one down and strung it.

Ash turned the bow in his hands, deferential to the artistry that had gone into its composition. "What wood is this?" he asked, testing its pull.

"Yew," Cat said. "English yew. All of these are yew bows."

Ash slid the upper limb of the bow between his thumb and index, noting the fine taper. "Alan's right. You do good work."

Cat's bows were a light shade of red-brown. All but one, which was so dark as to be almost black. Its gently curving lines showed a different architecture from the others. Even unstrung it appeared elegant lying on its pegs.

"That one's a beauty," Ash said.

Cat took it down, and they traded bows. As Ash rotated the bow the glassy finish flickered with white darts of reflected light. It reminded him of the river at night catching light from the stars.

"String it if you want to," Cat offered.

Ash did. Taking his shooting stance, he drew. It was powerful and perfect in its symmetry, the bend of the bow as pleasing as the feel of slipping into a favorite pair of shoes. Easing the string forward, he nodded his approval.

"That one's special," Ash said. He unstrung the bow and set it back on the rack.

"Hey," Cat said as he hung the other bow, "are you shooting in the homecoming tournament?" When he saw the question on Ash's face, Cat added, "Check out the poster in the lobby. Be a shame for you—of all people—to miss it."

Creeping back to earth in the elevator, Ash imagined a tournament taking place on his field. The idea pricked at him like needles. As soon as the doors parted he saw the poster. Against a background of autumn colors, an archer at full draw stood out in black silhouette. It was an eye-catching piece of artwork—Anne Metter's creation, no doubt. In old English script the text read: *Renaissance Days Archery Tournament*. The contest was scheduled for halftime during the Nacoochee game.

Juggling a slew of contradictory emotions, Ash turned away from the poster and walked to his dorm.

Chapter Fifteen

With all the graded tests handed out, Princeton Johns began a methodical survey of the students seated in the auditorium. The pivot of his head was like a cat's tail mesmerizing its prey. Ash sat at his usual desk, his hands empty. Mick sat behind him in his typical slouch. Princeton Johns never once deigned to acknowledge them.

"What an interesting array of test scores," Johns quipped in his shrill, acid voice. "Thirteen perfect scores. Seventeen more A's, twelve B's, four C's, three D's, and one F." He looked down at his notes. "Mr. Steinmetz!" he called out to the class at large.

"Yes, sir?" The weak reply came from the center section of the room.

Johns leaned on the podium and focused on his quarry. "What is the function of the endoplasmic reticulum?"

In the quiet of the room, Steinmetz cleared his throat and croaked, "Sir?"

"Does your inability to answer indicate default, Mr. Steinmetz?" Dr. Johns crossed his arms over his chest. "What did you score on the test, Mr. Steinmetz?"

"One-hundred, sir," he answered, his voice buoyed by the hope of redemption.

"How commendable," Johns purred. "Now, would you please bring your considerable knowledge to bear upon the function of the endoplasmic reticulum?"

Pages shuffled on Steinmetz's sinking ship. "Uh . . . that wasn't on the test, sir . . . was it?" Under Johns's unmerciful glare, the boy kept thumbing through his papers.

"Miss Boyles!" Johns purred, singling out his next victim.

"Yes, sir?" The reply was prompt, startled.

"Can you name the sequential phases of chromosomal alignment during meiosis?"

She managed to identify one phase but could shed no light on its place in the whole process. Johns leaned on his podium and propped a hand under his chin.

"And what did you make on the test, Miss Boyles?"

A little wiser to Johns's motives, she answered with less enthusiasm than had Steinmetz. "One-hundred." Her voice had the sagging intonation of a confession.

"Fascinating," Johns remarked to no one in particular. "Mr. Braswell!" he called to his next quarry. And so it went.

This performance continued with predictable results with eight more students, and all the while Ash prayed for a question to be tossed his way. He wanted to spit back the answers at Princeton Johns like a quiver full of arrows. But a question never came. Then without warning, Dr. Johns jumped full-tilt into the day's lesson, and every hand in the room clawed for notebook and pen. Princeton Johns had raised the red flag of war.

When the bell delivered its pardon to the class, Dr. Johns raised his voice to override the bustle of mass exodus. "Mr. Asherwood and Mr. Millerson, see me in my office before you leave." He walked off the stage and left the door open behind him.

As the other students shuffled out, Ash mounted the stage and walked into the hallway where he stopped at an open door. Dr. Johns sat behind his desk, his eyes closed, the fingertips of one hand touching those of the other. Mick sauntered up behind Ash and peeked around his shoulder.

"Come in and close the door!" Johns ordered.

Mick followed Ash into the room. There were two empty chairs facing the desk, but both boys remained standing. Johns sat back, threaded his fingers together over his stomach, and stared at Mick.

"Where did you get the test, Mr. Millerson?"

Mick swallowed, the sound like a small stone dropped into a well.

"Mr. Millerson, you know I do not bluff. If you choose to remain mute, I can arrange for your parents to come pick you up tomorrow." He leaned forward and propped his forearms on the desktop. "Where did you get the test?" he asked quietly.

A wet film now shone brightly on Mick's eyes. "I bought it."

Johns's voice remained controlled and articulate. "From whom?"

Mick's tongue darted over his lips. A tear curved down his cheek.

"From whom?" Johns repeated, his voice humming with patience.

Mick frowned down at his shoes and said nothing.

"*From whom!*" Johns screamed, causing Mick to totter backward as if the floor had suddenly tilted. The outburst mushroomed inside the room, making the space seem more confining. Still, Mick said nothing.

Johns's eyes cut to Ash. "Well? What about you, Asherwood?"

"I have no idea where he got it."

"Really," Johns whispered through a thin smile.

Ash was tempted to echo Dr. Johns's last word, but a deep, guttural sound turned him to Mick. Big tears welled in the boy's eyes as he began to sob.

"Sir," Ash said, "why am I a part of this meeting? I didn't—"

"Why?" Johns interrupted, his eyes catching fire. "Because I *have* you! I have *both* of you! Caught in the act by my eyes. Don't think for a second you can extricate yourselves from this." He sat back and gloated. "But this is much bigger than the two of you. I may be willing to bargain."

Mick muffled his crying, and his eyes turned hopeful. When Dr. Johns saw him nibble at this bait, the teacher softened his voice.

"Tell me where you got it, Michael . . . and perhaps we can negotiate."

Mick swallowed. "I told you . . . I bought it."

"Yes, but from whom?"

Mick raised his arms from his sides and stiffened them as if he'd been jolted by an electric current. "I don't know!" he insisted, the words scraping from his throat.

The room was very still but for a galaxy of dust motes floating in the light that angled through the window. The bell for next period clanged out in the hallway.

"*Who!*" Johns screamed. Mick jumped and began crying with a choking sound.

"Dr. Johns," Ash said calmly, "maybe Mick would be more comfortable talking if I left the room." Both Mick and Johns jerked their heads toward him, one out of despair, the other incensed. "Mick can tell you I know nothing about this."

"Nothing?" Johns snapped. "I saw you give the test to him, Mr. Asherwood. For all I know, *you* are the source."

Ash and Johns locked eyes. Without turning away, Ash said, "Tell him, Mick." But Mick's whimper had no chance against the acid blast that erupted.

"Why would I care to hear what either of you has to say about the other? You both had the test! You are caught!" He raised his hands, palms up, and made a slow exaggerated shake of his head. "The only choice you have is to talk to me. Neither of you will leave this office until I know where you got that test."

"Tell him, Mick," Ash said through clenched teeth.

Mick turned to Ash and fairly screamed his answer. "I don't *know* where I got it!"

Ash glared at him. "You have to know."

"Well, I *don't*! It was slipped under my door!"

"Whom did you pay?" Johns drilled quickly.

A stream of tears spread over Mick's cheeks. "I don't *know!*"

Ash gripped Mick's arm. "You can at least tell him about me."

Mick opened his mouth to speak, but Johns slammed his hands on the desktop. "You are not here to converse with each other. You are here to answer my questions."

The hopelessness of the meeting was fast sinking to panic. Ash wanted to shout that Dr. Leonhardt had pinpointed him as one of the few innocents in class. Ash was tempted to answer every question that had been posed in today's class, but Dr. Johns rose, checked his wrist watch, and then stabbed a finger down on his desktop.

"You have one last chance with me right here . . . right now!"

Five seconds passed. Then five more. When the bell clanged in the hall, Ash knew the ultimatum was sealed.

"Get out!" Johns shrieked and pointed to the door. "You will be hearing from the dean soon."

Mick started out, but Ash reached for his arm. "Ow!" Mick grunted. "That hurts!"

"Tell him, Mick!" Ash demanded.

Mick stared back with tears brimming in his eyes. "He won't listen to us, man!"

When Ash released him, Mick opened the door and walked out.

Ash looked at the top of Princeton Johns's head as the man wrote with a furious energy. "Dr. Johns, I had nothing to do with any stolen tests."

Without looking up, Johns stopped his pen and whispered. "Get . . . out!"

Skipping his other classes, Ash sat in the courtyard until noon. When finally Dean Oberleigh lumbered down the steps from the administration building, Ash rose to intercept him. The dean's haggard face mustered a show of irritation. It was all too clear that the dean had received notice of Ash's interrogation by Princeton Johns.

"What in heaven's name happened?" the dean wanted to know.

Ash related the story complete. As he did, Dean Oberleigh frowned at the sidewalk like an angry child having to sit through a parental lecture. When it was done, they stood side by side facing the lawn. A fragile silence hung in the air around them.

"Am I really thrown out of his class?" Ash ventured.

The dean almost laughed. "Son, I'm trying to determine if you're thrown out of the school." He looked out on the empty quadrangle. "Damn it," he growled, "I've been trying to straighten out the Leonhardt mess . . . and now this!"

Ash waited a beat. "What happens now?"

"Millerson has a hearing with the board in the morning."

"What time?"

The dean looked at him quickly. "It's at nine-thirty, but you are not to be there. I convinced the board to isolate the cases. I'm trying to buy some time for you . . . to sort this out. After Leonhardt's fiasco, Johns has the board's ear. *Your* credibility hangs somewhat on Dr. Leonhardt's word. And right now, his word—" The dean shook his head and left the sentence unfinished.

"But Millerson can explain what happened. He knows I didn't look at that test. I had it in my hand for maybe two seconds."

Dean Oberleigh made a humorless smile. "Do you really expect Millerson's word to carry any weight?"

"I'd like a chance to explain it to the board with Mick there to back me up."

The dean scowled and exhaled heavily. "Come by at nine-twenty in the morning, just in case. Right now, you should have a talk with Millerson."

Ash made a series of progressively louder knocks on Mick's door at Gamewell. The room remained quiet. He tried the knob, and the door swung open into semi-dark. A computer glowed from a corner desk, its screen turning with an endless galaxy of spirals. Someone lay on a bed with an arm crooked over his eyes.

"Mick? It's Asherwood."

A long heavy sigh came from the bed. "I'm fried," Mick said.

Ash moved toward him. "What did you expect, Mick?"

"I don't know," Mick said in an annoyed tone. He rolled his head to face the wall.

Ash pulled a chair closer and sat. "I need you to tell the board about me, Mick."

Mick's voice came off the wall inside the blur of an echo. "I talked to the dean. He said not to mention you unless I was asked."

"They're planning a separate hearing for me, Mick. I need you to be there."

Mick turned his head from the wall, his eyes pink-rimmed and teary. "Well, it better be soon. I gotta go before the board tomorrow at nine-thirty."

When Mick started to turn away again, Ash pulled him by the shoulder. "I need you there no matter when it is, Mick."

Mick's eyes filled with misery. "It's the first time I ever cheated."

Something in the boy's voice made Ash believe him. "What made you do it?"

"I don't know. I studied my ass off, but I couldn't risk a bad grade. I thought I might not pull it off with Dr. Johns." He let out a long breath and some of the bitterness left his voice. "My father said if I got through Greenwood and kept my scholarship, then he'd handle college. All I had to do was stay in this friggin' school."

"Mick, you bought a test. I didn't. I need to know you'll stand up for me."

Mick returned to the wall. "Yeah," he whined, "I know."

"Would you like me to walk with you tomorrow? Maybe wait outside?" When Mick didn't answer, Ash said, "I'll be here a little after nine. We'll walk over together."

Seated at the table with a book open before him, John Naylor made a two-fingered salute from his forehead when Ash arrived at their rendezvous room in the basement of the library. "Wasn't sure you'd show up. Did Dr. Johns kick you out of class?"

Ash slapped his books on the table and remained standing. "Out of school maybe. I've got a hearing before the disciplinary board sometime in the next week or so."

With his brow pushed low over his eyes and his ebony face lined with wrinkles, Naylor stared at him. "What you gonna do?"

Ash shook his head. "Hope that the dean and Millerson come through for me."

"How can the dean help?" John said. When Ash closed his eyes and slowly shook his head, John added. "Then how can I help?"

Ash opened his eyes to see Naylor's face transformed into obsidian. A fierce energy radiated from his dark skin. His eyes shone white-hot, just as they had in the sports page photographs.

Ash sat. "I guess the dean will be finding someone else to help you."

The fire in Naylor's eyes continued to burn. "Don't want someone else," John said. "You come to class and sit behind me up in back. Dr. Johns won't be able to see you. That way when this thing gets straightened out, you won't have to play catch-up."

Ash exhaled heavily. "I wish I could be so optimistic."

John raised his chin to Ash. "I'll be optimistic for both of us."

Chapter Sixteen

Behind John Naylor, Ash had survived most of the hour of biology unseen, but a disaster was in the making in the back row. One of the athletes was snoring so loudly that his friends around him were red-faced, their fists pressed to their mouths to keep from laughing. Twice Dr. Johns had paused in his lecture to glare at the jock section in back.

Five minutes before the bell was due to ring, Dr. Johns continued his oration and began slowly climbing the steps toward the back of the room. The students struggled to divide their attention between their note taking, his progress, and the hapless victim who napped in ignorant bliss. When Johns reached the top, Ash was bent low over his notebook, his pen hand scribbling away, his free hand pressed to his forehead like a visor above his eyes.

When the lecture stopped, the porcine snoring took center stage in the auditorium. Students on the lower tiers were turned in their seats and wide-eyed.

"Wake him up," Johns snapped.

Someone punched the sleeper's shoulder. Rising from a fog the boy cursed and then paled when he saw his teacher hovering in the aisle. Johns stretched out an index finger and curled it toward himself. The boy stood. He was big boned with a bulging stomach and his buzz-cut gave his head a bullet shape. He sidled out of the row and followed Johns down the steps. They stopped at one of the empty front row seats.

"This will be your seat for the remainder of the term. If you last that long."

The bell rang and the class made its first frantic leap to escape when Johns stopped them with a single, strident command. "Wait!"

He played the moment out by calmly taking the steps up to the stage. When he stopped to gather his things from the podium, his voice was almost pleasant.

"Mr. Asherwood, see me in my office . . . now." Then Johns walked briskly off the stage. Naylor turned around and looked at Ash, but neither spoke.

When Ash knocked on Johns's office door, ten seconds passed before his teacher's voice called out to enter. Ash opened the door to see Dr. Johns seated, his fingers laced together on his desk, one eyebrow frozen into a rigid tilde.

"Should I be flattered, Mr. Asherwood? Can you not bear to miss my lectures? Or are you keeping your hand in the business of selling tests?"

Ash clamped his teeth to hold down the words rising in his throat. Dr. Johns's eyes twinkled with amusement. Leaning forward, Johns ran his finger down a laminated page, picked up his desk phone, and punched in three numbers.

"When I dismissed you from my class, you lost your right to a place in it," Johns said, holding the phone to his ear. His eyes cut away and his voice sharpened. "This is Dr. Johns in the science building, room one-o-two. I need a security officer here." Johns listened, looked up at Ash and said, "A trespasser." The voice in the phone droned on until Johns interrupted. "Just send someone now!" he ordered and hung up.

"That wasn't necessary," Ash said. "What is it you intend to do?"

"I?" Johns said, sitting back. "Nothing. Security will escort you out."

Ash glanced at the wall clock and thought of Mick. "I have a meeting to go to."

"So do I," Johns sang, smiling as though they had something in common. Then his eyes went cold, and he pointed to a chair against the wall. "Sit!"

"Dr. Johns, if you would just listen to—"

"I don't have to listen to anything, Mr. Asherwood!"

Ash felt anger rise in his throat like a match struck against his windpipe. "I guess I'll just have to hope the rest of the disciplinary board is not as pompous as you are."

Johns smacked his hands together, the sound like the crack of a whiplash, and then he stiffened his arm to point at the chair again. "Sit!"

Ash sat.

"You will flunk my course, Mr. Asherwood. That is the least I can promise. At best, you'll be expelled along with your disheveled partner in crime."

For five minutes neither spoke. Johns went about his work. Ash watched the clock. At nine-twenty-five, three aggressive knocks rattled the door. A well-built, middle-aged black man leaned into the room. He wore the GDA security uniform.

"Come!" Johns snapped.

The guard stepped in, leaving the door open. He eyed Ash and waited.

"This boy has trespassed into my classroom!" Johns announced. "Remove him!"

The man eyed the GDA crest on Ash's blazer. "Where is he supposed to be?"

"I have no idea," Johns stated blithely. "He is not to be here."

"Where do I take him?" the guard asked.

Standing and taking his overcoat from the freestanding rack, Johns spoke as if the answer were obvious. "Out of here!"

To end the charade, Ash stood up and walked out on his own. The security officer followed. Without a word they walked the length of the hall and entered the auditorium stage from the rear. After hopping off the stage, Ash waited as the security man took the steps. The man's irritation seemed to be mounting.

"You wanna tell me what this is all about?"

Ash decided on a spare outline of the truth. "Dr. Johns asked me to go to his office after class. I did. I told him I had somewhere to be, but he made me wait for you."

"Are you registered in his first period class?"

"Yes, sir."

The man frowned. "Well, who, for Pete's sake, was trespassing and where?"

Ash looked at the man's nametag. "Mr. Dawson, Dr. Johns is hard to figure."

Dawson ballooned his cheeks, exhaled, and led the way out. "Come on," he said.

Outside a cold stiff wind cut through Ash's blazer. At the security car they stood on the sidewalk and hunched their shoulders against the weather and watched Dr. Johns hurry across the street, get into his car, and drive out of the lot.

"I've seen you around," Dawson said. He turned up the collar of his jacket to cover the back of his neck. "You're the archery fellow that shoots out on the west field."

Surprised, Ash nodded. "I got permission from phys-ed."

"Yeah. Coach Torrence cleared it through us. I used to do some shooting myself." He stuck his hands in his jacket pockets and looked Ash over. "What's your name, son?"

"Robert Asherwood."

Dawson nodded toward the building. "You wanna explain all this, Robert?"

"Mr. Dawson, I have no idea why he called you. It was totally un-necessary. All I know is I'm late for a nine-thirty meeting at the admin-istration building."

Dawson took a hand from his pocket, checked his watch, and pointed at the science building. "And you *are* enrolled in his first period class, correct?"

"Yes, sir."

Dawson stared across the valley and raked a row of very straight teeth across his upper lip. "He doesn't like to explain things much, does he?" He checked his watch again. "I got better things to do than walk somebody out of class." He frowned, made a little grunting sound and opened the car door for Ash. "Get in. I'll drive you up the hill."

The headmaster's receptionist stood her ground. "I am sorry, Mr. Ash-erwood, but if you were expected, I would have been told. Dean Ober-leigh mentioned nothing to me."

Ash walked back into the foyer and stood before the tall glass panes that faced the quadrangle. The day was gray. These buildings patterned into a rectangle around the lawn had always reminded Ash of the day he had enrolled at Greenwood. Now it was looking as though this courtyard would serve as the memory of his departure, too.

It was almost eleven when male voices filled the receptionist's room. The board members filed out the meeting room door, all dressed in dark blue-black suits, talking in genial tones as if they were walking off a golf course. In contrast, Princeton Johns strode through the crowd, his chin lifted and a smug smile skewing his mustache. His shoes clicked across the foyer until he marched out the door into the cold.

Dean Oberleigh came out of the room conversing with a bald man. When Ash approached, the dean immediately looked away to refocus on the bald man's words. As they passed by him, Ash heard the sharp tap of high heels right behind him.

"Well, hello, Robert." Ash turned to see his advisor of two years ago. Mrs. Alles looked much the same, alert and handsome with her strong jaw line and piercing blue eyes. She had been kind to him as a newcomer, helping him assimilate into the school. "I keep hearing good things about you from the teachers." She tilted her head. "I am curious. What in the world did you finally get your sharp claws into for a pre-major?"

"Still working on that, Mrs. Alles."

As she offered advice, Ash looked over her shoulder at the back of a woman entering the meeting room. Dressed in a rust-colored suit, she wore her hair piled on top of her head and pinned in place by a tortoise shell comb.

Mrs. Alles leaned to catch his eye. "Are you all right, Robert?"

He looked back at his former counselor. "Where's Mick, Mrs. Alles?"

She frowned. "Who?"

A quiet voice with an English accent pulled Ash's attention to the conference room. "Excuse me, ma'am," he said and eased around Mrs. Alles. At the threshold of the room he peered in and saw the profile of Marin's face as she sat in conversation with the headmaster. He could see enough of her face to recognize its wilt of regret. Mick was nowhere to be seen.

Ash hurried through the lobby, out the glass doors, and up the acorn-littered sidewalk. Dean Oberleigh, alone on the steps of his building, turned at his approach.

"What happened?" Ash said. "Where's Millerson?"

"Packing, I would guess," the dean replied testily. "He walked out five minutes into the meeting. It was clear to him, I guess, which way it would go. Where were you?"

Ash closed his eyes and shook his head. "Long story."

The dean knotted his jaws. "So was my opening statement to the board about hearing from another student." His glare was like a furnace, but Ash did not turn from it.

"So Millerson is expelled?" When the dean began to nod, Ash started backing away. "I'd better go find him."

The first person he saw in Gamewell's lobby was Alan Odell, who was bent before a drink machine feeding coins into the slot. "Young Asher," Alan greeted. "Ever the mystery. I just left you a note in your dorm—where there is no heat—and here you are dripping with sweat."

"Mick Millerson," Ash said between breaths. "You know him, right?"

Alan pointed to the front door. "He just hauled a big suitcase through here. I think he got in the cab that was parked out there. Must be a family emergency." When Ash only stared out the glass door, Alan's voice turned upbeat. "Hey, my note is about Cat wrestling today in the gym. At three o'clock." His face brightened. "Elaine's coming. She wants to meet you. Hey! Where are you going?"

"Today's not a good day, Alan."

"You're forcing me to play my ace, Young Asher." He popped the top of his soda can and bobbed his eyebrows. "There'll be a certain female archer there, too."

Ash felt a strong yearning to talk with Marin, but not at a sports event. "Sorry," he said and shook his head. "Not today."

Alan's eyes narrowed with concern. "Okay, young Asher, another time."

When Ash pushed out through the glass doors, the bell rang across campus, and students poured out onto the sidewalk for fourth period classes. Realizing he didn't know what to do or where to go, he stopped and watched the pedestrian traffic. Borrowing a little optimism from

John Naylor, he decided to go through his regular daily schedule and pray there might still be a chance to extricate himself from this nightmare and remain in school. Setting his pace with somber determination, he started for the cafeteria.

In the late afternoon, dressed in his sweats, Ash went to the gym for the hot shower that his dorm could no longer provide. When he saw a crowd filling the seats around the wrestling mat, he stepped up on the nearest bleachers to scan the seats for Alan. If Marin was there with him, Ash would know not to walk to Ten Point to find her.

The wrestling team was dressed out in its competition green and gold, the athletes scattered across the large blue mat, each team member stretching or rolling on his back or tightening his shoelaces. One was pumping out a set of rapid pushups. It was Guy Guisburn. His piston-like bursts of breath could be heard over the roaring seashell acoustics of the room.

Cat stood by the far wall, his feet together, spine erect, and arms hanging at his sides. His head hung forward as if he were examining his toes, but his eyes were closed. His head rose and fell slowly with the rhythm of his breathing. Over his dark green wrestling tights he wore a tattered, red tank top a shade brighter than his bronze-red hair.

When an overweight boy in baggy slacks and white V-neck undershirt stopped to speak to him, Cat looked up and smiled and then returned to his state of repose. The plump boy pulled a packaged sweet roll from his back pocket, took a bite, wrapped up the roll, pocketed it, and moved on to his duties.

Ash turned when he heard his name called. Alan stood waving from the top of the bleachers. Climbing the seats, Ash found Alan seated between two girls. One's face was smooth as fine porcelain, her golden brown hair parting over her shoulders and falling over her blazer to the swell of her breasts. The other was Anne Metter, who, apparently, was Alan's "female archer."

"Young Asher!" Alan yelled over the noise and beamed. "You came!" He wrapped his arm around the waist of the long-haired girl. "This is Elaine!"

The shy girl lowered her doe-brown eyes as though the mention of her name embarrassed her. She was perfectly proportioned, and Ash could imagine the attention paid to her by hormone-driven boys. With a pained smile she offered her hand. He reached forward and took it. It was like holding a small wounded bird.

Anne made room for Ash, and he sat. "I've been practicing!" she announced, pressing close to talk over the noise. Opening her hand she proudly displayed the chafed pads of her fingertips. Her smile brightened. "Have you seen the homecoming posters?"

He cupped his hand to his mouth and leaned to her ear. "Talk later," he said, "when it's quieter." She nodded enthusiastically, as if she had had the same idea.

"Do you know how this works?" Alan yelled pointing to the center stage mat. "They call it 'The Ladder.' It all goes by weight. The lightest man takes on the next heavier one in a one-minute round. The winner takes on the next heavier. Cat says it gets vicious. The lighter challengers have everything to gain. They want the coaches to see them perform well, beyond their weight class. And they want to let the big boys know that bigger isn't necessarily better. All the pressure is on the heavier ones. Nobody wants to get his butt kicked by a smaller wrestler, especially in front of the student body." Alan huffed his sardonic laugh. "Great for team camaraderie, don't you think?"

The shrill blast of a whistle quieted the room. Across the mat the wrestlers sat on their bench in a hierarchy of bulk, leanest on the far right, heaviest on the left. Snapping on headgear, the two lightest on the team walked out onto the mat and listened to instructions from the referee. Then they crouched for a standup start.

At the whistle they darted in, testing and parrying. Then, on a takedown, the contest slowed as one forced his opponent's shoulders to the mat. The crowd roared for a pin and got it.

After four more bouts, only once did someone defeat a heavier teammate, but his dream of climbing higher was crushed in the next round. At his turn, Cat rose from the middle of the bench, walked out onto the mat, and shook hands with his lighter challenger.

"Here's our boy," Alan announced.

The whistle blew, and the lighter boy feinted and shifted to another angle of attack. But Cat reacted as if he had expected the ploy. He melded with his attacker and immediately held the advantage, arching the boy backward as though easing him to the mat so as not to hurt him. And, just like that, it was over. Though it was not an exhibition that satisfied the crowd's bloodlust, a modest applause congratulated Cat's finesse.

When a heavier challenger was summoned to face him, Cat remained inside the mat's white circle with his hands resting on his hips. The newcomer strutted back and forth, and Cat watched him as though already dissecting his strengths and weaknesses.

The whistle chirped, and with two quick moves by Cat the contest was over in ten seconds. A roar of approval exploded from the stands. When the defeated boy stood and ripped off his headgear, Ash recognized one of Guisburn's sidekicks who had followed Anne to the archery field—the one named "Jeep." Jeep sat, and the boys around him offered words of consolation, but Jeep only frowned and rubbed at a shoulder.

Behind the bench, leaning against the wall with his arms folded across his gray work uniform, Troutman chewed gum, his jaws moving in a slow rhythm. Ash looked at Anne to see if she had noticed any of the trio, but she was bright-eyed, clapping her hands rapidly before her face, buoyant over Cat's victory.

Cat won twice more, and the white circle on the blue mat had now become his territory. The crowd was with him, now rooting for the underdog. But the weight differential took a leap that sobered the spectators. Guy Guisburn stripped off his warm ups and swaggered onto the mat like a bull in search of a red cape. His unblinking eyes fixed on Cat. Someone on the bench yelled, "Eat him alive, Cat!" and that prompted a counter-cry: "Trim his claws, Giz!"

Considering the weight Guy carried around on his simian frame, he was light on his feet, hopping in place while the ref ran through his compulsory spiel. When the talk was done, Guy stepped back and gathered himself like a predator about to make its kill. Cat stood upright, relaxed and expressionless, without any visible prologue to battle.

Like the timely boost of a dramatic movie score, a clap of thunder shook the building and then rolled across the sky with the resonance of bowling balls tumbling down a wooden alley. Rain drummed the high metal roof so violently that most eyes angled to the ceiling. Against this deafening soundtrack the whistle set into motion a scene reminiscent of David and Goliath.

Like a dancer, Cat glided to his left, then his right. In complete counterpoint, Guisburn bulled his way forward, trying to overwhelm Cat with sheer mass. Cat slipped through the attack and attached to Guy's back, pulling upward and back like a man uprooting a tree. Guy locked Cat's arms, lunged back and crashed to the mat with a bone-crunching slam. The crowd recoiled in a collective gasp that was audible above the sustained percussion of the rain. Guy made a quick turn to meet Cat chest-to-chest, but Cat rolled in a mirror image to Guy's pivot and was on his feet.

Guy rose as Cat assumed his familiar relaxed stance. Guy had received the takedown point, but another point had been made. Cat had not jumped to the advantage when Guy was down. He wanted more of Guy's tactless bravado. Cat was having fun.

Guy charged in again. Abandoning his smooth circling motion, Cat became a streak of aggression, attacking low. But Guy's repeat performance as a human battering ram was a ruse. He veered. Cat tried to adjust as Guy drove his shoulder into Cat's throat, the impact making a brutal smacking sound that carried into the bleachers. They hit on their sides, each vying for the advantage; but Cat's left arm was wedged in the meaty angle of Guy's neck and shoulder. Guy inched forward, taking the arm to an unnatural angle. Cat's face tightened as the referee hurried around them checking his watch.

With his free hand Cat pried at the hold, straining until his face approached the color of his hair. Slowly he opened a gap, and Guy began to lose ground, his broad, hairy back creeping closer to the mat. The spectators were screaming for an upset.

When the whistle blasted, the tension in the bleachers remained unbroken, for there had been no pin. In the next second—when it should have been over—Guy lunged, driving his weight into Cat's arm, wrenching it further from its natural range of motion. Only the people close to the mat heard the wet visceral snap, but all recoiled in unison. A collective dry intake of breath seemed to suck the air out of the room.

Cat clamped his eyes shut and bared his teeth. Ash was on his feet, and then others around him stood, all wanting a view of the injured athlete.

Guy stood panting and backed away, watching as two of the coaches knelt on either side of Cat. The overweight boy in the undershirt picked up a black kit and ran toward the mat. His plump, round belly bounced as he came to a stumbling halt. Panting and shifting his weight from leg to leg, he peered over the coaches' shoulders at Cat.

"Tucker, call an ambulance!" one of the coaches yelled to him.

Tucker started into a labored run toward the far side of the gym. He stopped, almost falling over the squeak of his shoes, retraced his steps, and set the black kit beside the coaches. Then he turned and hurried off again.

Ash climbed down from the bleachers and made his way to the edge of the mat. Cat's face was a mask of agony, his eyes squeezed shut as he breathed through clenched teeth. The trainer returned, bumping past Ash and stumbling to the coaches. Perspiration dripped from his face and spattered on the mat in big dollops.

"They're coming . . . to the back . . . entrance," the boy gasped between breaths.

The coach turned. "Go get the big doors open so they can park out of the rain."

"Right," the boy said, staring at Cat. "Is he okay?"

"Tucker!" the coach barked. "Go get the door open! Now!"

Tucker jumped. "Yes, sir!" He bowled past Ash in his awkward run.

Almost all the wrestlers stood, trying to get a look at Cat. Only Guy sat on the bench, working a stiffness out of his neck. Troutman sauntered up behind him, leaned, and said something that made both boys laugh.

Ash heard the slap of sneakers on the floor behind him, and he turned to see Tucker's pleading face. "Can you help me? I can't get the door open for the ambulance."

"Let's go," Ash said.

Tucker's anxious face collapsed with relief. Turning, he began running again, his shoes flopping on the floor in a labored rhythm. Ash followed at a fast walk.

They moved down a corridor to a garage with two big doors made of hinged aluminum slats that would open vertically along curved metal tracks. Outside rain pinged off the metal doors like popcorn.

"The switch isn't working," Tucker whined, slapping the black, half-sphere button with his chubby hand. Again and again he pushed the button.

"Is there another switch?" Ash asked.

"I don't think so. Do you think we can lift the door?"

Ash studied the ceiling and followed the tracks and cables, hoping to spot a manual device. Tucker had already squatted at the door to work his plump fingers under the rubber flange at the bottom.

"I don't think that's going to work," Ash said.

"Well, we have to at least try," Tucker snapped.

Ash knelt beside him and together they tugged upward. The slats rattled, but the door didn't budge. Tucker sat back, breathing hard, his heavy legs splayed before him.

"How do you open it when you're on the outside?" Ash asked.

Tucker frowned to think. "We use the remote in the van."

"Is there a van out there now?"

Tucker frowned at the door as if he could see through it. "I guess."

Ash pointed to the pedestrian door that led outside. "Okay," he instructed in a calm manner, "walk out that door, get in a van, find the remote, and open this door."

"But the vans are always locked."

Ash summoned patience. "Okay. Where do you keep the keys?"

Tucker's face lit up. "In the office!"

Ash offered a hand and hoisted him to his feet. With this new mission Tucker was off again, his shoes resounding in the corridor.

Ash walked to the pedestrian door and opened it. Raindrops rebounded off the blacktop like grease popping in a pan. Through the curtain of rain he made out three school vans parked side by side. At the sound of Tucker's slapping shoes, he turned to see the boy sucking in great gasps of air, dangling a ring of keys before him.

"I think these are the right ones." He held them out for Ash, but Ash pushed open the door for Tucker. In the distance a siren wailed from the direction of Naughton.

"Go!" Ash said and nodded out the doorway.

Tucker took a deep breath and ran out into the deluge. Stopping at a van, he went through the keys by trial and error. Failing that he ran to the next van and repeated the same procedure. By the time he was trying the third van, an ambulance wheeled into the lot, red lights flashing.

Ash ran out into the cold rain. "What's the problem?" he yelled to Tucker.

"These must be the wrong keys." Tucker whined. His clothes were sodden.

Ash pointed. "There's a window open a few inches in the middle van. Come on! I need to get on your shoulders." Ash tugged Tucker in place and began climbing his flaccid body. "Stand up straight!" Ash said when he began to lose altitude.

"I *am* standing up straight!" Tucker insisted.

The ambulance's red light swirled in the rain, coloring the side of the gym in a throb of stroboscopic motion. When the driver sounded his horn, Tucker lost his footing and slid down the side of the van until both knees were on the pavement.

Holding himself up by the top of the windowglass, Ash looked down at the boy on hands and knees on the wet asphalt. "Are you going to hold me up or not?!"

Tucker rolled to his side. "Why can't I get on *your* shoulders?"

Ash lowered himself to the pavement. "Are you hurt?"

Before Tucker could reply, a man yelled from the ambulance, "Hey, boys! How 'bout we get one o' these doors open?"

Tucker held up an index finger. "Give us just a minute. We're working on it." When he turned to Ash, he wore a pleading expression.

"All right," Ash growled, bracing himself against the van. "Climb on."

Tucker began clawing his way onto Ash's back, but he could not seem to get more than a few inches off the ground.

"This isn't going to work!" Ash yelled and eased the boy to the pavement. "Look, just brace yourself against the van like I'm doing, and let me try again."

They switched places, and Ash quickly gained the height he needed. Pushing one arm into the opening of the window, he reached for the door lock.

When the ambulance horn blared again, Tucker's feet went out from under him, and he fell. Ash barely had time to extricate his arm from the window, and now he tried to avoid coming down on Tucker. Landing off-balance, he stumbled toward the curb, hopped the concrete border, and then dropped feet-first into a ditch of muddy water. His right foot came down on something hard, twisting the ankle into a bright spear of pain that caused him to collapse.

Wiping the rain from his face, Tucker came running after him. In the next instant, he tripped on the curb and slid face-first into the ditch, zeroing in on Ash like a torpedo. After the collision, the water settled, and both boys sat up to glare at one another.

Crouched under an umbrella, a paramedic yelled down to them from the curb. "Can we get in through these doors? Or do we need to drive around to the front?"

Before Tucker could answer, the EMT turned to a steady grinding sound behind him. Ash crawled up the muddy slope in time to see one of the garage doors rising, its hinged slats clacking and rattling as they followed the curve of the track. Holding the button, one of the coaches stood just inside the garage looking out at the rain.

Following the ambulance inside, Ash hopped across the lot on one leg and stopped to catch his breath just inside the garage. Looking at the black button that controlled the door, he saw two white arrows engraved into the plastic: one up, one down. It was a button not meant to be pushed in but to be pressed up or down.

Breathing heavily, Tucker stepped next to Ash. Bending at the waist, he propped his hands on his knees and studied the switch.

"Oh," he mumbled and turned contrite eyes to Ash.

Chapter Seventeen

The rain migrated east across Naughton, taking its grumbling thunder so rare for mid-autumn. Under the hospital's entrance light, the street glistened like black ice. Ash dropped onto a wet bench at the curb and waited for the throbbing in his ankle to ease. The swelling had tightened the fit of his shoe. He shivered, stood, limped up the walkway into the warmth of the lobby, and inquired about Cat.

Coming off the elevator, he found Cat's room directly in front of him. After he knocked twice the door opened, and there stood Tucker, blinking, his filthy wet tee shirt crusted with mud and contoured to his bulging stomach.

"How is he?" Ash said.

Tucker wiped roughly at his cheek and tried to harden his face. "He's hurt!"

Ash limped across the floor, stopping when he felt a crunching under his shoes. Scallops of dried mud littered the floor like shrapnel.

Cat pivoted his head on the pillow and smiled. "Look who's here."

"Hey," Ash whispered and approached the bed. "How bad is it?"

"Don't know. It's back in the socket. They're taking me down for an MRI in a little while. Probably some torn ligaments. And maybe the rotator cuff."

"It was stupid," Tucker blurted out behind Ash. "Stupid coach! Stupid contest! Stupid Guisburn!" When Ash turned, Tucker's face turned defensive. "Well, it was! Why do you think we have weight classes?"

"Maybe we should find a broom before the nurse comes in here," Ash suggested.

The door swung open and brought in the soft swish of fabric and the padding of rubber soles that quickly converted to crunches. The nurse was heavy-set with battle-weary eyes. She stopped and lifted up the tray in her hands to inspect the floor.

"Where in heaven's name did all this come from?" Her face compressed like a fist when she took in the appearance of the two visitors. "You two go back to that school of yours and get yourselves decent. My Lord! This is a hospital, not a hog pen!" She set down the tray and herded them out the door with a fluttering of her hands. "I'll have to clean this up before carting him to X-ray! For the Lord's sake!"

Ash limped out behind Tucker, who mumbled to the hall. "I'm coming right back after cleaning up." He pushed the elevator button and waited. They stood without talking, and then the elevator chimed and opened. Tucker marched in and Ash followed.

As the elevator started down, Tucker glared at Ash. "Why are you here, anyway?"

"I'm a friend of Cat's. My name is Ash."

Tucker's mouth opened but then closed. The doors glided apart, but he made no move to exit. When the doors started closing, Ash blocked it with an arm.

"You're Ash?" Tucker asked, his tone now softened. Ash hobbled out and Tucker hurried to walk beside him. "Did Cat tell you I'm going to be in the homecoming tournament?" he began babbling. "I'm going to be a king's archer! Are you?"

Ash could barely walk now. His limp across the lobby had become a rhythmic lunge. At the first sofa he collapsed onto the cushions and propped up his injured foot.

"I'm not going to be in the tournament," Ash informed him.

Tucker's bushy eyebrows came together as a single fuzzy line. "But you've got to! Cat says you're the best archer at school! And Mrs. Fitzwalter said—"

The sudden intensity in Ash's eyes stilled Tucker's tongue. "You know her?"

"Sure," Tucker chirped. "She was my teacher."

Ash stared at him. "You're part of the Fitzwalter program?"

Tucker nodded but pressed his point. "You've got to be in the tournament! Cat said you'd probably win it! I'm a theology pre-major, and I get to do the benediction!"

"How'd you get here to the hospital?" Ash asked.

Tucker beamed with pride. "In the ambulance . . . since I'm a trainer."

Closing his eyes, Ash eased his head back to the cushion. "I need to sit a while."

Tucker frowned. "How are you going to get back to school?" When Ash made no reply, Tucker spoke in an earnest voice. "Maybe I could carry you on my back."

Ash opened one eye. "I think we've tried enough of that." When Tucker stared at the door, Ash added, "You go on. Cat'll be expecting you to get back here."

Tucker's face brightened. "I could call a taxi for you."

Ash shook his head. "No money. Go ahead. But could you do me a favor? Would you call the library and ask someone to go down to the basement and tell the student waiting there that his tutor can't come tonight?"

Tucker frowned and mouthed the message to himself. Finally, he nodded and marched out into the cold night in his soiled undershirt, leaving a trail of dried mud behind him. Ash raised his pant leg to check on his ankle. It was the size of a softball. It burned as if his sock had been stuffed with raw nerves and broken glass. Again he shut his eyes and lay back his head.

Within a minute, a draft of cold air poured over him, and he opened his eyes to see three people file past him into the lobby. It was Guisburn, Jeep, and—lighting a cigarette—Troutman.

"Hey, Jeep, whataya get when you wrestle a chipmunk against a bear?" Guy joked as they walked to the front desk. "A bear!" Guisburn said, answering his own riddle. He laughed. "Tell that one to Scathlock, why don't you."

The woman on duty looked up when Jeep leaned over her counter, but her eyes cut to Troutman. "There is no smoking in the hospital, sir."

Troutman plucked his cigarette from his lips and blew smoke. He shrugged and started back toward the front door. Guy strolled into the waiting area and sat on a sofa across the room.

"Hey, Guy!" Jeep called. "Aren't you coming up, too? You oughta come."

"Go be a boy scout if you want to, Jeep. I'll be down here checking out the nurses." Guisburn, now dressed in green sweats, spread his legs out before him and spread-eagled both arms on the back of the sofa. Troutman stood just outside the door, holding his cigarette down by his leg.

Ash pulled his sweatshirt hood over his head, forced himself up, and limped past Troutman into the cold night air. He made it to the bench at the curb and sat. There he lifted the throbbing ankle up onto the wet wooden slats. It would have to go like this, he knew—a short walk, a long rest. The temperature had dropped, and already he was shivering. He pulled the draw string on his hood and bundled up as best he could.

Within seconds Guy and Troutman came out of the building, arguing about something. Ash looked back to see Guy feint toward Troutman with a wrestling move. Troutman sidestepped, almost falling and flipped his cigarette at Guy.

"Oh, I don't think you wanna do that, Trout ol' buddy," Guy laughed. "You wrestle a bear against a skinny dumb-ass fish and you get the same answer." When Troutman said nothing, Guy made another quick feint. This time Troutman did not react.

Ash tried putting weight on his ankle, but it was no good. He hunched over on the bench and fought the shivers that wedged into the center of him. Twenty feet away, Troutman stopped to light another cigarette.

"He's getting X-rays or something," Jeep yelled from behind them. "Then they're not letting in any visitors after that."

"Go get your van, Trout," Guy said. "Bring it around here."

Troutman huffed a laugh that made his head bobble. "What . . . you can't walk?"

There was a beat of silence before Guisburn's voice came back with an edge. "I don't feel like walking two blocks because you didn't feel like paying for parking."

Troutman shrugged. "Wasn't me who wanted to come here and cry about—"

Guy locked an arm around Troutman's neck, bending him forward from the waist. Troutman's feet scrambled for purchase on the wet sidewalk.

"I swear, Trout!" Guy crowed. "Sometimes you talk like *you're* the bear." When Troutman continued to struggle, Guy tightened his grip and jerked him in a half-spin.

Troutman coughed and pried at Guy's arm. "Leggo, dammit!" The cigarette dropped to the sidewalk in a tiny burst of sparks.

Jeep hurried toward the scuffle but stopped short of intervening. "Let 'im go, Giz! Come on, man! You're chokin' 'im!"

Guisburn put his head close to Troutman's. "Now would you like to go get your van . . . the one I put gas into last night?" Troutman whispered something Ash could not make out, but it was not the sound of submission. When Troutman's legs buckled Guy let him fall to his knees. Jeep went to Troutman, but the older boy pushed him away. When Troutman got his legs, he walked stiffly through the lot.

Guisburn and Jeep stood at the curb like two strangers and waited. Ash lowered his chin inside his sweatshirt and kept his face covered by the hood.

"What's eating you?" Guy finally said to Jeep. Jeep just shook his head.

After five minutes a vehicle cruised up the street and turned into the circle, its headlights carving the two wrestlers out of the night with razor sharp clarity. When this light fanned over the bench, Ash felt like he was on center stage under a spotlight.

"He-e-e-e-y," Guy said, stretching out the word like the sound of a rusty door hinge. "Whatta-ya-know! It's Chief Smart-mouth!"

As Troutman's van braked at the curb, Jeep stepped in front of Ash and read the pain in his face. "What happened?"

Shivering, Ash nodded to his ankle. "T-took a fa-fall," he said.

Jeep frowned and nodded toward the hospital. "Didn't they give you some crutches?" Ash shivered and shook his head. "Hey, man, you need a ride?"

The white van's horn blared. Ash looked up and saw painted in blue on the side panel a logo of a computer monitor and keyboard. A caricatured doctor listened to the monitor through a stethoscope. *The Office Doctor,* it read in big block letters. The engine revved. Guy swung into the front seat and slammed the door.

Jeep helped Ash hop over to the van, opened the sliding door, and eased Ash inside. Troutman turned and squinted through a haze of cigarette smoke.

"What the hell're you doing, Jeep?" Troutman complained.

Guy looked back and blew a flutter of air through his lips. "Jeep's going for two merit badges tonight." He shook his head as he settled back in his seat.

"Turn the heat up, Trout," Jeep said. "He's cold. He's wet all over."

"Looks like he was buried and dug up," Troutman said. He bounced with a quiet laugh. Watching Ash in the mirror, he smiled. "Too cold for you, great white hunter?"

Jeep reached to the dash and flipped the heat on high, but Guy clicked it down two notches. "Shut the damned door, Jeep, and let's get going," Guisburn said.

The van lurched forward and sped through the business section of Naughton. "God, what a hick town," Guisburn mumbled, looking out his window. Then he turned his head. "Hey, Jeep you wanna look for some homeless bums and take 'em back to your room?" Guy punched on the radio and spun the dial until he found hard driving music. Jeep repositioned Ash to better receive the current of heat blowing from the front.

Jeep pointed to the dashboard. "Giz, aim that vent back here, would ya?"

Guisburn ignored him, but Troutman spoke up. "Where're we takin' 'im?"

Guy turned with a comic smile. "Yeah, where's your tipi, Chief?"

When Ash did not answer, Jeep quietly asked, "What dorm do you live in, man?"

Ash shivered as he worked up a voice. "Hu-Huntington."

Guy turned again. "T-Toad H-Hall?" he mimicked. "God, what a dump!"

Laughing, Guy turned up the radio and thrust his chin to the beat of the music. When Troutman turned it down, Guy stared at him with challenge in his eyes. With his cigarette dangling off his lower lip, Troutman ignored him and watched the street ahead.

Jeep tapped Ash's shoulder. "How come Dr. Johns is on your case, man?"

Ash struggled to regulate his breathing. "H-how'd you know about th-that?"

"I'm in your class . . . first period."

Ash nodded. "He w-wants to fl-flunk me."

Guisburn turned down the music and leaned back in his seat.

"You and everybody else," Jeep said.

"If he could," Guy muttered. He exchanged glances with Troutman.

Ash spoke to the back of Guy's head. "Yeah, but he *told* me he would flunk *me*."

Jeep's face wrinkled like a twisted rag. "Man, you oughta turn 'im in. Teachers aren't s'posed to say stuff like that."

"W-we w-were alone when he s-said it. It would be my w-word against h-his."

"What'd you do to piss him off?" Jeep asked.

"Told him he was p-pompous."

Jeep rocked with delight. "Really? You said that?"

Troutman turned into the campus entrance with wheels squealing, causing everyone to brace. The guard on duty yelled something through his closed window, but Troutman ignored him. The van fishtailed on the wet pavement and then straightened.

"Geez, Trout!" Guy sniped and squirmed in his seat. "You tryin' to kill us?"

Troutman made a snide smile and beat out a rhythm with his thumbs on the top of the steering wheel. Guy turned off the radio. Troutman drummed on.

"You don't have to flunk, you know," Jeep confided to Ash.

Troutman glared in the mirror, and Guy turned partway around to give Jeep the side of his face—both looks a warning. They cruised down Academy Drive and took the turn at Valley Road on another skid and then slid to a stop in front of Huntington.

"Slums!" Troutman announced like a jaded train conductor. He stared straight ahead and tapped his thumbs on the wheel like a clock ticking away his valuable time.

Guy leaned to look out Troutman's window at the old dorm. "God," he laughed, "it's a war zone out there. Are they finally tearing down that rat trap?"

From a flatbed trailer a spotlight shot a tubular beam through the misty night, burning a bright round sun onto the exterior wall where men worked on a scaffold. They hammered at the brick, their frustration readable even at that distance.

The sliding door opened, and Ash eased out, testing his ankle on the street. Pushing himself upright he almost collapsed from the pain. Before he could thank them, the tires spun and Jeep fell back on the floor and cursed. The engine whined and laughter cascaded from the open door— Guy and Troutman, allied once again over another person's misery.

In the lobby Ash dropped into an armchair. Outside a generator purred, and the hammering and voices of workmen echoed through the empty halls. Otherwise, the building was cold and still. Tacked above the mailboxes was a sign: *Huntington residents: No heat, no water, no electricity. Go to the gym for sleeping arrangements.*

Ash scaled the steps between phases of rest, and then he hopped the home stretch down his hall. Inside his room he found a flashlight and lay on his bed. His heart pounded in his ears, and the ankle throbbed with a consistency that matched the sledgehammering outside. When he flicked on the flashlight, its weak orange beam faded and died, and he remembered his extra batteries and candles were at Beechwood.

He hopped across the hall, knocked on the door, waited several seconds, and then poked his head inside. "Crawley?" When his eyes adjusted, he could make out a candle on top of the desk. But an outline in the corner of the room drew his attention. Crutches. Ash fitted them under his armpits and pendulumed to the desk, where he appropriated the candle. Swinging back to his room he set the candle on his desk and struck a match. When the flame settled, he frowned at a black book lying on his desktop. He parted his lips as if to speak, but then his breathing stopped. It was Marin's book.

Holding the burning candle high, he turned to the opening lines and read on the *verso* page the two faded lines handwritten in ornate cursive: *The Journal of Maryanne Fitzwalter, 1199. Notes on Robert of Sherwood.* The same words were typed on the facing *recto* page. He leafed over to the next page and found an introductory quote, again handwritten on the left, typed on the right. He read out loud in a whisper.

"Injustice is a poison difficult for any man to swallow . . . but its bitter taste lingers longest on the tongues of youth." The quote offered no attribution for its author.

The sledgehammer outside the dorm picked up its bone-jarring tempo, but it registered in his senses no more than the ticking of a far-off clock. After a stoic shower under a dribble of icy water, he dried off, wrapped his ankle with an elastic bandage, and pulled on his spare sweat clothes. The black book fit nicely into his backpack. After slipping his arms through the straps, he jockeyed with the crutches down the stairs.

Once again he confronted the damp cold of the night. It was a long haul to Beechwood, and he was tired; but he knew he would be reading all night. He would be reading when the birds announced the dawn.

Chapter Eighteen

At midmorning on the following day, Ash knocked on the oaken door of Ten Point. When Marin opened it, she held a red rose in one hand. Her welcoming smile snapped off as she took in the crutches and the bandage wrapped around Ash's foot.

"What happened?"

Without speaking he swung past her and crossed the room to the table. There he propped the crutches and squirmed out of his pack. Marin watched as he sat, slid the book from the pack, and opened it to a page marked by a leaf that shone like copper foil.

When she sat across from him, he swiveled the book around for her to see. Then he outstretched his arm to the southwest corner of the cabin and pointed.

"Marin, I built an underground home in the forest. And I gave it a name." He stared at her in silence until she lowered her gaze to the book. "Beechwood!" he said, hurling the word at her like an accusation.

Her eyes came up. "You named it that because of the book?"

Ash shook his head. "I named it weeks ago." He propped an elbow on the table, closed his eyes, and pinched the bridge of his nose. "I don't even know how to begin to ask what I need to ask you," he whispered in a soft sigh. Dropping his forearm to the table, he met her steady eyes. "Sometimes I think I know you as well as I know myself. But the truth is . . . I don't know you at all."

She nodded. "I know," she whispered. Laying the rose aside she laid a hand lightly on his forearm. "I'm in this, too, you know."

He pulled back from her grip. "Why am I at this school, Marin? Me and practically everyone I know? What am I supposed to think about all this?"

She picked up the rose and turned it in her hand. "My husband, Hubert, knew things, Ash. I don't know how he knew them. He just did."

Ash watched her carefully, scrutinizing her every word and gesture. The question of her sanity came to mind. It was like the scent of something burning in the room.

He swept a hand toward the book. "Are we talking about . . . reincarnation?"

The word took its place in the room like a stranger come in from the cold. Arming himself with steely logic, Ash was ready to challenge any argument she might offer.

"I don't have all the answers, Ash." Her voice was gentle and frank, her gray eyes like droplets of water flooded with light. "Hubert said that sometimes there are rare bonds between extraordinary people . . . bonds so strong they cannot be broken . . . not even by death." She smiled and shrugged a shoulder. "That's what he said."

Ash spread his hands. "So we're supposed to *what*? Remember each other? From some other life? Is that what this is? Do *you* feel anything like that?"

Her smile faded, and she looked away. "No," she admitted.

Relief washed through him, and he tried to calm his voice to match hers. "So, you just followed him on this . . . what . . . to humor him?"

She shook her head. "No, it was more than that."

"So you don't believe all this . . . about reincarnation . . . right?"

"I don't believe it . . . and I don't *not* believe it. I just don't know."

He spread his hands. "Is this what the scholarship is all about? Bringing people back together?" He glared at her, but her gaze lowered to the rose turning in her hand. "What's the point, Marin? Didn't you need a little bit of explanation?"

The rose stilled. "Hubert said it was about need," she said quietly.

"Need?!" Ash laughed, pushing the word back at her.

"Hubert said sometimes the world has need." She nodded toward the book. "How much did you read? You would have to read it all to understand what he meant."

"Marin, it's just a book!" he said, hearing the impatience in his voice.

Her eyes flashed with challenge. "No, it's flesh and bone. It's people's lives." Marin reached for the book, but he pressed one hand down on the cover. "Ash, you can't see a truth if you're not willing to look at it."

He leaned toward her. "Now you're calling it the truth?"

Surprised, she lowered teary eyes. "I just want you to look at it. Give it a chance. You didn't know Hubert, Ash. If you had known him, you would *want* to look."

When he did not reply, she stood and donned a gray wool coat. After picking up the rose off the table, she turned and walked out the door. When the door closed, he felt the emptiness in the room swallow him.

This was his chance to leave, to deny the arcane agenda conjured up by an old man he didn't know. Yet he could not go. Not with anger being her last memory of him.

He found her behind the cabin sitting by the mound of earth—the place where he had slept when the dream had come to him. Beside her on top of the berm lay the red rose, and strewn over the mound like encryptions of past prayers were other roses, now black and limp. He lowered himself by the crutches and sat next to her.

"I didn't realize what this was," he said, looking back at the grave. "You buried your husband here, didn't you?"

Marin gazed out from the promontory in the direction of the archery field, her eyes dry and alert. She nodded. Ash took in a deep breath and looked up through the branches of the dead pine above. The sky was cold steel, and the wind sleaved through the branches with a thin incisive whisper. From the valley came the distant static of water breaking over the shoals. All of it came together like an elegy.

"I married him when I was sixteen," she began. "Hubert was much older. He was a Fitzhugh and I a Fitzwalter. He insisted I keep my family name and that the scholarship bear that name, too. He had been my tutor for a decade. I don't remember how that started—if I had asked Father for it or if Father had arranged it. Knowing what I know now, Hubert probably approached him."

"When Father died, Hubert took care of me." Marin smiled. "The marriage was in name only, Ash." Her eyes came up like a plea for understanding. "I was groomed for this from such a young age. It seemed to come as the natural unfolding of my life."

"Groomed for what?" he said. "I mean . . . what is all this headed toward, Marin?"

Staring off at the horizon, she seemed to be looking far beyond these hills. "Just tell me this, Ash. Have you felt anything at all that might help me to know that my life has not been a fatuous exercise of futility?"

He wanted to put this notion of recycled lives to rest, but with this grave at his back, he could not lie to her. He took in a lot of air, exhaled, and let his head sag.

"I came up here one day . . . looking for you. While I waited I fell asleep." He laid his hand on the curve of the mound. "My head was right here. And I had a dream about shooting my bow." He turned to watch her face. "It was the same one I'd told you about . . . from my child-hood."

She made a faint smile and nodded once. For a time they sat staring out over the treetops, listening to the wind and the river. Ash felt somehow cleansed, absolved by what he had said.

"I do know this, Ash," Marin said, her voice now somber. "Meeting you—even at a distance—meant everything to Hubert." He turned to see her gray eyes hardened to stone. "Everything," she repeated.

Chapter Nineteen

Sitting across the auditorium from Naylor, Ash hunched over his desk behind a basketball player and listened as the jocks taking their seats around him talked of the homecoming game that was two days away. He peeked at the stage to see if Dr. Johns had made an appearance. The podium was empty. When someone tapped his shoulder, he flinched.

"Hey, man, I see you got some crutches." Ash turned to find Jeep leaning toward him. "Did Johns let you back in class?"

Ash shook his head. "I figure if I don't come to class, I'll flunk for sure."

Jeep leaned closer. "What if I could get the next test for you?"

Ash gave him a doubtful look. "What would that cost me?"

Jeep's voice took on a defensive tone. "Look, man, I'm just trying to help you out because—?" Jeep fell silent and fixed his gaze on the stage. "There he is," he whispered.

Ash ducked and turned back to his desk. As he began taking notes from Dr. Johns's lecture, a folded scrap of paper fell on his notebook. Opening it, he read: *No charge for the first one. Next time $50.*

An unexpected pang of guilt gnawed at Ash's gut. In Jeep's offer there had been a trace of generosity. It was the boy's second act of kindness toward Ash.

The hour was an avalanche of information. One minute before class was to end, Johns closed his notes and stiffened both arms on the podium as he panned his audience. "As you know, there are no classes tomorrow due to preparations for the *holy* homecoming," he said with a sneer. "You will have to read chapter nine over the long weekend. It will be included on Monday's test."

A communal groan rose from the room. When the bell rang, Johns left the stage at a brisk pace. The students were slow and aimless, like shell-shocked survivors finding their way off a battlefield. Naylor met Ash in the aisle and arched his eyebrows.

"What happened to you?" he said, nodding at the crutches.

"Turned an ankle," Ash replied.

Naylor nodded and looked around casually. "Can't meet tonight or the next," he mumbled. "Got evening skull sessions for the game with Nacoochee."

Ash tore several pages from his notebook. "Here, I've improved my handwriting for you." Handing over the papers, Ash added, "Good luck."

Naylor scanned the notes. "I can read it okay."

"I meant the game," Ash said and climbed the stairs to the upper level exit. Just inside the hallway he saw Jeep leaning on the wall, waiting. When Ash crutched past him, Jeep fell in alongside him.

"Listen, man, I can't guarantee Monday's test. It depends on how Johns does it."

Ash kept plodding ahead in his swinging rhythm. "What do you mean?"

"He might not type it out," Jeep explained. "If he writes it up on the board, we're busted." He shrugged. "Look, don't sweat this test. If you ace the big ones you'll pass. But if Johns types this one up, I'll get it to you." Jeep's face lit up. "Hey, and it comes with the answers. You're just s'posed to word it your own way, you know? You might wanna even miss one or two on purpose."

"How can you get the test?" Ash asked.

Jeep shrugged that off. "First one's a freebie. I'll bring it by Toad Hall, okay?" With a bounce in his step, he strode down the hall and out into the bright autumn day.

On the sidewalk Ash put enough weight on his ankle to feel improvement, so he decided to stop by his dorm to return the borrowed crutches. At Huntington he swung past the repairmen on the outside scaffolding, entered the dark lobby, and paused as the light above him flickered and made a buzzing sound like a bee trapped inside a bottle. Then the building seemed to resurrect. The light burned steadily, and the water cooler hummed. Outside a cheer rose from the workmen. In that moment of illumination Ash saw a letter in his mailbox, and his heart sank. Extracting the letter he found a handwritten message on the dean's stationery.

> *Robert,*
>
> *Dr. Johns has prevailed in his efforts to convene a board hearing for your expulsion. It will be held in eight days, Friday next. Meanwhile your suspension from biology class is in effect. I'm trying to contact Millerson to request his presence at your hearing. He seems like your best defense.*
>
> *Richard Oberleigh*

Overhead, the light bulb made a hollow *pop* and died. The water cooler ticked off. One of the workmen outside cursed so loudly that the others broke into a cathartic laugh. Then silence claimed the building.

In his room he lit a candle and stared at the disturbing black book that he had agreed to finish reading. As soon as he opened it to the page marked by the copper leaf, the word "Beechwood" flew up at him, and with it came all his doubts.

Outside, the generator sputtered to life and began churning out a monotonous hum. A power tool whined. Adding a rhythmic beat to this ensemble, someone started pounding with a sledgehammer. Ash decided to skip classes and go to the forest.

Leaving the book on his desk, he stuffed his pack with schoolwork, a water bottle, and a few extra clothes. After returning Crawley's crutches, he slipped into the pack, collected his bow and quiver, and struck out for Beechwood.

In the peace of the woods, he read and dipped his ankle into the Salacoa as the steady whisper of the shoals upstream and the occasional fluting of a thrush kept him company. Later in the afternoon he put finishing touches to his roof and added fresh leaves to his bedding. At twilight he lighted a fire and warmed soup for a meal.

After eating he lay down to watch the flames lick upward from the hearth. The radiant heat stroked his skin like the soft fur of a cat. When he closed his eyes, a parade of faces marched across the screen of his mind: Guisburn, Troutman, Tucker, Princeton Johns, and Mick. Then John Naylor. Next came the dean's disapproving glare Finally, he saw Marin's expectant eyes, the way they had shone when she had begged him to finish the book. All of it seemed too much to comprehend. Throughout the night these images haunted him, allowing only short, fitful naps.

*****

As the birds sang to the morning he made his way to the river, where he sat on a mossy bank, read, and repeated the cold water therapy for his ankle throughout the day. When evening came, the images of the previous night returned to haunt him, so that he tossed in the leaves and spoke out loud, waking himself after brief snatches of unrestful sleep.

On the following morning he repeated the cold treatments at the river and felt his ankle much improved. Bleary-eyed from two restless nights, he lasted only a few hours before returning inside the shelter. There, curling by the fire, he finally slept.

*

He ran until his lungs burned and his legs began to fail. He knew the forest well, but his pursuers had hounds! Trained for the hunt, these dogs might catch him before he could find help. At a high point of land he tightened his fingers around the smooth curve of a hollowed-out ox horn that he carried by a shoulder strap. Raising the instrument he pressed the circular opening to his tightened lips and blew for his life.

The note broke and rose in a soulful wail, blossoming pure and full, aborning through the forest with a message of urgency. He blew until his lungs screamed for air.

*

Ash sat up gasping, rubbing his eyes, confused as the dream-note continued to shriek in his ears. Even fully awake he could not turn it off. Crawling outside, he frowned at the sky. Time had gotten away from him, for the sun was high. The wailing note from the dream now frayed into multiple high-pitched whines, and he realized he was hearing sirens somewhere to the east.

Then he remembered that it was homecoming weekend. The sirens, he guessed, were a part of a celebration. Exhausted, he backed into his shelter, wrapped in his blanket, and fell into a deep sleep, this time free of dreams, faces, or worries.

It was late afternoon when he awoke. After a meal of hot soup, he gathered his bow and quiver and struck out for the archery field. As he approached, he heard the school marching band pounding its war drums in the stadium. The drumming stopped abruptly, and a loud cheer erupted and spread over the campus. Then the drums began again. Anne Metter's homecoming festivities were underway, pumping up the crowd for the coming game. Ash remembered this was an important night for John Naylor. College scouts were expected to see "the Hammer" nail his opponents to the turf.

As Ash stepped from the woods, he noted that the cloudless sky showed a dirty pink cast in the east. When the wind shifted, the acrid scent of smoke piqued his interest. Picking up his pace he passed through the border of pines to look from the curb. A lazy column of black smoke rose from the bottom of the valley, tearing into wispy shreds that spread like tentacles into the sky. His legs began to move of their own accord, down the hill, past the rows of cars lining the street. At the intersection the sharp bite of the smoke caused him to pinch the collar of his sweat shirt over his mouth and nose.

Three bright red fire trucks spoked around what remained of Huntington Hall. Men in bright yellow rubber suits and GDA maintenance workers milled around the lawn inside a yellow tape that cordoned off the area. Above them long parabolas of water arced from hoses over the partially collapsed walls, raining down on steaming brick and timber. The building was destroyed.

Ash stared into the emptiness above the front right corner of the blackened ruins—the place where his room had been. Now it was an anonymous space in the air. A ghost room. Smoke billowed through it without regard for what had been.

He sat down on the grass to ease the throb in his ankle. Next to him steam lifted from a chunk of damp charred wood. He picked it up, feeling its residual heat, crushed it into powder, and let the black debris sift through his stained fingers.

Chapter Twenty

The stadium was filled. It looked like an enormous ark adrift in an ocean of noise. The student bodies of Greenwood and Nacoochee faced one another across the width of the chalk-lined field, where the two teams approached the line of scrimmage under the brilliant lights. In mirror image they poised motionlessly, like playing pieces of a giant board game, green against red. Then they scattered, spreading into the momentary chaos of a rack of billiard balls broken on green felt. The play ended with a collective "Ooh!" from the stands as the ball carrier crashed onto his back with a *clack* of shoulder pads.

The male voice on the loud speaker rose above the sound. "And it's Naylor again! Stopping number forty-four at the line of scrimmage! That's the end of the half, folks! Keep your seats for a unique half-time show! You're in for a real treat tonight!"

Ash stood in deep shadow beside the stadium seats and watched a hodgepodge of yeomen, royalty, and maidens tinker with their items of period dress on the near sideline. Mounted on a wheeled platform was a giant red target with a generous bull's eye—a painted white circle whose template might have been the round lid of a trashcan.

Under Anne Metter's orchestration, a squad of king's soldiers followed a cartwheeling jester who flashed over the grass in piebald rags. The soldiers trundled the huge target out onto the field, wheeled it around at the fifty yard line, and faced it toward the Warriors' end zone. The band performed an auspicious fanfare as an army of yeomen and fairy-like maidens dashed out carrying long poles that trailed pennants of green and gold crepe. They swirled through a choreographed pattern that eventually assembled them into two lines forming a V with the target at its point. At a flourish from the French horns, they raised their poles, stabbed them into the ground, and ran off the field. The slight breeze lifted the colorful streamers atop the two lines of poles, all fluttering toward the east like flickering flames.

The sound system came alive, popping and crackling like dry sticks tossed on a fire. After a moment of confusion, another fanfare—this one by trumpets—signaled the commencement of the contest. Then a student's voice welcomed all to the festivities and explained the details of the archery tournament to follow.

"And now to witness this contest," the voice continued, "and to bestow the prize to the champion archer!" Snare drums rolled. "Welcome the new queen of Greenwood Downs Academy homecoming . . . Elaine Perrin."

The trumpets broke into a longer fanfare as four veterans of the weight room carried out the homecoming queen in her royal sedan. The home side of the stadium came alive, drowning out the instruments. The porters carried the queen in her boxy cart onto the field and set her down on the grass.

"And now, ladies and gentlemen, please welcome the contestants."

The naming of the archers began. They came representing sports teams, dorms, honor societies, academic departments, and school clubs. This motley group assembled along the Warrior's thirty yard-line and faced the target twenty yards away. Their colorful attempts at authentic costumes were, in most cases, comical. Some looked more like pirates or Roman centurions than medieval archers. The introductions went on.

"And next, representing the Warrior wrestlers, Sir Guy of the Dark Dung."

Guy Guisburn, with a leather bow case in tow, had begun his strut out onto the grass, but he stopped and glared at the announcer up in the booth above the seats. Guy wore a toga cinched at the waist by a length of rope. Dark leather thongs crisscrossed his rounded calves. He scratched his cheek with his middle finger, and those students who were close enough to see it howled with laughter.

"Uh . . . sorry," the announcer said. "That should have been: 'Guy of the Dark Dungeon.' " Then the speaker's voice became upbeat. "And last, our sole competitor from Naughton: ten-year-old Bobby Seabolt!"

The Nacoochee fans came to their feet and roared their approval for one of their own. A small boy wearing a green costume ran onto the field carrying a thin fiberglass bow, his arrows rattling in a cardboard quiver fastened to his belt at one side. When he stood among the other archers, the tall feather in his cloth cap barely topped out at the shoulders of his neighbors.

"And now," the speaker purred with high drama, "the highly kept secret of the night." Another brass fanfare ushered in the news. "The champion will receive from the hand of our queen—" Snare drums rolled in waves then pulled back to a low rattle. A caped man ran across the field hauling a burlap bag, so hefty that it swung out of sync with his stride. "From the coffers of our generous alumni—" The drums silenced. "One! . . . Hundred! . . . Silver! . . . Dollars!"

The audience yelled its approval, and the archers began talking excitedly to one another. Guy jogged back to the chain-link fence and called out across the track. Ash followed his gaze to see Troutman leaning against the concrete wall, one leg bent, the foot propped behind him, a cigarette held limply over the jackknifed knee.

"Let's go, Trout!" Guy said. "It's time."

Troutman drew on his cigarette and blew a long stream of smoke toward the proceedings on the field. "You wanna make a ass of yourself, be my guest . . . *Sir* Guy."

Guisburn vaulted the fence. Ash could not hear Guy's words, but the tone of threat was clear. As they argued, the tournament rules were explained over the loud speaker.

A boy in Ash's art class carried a clipboard as he jogged over to the fence and yelled out to Guy. "Guisburn! Are you going to be in the contest or not? You're up!"

Guy approached, reached over the fence for the tie-cord at the boy's throat and pulled. "How 'bout I borrow this for my designated shooter?" The boy's hand came up but stopped short of touching Guisburn's wrist. His cape slipped off him like the unveiling of a statue.

"Let's go, Trout! Hundred bucks!" Guy prodded. "Fifty-fifty, remember?"

Troutman muttered something, flipped his cigarette to the track, and pushed off from the wall to amble toward the gate. Guy whipped the cape around Troutman's stiff shoulders, and together they marched onto the field.

"Mr. Geoffrey Tucker, a senior theology student, will deliver the benediction."

As the crowd grew quiet, the microphone bobbled, and Tucker's breathing came through the system like a bellows. "Father, we look tonight to the steady hand and the unflinching eye. May we shoot not for silver but for the honor of competing, just as we strive to live our lives not for our own glory but for the glory of God. Amen."

The murmur of the audience built again then hushed as the emcee called five names—Guy's among them. All the other archers were herded back into the end zone. Guy knelt and opened his leather case. When he lifted out a bow and pushed it on Troutman, Ash saw the weapon's pulleys, cables, counterweights, and sights—an assortment of high-tech gadgets that blatantly violated the spirit of the antiquated contest. Troutman counted the yard-lines between him and the target and adjusted the sighting pin.

"Ready!" Snare drums rolled and the five archers set arrows to strings. "Raise!" The bows rose up in unison. "Draw!" The drum major raised his baton, and the drums fell silent. "Shoot!"

Troutman's arrow rocketed to the white circle—so fast that the *smack* of the shot was lost on the crowd. The ping of the other bow-strings came in staggered time, and the target spat out three more reports. One arrow missed the target entirely. The tuba player blew a sliding note that bottomed out with laughter from the stands. The jester retrieved the arrow in the grass and then ran to the target, where he pulled two arrows from the white and two from the red.

The announcer's voice moaned. "Fare thee well, ye three archers who missed the mark."

As the next archers were named, Anne Metter ran out on the field to inspect Troutman's bow. Guy stepped into the conversation and his voice rose half an octave.

"But it *is* wooden, Anne. That was the only rule on the poster!" Guy pointed at the little boy with the child's bow. "That one is fiberglass! You gonna kick out the kid?"

Anne frowned at the Seabolt boy taking his place with the second group of shooters. She shook her head in frustration and walked away without another word.

Bobby Seabolt stood next to Tucker and three others. Again the drums rattled at the "ready" call. At the command to draw, the drums quieted. Bobby appeared to angle his bow to the top tier of the stadium. At the signal to shoot, his arrow arced high above the others and was last to drop into the target. When it fell into the circle of white, the Nacoochee crowd exploded with a cheer that lasted half a minute. Two other arrows had found the bull's eye. Tucker's arrow had struck in the red several inches too high.

After the first round, the surviving archers watched the target be carted five yards further. In the next round, Troutman and one other archer hit the white mark, while two others pinned the red. Bobby Seabolt again launched an arrow into the bull's eye, drawing another cheer from the crowd. The boy spun to the track, where an elderly man smoking a pipe slid his hands into his back pockets and nodded. The woman standing with the old man clapped before her chin and then pressed her fingertips to her mouth.

The target was wheeled back again. "This is pathetic," Troutman snorted to Guy. "They even got the distance marked off for us."

With six archers left, they now shot in trios. In the first, Troutman hit the white, as did one other contestant. Bobby Seabolt was last to shoot as he angled his bow so high that he subtracted yardage from his arrow's flight. The crowd groaned when his arrow sailed short into the grass. Bobby walked to the remaining archers and shook their hands. Then he walked off the field to thunderous applause. Whistles shrieked and fans yelled as he joined the elderly couple and became a spectator even as the audience continued to cheer him.

Ash began grinding his soot-stained hands into his face. Then he pulled up his sweatshirt hood, and limped from the track into the bright lights illuminating the field.

In the next round, when Troutman fired an arrow that cut the lower edge of the white circle, Guisburn hurried to him. "What the hell was that? You almost missed."

"Keep your panties on," Troutman purred. He tightened his lips and shot a squirt of saliva into the grass. Only two other archers had managed to hit the white.

Guisburn frowned at the crew moving the target. "Hey! Did they move the target back one or two lines?" He poked his finger at the air, counting the yardage.

Troutman's head came around alert and angry. "What? It's forty, ain't it?"

"I make it at forty-five yards," Guy said excitedly. The drumroll began.

At the command to shoot, Troutman's arrow hit low again, just nicking the white. Another arrow hit closer to center. The third hit outside in the red.

"It *is* forty-five," Guy huffed. "I told you!"

Troutman glared at Guy. "How about shuttin' your fat trap when I'm shootin'."

Guy walked up to the line and stuck his face into Troutman's. "If you'd 'a listened to me you'd 'a known they moved it back ten yards instead of five."

The sound system crackled. "The Baron of Basketball drops out and now, ladies and gentlemen, two archers remain! This will be the final shot for the bag of silver coins. The champion will be Eric the Debater or Sir Guy of the Dark . . . that is, his cohort."

"See!" Guy pointed downfield. "I think they did it again! It's fifty-five now!"

Troutman's fingers stalled on the sighting pin. "What?!"

"This is the final round, folks," the announcer declared. "The Warriors and Skyhawks are about to come back on the field. Ready, archers?" The drums buzzed. Flustered by the counting of lines, Guy stepped back and was bumped by an archer, who moved past him and stepped between Troutman and Eric. The two archers glanced in mirror image as Ash loaded his bow.

"Looks like we have a latecomer, folks!" the announcer chirped. "Ready!"

Ash stood relaxed, his mind empty, his eyes hidden in hooded shadow and fixed on the target. At the command he drew and sighted down the shaft.

"Reckoning arrow," he said under his breath.

At full draw, he saw a puncture at the dead center of the white circle crystallize in minute detail. And then a rusty voice whispered to him from memory.

Don't lock up on me now. You're not a statue. You're still pushing and pulling.

"Shoot!" came the command.

The three arrows soared through the air and smacked the face of the target in quick succession. The jester ran to the target, jerked an arrow out of the red and pointed to Eric, who bowed and took three steps backward. The jester then pried out an arrow that had buried to its fletching two inches below the white circle. He turned to point, but Troutman was already walking away. The jester shrugged, turned back to the target and pointed at the white. He did a standing vertical jump, spread-eagled, and touched his toes with his fingertips before landing. After pulling out the red-fletched arrow from the center of the bull's eye, he ran to the shooters' line, went down on one knee, and returned this shaft to the hooded archer.

Ash could hear nothing over the roar of the crowd. He received his arrow and limped toward the track, where the homecoming queen was carted into his path. It was Alan's Elaine, who—with the help of one of her attendants—presented him the bag of coins. As Ash took it, her eyes narrowed. She leaned to peer under his sweatshirt hood.

"Ash?" she whispered.

The presentation of the prize was quickly upstaged as the Warriors filed out of the stadium tunnel and poured onto the field. The players broke formation to dodge the people hauling away props. Ash was moving against the current of bodies when little Bobby Seabolt stepped before him. His costume was hand-sewn. The little fiberglass bow was one Ash often saw in the toy section of stores. Three arrows with plastic fletching jutted from his quiver.

Bobby looked up at the darkened face, then down at the bow that had won the day. The old man and woman approached and stood behind the boy.

"One shot!" Bobby whispered like an exhalation. His face was slack with awe. "How come you've got all that black stuff on your face? Are you like . . . s'posed to be a outlaw or somethin'? Like Robin Hood?"

"Guess I am," Ash said and nodded to the boy's bow. "You're ready for something a little stronger." Ash dropped the sack of coins next to the boy's moccasins. The heavy prize hit the track with a solid, collective *ca-chink!* "That ought to do it."

The boy's wide eyes fixed on the prize and then rolled up in disbelief. His mouth opened and closed. He twisted around to check the faces of the couple behind him. The man stepped closer and rested his fingers on the boy's shoulders. The woman pressed a wadded tissue to her mouth. Tears welled in her eyes.

The boy squinted up at Ash. "You mean you're givin' me the hun'erd dollars?"

Ash nodded. "For a new bow and arrows with real feathers." When the old man took his pipe from his mouth, Ash locked eyes with him. The man reached over the boy, and Ash took his hand. The woman laid her hand on top.

"Bless you," she said.

Ash crouched to look into Bobby Seabolt's big brown eyes. "You're off to a good start. Keep practicing. You've got what it takes to be a great one."

Ash nodded to the old couple and limped past them. As he made his way to the tunnel that led into the locker rooms, someone called his name from the stands. He looked up to see Alan standing three rows up, his arm raised high. Ash nodded and kept walking.

Halfway down the ramp into the tunnel, he heard his name again. He turned to see Anne Metter coming down the ramp. Ash waited as the GDA team continued to stream past him.

Stopping before him, Anne studied his blackened face, her eyes wide with alarm. "Were you in the fire?"

He barely heard her question. "Anne, are you part of the Fitzwalter, too?"

She frowned. "The what?"

At the top of the ramp the homecoming crew eased the rolling target to the edge of the slope. Its spoked wheels appeared salvaged from an old wagon. Anne turned to the sound of rumbling behind her. The cart was coming too fast. A lineman, on his way out, sidestepped, knocking Anne off balance. He reached for her as she grabbed for Ash, and the three of them tumbled together. Ash's bow bounced off the concrete into one of the wheels, and the bow whipped two circles in the air until it jammed hard against the axle and splintered like a dry oak branch.

The football player cursed and rolled off the pile. Then Anne peeled away, and Ash sat up on the concrete, watching the cart pick up momentum again and finish its run with the ruined bow limping alongside, slapping the concrete like a broken wing.

"Oh, no!" Anne gasped and clapped a hand over her mouth.

Ash kept his face emotionless. His voice was a flat monotone.

"Do me a favor. Don't use my name . . . about what happened out there." He nodded toward the field.

Anne's face screwed up with a question, but she felt too heartsick to venture a word. Leaving the ruined bow behind, Ash turned and walked down the corridor into the dark of the hallway.

PART THREE

The Outlaw

On Monday morning Ash entered the cafeteria and paused to glance at the newspapers stacked on the floor. *The Greenwood Leaves* headline paid a minimal tribute to its oldest dormitory: *The Toad is Toast*, it read. He picked up a copy. An inset covered temporary sleeping quarters and availability of new sweat clothes for Huntington's refugees. The school's dress code would be relaxed until further notice.

Another article caught his eye at the fold on the page. *Mystery Archer Takes $100 Prize*. Ash dropped the paper back on the stack and crossed the room to the serving line.

He was rubbing at the charcoal stains around his fingernails when he heard a familiar voice that stilled him. "Who gives a flying fart! It was just a hundred bucks!" In the line, up ahead, Guisburn was holding court with a stocky boy with a buzz-cut. "It was worth going out there just to see those gazongas on the homecoming queen. Man, they shoulda skipped the stupid bow and arrow stuff and held a wet tee-shirt contest."

Guy's lewd smile upped the wattage in his face. Pleased with himself, he scanned the room. Then his eyes suddenly locked on one of the tables.

"Well, look who's here." He nodded out into the room. Ash looked, too. Elaine was seated, talking with two other girls as they ate. Like her friends, she had taken the change in the dress code to heart. She wore a raspberry, long sleeve pullover that conformed to every nuance of her finely sculpted body.

"Hey, Beezer," Guy growled. "Ten bucks says you won't accidentally spill water on the queen's royal chest." Guy's teeth flashed white when he widened his smile.

Guisburn picked up his tray and approached the girls' table. Ash couldn't hear what he said, but he set down his tray opposite Elaine and took a seat. Elaine's eyes lowered to her tray. The other girls exchanged glances and grew quiet.

When the one named Beezer carried his tray to another table, Ash chalked it all up to male braggadocio. He took his breakfast to his usual place by the window, opened up his biology book, and lost himself in study.

Five minutes later a high-pitched shriek quieted the room. Ash looked up to see Beezer standing over Elaine, trying to squelch a smile, holding an empty glass in one hand as he pretended to bobble his tray.

Elaine was frozen in space, mouth open, hands splayed, and her shoulders hunched around her ears. A lock of her hair was plastered to her forehead and her shirt showed a wet streak over her heart. Beezer made an attempt at an apology, but his performance was transparent. Some of the students at neighboring tables were snickering.

Guy half-stood and offered Elaine his napkin, but she leapt up and ran for the door. Guy sat back down and fell into conversation with the other girls. Catching Guy's attention Beezer mouthed, *Ten bucks.* Ash turned in his tray and left for his class.

Because of the fire that had devastated Huntington Hall, the biology test was postponed—a concession not of Dr. Johns's choosing but issued by the headmaster, as Johns was quick to share. He traded this sacrifice for another hour of nonstop lecture. At the bell, Ash melded with the crowd at the upper door and exited unseen.

In the bathroom he set his books on the bench to work on the remnants of charcoal smudges on his face. After rinsing at the sink he spotted a folded sheaf of papers now extending from his biology text. He dried his hands and pulled out a typed three-page test. The answers—

also typed—were included on a fourth page. At the top of this last page was a hastily scrawled message: *Couldn't deliver to your room.*

When the door opened, Ash folded the papers and watched in the mirror as John Naylor appeared. Each stared at the other's image in the mirror.

"Had me a little worried," Naylor said. "Thought maybe you'd chosen a Viking funeral in the Toad."

Ash turned around and held out the test. "Take a look at what I just got."

John took the papers, scanned the top page, and pulled out an identical packet. "How much for yours?" he asked.

"Free, this time. They'll expect me to come back for more at fifty dollars a pop."

John whistled a thin note through his teeth. "Just ten for football players." He raised his chin to Ash. "Where'd you get yours?"

Jeep's earnest face flashed in Ash's mind. "I got word out I needed the test. I found it folded inside my book. I never saw it delivered. What about you?"

"Same. Found it in my locker. So, what now?"

Ash took his test and folded it. "I'll get it to the dean today. Maybe this will help me on Friday when I meet with the disciplinary board?"

"Might as well take mine, too," Naylor said and handed over his test. "Can't meet at the library tonight. College scout's taking me out to dinner."

Ash stuffed the papers away. "What school is he from?"

Naylor's eyebrows lifted when he smiled. "*She's* with UGA. Black. Used to be a sprinter." Then his face sobered. "Gotta good veterinary program there." He set his gaze on Ash's pocket and shook his head. "Damn," he said, "it's all right there, every damn question of the test.

But us Boy Scouts? We'll be studying our asses off and chasing our tails."

Ash offered a sly smile. "The price of virtue," he said and walked out.

As he started up the hill toward the administration buildings, a white van wheeled hard into the parking lot behind the cafeteria. On the steep ascent into the lot the van belched a cloud of black smoke, and the sun glinted off its side panel lettering: *The Office Doctor*.

From the shade of an oak Ash watched Troutman—dressed in his gray uniform—slide out of the van and carry a black satchel through the side door of the history building. In less than a minute he reappeared, cranked his van, and roared out of the lot.

Ash crossed the parking lot and entered the history building. At the room marked *Department Head*, he confronted a smartly dressed woman with hair as black as his own. She looked up from the open drawer of a file cabinet.

"Can I help you?" she asked, her smile welcoming.

"Ma'am, I was wondering . . . did a repairman just come in here?"

Her smile relaxed, and the lids of her eyes hooded. "Are you a friend of his?"

"No, ma'am. Actually, I'm checking up on him. What was he doing here?"

A look of triumph tightened her mouth. "Really." She pointed at the copy machine. "He worked on that . . . supposedly," she said.

Ash frowned. "He fixed it that fast?"

She banged the file drawer shut. "He *said* it was a routine mainte-nance check, but I don't think you can do that in five seconds, do you?"

Ash studied the copier. "What exactly did he do?"

"What he usually does. He comes in like a whirlwind, tinkers with something or other, then leaves. I don't know why the school would want to pay for that kind of service. He never fixes what I ask him to. The counter always messes up."

"The counter?"

"The numbers that tell you how many copies you've made," she said.

Nodding, Ash backed out the door. "Thank you."

With Jeffrey Hall so close, he detoured again and tiptoed past classes in session to the little room under the stairwell. Marin stood just inside her classroom, listening to a female student read aloud from a text as the others scribbled notes. As soon as he appeared in the doorway, her eyes locked on him.

"Keep reading, Marcie," Marin instructed and stepped out into the hallway. She studied Ash's face with an intensity that surprised him. "I've been worried about you."

"Marin," he began and swallowed. "Your book . . . it was in my dorm room."

She nodded as if she had expected this. Her gray eyes shone when she smiled.

"It was just a book," she whispered.

Inside the room the reader paused. "Mrs. Fitz? Should I read all the parts?"

"I'm coming," she said. Still holding grateful eyes on Ash, she took a step backward. "Come to Ten Point tonight. For dinner. Please?" Then she was gone.

When Ash learned that Dean Oberleigh might not come in to his office, he started for Maple Drive off campus. Ten minutes later Dory Oberleigh opened her front door and managed a strained smile. Her eyes were red-rimmed and her face pinched with worry.

"Hey," Ash said, "could I see the dean?"

She leaned against the doorframe. "It's been a rough day, Ash." Her voice was whispery and trancelike, lacking its usual melody. When she opened the door wider, Ash entered the hallway and walked into the dining room just as Dean Oberleigh pushed through the swinging door from the kitchen with two glasses of iced tea in his hands. Seeing Ash, he paused but made no gesture of greeting.

Dory broke the silence. "Do you have a place to stay, Ash?" When he nodded, she did the same. "I'm just setting out some lunch. Why don't you stay and eat with us?"

"Thank you . . . but no." He watched the dean set down the glasses. "I just need a moment with your husband."

Dean Oberleigh leveled haggard eyes on Ash. "Let's go into the study."

An uncomfortable quiet followed them into the room. The dean sat at his desk and pinched the bridge of his nose between his eyes. Ash took the sofa.

"Dr. Leonhardt is in the hospital," the dean reported. "Heart attack."

Ash had begun unfolding the tests, but now his hands stopped moving.

"Doctors say he'll make it. It's all this damned stress." The dean sat forward as if he had been jerked by a rope. "Damn it all!" He glared at his desktop. "On principle he chose to be fired rather than retire. Except for one year abroad, he's taught here for thirty-eight years. Now he's lost his pension and insurance. He doesn't have any family."

Ash stared at the tests in his hand, the papers now seemingly tainted with a malevolent power. "That's not right," he said quietly.

The dean looked up. "Nothing's been 'right' about any of this." He rubbed his palm across his mouth and then let his hand slap down on the desk. "All he did was try to find out who was cheating. Now the hospital bill is eating up his life savings."

"What happens now?" Ash asked. "Who is going to help him?"

The dean sat back and stared at a framed picture on his desk—Dory smiling on a boat deck. "I am," he said and showed dead eyes to Ash. "I've gone into our savings."

In the quiet that followed, Dean Oberleigh closed his eyes and inhaled deeply.

"I was counting on Dr. Leonhardt to speak for me at my hearing," Ash said.

The dean huffed a humorless laugh and opened his eyes. "Don't you see that his word would have no weight? And I have to tell you . . . Millerson is not coming." He shook his head. "I'm all you've got." His smile was a discouraging twist of the mouth. "But remember, I wasn't there when you and Millerson were handling that test."

"But you know what I was doing for you . . . for Dr. Leonhardt."

The dean's eyes turned cold. "But remember, you had turned me down."

And there it was: the immutable fact that ran through the heart of Ash's fiasco. He felt the sense of pending doom that he'd been carrying around for days now congeal into a tangible presence in his gut. The ticking of the clock in the hallway was eating up his time at this school. He stood and dropped both sets of test papers on the dean's desk.

"For what it's worth, it costs fifty dollars." Ash turned and walked to the door.

"Where did you get this?"

With his hand on the doorknob, Ash chose his words carefully. "I never saw who delivered it. Naylor got one the same way. That's all I know."

Ash trekked out to Beechwood to soak up the solace of the forest. There was nothing he felt like doing. Even if he still had a bow, he would not have wanted to shoot. Sitting under the beech tree, he watched the river slide past him, envying its purpose and direction, neither of which seemed to exist in his own life now.

When twilight ushered in its softening shade to the forest, he stoked his fire inside the shelter, grabbed his coat and flashlight, and limped off to Ten Point.

It was fully dark when he reached the top of the hill. There he stopped and stared at the dimly lighted windows of the cabin. When he rounded the corner of the building, he discovered a car parked in front. He flattened his hand on the hood of the car. It was still warm. A faculty parking sticker showed on the window. Only then did Ash recognize Dr. Leonhardt's old Buick.

He stared at the lodge, listening for voices. There was nothing to hear but the wind whispering in the pines above him and the river hissing from the valley below.

When Marin opened the door to his knock, Ash stepped in to see Alan and Tucker seated at the big oak table. Cat stood by the heater, his arm trussed in a sling. The rich aroma of meat and onions filled the room.

"Thank you for coming," she said for his ears only.

Alan stood and gripped Ash's shoulder. "Young Asher, I was so relieved to see you at the football game. I was afraid you'd been camping out in the lightless Toad Hall when the fire broke out."

So began an interrogation about the fire and its aftermath. Answering questions, Ash was unanimated and spare with words. He watched Marin set the table. She worked quietly, pouring tea and serving portions from a meat pie. Finally, she laid down a basket of warm bread nestled in a towel.

When she declared the meal ready, Tucker delivered a plodding grace, capped off by a quick "Amen." He tore off a chunk of bread and slathered its steaming white core with a generous smear of butter.

"I haven't had a pasty since I left England," Tucker said, digging into his meal. And with that, the conversations shifted to lighter topics—the charm of the cabin, the coming holidays, the food. But Ash remained remote and disconnected, eating quietly like a stranger brought in from the cold.

Marin set the last contents of the baking dish before Alan, but Tucker snatched it up and held it out to Cat. "If anybody needs more, it's Cat," he said. "For healing."

Cat raised his good arm, palm out. "Not me, Tuck."

"I'm stuffed, too" Alan said.

Tucker continued to hold the dish. "Ash?"

Ash was wiping his plate clean with a scrap of bread. At his name, he stopped the motion and looked up. He took the platter and spooned half the remains into his plate and returned the dish to Tucker. The others watched these two finish their meal.

Everyone helped clear the table. The arc of easy conversation was gone from the room. All tried to minimize their sounds as they washed and stacked dishes. Marin was first to return to the table, and then one by one the others joined her.

Chapter Twenty-Two

Marin produced an envelope from the pocket of her blouse, removed a letter, and read silently for a few moments as the others watched. "I received this from our bookkeeper in England. I'm afraid there is a problem with the scholarship money." No one spoke as she folded the paper and returned it to the envelope. "There are debts. I had no idea how serious it was. The bookkeeper has advised me to return to sell some of the property."

Ash felt a cold chill. News of her leaving hit him to the core.

"Hubert handled all this before," Marin continued. "I'll have to study the finances. I want you to know I will do whatever it takes to continue the program."

"Mrs. Fitz," Alan said. "It's not that important. We can go to public schools."

"It *is* important," she countered, her voice resolute.

"Alan's right," Cat said. "We can go to other schools."

Marin shook her head. "No, this is the place. Hubert knew."

"Knew what?" Tucker asked.

Watching them, Ash felt like a contrived "spirit" hiding behind a curtain at a séance.

"Hubert had good reasons to choose this school, just as he did in choosing you." She looked at each face around the table . . . all but Ash's. "You remember the book we studied together in England—the journal. Finding it was Hubert's finest hour of research. In it he found the link between the Huntingdons and their descendants, who were forced to forsake that surname for another."

"I remember all that," Tucker blurted out. "I liked your classes a lot."

"Too late, Tucker," Alan quipped. "She won't raise your grade now."

Marin smiled. "You see, there are many genealogical dead ends in the three centuries after the Norman invasion. Records are difficult to piece together because Saxon estates were torn apart and new boundaries were drawn. Huntingdonshire, for example, is today a district of Cambridgeshire. You see, Saxon insurrectionists became an embarrassment to their Norman overlords. After so much oppression, some of the 'pet' Saxons gave up their token nobility granted by the new king and galvanized commoners into rebellion."

"You're talking about the seed of the Robin Hood legend," Alan said.

Marin nodded. "Robin o' the Hood, as he was called. That legend, as I'm sure you know, is a composite of several people with similar plights. People like Hereward the Wake, Fulk Fitzwarren, Eustace the Monk, and . . . Robert of Huntingdon."

"We did papers on them," Tucker said excitedly. "I wrote mine on Hereward."

Marin steepled her hands and looked at Alan. "And you researched Robert of Huntingdon. Do you remember by what name he was first called as an outlaw?"

Alan nodded. "Robert o' Sherwood." A beat passed as the sound of Alan's voice circled around the table and returned to him. The skin on his brow flexed, and his eyes tracked to Ash and held there as if seeing his friend's face for the first time. "Robert o' Sherwood," Alan said again, this time without accenting any syllable over another.

"But what does all this have to do with the scholarship?" Tucker asked, blinking.

Marin spread her hands. "Hubert traced his ancestry as well as yours. He was descended from the Huntingdons. Each of you—in fact, everyone in the Fitzwalter program—is similarly connected to other people who were part of this story."

"Are you saying we're related to them?" Cat asked.

Marin eased out a long breath. "That is part of it."

Tucker beamed. "Cool!"

Marin leaned forward. "This is the difficult part . . . the part Hubert needed to handle." She offered a tentative smile. "I'll try to tell you as best I understand it."

She pushed up from the table, and they turned in their seats to watch her move to the woodstove. All but Ash. Staring at the window, he could see the room's dusky reflection and in the old warped glass their faces were distorted. The dark night behind the glass made them appear transparent and wraithlike. His own image was no different.

"It is more than being related to the people of this story," Marin continued. "Do you remember in the journal? The bond between them? Individually, they were good people, but ordinary ones. When they came together, it was something rather remarkable. What they shared was a collective energy fueled by a fierce loyalty. And that was what the times called for." She looked at each of her guests. "We are that energy," she said quietly. "Here. Now. Returned. Huddled together in an old cabin on another continent."

No one moved or spoke. Ash tried to hold on to the distant sound of the river like an anthem of sanity, but Marin's words pried into his head and replayed in echoes.

"Wait a minute!" Alan laughed. "This sounds a little like reincarnation." He started to laugh again, but Marin's expression held him in check.

"Is that it, Mrs. Fitz?" asked Cat. "Are you saying you have some knowledge about a previous life for yourself?"

Marin smiled. "I honestly don't know. But Hubert said I *would* know . . . in time."

"What about Dr. Fitz?" Alan asked. "Did he have this awareness about himself?"

Marin nodded and looked Alan in the eye. "Yes," she said quietly. "He did."

The room stilled. Ash waited for someone to balk at Marin's words, but the silence drew out as the others seemed to wait for more.

"But how did he know?" Tucker demanded. "How can anybody know that stuff?"

Marin let the silence gather around them again before answering. "Dreams," she said without apology. "That's one way."

Still gazing at the window, Ash finally spoke up, the force of his voice surprising even himself. "That's convenient. Dreams are the most abstract playground of the mind." He turned to face Marin. "So you believed him? Just like that?"

"I always believed him," she said softly. "But I'll concede this: I was exposed to his beliefs by spoonfuls from an early age. I didn't know his stories were meant for a purpose. My child-questions were just story-book curiosities. Later, when I was older, the bigger questions did start to perplex me, but it was like questioning Hubert's thinking, and I had come to respect that dearly. He was my teacher, you see. Then my husband." She had been speaking to all of them, but now she singled out Ash. "There was a fire inside him. Anyone close to him felt it."

"That's for sure," Cat said. Both Alan and Tuck nodded in agreement.

"I became absorbed in my part of the research," Marin continued. "In transcribing Maryanne's journal, I found myself swallowed up by the story. I became invested in it. But I did not yet see the big picture. I was utterly shocked to learn that we were uprooting ourselves and coming to live here in America."

"So, what *is* the big picture?" Tucker asked.

Marin looked at the bare bed in the corner. "Hubert never put a name to it. He talked about the synergy of the people in the journal. And the return of it by need alone." She shook her head. "I'm not sure what that means."

"He was a great teacher," Cat said. "The most believable I've ever had."

"I know," Marin said. "We who knew him . . . knew *that*."

Tucker scratched his fuzzy head of hair and let his arm flop down on the table. "I still don't get it. What's all this got to do with us being at GDA? Why are we here?"

Marin walked to the back window that overlooked her husband's grave. When she spoke, her words came off the windowglass with a hollow sound.

"Everyone who was offered the scholarship in England did not accept," she explained. "We had to go where we would all be together."

Alan pressed his hands together prayer-like, and softly bounced his index fingers against his lips. When he stopped the motion, the lines in his face deepened. He angled his eyes to Ash. Cat did the same.

"But why here?" Tucker persisted.

When Marin did not answer, Tucker looked to Cat and followed his gaze to Ash.

"Because of me," Ash said in a flat tone. "I wouldn't come to you, so all of you had to come to me."

The room felt suddenly heavy. The woodstove made a faint whistling sound.

"And because Dr. Leonhardt left England to return here," Marin added. "That, too."

Ash glared at her. "What is the point, Marin?"

Marin tried to offer a calming smile. "Hubert said there would be a need for us."

Ash swept a hand toward his friends. "How can you pull people from all over the country and dictate their lives based on dreams?! *Everybody* has dreams!" He coughed up a sarcastic laugh. "In four days I'm gone! What then, Marin?"

A tear ran down her cheek. "All I know, Ash, is that I believed in Hubert. I can't tell you what we do with all of this. I don't even know that Hubert knew."

"Well, whatever it is, it's a little late now!" Ash said rising from the bench. He walked across the room, punched his hands into his coat sleeves, and pulled his flashlight from his pocket. At the door he hesitated and calmed his voice for what he needed to say. "Marin, I'm sorry for your loss. And that you're all alone in this. I don't believe you would willingly deceive us. But I can't believe in this thing you believe in. It doesn't make any sense to me." He looked at the rest of them, and he could see that he was the only one who refused this one step based on blind faith.

"Ash," Marin said, "those dreams you told me about. Don't you think—?"

"No," he interrupted. "They're just dreams." He met all their eyes one last time and walked out into the night.

Chapter Twenty-Three

As four monitors handed out the biology tests, groans began to rise from the auditorium. Several rows behind Ash, someone dared an obscenity that carried all the way to the front of the room. Ash peeked over a shoulder at Princeton Johns, who stood legs parted, fists on his hips, a sneer fixed on his face. He approved of the expletive. He had drawn blood.

Ash received his test and dove in, writing through the hour with a fierce and confident energy. When the bell rang, Johns barked out orders for leaving class through the lower level door only. The top doors, he informed everyone, would be locked. Even as he spoke the words, one of the monitors jangled a ring of keys as he climbed the steps to the top and set the locks on the doors.

The aisles filled with students shuffling down the stairs. The teacher waited at the door to personally take a test from each student. Reaching ground level, Ash joined the crowd and found himself behind Naylor. John turned and arched an eyebrow.

"You expectin' him to grade *your* paper?"

"I didn't sign my name," Ash said, his voice unconvincing. "But I wasn't counting on this." He nodded toward the bottleneck at the exit.

Naylor studied the situation at the door and then reached back and snatched up Ash's test. "You better get lost," he said and stacked the two tests together.

"Thanks," Ash replied and moved against the traffic to the aisle. Six tiers up he sidled into a row and bent as though to pick up something. There he crouched and prayed that the monitors would not climb the stairs to check the rows of desks.

As Naylor inched toward the exit he came shoulder to shoulder with one of his teammates. "Gunter," John whispered, "where's your test?"

The thick-necked boy made a sour face. "Wadded up in my damn pocket." He glowered at the door. "I'll just say I wasn't here today. I can get a doctor's note from the trainer." His lip curled into a scowl. "Johns changed the damn test on us."

"You think about how you're gonna get past him without a test?"

When Gunter's worry lines cut deep into his brow, John slipped out Ash's test. "Here, give 'im this."

When the last students left, the monitors followed them out the door. Johns vacated the stage and disappeared into the hallway. Ash waited thirty seconds and then hurried out of the empty auditorium.

Tires squealed at the bottom of the hill, and a van accelerated toward him. Ash backed into the tall shrubs and watched The Office Doctor van roar past him and skid to a stop. Troutman jumped out and hurried into the science building. In less than a minute he was back, running to the van. He fired it up, U-turned, and raced back down the hill, barely slowing at the stop sign. As it climbed the hill the van whined through its gears, spewing black exhaust all the way.

At lunch Ash went to the gym for a shower. As he walked the perimeter of a pick-up basketball game, the booming reverberations of the ball stopped and the echo of voices died. Footsteps squeaked on the floor and stopped just behind him.

"Hey, man. Sorry 'bout the test." It was Jeep, glowing with the heat of exercise. He put his hands on his hips, scowled at the floor, and shook his head. "Johns pulled a switch." Jeep snorted an embarrassed laugh. "Too bad we aren't in Johns's afternoon class, we could'a got the right test." He looked back at his friends waiting on the court, and they began honking his name like a flock of geese. Out of boredom one boy bounced the ball, then took a shot. The others reacted and fought for the ball.

Ash held his eyes on them, but a silent movie was running in his head: Troutman hurrying toward the science building, The Office Doctor van tearing across campus.

"I'll make it up to you," Jeep said. "It's the midterm and final that'll count."

Ash could see the good will in Jeep's eyes. "Funny," Ash mused, "you don't seem like the sort to follow someone else's lead and get into something like this." It was a lie, but Ash knew it was the kind of lie that might contribute something of worth to the boy.

Jeep's face turned defensive. "What's that supposed to mean? I'll bet you didn't mind too much when you found that test in your book."

Ash conceded the point with a sway of his head. "True."

"Jeepster!" a boy yelled from the court. "Come on, dude! Let's play!"

Jeep ignored the boy. "I'm just trying to help you out, man."

"It's Ash."

Jeep turned his head to watch the players fight for the ball and make random shots. "Mine's Gilbert," he said and met Ash's eyes. "But everybody calls me 'Jeep'."

"What do you prefer?" Ash asked.

"Bert," Jeep said without hesitation.

The play on the court was disorganized, but it gave them a thing to look at in the awkward quiet. Jeep started to rejoin the game but stopped after two steps.

"So what'd you mean about me not following somebody else's lead?"

Ash closed the distance between them to keep their words private. "Well, you're in something chancy with these tests . . . with pretty severe consequences if you get caught. Just kind of surprises me you'd take that kind of risk with someone who doesn't have your best interest at heart."

"Whatta you mean? Are you talkin' about Guy?"

Ash let his eyebrows rise. "You're pretty loyal to him, aren't you?"

Jeep frowned. "What's wrong with loyalty?"

"Depends on where you place it. If you got caught, would you rat on Guy?"

Confused at the change in direction, Jeep frowned. "Hell, no!"

Ash nodded. "What if it were the other way? Would he rat on you?"

Jeep looked away. The loose basketball rolled toward him, and with a dancer's grace he trapped the ball soccer-style under one foot. The players froze and looked at him expectantly. Jeep picked up the ball and spun it in his hands, watching the seams whir and stop, whir and stop. When the players started honking his name again, Jeep flung the ball from his chest like a rocket, and one player fumbled it and gave Jeep the finger.

"You got many friends?" Jeep asked as he watched the players.

Ash stepped beside him and watched a boy take a long jump shot. "No."

Jeep turned quickly. "That doesn't bother you?"

Ash shook his head. "No."

Jeep watched the boys fight for the ball. "Guess I better get back to the game."

Ash let him go a few steps. "So long, Bert."

Jeep turned, his eyes wide with surprise. "Yeah . . . see you."

Ash crossed the parking lot for the science building. After entering the empty auditorium he climbed the stage steps, tiptoed to the stage door, and peered through the small window of pale green glass. Entering the hallway of offices, he walked briskly and turned right into the secretary's office.

Juanita Esparza was tiny with sharp cheekbones and angular shoulders. Her white blouse and simple black skirt complemented her darkly golden skin. Her black hair threw off a sheen of light like the dark mane of a horse.

"Can I help jyou?" Eyes wide, she sat upright at her desk, eager to be of service.

"Yes, ma'am. Did The Office Doctor repairman stop by here today?"

She glanced at the copy machine. "Jyes, he deed."

"Did you call for him, ma'am?"

"No, he joss stop by." Her eyes turned curious and waited for his next question.

"Could you tell me what he worked on?"

She pointed to the copy machine. "He comes around for the maintaining. But I tell jyou what. I don't know what he can do so quick." She leaned her elbows on the desktop. Now she was engaged in the conversation as if they were old friends confiding secrets.

"Before this morning, when was the last time he came by?"

"See, that's the thing. He was joss here yesterday."

"Did you call for him that time?"

"I never call heem! He joss always comes by."

"Do you mind if I take a look?" Ash gestured toward the machine.

She shrugged with a quick jerk. "Ees okay with me."

He stood over the copier and, for lack of anything else to do, raised the seal on the window. Then he knelt and opened the front panel. He knew she was watching him.

"And . . . who are jyou?" Ms. Esparza finally asked.

"My name is Ash. I'm in first period biology class." He peered into the machine's inner workings. "What exactly did he do here?"

"I donno. He joss go behind. I hear the tools, and, poof, he ees gone!"

Ash looked behind the machine, where a thick wire coiled on the floor and connected to a wall socket. "Did he move it from the wall?"

She got up and came around her desk. "Jyes . . . some. Ees it okay?"

"Can we try it?"

She lifted a sheet of paper from her desk, placed it on the glass and pressed the button. They waited as the rolling light of the scanner captured the image. Then the machine churned out a reproduction.

She checked the copy. "Ees okay," she said, handing him both papers to compare. "I tell jyou what," she said, lowering her voice to a whisper. "I don' think I trust heem."

"Same here," Ash said, and they looked at one another across their new common ground. In the hallway the stage door opened and footsteps approached. When the door behind Ash opened, he turned his back and bowed his head to the papers.

"I have one more test next period and then I'm leaving." Princeton Johns's voice was like a nest of spiders creeping up Ash's spine. "If the man from Fox News calls, you can give him my cell number."

Juanita Esparza nodded with the energy of a woodpecker. "Jyes, sir. I will."

The door closed. Footsteps trod back to the stage, and Ash breathed again.

Ms. Esparza frowned. "The thing *I m* wonnering ees why he comes by so often when I don't call heem. The only thing wrong he never fixes."

"What's that?" Ash asked.

"The nom-bers. Jyou know, the ones that tell jyou how many copies jyou make."

Ash checked, and the digits read *001*. "It worked just now," he said.

"Jyes, but not when jyou do the big nom-bers."

Ash nodded and backed to the door. "Well, I'd better get to my class."

She looked him up and down, studying his clothes. "Were jyou in the building that burned?" When he nodded she gave him a compassionate smile but quickly replaced it with a question mark. "Do jyou think I should tell Dr. Johns about the repairman?"

Ash shook his head. "Probably not a good idea to bother Dr. Johns unless it's absolutely necessary." She was still nodding at his wisdom when he left.

Through the stage door window Ash saw Dr. Johns hunched over the podium, writing. The first bell rang. Backtracking, Ash crept past Ms. Esparza's door on his way to the building's front exit, but he stopped when he saw the door's lock and chain. He tried Dr. Johns's door and found it unlocked. With no other option, he went in.

Wasting no time he cranked the window open just wide enough that he could fit through, but he hesitated, wondering how he would close the window from the outside. Looking around for a makeshift tool, his eyes fixed on the desk. Weighted down at the corners by various objects, a large blueprint showed a two-story floor plan. At the bottom of the paper were two words: *Residence Series*. This was, Ash guessed, the faculty housing project that would usurp Dr. Leonhardt's chapel funds.

Curious about the word "series," Ash lifted a coffee mug from a corner of the plat and let the top sheet curl up to reveal a drawing of a building front. Beneath that sheet was a drawing of three buildings surrounded by cloud-shaped figures labeled with names of trees. The eye-catching feature was two parallel lines that meandered across the map and made a sharp curve near the buildings. One word was written inside them: *river*.

Ash felt his stomach open up like a trap door. On the south side of the bend was another scalloped cloud shape with the word "beech" printed inside. He knew he was looking at Beechwood.

In the hallway a door opened. Heels clicked on the floor. Ash let the papers curl up as he hurried to the corner of the room where an overcoat hung on a rack. Slipping behind the coat he held his breath as a coat-hanger rattled against his head. The wire settled just as the door opened. The tap of heels softened on the carpet. When the second bell rang, the shoes padded out of the room, and the door closed. More clicks in the hall were followed by the sound of Ms. Esparza's door closing.

He peeled out of the coat rack, taking the wire hanger with him. Un-twisting the hook he fashioned a closed loop. Before crawling out the window he took one last look at the blueprint to see the architect's name: *Norman Creed and Associates, Atlanta, Ga.*

After climbing out into the shrubs, he worked the wire over the crank handle and began alternating pushing and pulling as he leaned on the glass to coax it shut. After a few minutes there was still a two-inch gap. It was the best he could do.

Ten minutes later, Ash picked up the telephone in the cafeteria and thickened his voice. "This is maintenance. Is this Miss Esparza?"

"Jyes!" she said, sounding delighted that someone would know her name.

"Ma'am, I wonder if you'd do me a big favor? Dr. Johns called this morning and said there was something wrong with the heat in his office."

"He deed?"

"The thing is, Miss Esparza, this has happened a couple of times be-fore . . . and each time . . . well, I'm sure Dr. Johns is a busy man . . . but he'd left his window open. Would you check it out for me? Maybe save me a trip over?"

"Jyes," she assured him and laid down the phone. In thirty seconds she picked up on the line. "That was it. I'm in his office now. The window was open, but I close it."

"Thank you kindly. Oh, Miss Esparza . . . it's probably best not to mention this and embarrass Dr. Johns, if you know what I mean."

"O-o-oh, no-o-o," she agreed gravely. "I don't say a word."

Chapter Twenty-Four

Friday came too fast. After two days of interviewing department head secretaries, Ash had learned nothing new about Troutman's tinkering with the copy machines. Now, in the headmaster's conference room, he stood before the same board members from Mick's hearing. They sat behind the railing at a long table—the men in dark suits, Mrs. Alles wearing gray. All listened as Dr. Johns held court.

"Mr. Millerson was guilty. He is no longer with us. Mr. Asherwood is equally guilty. Both students were in possession of the test. I saw them share it with my own eyes." He pinned Ash with a vindictive glare. "Mr. Asherwood cannot deny this."

When Dr. Johns sat down, the chairman's voice turned every head at the table as if a single string had been tied to a row of puppets. "Thank you, Dr. Johns. I will add that Dr. Johns has submitted an affidavit which corroborates his data—signed by five students who sat around Mr. Asherwood and Mr. Millerson." He raised his eyebrows to Ash. "May we hear your version of that same morning, Mr. Asherwood?"

The puppet string jerked again as all eyes settled on Ash. Silence gelled in the room. Ash stood up straight, striving for dignity in his sweat clothes.

"Nothing Dr. Johns saw will I contest. But I'll correct his assumption. I did not know Millerson's papers were the test. I held them only a few seconds. That's all."

The board members sat without expression, and Ash could see they needed more.

"I'd like to say something," Dean Oberleigh said, clearing his throat. "Mr. Asherwood enjoyed a certain reputation with Dr. Leonhardt as a student who—"

"Leonhardt is no longer with us," Johns interrupted, "because he gave some students an easier test. Perhaps Asherwood was one of those."

The chairman looked down and spoke to his yellow legal pad. "This is ground we've covered, Richard. We can't argue Dr. Leonhardt's case again."

The tendons in Dean Oberleigh's jaw knotted. "May I finish what I want to say?"

The chairman forced a smile. "As long as we steer clear of Dr. Leonhardt. This hearing is about a current student and a current teacher." With this clarified, he swept a hand as a gesture to let the dean know he had the floor.

The dean bristled. "I remind you that Leonhardt shot the first flare. He—"

"Richard!" the chairman interrupted, his head canted in a show of strained patience. "We have already heard these arguments from you."

Dean Oberleigh began to nod. "All right, then let me start this way." He leaned forward to go eye to eye with the chairman. "I initiated a meeting with Robert Asherwood for the purpose of securing his assistance in exposing the cheating problem."

"And how did you propose to do this?" asked Mrs. Alles.

"We wanted to know how students were getting hold of the tests. I thought it would be helpful to have a student—one I could trust—try to obtain a test."

Mrs. Alles perked up at this news. "Is this true, Robert?" Ash was nodding, his mouth open to answer, when she added, "Did you agree to do this?"

With this last question, his hopes sank. "The dean did ask me to help," he said and felt the tension in the room loosen. In that moment when the world could turn in his favor, he sensed that some of the board wanted to believe him. But there was more to say, and he knew he must say it. "But I didn't sign on."

As the other board members looked at one another, Dr. Johns smiled.

"*But*," Dean Oberleigh added with enough volume to still the room, "only a day or so later, Asherwood returned to me with a different answer. He wanted to help."

"Why the change of heart, Robert?" Mrs. Alles asked.

"I'd heard about Dr. Leonhardt being accused," Ash began. The chairman glanced at him quickly, and Ash realized too late that it was the wrong thing to say.

"That would be an opportune time to jump the fence," Princeton Johns purred.

"Well, now, wait a minute," Mrs. Alles said and turned to Dean Oberleigh. "Did you instruct him to get one of those tests into his hands?"

It was a good question—one calculated to give Ash a technical way out of his predicament. But as he and the dean well knew, this question had the wrong answer.

"No," the dean said, "but he knew what we were after."

"Let's make this perfectly clear, Richard," the chairman said. "Was Mr. Asherwood authorized to seek out, obtain, or hold in his possession an illegal test?"

The dean clenched his jaws. "Not in so many words." There was a beat of silence. The dean broke it by slapping both hands on the table. "Look. If this boy was interested in getting away with cheating, why would he bring to my home the biology test scheduled for the next day?"

Princeton Johns jumped to his feet. "Why wasn't I informed of this!?"

The dean calmly looked at Johns. "It had to be verified. How could I be sure it *was* the test?"

Johns spun to Ash. "What was the first question on that test?"

Ash shook his head. "I don't know. I didn't read it."

Johns sputtered a cynical laugh. "Of course you didn't."

"I read it," said the dean. "As I recall, the first question dealt with DNA."

"Ha!" Johns shrieked. "It was the test I had originally planned. On the morning of the exam, I changed it. Which is why ninety per cent of the class failed."

Ash stood. "And what did I make on that test, Dr. Johns?"

"You?" He waved Ash away with a hand. "You are no longer in my class."

"But I was there. And I took the test."

"Nonsense. I took up a test from each student. I did not take one from you."

"Do you remember a test with no name on it? That test was mine."

Dr. Johns blinked. "There was one, but it was accounted for."

The chairman folded his arms on the table. "Mr. Asherwood, did you hold in your hand—not once but twice—a test prior to its scheduled exposure to the class?"

Ash closed his eyes and shook his head at the inflexible nature of the question. "If the paper I was handed from Millerson was a test . . . and if what I handed the dean was the test, then the answer is 'yes.' But—"

Holding up a hand to cut off Ash's explanation, the chairman faced Dean Oberleigh. "Richard, did you ask Asherwood to obtain either of these?"

Dean Oberleigh eased out a long breath. "No."

"Wait a minute," Mrs. Alles broke in. "Robert, if indeed you gave Dean Oberleigh the test the night before, where did you get it?"

"I put out the word that I was in the market for a test. It showed up in my books."

"And how was this arranged?" Mrs. Alles pressed. "Did you pay for it?"

"No, ma'am. But after the first time it's supposed to cost fifty dollars."

The board members exchanged shocked glances. Behind him Ash heard the door quietly close. He was unprepared for the voice that graced the room.

"Mr. Chairman, if I may speak?"

Ash turned to connect the melodic English accent to the face. Marin was dressed in a dark brown suit, her hair gathered in back, her hands clasped before her.

"Mrs. Fitzwalter?" Mrs. Alles said. "You have something germane for us?"

The chairman squirmed in his chair. "Mrs. Fitzwalter, I'm afraid this is a closed hearing."

"Yes," Marin said, "forgive me for listening in. But the gravity of this gathering as it concerns Robert is much too important for any qualms over protocol."

"Is Mr. Asherwood a student of yours?" the chairman asked.

"No, he is not."

"With all due respect, madam, I fail to see how your presence here is pertinent."

Mrs. Alles propped her elbows on the table. "What's the harm, Jack? Better to hear it and reject it than not hear it and make a decision without all the data."

Marin walked to the wood rail. "I have a simple suggestion." She turned to face Dr. Johns, her expression pleasant. "Why don't we all go to your office and look through the tests until we find that paper with no name that bears Robert's handwriting so we can see what kind of student he really is. After all, by your admission, if, indeed, Robert took this test, it was one he could not have seen beforehand."

Johns stiffened and turned to the chairman. "As you said, this is a closed meeting. She should not be present."

"Mrs. Fitzwalter," the chairman began with a pained smile, "Is there anything substantive you can offer us in regard to this matter of cheating before you leave?"

Marin slowly closed her eyes and opened them. "Just this," she said. "You have probably never before had a student like Robert Asherwood. Perhaps you never will again." She took time to meet every board member's eyes. "None of you know him. And that prevents you from knowing what I know without any doubt. Robert has his own code of honor. Do you find it hard to believe he could carry in his pocket a test that would be given him the next day, yet he does not look at it? I don't doubt that for a second." She gave them a sad smile. "If you lose him, you will have lost *two* jewels in your crown."

"Are you threatening to resign, Mrs. Fitzwalter?" the chairman asked.

She shook her head. "I am talking about Dr. Leonhardt."

The chairman inhaled sharply through his nose. "I'm sorry. You'll have to leave now. Please, Mrs. Fitzwalter."

"Please," she echoed. "Don't make a mistake here today. Injustice is a hard poison for any man to swallow . . . but its bitter taste lingers longest on the tongues of youth."

"I am not familiar with the quote," the chairman admitted, clipping his words with authority. "But that also has the ring of a threat."

Marin shook her head. "I am not here to threaten. I am here to speak for Robert." When she looked at Ash, her faith in him sank to his core. "You need to hear this from someone here today," she said, looking at Ash as if the two of them were alone in the room. "I believe you, Ash. I know you are innocent of these charges."

The chairman rapped his knuckles politely on the tabletop. "Mrs. Fitzwalter, please, if you would allow us to finish our business?"

When Marin walked back down the aisle and out the door, Ash felt something pull at him. He wanted to go to her now . . . to walk beside her . . . just to be near her.

"Unless someone has additional information?" the chairman said to either side of him. He glanced at Ash, then looked down and spoke to his unmarked yellow legal pad. "Please give us a few minutes, Mr. Asherwood, as we deliberate."

Ash stood and walked out of the room. Closing the door behind him, Ash found John Naylor seated on the sofa in the foyer.

"How'd it go?" Naylor asked. "The dean stand up for you?"

"He tried, but—" Ash shook his head and sat.

John cocked an eyebrow. "You made a ninety-six on the test. Highest grade in the class. Friend of mine claimed it."

"How did *you* do?" Ash asked.

Naylor beamed. "Ninety-four . . . second highest." He held out a fist and they tapped knuckles.

"Did you see Mrs. Fitzwalter?" Ash asked. "Did she look okay?"

John chuckled. "She looked like other women her age would wanna look."

"Do you know about the scholarship drying up?"

"Yeah, she called me." He shrugged. "I'll be okay. Lotta colleges wanting a big black dude to come knock heads on their football field."

Ash leaned forward, rubbed his temples, and then looked at Naylor. "John, do you ever dream about being chased through the woods? By people . . . with dogs?"

John's head came around slowly, his face shining like black marble. "How the hell'd you know 'bout that?"

The door opened and Dean Oberleigh's somber face appeared. He took in Naylor's presence without a sign of recognition and then leveled his eyes on Ash.

"We're ready for you," he muttered and turned, leaving the door open.

"I'll wait on you," John said. "Be right here."

Ash rose and walked back into the conference room. Now, none of the board members would look at him. Even Mrs. Alles, who kept her eyes down on her clasped hands that tapped steadily on the table.

"Mr. Asherwood," the chairman began, "we have been talking at length about a point which seems to lend an extenuating circumstance to your complicity in this matter. The test paper handed to you by Mr. Millerson did have *his* name on it. But what was the initial direction of transfer of that test? That's the question. A test being delivered *to* Millerson could conceivably have his name on it, correct?"

Ash started to speak but Dean Oberleigh stood. "If we're to consider what-ifs, *what if* Millerson was luring him into the test market; *what if* Millerson was showing the test to everyone around him; *what if* Asherwood has told us exactly how it happened?"

"Richard," the chairman said quietly, "we are not offering this hypothesis as a working theory but merely as a way to show that there are many possible interpretations to the same scenario. Now please, I will ask you again to stand by the majority rule."

And there it was. They had made their decision. What remained was merely a formality. Ash waited to hear the words that would end his career at Greenwood Downs.

"We are obligated to deal with facts," the chairman continued, "as they apply to the scandalous atmosphere presently pervading our school. To make an exception in your case after the dismissal of Mr. Millerson would be unjustified, and we would, as a governing body, be lax in our duty if we did not act impartially and expediently."

The chairman leaned on his elbows and counted off on his fingers. "Fact: Dr. Johns saw you with a test. Fact: You admitted to having possession of one other test. Fact: You were under no umbrella of protection or exemption to hold such a test." He removed his glasses to play out the courageous moment that comes to all adjudicators. "Therefore, Mr. Asherwood, it is my duty to inform you that you are now—"

The door slammed. Every board member's eyes fixed on the back of the room. Ash turned to see John Naylor walking toward them in his long, aggressive stride—his presence there a little jarring . . . like a panther strolling down the aisle of a church during service.

"Mr. Naylor?" The chairman's voice managed to ask a question while still chiming with deference. "What, uh—?" He pasted a smile on his face, and the two men next to him responded in kind. Their expressions cycled through uncertainty to recognition and finally to homage. The room's focus had shifted. Mrs. Alles, obviously irritated at this fawning of her peers, looked on in disbelief.

"Excuse me," Naylor said in his deep, resonant voice.

Three men behind the railing showed a phalanx of forgiving smiles, while Mrs. Alles and Dr. Johns appeared annoyed. Dean Oberleigh lowered his forehead into his hand and pushed out a long sigh.

"Excuse *me*!" Mrs. Alles countered. "And you are—?"

"John Naylor, ma'am." He nodded toward Ash. "I'm in his biology class."

Mrs. Alles carried her skewed smile to the chairman as if she were tolerating a bad joke. The chairman leaned forward and arched his eyebrows at Princeton Johns.

"Dr. Johns, did you ask Mr. Naylor—?"

"Certainly not!" the professor snapped.

"Nobody asked me," John said and nodded toward Ash. "I came 'cause he needs somebody to back 'im."

Mrs. Alles bristled. "Young man, though your intentions may be admirable, this is not the way a disciplinary hearing works."

"Ma'am," John said, "as I see it, this hearing is not working at all."

The men at the table closed their mouths and cut their eyes to Mrs. Alles.

"Mr. Naylor," she said, "if you have information relevant to this hearing, I suggest you present it quickly as your presence here is fast coming to an end."

The chairman cleared his throat with a nervous laugh. "What she means, John—"

"I said exactly what I mean," Mrs. Alles broke in.

John pointed at Ash. "He's been tutoring me. Without him I wouldn' have a prayer." He tapped his ear. "Got tinnitus. Can't hear Dr. Johns's sibilant voice."

" 'Sibilant'?" the chairman muttered.

"Means: kinda high and hissy," Naylor explained. "I had a D average a week ago. Last test I made an A." Several men nodded their approval at this announcement.

"Very heart-warming, Mr. Naylor," Dr. Johns cooed. "It proves nothing."

"Yes, it does," Naylor replied in a calm voice. "He answers my questions. How could he do that without him knowing the subject?"

Johns pounced on this opportunity. "Simple. Perhaps your test scores are improved because you are being coached by someone who has access to the tests."

Naylor shook his head. "Why would he turn a test over to the dean the day before the test? If the dean reports it . . . test gets changed . . . Ash is up the creek. Only he *ain't* up the creek! Why? 'Cause he knows the material inside and out."

"Mr. Naylor," Johns said in a smug tone. "your friend is no longer in my class and hasn't been for some time now. He didn't have to face the test on Tuesday."

"But he did 'face the test,' " Naylor informed him. "And he scored the highest."

"He was not there!" Dr. Johns insisted. "I took the tests up one at a time. I would certainly remember his face." He threw a hand in Ash's direction. "There was—"

"I turned it in for him!" John said loud enough to drown out his teacher's attack.

"Gentlemen," the chairman pleaded, "can we—"

"You what?" Princeton Johns laughed. Turning to the board members he presented his there-you-have-it smile and spread his hands. "Our den of thieves grows!"

Naylor folded his arms over his chest and stared at his teacher. "Would you say you successfully out-maneuvered the ones who were cheatin' in your first period class?"

Dr. Johns made a modest bow of his head. "Yes, I would say that I did."

Naylor nodded. "What about your other classes?"

When Princeton Johns only glared at him, Mrs. Alles spoke up. "Dr. Johns?"

Johns shrugged. "The grades were higher," he admitted.

Naylor nodded. "What was the first period average for that test?"

Dr. Johns sniffed. "I don't remember."

"Average was fifty-nine," Naylor said. He let that number hang as he studied the board members' faces. "What was the average for the fourth period class?"

Dr. Johns wiped at something in his lap. "I'm afraid I don't know that either."

"Eighty-four," Naylor informed him. Everyone was watching Dr. Johns now. "Fifth period was eighty nine," Naylor added. The board was mesmerized by these statistics. "Who made the highest score in first period?"

Johns raised his chin quickly. "A Mr. Gunter, I believe."

Naylor shook his head. "Nope. Gunter didn't take your test." He pointed to Ash. "Asherwood made a ninety-six. His test was turned in with no name, and you assumed it belonged to Gunter since you had no test with his name." Dr. Johns opened his mouth but did not get a chance to answer. "Who made the second highest grade?" Naylor waited only a beat before tapping his thick thumb against his chest. "Me. Made ninety-four."

"Mr. Naylor," Dr. Johns said, collecting himself, "what I am hearing from you is that perhaps you were supplied the test information, too." When the board members shifted in their seats, he added, "Whether knowingly or unknowingly, I cannot say."

The chairman cleared his throat. "I think this has gone far enough. We all appreciate what you've tried to do, John, but I'll have to ask you to leave."

Naylor stepped to the rail. "I came here as proof that you're making a mistake."

"It is not proof at all," Dr. Johns snapped. "If anything it implicates both of you."

"John," the chairman said, rising. "You'd best leave now, son."

Naylor stepped beside Ash, who numbly awaited the inevitable. "In that case," John said, "I'm here to let you know that I'm guilty of doin' exactly what he did."

The males seated at the table appeared stricken. All but Dr. Johns, who made a sly smile, raised his hands, and pantomimed a slow applause.

"John," Ash whispered, "don't—"

"What are you saying, Mr. Naylor?" Mrs. Alles asked.

"I'm saying . . . the day before the last test, I acquired a copy, too . . . with the answers all typed out. And like him, I didn't read any of it."

Mrs. Alles folded her arms across her chest. "And did you have permission?" She nodded toward Dean Oberleigh.

"Nope," John said. "The Dean just wanted me to ask some questions . . . see if I could find out who's makin' these tests available."

Mrs. Alles narrowed her eyes at the star athlete. "Are you trying to blackmail the Academy, Mr. Naylor?" she challenged.

Naylor shook his head. "I'm not coming back here for one of these so-called disciplinary hearings. If we're kicked out of school, tell us now."

The room was as still as a photograph. No one spoke, until, finally, John Naylor tapped Ash's shoulder.

"Come on. We got classes to get to."

Naylor walked out of the room, leaving the door open. They heard his footsteps in the hallway, and then the glass door at the front of the building thumped shut. In the quiet that followed, Ash stood and duplicated John's exit. No one stopped him.

Before he left the building he heard Mrs. Alles say, "Gentlemen, I for one will not be bullied. I don't care if that was our ticket to the state championships. Now let's get on with our business."

PART FOUR

The Gauntlet Down

At four o'clock Ash left the art building with Beechwood on his mind. On the sidewalk out front he turned when he heard his name. Anne Metter, carrying a long box under her arm, marched toward him as if she were walking into an argument.

"I need to talk to you, Ash," she said and continued past him to the bench on the lawn. There she sat and waited. He followed and stood before her troubled face. "Ash, I worked hard on homecoming. I raised money, enlisted volunteers, made props, printed posters, choreographed the whole thing, and lost seven pounds from worrying."

Ash lowered his eyes. "Anne, I apologize for the way I disrupted your tournament. I don't know why I—"

"Are you kidding?!" she laughed, her eyes shining like bright coins. "It was everybody's favorite part of the whole weekend!" She patted the bench. "Sit down."

When he sat she laid the box across both their laps. "Open it." she ordered.

After unsealing one end of the box he pulled out wads of newspaper stuffing until he saw the notched tip of a bow. He slid out the dark yew bow he had admired in Cat's room, its polished wood reflecting the afternoon light like black glass.

"Before you say a word, Ash, we had four hundred dollars left over in the budget. Plus, I sold the big target to Bobby Seabolt's grandfather. We had only one mishap: destruction of personal property. So, I used the surplus money for that. It's a done deal."

"Anne—" Ash said quietly.

The Office Doctor van pulled into the shade of the big hemlock tree in front of the building. Troutman jumped down from the driver's seat, slammed the door, and jogged to the front entrance of the building, leaving the van idling and belching intermittent bursts of black exhaust.

"Anne, is there a test coming up soon in an art class?"

Anne pursed her lips. "Mrs. Rainey's art history test is on Monday. Why?"

Ash slid the bow into the box. "Will you wait for me a few minutes?"

Her eyes slanted with a question as she took the box from him. "Okay," she said.

Inside the building he climbed the stairs and listened in the second floor hallway until he heard a metallic *clunk* from the copy room. Walking past the door, Ash caught sight of Troutman, kneeling, twisting a screwdriver into the panel of the copier. When Mrs. Rainey approached from the far end of the hall, Ash turned and buried his face in the water fountain as she moved past him and entered the copy room.

"Is there something wrong with the machine?" she asked Troutman.

"No' ma'am, this here's a reg'lar service call. Go ahead an' use it. Then I'll clean it."

"Maybe you should clean it first. It may take me a while."

"No' ma'am, it'll copy for you fine. Besides, I ain't in no hurry."

A beat of silence passed. "Then why are you cleaning it?"

"I gotta schedule to follow. Part o' the service plan. You go ahead."

Ash leaned over the fountain again as Troutman walked from the room and down the hall to the stairwell. When the machine started, Ash entered the room.

"Test coming up, Mrs. Rainey?"

"Oh, hello, Robert. Yes, Greek architecture."

He watched the machine slowly spit out her tests. "Copier working okay?"

"We'll see," she said. "So far, so good."

"Does the counter work okay?"

She made a face. "Well, *that* never works. I always have to make a few extras."

He walked to the front window and looked down at the curb. There was no exhaust coming from the van's tailpipe now, but a thin stream of cigarette smoke curled from the driver's window. Leaving Mrs. Rainey to her work, Ash walked across the hall into an empty classroom and closed the door an inch shy of shut.

Finally the machine rested, and Mrs. Rainey's shoes clicked down the hall. Ash returned to the copy room and moved to the window. Smoke still rose from the van window. Ash turned and surveyed the room. Cartons of paper were stacked along one wall, and in one corner stood a large cardboard box showing a drawing of an ergonomic chair. He lifted out the chair, and rolled it on its casters to the window.

A cheap screwdriver was taped to the chair's arm. After peeling the tool free he climbed inside the empty box, knelt and, using the screwdriver, reamed out a peephole the size of a nickel. As soon as he had pulled the top flaps closed over him, footsteps clicked at the door. Through the hole he saw Mrs. Rainey's blue dress appear. The machine turned on. Right away a second set of footsteps scuffed to a halt at the door.

"Why does this counter never work right?" she said.

"Aw, it's these old models." Troutman's voice was so close to the box that Ash stopped breathing. "First thing to go bad. How much longer you gonna be?"

The machine rested. "I'm done," she said with a curt finality.

When she had gone, Ash watched Troutman kneel and work the panel free. Inside the copier he tripped a latch, removed a plastic plate, and turned his face directly toward Ash as he reached into the heart of the machine with his right arm. After extracting a small stack of papers, Troutman pivoted on the balls of his feet and flipped the catches on his tool case. He stuffed the papers inside the satchel and then set the plate back into place and closed the panel. A long quiet followed as he replaced the screws. Then he was gone.

When he heard the van start up outside, Ash pushed out of the box and knelt before the panel. Using the screwdriver he backed out the screws. With the panel open he sprung the latch Troutman had turned. In the dark recesses of the machine, he found the plastic plate and popped it out. There was nothing else of note that he could see.

"This is my last batch then I'm gone," a voice said from the door.

Ash banged his head on the frame as he tried to back out. Rubbing his head he faced Mrs. Rainey, who stood in the doorway holding a stack of papers.

"Robert?" She winced. "Are you all right?"

Ash stood. "I'm fine."

She looked around the room. "Where's the repairman? He couldn't have cleaned it that fast." Then her frown deepened. "What are *you* doing under there?"

Ash looked at the machine. "Trying to see what's wrong with this counter."

She exhaled her exasperation. "Well, I wish someone would. That repairman can never seem to fix it." She scowled. "Let's just see if he really cleaned it."

She loaded a paper, punched in commands, and waited for a copy to emerge. When the first sheet floated into the collection tray, she snatched up the paper and examined it.

"This is no cleaner!" she scoffed. "Look at these smears." At the bottom of the page was a grainy sketch of the Parthenon. When the machine finished its work, she counted the papers in the tray. "See there? It happened again! I'm one short!"

She punched the buttons again to make up for her missing copy, and then she left the room saying, "If you figure out what's wrong with it, maybe we'll hire you instead."

Alone again, he knelt and peered into the machine. Now something glowed white deep inside. He reached in, turning his head just as Troutman had, and felt a single sheet of paper nestled in another tray situated deep inside the machine. He extracted it and found himself looking at the Parthenon.

Ash laid the paper face down on the glass and punched the buttons to make more copies. After a series of experimental runs, he determined that every thirtieth copy dropped into the hidden tray. He laughed quietly—a single breath of revelation—and then he laughed again for the implications of this moment, as he once again illegally held a test in his hands. He jumped when Anne Metter appeared in the doorway holding the long box.

"What in the world are you doing?" she asked.

He turned a paper for her to see. "The Office Doctor is smarter than I thought."

When Mrs. Oberleigh opened her front door, her eyes were red-rimmed and puffy. "Richard is not here, Ash," she said, her voice hollow, automatic.

"I know how they're getting the tests," he said.

She seemed not to hear him. "When did you last talk to Richard, Ash?"

"This morning at the hearing. But listen, I just—"

"Ash, the board expelled you. John, too." She sagged against the doorframe. "We are all trying to help each other, and it looks like we're all going down together." Dory stepped out onto the porch and looked out at her neighborhood. She began to cry. "I'm afraid you're not the only one with troubles. We are seriously over-extended. Richard went into our savings to help Dr. Leonhardt with his bills."

She wiped at her cheeks and made a pained smile. "Because Leonhardt confided in him, Richard feels responsible for his dismissal." She shook her head. "I know this is selfish, because Lord knows Dr. Leonhardt needs the money. God, he might even die without it. But this is money we saved for our lives. We'll never see it again."

The dread smothered her, and she began to sob. "Richard feels guilty about you, too," she managed to say. "And John. The board members just wouldn't listen to him."

"Dory, I know how the tests are stolen."

She sniffed twice and looked at him, squinting through her tears. "What?"

"Tell the dean that John and I will be at his office at nine in the morning."

"Saturday?" She wiped her eyes. "All right, I'll tell him."

The rock music across the hall was so loud that Ash had to pound on John Naylor's door with the pad of his fist. The music shut off, and the door behind him opened. A stocky boy reached up to his doorsill and leaned forward to arch his back.

"Naylor hasn't been back since practice," the boy said and huffed a laugh. "Neither have his victims. Try the library. He goes there a lot at night." He turned back to his room and closed the door, and the music boosted up again.

Ash walked to the end of the hall and cupped his hands to the tall glass window. Across the road the stadium was visible. At one end of the field a lone security light glowed. Then he saw a dark vertical line race up the field, dragging a shadow with it.

Five minutes later Ash stood on the track watching John Naylor sprint to the far end of the field, his arms and legs pumping like pistons, his body tilted forward in an aggressive attack against the night. Naylor walked a half-circle in the end zone and charged back with the same fury, his eyes bright behind the steam blowing from clenched teeth. He walked around the near goal post, turned his head to spit, and saw Ash's approach. Naylor stopped, his chest still heaving as he sucked in air.

Ash stepped before him, and the two ex-students locked eyes. "I know how they're doing it. It's the copy machine."

John spat off to one side and stared at Ash for a time. "Tell me."

And Ash did. When he finished, he dropped the sweatshirt hood onto his back, stepped up to the goal line and crouched, hand on knee, poised for a start.

"One more?" Ash said.

Naylor nodded, joined him, and took his sprinter's stance.

"Go!" Ash called.

They flew down the field like animals sprung from a cage. By the fifty yard-line they were laughing, every fiber of muscle and sinew bursting with the righteous energy to drive out the demons that had recently taken up residence in their lives.

Chapter Twenty-Six

Looking out of uniform in his red plaid shirt, Dean Oberleigh sat on the edge of his desk and rubbed the sides of his square chin, the sound like sandpaper. "All right, I'll get surveillance cameras," he agreed. "But we'll need to follow this to the actual selling of the tests. To see who else is involved." He ballooned his cheeks and exhaled. "This will prove Leonhardt right. He'll have to be reinstated." The dean arched his eyebrows. "It will solve a lot of other problems, too."

"If it doesn't reinstate him," Ash said, "I have a friend who writes for the school paper and for the *Clarion*. He would love to put this story into print."

John Naylor chuckled. "Blackmail's gettin' to be our specialty."

Ash waited for the dean to look at him. "I've seen a blueprint for Dr. Johns's housing. It cuts into the woods west of campus. Six buildings. One looks like a mansion."

The dean huffed a quiet laugh through his nose. "That mansion would be for department heads." He frowned out the window. "Who gave him the go-ahead on this?"

"Prob'ly nobody," John said. "He's already got a bad case of 'department-head.' "

"His architect," Ash continued, "is Norman Creed in Atlanta."

Dean Oberleigh leaned over his desk and pulled a telephone book from a drawer. "Creed," he mumbled to himself. "Where have I heard that name?" He dialed a number and stood before the window with the phone to his ear. Ash and John remained quiet.

"Yes, this is Richard Oberleigh, Dean of Students at Greenwood Downs Academy up in Naughton." The dean's voice was business-like, self-assured. He listened for several seconds, and then his eyes locked on Ash and hardened like glass. "Oh, yes, Pam," he said with the lilt of courtesy, "I do remember meeting you. Is Norm around this morning?"

Ash could hear her tiny voice rise and fall from ten feet away.

"Well, perhaps *you* can help me, Pam," the dean interrupted. "Please remind me: Who is Norm's main contact here at the school concerning the new construction?" The dean listened and began to nod. "Well, thank you, Pam. Maybe we'll see you at the Christmas program . . . all right . . . you, too . . . goodbye."

Dean Oberleigh hung up and stared out the window "Now I remember. Norman Creed is the brother-in-law of the school attorney, Candler Reeve. Reeve sat in on Leonhardt's hearing. He counseled for dismissal." The dean's jaw knotted as he turned to Ash and John. "And Norman Creed is not only the architect . . . he's a builder."

"Doesn't the school charter forbid development in the forests?" Ash asked.

"I'll check on that," the dean said. "Meanwhile I'll have maintenance install the cameras this weekend. Sunday night we'll finalize our plan at my house. Eight o'clock."

*****

On Sunday morning Ash left the warm womb of Beechwood and moved at a brisk pace along the river's edge. The air coming off the water was like cold metal touching his skin. Just shy of Painted Rock he crossed the bridge and climbed the trail to Ten Point.

Opening the door Marin peered over her reading glasses and gave him the smile that etched crow's feet around her eyes. As soon as he witnessed this warmth from her, he realized that part of his reason for coming was to receive that smile.

"Tea is ready," she said and welcomed him inside.

As she poured, he pulled the bench closer to the stove. Each with a cup, they sat.

"Things are looking better," he said and told her about The Office Doctor and the copy machine. "We might be back in school soon. Dr. Leonhardt, too."

"I talked to him last night," she reported. "The doctors are optimistic. But the real optimism, I think, will come from you. When he hears what you have found out."

Ash laughed quietly at the irony. He had made a concerted effort to win Dr. Leonhardt's respect in the classroom. He was having a better go of it from a distance.

"Marin, I saw some blueprints on Dr. Johns's desk." As he described the scope of the housing development, a blue vein stood out on her temple, and her jaw set.

"I'm certain about the charter's provision protecting the outlying woods," she said. "Hubert had a copy sent to him, but we didn't bring it to the States. It was so bulky; and, of course, he knew the original was here." She checked her watch and smiled an apology. "I have to be off. I have a student coming to my classroom to make up a test."

As he watched her gather her things, he wondered how much longer she would stay at Ten Point. Or for that matter, in America. They walked out together, and she got into Dr. Leonhardt's Buick. When Ash stood watching her, she rolled down the window.

"Would you like a lift to school?"

He shook his head. Before she could raise the window, he stepped closer and leaned on the car door with both hands.

"I'll never forget what you tried to do for me at the hearing." He lowered his eyes. "As to this other stuff . . . our pasts . . . I don't know what to say." His eyes began to sting, yet he could not help looking at her. "I don't know what to do with all that, Marin. But I know it's important . . . because you say it is."

"I don't know what to do with it either, Ash," she said and started the car.

Standing by the big cafeteria window, Ash listened to the dean's telephone voice grow more exasperated. "The school charter is not in the library's records room, where it belongs. As it turns out, the charter is undergoing restoration. Reeve initiated the project and hired a documents-specialist. I'm told there are no copies."

Ash looked out at the low clouds graying the sky. "Actually, there is one."

Ash waited outside Marin's classroom until her student left. Stepping inside, he found Marin standing at the window, her eyes closed, the muted light bathing her face.

"Marin," he said. She turned to his voice. "We need your copy of the charter."

Her eyebrows lowered and she began to nod. "Our secretary is on leave. There is a groundskeeper, but—" She shook her head.

Ash took a deep breath and eased it out. "Is this why we've all come together, Marin? To save this forest?"

She turned back to the gray day beyond the windowglass. "Sometimes when I could not see things Hubert's way, I asked questions like that. To know what this so-called 'homecoming' was about. He would say, 'Nobody knows the way of it.' And I would ask 'Then how do you know it at all?' And he would say, 'Ah, now there's a different story. I know it in my bones.' And I would say, 'Why don't I?' And he answered, 'Your bones have to get used to it.' "

She shook with a private laugh. "Once, during one of these exchanges, I got quite angry with him. He never raised his voice, but to prove a point we drove to Nottingham and rented a cottage near the old Lenton Priory. He settled in to read, telling me to look over the countryside. I had expected more from him, so I suppose I was in a snit when I began to walk the streets with the vague notion of searching for a complete unknown."

"My day was so uneventful that, by late afternoon, I was embarrassed to return to the cottage. I felt like a puppet shorn of her strings . . . someone who could do nothing on her own. Weary of strangers' eyes I left the thoroughfare for the footpaths. At twilight I crested a hill and looked back at the lights blinking on beyond the priory. There I experienced a profound sadness. Yet at the same time, I felt solace in the land.

"When I returned to the cottage, I was spent. Hubert was very kind to me that night. He said very little beyond asking if I needed anything. I woke up late in the night, cold and crying, and he built a fire and bundled me with blankets. Then he began to read to me from the book—the last pages I had not yet transcribed. He read of the death of Robert of Huntingdon, Maryanne's lover, who was by then a wolf's head with a bounty offered for his death. Because he was hunted so, there had been a long separation between Robert and Maryanne. He became ill and, fearing he would die, went to her at Kirklees, where she had joined that order."

She paused for a time and cocked her head. "I had always believed that Kirklees had been in Yorkshire, for there is a Kirklees Abbey there today. As it turns out, Lenton was once known as 'Church Fields,' which in Old Saxon is written as 'Kirk Leas.' While Robert was there, one of the sisters betrayed him. We don't know why. He died in Maryanne's arms and was buried nearby."

Marin returned to the bench and sat. "It was then that Hubert showed me in the book a crude hand-drawing of the shire. He pointed out a little square with a cross, just north of Nottingham. It was labeled 'Kirk Leas'—the place Lenton Priory is situated today. North of that was another cross—this one smaller without a square. It was labeled with the letters 'RH'. This was the grave of Robert of Huntingdon. The journal tells how he chose the site by shooting an arrow from his bedside window."

She turned to face Ash. "That spot—that grave—that's where I was standing that night, Ash. Sister Maryanne's room was on the north side of the abbey. She wrote by her window, prayed there. She described the mountain vista outside her window as the 'Sleeping Angel'. Its outline against the sky resembled a reclining head and torso. One downward sloping ridge swept from the shoulder like a folded wing."

"The next morning Hubert and I walked out to the gravesite. There was nothing there to mark it. I looked out at the 'Sleeping Angel' . . . at the comforting rise and fall of the land. Ash, I felt that my private life had been stolen from me, and yet I did not know who had taken it. I guess I had begun to feel it in my bones."

Rain tapped the window. As Ash watched the glass blur, the memory of the dream surfaced in his mind. An old man standing at his back, hands clamped to his wrists, bending the bow. And then a rusty whisper in his ear: *Did you feel it? In your bones?*

"I wish I could have known your husband, Marin."

The rain fell harder now, and the wind swept droplets against the glass, distorting the outside world.

"He knew you," she said. "More than you might imagine."

He looked at the profile of her face. Her iris was the color of the rain.

"If I understood it better," he said, "I might feel we're on the same side in this."

She smiled. "We've always been on the same side, Ash."

234

When the rain stopped in early afternoon, Ash shot his new longbow, adjusting to its length and power and mystified by its appeal. He liked that it was made by Cat's hands from wood that had grown in Marin's England. Already, his confidence with the bow was equal to what he had felt with his old bow. Each shot that he made was performed first in his mind, and then the physical flight of the arrow followed as an after-thought. After three hours of this he stowed his gear at Beechwood and walked to the gym to shower.

As he was leaving the gym, two maintenance men rolled out the big blue mat at the center of the basketball court. Students were trickling in, taking the best seats in the bleachers. At the front entrance he saw a notice taped to the glass announcing a wrestling match against Rabun County. His eyes were pulled from the poster when The Office Doctor van climbed into the lot and pulled into a parking space. Guy rolled out of the van, followed by Jeep. Both were dressed in school sweats. Troutman emerged from the driver's side wearing camo jacket and jeans.

Guy and Troutman swaggered past Ash, but Jeep stopped, his open face holding no secrets. "You staying for the match?" he asked, his expression hopeful.

Ash shrugged. "I need to study."

Jeep turned Ash by his arm. "Hey, I'm gonna fix you up with the next test."

"Bert, I don't want to depend on that and be disappointed again. Anyway, I've decided it's all a dead-end."

Jeep appeared hurt. "Whatta ya mean?"

"What happens later in life when we need some of this stuff we've skipped?"

Jeep spewed air through his lips. "It's not like I'm gonna be a scientist."

"What if you change your mind? You're narrowing your choices."

Jeep's face lost its innocence, and he looked away. "I'm sick of this school's fixation on pre-majors." Then he turned quickly to Ash. "What? You think that's funny?"

Ash held his smile. "We have more in common than you know."

A yellow bus pulled into the lot and parked at the curb. Dressed in red sweats, the Rabun County athletes began to file out, their sports bags in tow.

"If you don't know what to pre-major in, maybe it's because you're too smart to narrow your choices right now."

"Jeep!" Jeep turned to see Guisburn yelling from the locker room door. "Get your scrawny butt in here and get dressed! Tell Chief Broken Foot to take a hike."

Jeep raised his chin to Ash and started away.

"I changed my mind, Bert," Ash said. "I will watch your match."

Jeep's boyish smile flashed, and he waved as he jogged away.

As soon as he had taken a seat in the bleachers, Ash saw Cat climbing the seats toward him. "How does it shoot?" Cat asked and sat.

"With authority," Ash replied. "It's everything I could hope for in a bow." Ash plucked at Cat's scrimmage vest. "Are you wrestling already?"

Cat shook his head. "Just dressed out with the team. Therapist says three more months." He laughed quietly. "*If* I can handle all the rehab work ahead, she says." He smiled. "My therapist doesn't know me very well."

They watched Tucker set out bottles of water at the Warriors' bench.

"Can I ask you something, Cat?" Ash said and lowered his voice to a whisper. "How do you deal with this whole premise for the Fitzwalter scholarship?"

Cat laughed. "Me?! How do *you* deal with it? It all centers around *you*. If you were in school at the South Pole, I guess that's where we'd all be right now."

When Ash did not laugh, Cat's smile relaxed.

"Listen," Cat said solemnly, "I put a lot of trust in Mr. Fitz. And Mrs. Fitz, too."

Ash stared across the mat as the teams filed out of the locker room and took their places at their respective benches. The bleachers had filled now, and the gym buzzed with an ocean of chatter. Two names were announced over the speakers, and a wrestler from each team walked onto the mat.

Ash turned to Cat. "Are you saying you buy all this? About all of us?"

The referee's whistle pierced the air, and the first bout began. Amid the echoes of cheers bouncing off the walls, Cat didn't try to respond. After just a minute the GDA wrestler was pinned, and the Rabun wrestlers came off their bench, punching the air with their fists, filling the gym with howls of victory. When the noise subsided, Cat leaned his elbows on his thighs and looked at his hands as he rubbed his flattened palms together.

"Whatever all this is about, Ash, it's worth knowing that a man like Mr. Fitz would take an interest in you. Or plan his life around you." Cat shook his head. "Man, I can't believe the two of you didn't get to meet."

For the next match, Jeep stepped onto the mat and went to hands and knees for the start. The ref's whistle blasted, and the Rabun wrestler quickly gained the advantage. On the defensive, Jeep worked mechanically without innovation. With his eyes locked on some distant point, he splayed his hands and knees as though digging in for the duration—a portrait of his four-wheel-drive nickname. The green team cheered him on, all but Guisburn, who was talking with Troutman by the wall.

When it was over, Jeep walked back to the bench, oblivious to the coach's pat on his back and the consoling comments from his teammates. He sat, pulled off his headgear, and looked back at Guy, but Guy and Troutman were deep in conversation.

"Hey," Cat said to Ash, "let me ask *you* something?" He narrowed his eyes. "Is Anne Metter a person of interest to you? I mean . . . romantically?"

Ash shook his head. "She's a good person, Cat. Anyone who is interested in her, and vice versa, would be a lucky man. But that's not me."

Cat nodded and shifted his attention back to the match. "Good to know," he said.

Ash nodded. "Sounds like a good . . . project . . . for lack of a better word." He stood. "Guess I'll go. You staying to the end?"

"Yeah," Cat said without hesitation, but there was a tone in his voice that made Ash hesitate. Cat raised his chin toward the mat. "I want to watch Guisburn." Cat smiled and looked up at Ash. "He's my other new project . . . for lack of a better word."

Chapter Twenty-Eight

"There are five motion-activated cameras in place," the dean said, closing the door to his study. "One for each department giving a test tomorrow. By my instruction, the teachers made up new tests and copied them today. Then the copy rooms were locked, not to be opened until seven in the morning. Here's the list." He set a paper on his desk and sat.

Ash read the list and passed it to Naylor. "Security men at each building?"

The dean shook his head. "There are not five to spare. You two will use my car to play lookout." He set car keys and a cell phone on the desk. "You know this repairman's face. He may not use his van. Call my office when you know which machine he's going to, and I'll get security there."

*****

The dawn bloomed to a cold hazy pink. Ash killed the Pontiac's engine on the shoulder of the highway across from the front gate, and the two ex-students kept watch on the crest of the road sixty yards distant. As the car's residual heat slipped away, Naylor hunched forward in his seat and blew into his hands. Ash folded his arms and fought a shiver.

When a sheriff's cruiser pulled alongside them, both boys sat up straight. The driver lowered his window and motioned for Ash to do the same.

"Any trouble, boys?"

"No, sir," Ash replied. "We're waiting for someone."

The officer eyed the car from grill to taillight. "This your car?"

"It belongs to the Dean of Students," Ash answered. "We're from GDA."

The two men exchanged a few words, then the cruiser's passenger door opened. A tall deputy stepped out and carefully set a Styrofoam cup on the roof of his car. His shoes crunched on the cold ground as he approached. Through the cruiser Ash watched a VW slow and turn into the gate.

"Which dean was that?" the tall man said, stopping at Ash's window.

"Oberleigh," Ash said, leaning to look around him. It was a woman in the VW.

"Would you take out your license, please." The policeman leaned down to look past Ash, and his mouth dropped open a half inch. "That thuh Hammuh?" he sang out.

"That's me," John said, matching the man's melodic surprise.

"What ya'll doing out heah, Hammuh?"

John smiled. "Dean asked us to meet somebody at the gate this morning."

Another car slowed at the gate. Ash strained to see it as he held out his license. It was a BMW driven by a portly man. Ash recognized one of the computer staff.

"No trouble then?" the officer asked, hardly glancing at Ash's license.

"No trouble," John assured him.

"Aw-right, then. Ya'll be careful, now." He returned the license and got back into the cruiser. John made a little salute with two fingers from his brow. Both men returned the flourish. As they pulled away, the coffee cup balanced on the roof of the car until they had sped halfway up the hill, where it spilled down the rear windshield and spiraled in the wake of the car. The brake lights flashed briefly, then the car accelerated.

Ash tapped his license on the steering wheel and eyed John. Smiling, Naylor began singing in a soft falsetto, bobbing his head to an internal beat.

"Fame . . . I'm gonna live forever . . . I'm gonna learn how to fly."

A van crested the hill and downshifted with popcorn bursts from the exhaust. Hardly slowing, it careened through the gate.

"Office Doctor," Ash said and fired the engine. "That's him."

Troutman sped down the tunnel of oaks lining the entrance drive. Just past the quadrangle he turned into the parking lot behind the cafeteria. When Ash and John passed the entrance, they saw Troutman lugging his black tool case across the lot. John punched numbers on the phone as Ash pulled to the curb and idled.

"This thing is dead," John said, scowling at the phone's screen. He tried again and got nothing.

Ash opened his door. "I'll go inside the cafeteria and call."

Naylor pointed toward the quadrangle. " 'Bout as fast to run to his office."

Ash stepped out on the pavement, but right away he ducked back in. "He's already coming back out!"

The van's consumptive engine fired, and the tires screeched as Troutman backed out of his parking space. Ash jammed the gear stick into reverse, backed up ten yards, and turned off the engine so that they blocked the exit. Troutman skidded to a stop at the top of the slope, glared through the windshield, and laid on the horn.

Ash pulled up his sweatshirt hood, popped the hood release, and got out. Keeping his face hidden, he leaned over the engine. Again, Troutman's horn blared from the lot.

By reflex, Ash glanced at the van. In that split second he saw the unmistakable squint of recognition in Troutman's face. The van roared and its rear tires clawed backward until the van lurched to a stop. The gears grated with a metallic whine, and Ash saw Troutman craning his neck high, eyeing the grassy slope beside the drive.

The Pontiac fired up. Ash slammed down the hood to see John in the driver's seat, one big blocky fist clenching the steering wheel. When the van charged forward and tilted off the pavement, Ash backpedaled into the street. John ratcheted the gears and punched the gas, and the Pontiac rocketed forward in a perfectly choreographed collision, the van ramming the dean's car broadside. The crash of metal and glass sounded like a small house dropping to earth.

Ash's entire body flinched. He ran to the dean's car and opened the door to find John sprawled across the seat, cradling an arm, his teeth clenched like a stone wall.

"Go!" Naylor grunted. "Don't let him get rid of the tests!"

When Ash reached the van, Troutman was draped over the steering wheel, catching his breath. A glistening black ink stain spread from his shirt pocket.

"Are you hurt?" Ash said, opening the door. Troutman only glared at him.

A campus security car arrived with flashing orange lights and skidded to a halt. Another was on its way from across the valley. The first man out of the car went to Naylor and then yelled to his partner to call an ambulance. Next, he ran to the van.

"You all right, fella?" he inquired, leaning into the van. Troutman probed the raw scrape mark on his throat and kicked at the door, pushing the officer back a step. "Just take it easy, son. Ambulance is on the way." Still seated behind the steering wheel, Troutman stretched his chin high to view himself in the rear view mirror.

Ash looked at the man's nametag. "Officer Purley . . . the toolkit?"

Troutman turned from the mirror, his cautious eyes fixing on Ash.

Purley pointed into the van. "You wanna hand me that satchel, son?"

Troutman's laugh was a raspy croak. "Hell, no!" He removed a leaking pen from the blackened pocket. "These morons blocked my way outta the lot!"

The students who had gathered in the street now made way for an ambulance. An EMT jumped out, ran to the van, set his kit on the running board, and began questioning Troutman. Another EMT—a female whose head leveled off at Naylor's shoulder—helped John to the ambulance. Another security car arrived with the dean glaring out the window from the rear seat.

The EMT with Troutman zipped up his bag and announced to Purley, "He's okay. I think he just had the wind knocked out of him. Caught his throat on the steering wheel." Then he addressed Troutman directly. "We'll get some X-rays just to be sure."

"I don't want no damn X-rays," Troutman shot back.

The dean stepped before Ash, his big jaw set like angle iron, and his eyes glued to the wrecked Pontiac. "Sir?" Ash whispered and tilted his head sideways toward the van.

Dean Oberleigh turned to Purley. "I want this driver and his van searched."

Troutman turned angry eyes on the dean. "What for?!" he challenged.

Purley put some steel in his voice. "I need you to step out of your vehicle, sir."

"I don't feel like steppin' out. I was just rammed by these morons."

Purley worked up a hard stare and slapped a hand to the door. "Outside! Now!"

"You ain't got no badge or warr'nt. Go an' play cop with someb'dy else."

"I've got all the warrant I need," the dean boomed, causing both Purley and Troutman to look his way. "You are on school property. You have driven off the driveway and crashed into *my* car. I suspect there's alcohol in this van. If you're not down out of that seat in three seconds, I'll help you down."

Troutman threw the broken pen to the floor and stepped out. He tried to meet Dean Oberleigh eye to eye but the stretch of his throat that this required made him cough.

The satchel rattled with loose hardware when Purley set it on the grass. Opened, it revealed tiers of wrenches and screwdrivers and other tools, but no papers.

"Go through the van, officer, and I want you to administer a sobriety test."

"Yes, sir," Purley said and called down to the other officer. "Leo!"

The black security man, Dawson—the same man who had escorted Ash out of Princeton Johns's office—joined them. Troutman held open his jacket and submitted to a frisk while his van was examined. When it was over, Dean Oberleigh glared at the van with disgust and held that expression when he shifted his gaze to Ash. The dean walked away and began talking with the security men on the street.

When Purley returned from his car with the balloon kit, Troutman balked. "You gonna give that coon who ran into me a test, too?"

Officer Dawson stepped out of the van, stood between Purley and Troutman, and spoke in a low hum into the Office Doctor's face. "Sure we are. But we'll have to get the other kit for him . . . the one we keep sanitized." Dawson turned away, mumbling as he walked past Ash, "Damned redneck coon-ass cracker."

When the ambulance pulled away, Ash joined Dean Oberleigh on the street. "What in the hell happened?" the dean asked.

"We couldn't get through to you, and he was in and out so fast I blocked the drive so he couldn't leave. I got out of the car like something was wrong with the engine. John stayed inside. When Troutman tried to go around us, John pulled forward."

The dean exhaled a blast of air. "Did it occur to you to get him at his next stop?"

Ash looked at the growing crowd of students. "I guess not," he said.

The dean sucked in his cheeks as if he were about to spit.

"We need to look at the film," Ash said.

The dean glared at the Pontiac. His nostrils flared, and a vein pulsed in his neck.

"All right," Purley called to Ash, "I need your story."

Leo Dawson stepped into Ash's path. "Odd, isn't it?" Dawson said.

Ash frowned. "Sir?"

Dawson nodded toward the wrecked vehicles. "Your friend, Naylor, just trying to free up the driveway to let the van exit the lot." His deep brown eyes began to shine with an inner light. "And then this repairman drives over the grass to T-bone the Pontiac." Dawson's eyebrows floated up, and then he strolled away.

After writing up a report, Purley led Ash to Troutman for a conference. As the three stood together, Troutman lit a cigarette and glowered off into the distance.

"Since this involves a vehicle from a Naughton business," Purley began, "we're calling in the county. Wreckers are on the way. Just be patient, and we'll try to get this sorted out."

"Sorted out?" Troutman sniped. "These morons blocked my way out."

Leo Dawson joined the parley and very casually removed the cigarette dangling from Troutman's lips. "Smoke-free campus," he said through a smile.

Troutman tried to outstare Dawson, but he was no match for the man. "I got a business to run!" he complained to Purley. "I got appointments to get to. I had to pull around that big nig—" Troutman's eyes darted to Dawson. ". . . the big black dude. He blocked me in!"

Composed, Dawson pursed his lips as he studied the wreckage. "Funny," he said in a wistful voice. "Looks more like you ran over the grass to hit him."

The first wrecker arrived and began hoisting the Pontiac onto its flatbed. Then a county cruiser pulled up at the curb. Ash recognized the deputies by the brown stain that covered their car's back window. Dawson beckoned Ash and the dean aside for a parley.

"There is nothing in the van. Be a good idea not to mention the tests to the county cops. Stick with the alcohol search."

"Whatcha got here, Leo?" the tall deputy said as he unfolded from the car. When the cop recognized Ash, his face went slack, and he turned to the crumpled Pontiac being strapped down on the trailer. "The Hammuh in this pileup?"

Dawson nodded. "Gone to Nacoochee General. Probably a broken arm."

The deputy frowned at the shattered glass sparkling on the sidewalk. "What thuh devil's that van doin' drivin' off thuh road like that?"

"In a hurry," Dawson said in a low, flat tone. "Businessman's got people to see, places to go."

The cop pointed at Troutman sitting on the running board. "Can he walk?"

"I can walk," Troutman answered for himself.

The deputy whipped out a citation pad. "Then how 'bout walkin' over heah. Time to talk."

After a second wrecker hauled away the van, a white station wagon carrying The Office Doctor logo arrived and idled at the curb. The driver was a skinny boy with long hair. Music throbbed from his radio, making his stillness appear like a coma.

"Can I go now?" Troutman said in a flat voice.

The deputy held Troutman's driver's license between two fingers like a clothes pin and slid it into the pocket next to his badge. "I'll hold on to this till I can have a talk with the driver of the Pontiac. Be at the sheriff's tomorr'r at fo-ah." Troutman walked to the station wagon without looking back.

As the wagon drove away, the deputy said to Ash, "You, too. Fo-ah o'clock."

The dean's computer screen fluttered to life with a view of Troutman's back as he approached the copy machine and set down his tool kit. Digging a hand into his pants pocket, he pulled out a stick of gum, unwrapped it, and began chewing. Crumpling the wrapping he looked around the room until he spotted an off-screen target below the camera. He cocked his arm like a prelude to a free-throw. Then his eyes rose, and his eyebrows lowered. Ash felt as if Troutman were looking right at him from the screen.

"He saw the camera," Ash said.

Hardly missing a beat, Troutman tossed his trash and spun to the copy machine. After loading a sheet of paper he pretended to check the quality of the copy. Then grabbing his case he walked out, his eyes fixed in their sockets, looking straight ahead.

Dean Oberleigh turned off the video. Ash closed his eyes and exhaled heavily.

"I'm going to check on John," Ash said.

The dean kept glaring at the monitor. "Well, I would offer you a ride, but—"

The receptionist in the emergency room told Ash that John had been released and a sheriff's deputy had given him a ride back to school. Ash took the elevator to the hospital's sixth floor, where he stood outside Dr. Leonhardt's door and listened. After a long silence, as he turned to leave, he heard the dry scrape of paper. Ash knocked lightly.

"Come in," said a feeble voice.

Ash entered to see Dr. Leonhardt's head sunk into a pillow, a tube running to his nose, and a book propped on his chest. The man's hollow cheeks were blue with shadow, and the skin on his face sagged. With an effort, the old man turned his head to Ash.

"Ah, Mr. Asherwood. How went the ambush?"

Ash approached. "Badly, I'm afraid." He related the story, stopping whenever the old man's eyes closed. At each pause, the eyes opened as a silent cue to continue. When Ash finished, Dr. Leonhardt laced his fingers over his stomach and stared at the ceiling.

"Well," the professor summed up, "the two questions are: What are they going to do now? They know their system is exposed. But more importantly: What are *you* going to do now?" Leonhardt fixed his eyes on Ash. "Let's look at your options. You could have a heart attack." He chuckled. "That was my first choice, it would seem." The mirth left his face. "Or go home with your reputation in shambles." He pushed himself higher on his pillow. "Or fight it!" Now his color was up, and his lip quivered.

"Sir, you ought not to be getting excited right now."

"But I am excited. About cutting this cancer out of our school. Plus, I've got a chapel to build, Robert. I'm going to need your help."

Ash saw the fire in the old man's eyes. "Sir, you know I've been expelled, right?"

Leonhardt raised himself on an elbow. "But you're not going to walk away, are you?" He said this as if it were fact. "I can offer you this: a place to stay and three meals a day." When Ash did not respond, Leonhardt knotted his frail hand into a fist and shook it. "I want to clear my name, too!" He started to lie back in the bed but stopped and pointed at Ash. "And your friend . . . the football player."

"John Naylor," Ash said.

Dr. Leonhardt reclined. "That's the one. Linebacker isn't he?"

"Yes, sir."

Leonhardt chuckled. "I hear he stopped an end run today. Is he all right?"

Ash nodded. "He must be. The hospital already dismissed him."

"Well," Leonhardt sighed, "soon as I can get out of here, too, we'll put our heads together and figure something out." He locked eyes with Ash. "All right?"

"Yes, sir," Ash replied automatically.

When the old man closed his eyes, Ash watched his chest rise and fall in a steady tempo. Soon his breathing took on the long relaxed abandon of sleep.

Ash was not convinced that this feeble old man could provide any help in the debacle that had fallen upon them, but he did feel a bubble of redemption rise inside him. After all, just weeks ago he could barely tolerate this man for an hour-long class, and now Dr. Richard Leonhardt seemed to have chosen him to champion their cause.

PART FIVE

The Blood in the Bond

Ash knocked on John Naylor's door and listened. The athletic dorm was quiet in the late afternoon. When he tried the doorknob, it turned. One desk was heaped with magazines, CDs, and food wrappers. The other by the window was bare but for a telephone and a scrap of paper.

Two of the four shelves between the desks were empty. One of the closets contained only a row of wire coat hangers and worn-out running shoes—big ones. Ash picked up the torn paper from the desk. Two telephone numbers were scrawled in ink. One was prefaced by the letters "HI" and the other by "TX." Both numbers were local. He dialed the Oberleigh's home, and Dory picked up.

"It's Ash. Have you heard from John Naylor?"

The pause prepared him for bad news. "He called here about two hours ago and left a message," she reported. "He sounded dejected. His arm was broken in two places; he'd wrecked our car; and he was expelled. All of it seems to have overwhelmed him. John said he was going home."

Ash thanked her, hung up, and stared out the window toward Naughton.

"Help you?" came a voice from behind him.

Ash turned to see a stout, gray-haired man dressed in khaki slacks, polo shirt, and bedroom slippers. "I'm looking for John Naylor."

The man frowned as he looked around the room. "He went to the hospital." He fixed questioning eyes on Ash. "Looks like he took everything he owned."

"The hospital released him," Ash said. "Are you his coach?"

The big man shook his head. "Hall monitor." He pointed to the closet that was not bare. "Someone else lives here, too, you know. You can't just waltz into someone else's living quarters."

"If I could just use his phone. I need to find John."

He waved Ash toward him as he stepped out the door. "You can use my phone. Come on."

Ash snatched up the scrap of paper from the desk and followed the man down the hall to a room wallpapered in newspapers articles and photos of the football team. "Right there by the bed," the man said and crossed his arms as he leaned against the doorframe.

Ash read from the paper and punched in the TX number.

"Mountain Taxi," announced a woman's nasal voice. Behind her breathing, Ash heard a car horn echo inside an enclosure.

"Can you tell me if you picked up John Naylor at Greenwood Downs Academy?"

Papers shuffled. "One o'clock. GDA to the Holiday Inn out on the highway."

Ash hung up and called the HI number. There was no Naylor checked in.

"He's a tall black athlete. He might have a cast on his left arm."

"Oh, yeah!" the girl said. "He was in the lobby. We're a bus stop, too, you know."

"Which bus did he take?" Ash pressed.

"Something southbound. Everything this afternoon goes through Atlanta."

When Ash hung up, the waiting man narrowed his eyes. "What's this about a bus?"

"Naylor was expelled today," Ash informed him.

The monitor's face compressed and filled with lines. "What for?"

252

"The wrong reasons," Ash said and hurried past the man to the elevators.

Twilight was settling in over campus. Praying that Marin would be at Ten Point with Leonhardt's Buick, Ash started toward the west field at a limping run. When he was halfway up the hill on Valley Road, two joggers appeared from the Loop, leaning into the turn and coming his way. As they got closer, Ash recognized Jeep and Guisburn.

Jeep raised a hand in greeting and continued down the hill, but Guy checked his pace and ran in place, bouncing effortlessly on his muscular legs before Ash. Then he stopped, propped his fists on his hips, and cocked his head.

"You're puttin' your nose where it don't belong, Chief!" Guisburn growled. He started to reach for Ash, when the bulk of his body was suddenly outlined by headlights from down the hill. Squinting into the lights, Guy hesitated.

The car stopped just below them, its lights holding on both boys. "Ash?"

Guisburn straightened. "Well, howdy there, Mrs. Fitz," Guy said, his voice now full of melody. He turned back to Ash and, holding his specious smile, lowered his voice. "You won't always have Mama with you, Chief." He began jogging backward down the hill. "Hey, we got a Driver's Ed class here. Maybe you and your buddy could take a correspondence course now that they've kicked you out." His smile stretched until his teeth glowed against his dark silhouette. Then he turned and jogged down the hill.

Marin stepped out and stood in the open doorway. "I've been looking for you."

Ash ran to the passenger door. "John's on a bus. He's on his way home."

They looked at each other over the roof of the car. Without another word they ducked inside and slammed their doors in unison. Marin U-turned and sped down the hill.

A light rain met them at the front gate. Out on the highway they drove into a downpour. The halo of pink light from Naughton passed behind them, and the darkened countryside alternated with fields and forests and the occasional farm house set back from the road.

Ash related the events of the morning: the stakeout, the wreck of Dean Oberleigh's car, John's subsequent trip to the hospital. As he talked, he kept his eyes on Marin's profile. In the warm cubicle of the car, the dashboard lights sculpted her face until once again she seemed to slip out of time. She could have been seventeen.

"Which way do we go?" she asked.

"The bus will take highway four hundred. Turn left up here. We'll cut a corner."

Marin made the turn, and the tires squealed. "How do we stop a bus?"

"I don't know, but using these backroads we should get ahead of it."

In forty-five minutes they intersected 400 and pulled over on the shoulder. For five minutes the rain hammered the roof as they watched the traffic. Then a gray bus dotted with orange running lights roared in front of them, its tires hissing, throwing up sprays of water from the wet pavement.

"That's got to be it!" Ash said.

Pulling out onto the highway, they followed in the bus's exhaust for a mile before Marin became desperate to escape the fumes and pulled alongside the bus. Ash rolled down his window, and a rush of cold air and rain invaded the car.

"I see him!" Ash yelled into the wind. "He's asleep. Blow the horn."

Marin pressed the heel of her hand to the center of the steering wheel. "I forgot! It doesn't work!" She jerked her head around to the backseat. "Ash! That box behind you!"

He turned and saw the wooden box she had wanted to open for him at Ten Point. Setting it in his lap, he lifted the lid and worked through a mass of crumpled paper until the smooth curve of something cool and hard filled his hand. A hefty old animal's horn lay nestled in the paper. He lifted it out and gave Marin a doubtful look.

"Just try!" she insisted, and the confidence in her voice was like a jolt of adrenaline. With the rain soaking his head he leaned out the window and lifted the horn to his mouth. Tightening his lips against the mouthpiece, he blew a thin but forceful burst of air. A grace note broke into a higher pitch that bathed the side of the bus in an extraordinary hollow wail that drowned out the sound of the rain and the tandem vehicles. The bus swerved right a few feet, and faces pressed against the windows. John Naylor leaned into the glass, his eyes darkened between his cupped hands.

When John moved up the aisle of the bus, Marin dropped back and followed. At the next exit the bus flashed its blinker and took the ramp to a gas station, where it pulled into the parking lot and braked. Marin pulled up ten yards away. When the bus door opened, John emerged in a yellow poncho. Ash stepped out in his sweat clothes and met him halfway as the rain drummed the lot around them.

"We're taking you back!" Ash yelled over the bus's motor. "This is not over!"

Naylor said nothing. His gaze fell to the horn still clutched in Ash's hand.

"Be damn," Naylor breathed. " 'Member when you asked me if I dreamed 'bout being chased in the woods? Man, I was having that dream just now . . . with those damn dogs . . . and that." He pointed to the horn.

"Same sound . . . like a wounded bear." The rain came harder at a slant, pulsing in sheets. Ash's clothes were sodden.

"We're going to fight this thing, John. Dr. Leonhardt is going to help us."

For a time Naylor just stared at Ash. Finally, he jogged to the bus and conferred with the driver, who stood waiting just inside the door. The man popped an umbrella and opened the cargo hold, where he stacked John's luggage on the pavement.

The Buick journeyed back toward Naughton with the heater fan blowing on high, but the best the old car could do now was to blow out a stream of lukewarm air. Ash's wet clothes proved too much for him. They had just entered Nacoochee County when Ash began to shiver.

"We need to get you warm," Marin said.

John pointed. "Pull over up here. I got a whole duffel of dry clothes."

Under the drive-through awning of a gas stop, John got out and went through his bag as the rain pounded the plastic roof above. The door to the store swung open.

"Y'all doin' all right?" an elderly woman called out. "It's a-coming down, ain't it?" She held a newspaper over her head against the swirling blow of the rain.

"Need to change clothes, ma'am," John called out. "Got somebody wet and cold."

"Well, gracious me, y'all come on an' get on in here." She opened the door wider and waited. When they were all inside, Ash crouched before a gas heater hissing with a row of steady blue flames. The ceramic reflector plates glowed orange-red, and the room was mercifully warm. When Ash faced the woman, he saw that she was staring at him.

"Well, Lord help me," she said. "It *is* you." When she smiled, her cheeks dimpled, and her hazel eyes shone. "You're the one give my gran'son that big ol' bag o' money." She pointed to the back of the room. "You go on back and change in the john. I'll have something hot for you to sip on when you're done."

When Ash returned from the bathroom, the woman was handing out steaming porcelain cups to Marin and John. "Where're you from, honey?" she said to Marin.

"England. I'm teaching at the Academy this year."

The woman saw Ash, picked up another cup, and held it out for him. "Lordy, I believe you could git lost in them clothes. You drink this now, hear?" She walked behind the counter and picked up a telephone and pecked at numbers. She waited, straightening items on the countertop, and then her eyes fixed on nothing and her voice became animated. "Well, you're not gonna b'lieve who's a-settin' here in the store . . . that young feller give Bobby the prize money for his bow-n-arrs . . . I know it . . . well, can you go an' git him?" She turned and read the clock on the wall. "Well, I know it is, but . . . all right . . . oh, Harland? . . . tell him to bring his book." She set the phone in its cradle and eyed the shelves of food. "I know y'all got to be hungry."

John ate two cinnamon rolls, and Marin accepted a package of crackers. Ash sat by the heater, content to sip the bitter coffee for its warmth. In fifteen minutes flashing lights swirled outside the front window where a county sheriff's car eased under the awning. A small head barely showed in the passenger window.

The store's door opened and Bobby Seabolt ran inside, his eyes eager, searching the room, then locking on Ash. He held some papers to his chest. When the boy's grandfather entered wearing a Nacoochee County sheriff's uniform, Ash had to look twice to remember him.

"Didn't know you was throwin' a party, Luler." The sheriff's eyes crinkled when he smiled. "Harland Seabolt," he said and offered his hand to each of them. When he got to John, he paused. "Mister Naylor. I believe you boys are due in my office tomorrow."

Marin knelt in front of Bobby and waited for the boy's eyes to peel away from Ash. "Hello," she said, "I'm a big fan of yours. I heard all about the tournament."

Bobby blinked. "Are you a teacher at that school?"

"Yes, I am."

"Do you teach him?" he said pointing at Ash.

Marin's smile softened. "Robert and I are friends," she said. "Old friends."

Mrs. Seabolt swept hair from the boy's eyes. "Show'm your book, Bobby."

Bobby thrust the book forward to Ash. Two sheets of cardboard were bound along one border by a running stitch of green yarn.

Ash read the cover aloud. " '*How I Met Robin Hood* by Bobby Sea-bolt.' "

"Is your name really 'Robert'?" Bobby asked.

Ash nodded. "Sure is."

Bobby's head swiveled quickly to his grandfather and then back to Ash. "That's my name, too!"

Chapter Thirty

At the sheriff's office, Harland Seabolt presided over the questioning. Present were Ash, John Naylor, Jarvis Troutman, Leo Dawson, and the two county deputies. The meeting was brief and the culpability not open to debate. The van had left the road. Troutman left the meeting without his license and with a summons for a court date.

During Thanksgiving holidays John Naylor settled into Dr. Leonhardt's basement with mixed feelings. In the room next to his were twelve glass cages, all lighted by the eerie red glow of long fluorescent bulbs that warmed a menagerie of native snakes. "Sleeping with snakes" became Naylor's long-suffering mantra.

"You got snakes where you live in the woods?" he asked Ash one night over dinner in the Leonhardt kitchen.

"It's almost December, John. Snakes are denned up for the winter."

John huffed at the irony. "So I'm in a house in town in winter . . . and I got a dozen snakes sleeping downstairs with me. And you're in the woods . . . home free."

"Home free," Ash said and smiled.

*****

They lay low for weeks, giving Guisburn and Troutman time to believe they were free to open up business again. During this time Ash wandered through his forest, practicing with his new bow and stopping often to observe the daily goings-on of wildlife. It became his habit at twilight to walk to Ten Point, where he and Marin talked late into the nights—their conversations wandering through a variety of subjects—all of it weaving into the fabric of their strengthening bond. She would be leaving soon, and their time together became compressed, as though it could not contain all Ash needed to put into it.

John spent his days reading and doing sit-ups and one-arm pushups with his cast pressed to his chest. At night he ran the streets of Naughton with his sweatshirt hood covering his face. And so went most of December.

When Christmas neared, the two ex-students boarded buses for home—John to Texas, Ash to his mother's. They planned to meet three days before the new term and return to Naughton together. Marin left for England to fetch Hubert's copy of the school charter, and with her departure a hole opened up inside Ash that nothing could fill.

For Ash, home was an adjustment. Being with his mother and his dog was comforting, but he was an outsider in his hometown. Neighbors had not spoken to him about his scandal, but the knowledge of it was in their eyes and in the tone of their voices. His thoughts constantly returned to a grisaille portrait—a handsome woman reading by oil lamp inside the walls of Ten Point, until it seemed that she was all he thought about. She had no telephone, so he waited for her call. It came on Christmas Eve.

"How is home for the holidays?" she asked in her English lilt.

"I'm feeling a little stagnant," he said. "But I've been shooting a lot." He opened the book before him to the inscription written in Marin's hand. "Your present came today. Thank you." He waited, sensing her silence as a portent of bad news.

"Ash, I've had no luck with the charter. There's been flooding in the basement, and some of the boxes are quite the mess." He leaned against the kitchen counter, content just to hear her voice.

She was quiet, and he heard a sheep bleating in the background. "Ash? Do you take the Atlanta newspaper?"

"There's one in the next room. Why?"

"I thought you might want to have a look. Page four in section M."

"What's it about?" He waited, listening to the trans-Atlantic static over the line.

"Ash?" she said ever so quietly. "I'm glad you're home."

"Marin, I wish—" He didn't know how to finish his thought.

"I know," she whispered. After a time she asked, "What time do you shoot?"

"Just before dusk."

"I will, too," she said with resolve. "It's been too long since we shot together."

"Isn't your dusk a little earlier than mine?"

"It's still dusk," she said. "Just a little time separates the two. Merry Christmas, Ash." The connection broke.

The thick Sunday edition of the *newspaper* was fanned across the table in the den. A half-page article dominated M-4. "Our Past Selves" the title read. It featured Dr. Sibyl Tanenbaum, whose research with purported passengers through multiple lives was getting attention in the scientific community. At the end of the article, Ash read out loud.

"Dr. Tanenbaum will speak at the University of Georgia Center for Continuing Education Building at 9 a.m. on January 6. Admission is free."

*****

When John Naylor arrived, Ash made up a bed for him on the den sofa. When he had finished, Ash's dog, Archer, climbed up on the blankets and curled into a ball.

"Got my own bed-warmer, huh?" John said. He sat and stroked the dog along the curve of its spine. "Been having more of those dreams," he said. He leaned for his duffel. "Got this in the mail from Mrs. Fitzwalter." He pulled out a book—the same one she had sent Ash, *Robin Hood, the History and the Legend*. He opened it to a marked page. "Not sure what I think 'bout all this." He held up the illustration of two men sparring with quarterstaffs on a log bridge. "You ever think 'bout that night we met at the pool?"

Ash sat down and stared at the picture. "Yeah, I know. I don't get it. Are we supposed to believe that events reincarnate, too?"

Naylor tapped his finger to the larger man fighting on the bridge. "Know what this dude's name was? Book says 'Naylor.' "

Ash picked up section M off the table and dropped it in John's lap. "This lady, Sybil Tanenbaum, researches past lives." John picked up the paper, and the room went quiet as he read. When he looked up, Ash said. "Wanna go hear her talk?"

Naylor looked back at the article and pursed his lips. "Yeah, I do." Archer stretched, forcing John to slide over. "I really gotta sleep with this dog?"

Ash scratched the dog's belly. "Hey, what if she was Cleopatra in another life?"

Naylor studied the dog and let his eyebrows rise. "Or Lizzie Borden."

*****

Dr. Sibyl Tanenbaum walked to the microphone amid enthusiastic applause. She raised her hands three times to quiet the audience. In her mid-forties, she was slight of stature and smartly dressed. There was a businesslike air to her as she waited for quiet.

The audience had its share of college students, but mostly the seats were filled with middle-aged women with graying hair and necklaces that hung over gossamer blouses. To her credit Dr. Tanenbaum did not play to the affirming nods of followers. She spread her attention to everyone, including the blue-clad janitors who lingered by the door. Her lecture led both the skeptical and the devoted through an array of suppositions as to why certain cultures had embraced reincarnation. She was careful to avoid leaps of faith as she laid down the historical groundwork. She wanted each person to think independently, to arrive at a common jumping-off point for the coming blind-step.

"The great impediment with a study like this," she explained, "is that it cannot be measured quantitatively. If someone claims, as many have, to possess insight into this elusive dimension, we must resort to a simple, private judgment: Do we believe them or not? History has paraded a long line of charlatans before us. So how do we know? Is it possible to remember a past life? Is there a conduit for such memories that can preserve a legacy begun before our present physical lives were hatched . . . or re-hatched?"

Closing her notebook, she signaled someone, and a screen lowered behind her. The lights dimmed, and a projector beamed onto the screen a still shot of a balding man wearing thick glasses. In his hand he held an antique pistol.

"Nineteen eighty, Oneida, New York. This man—a CPA—takes apart, cleans, and reassembles this old model revolver in front of my staff. It is a gun we have supplied him after his three-week session with us. At a shooting range, he shoots five bullets into an index card at twenty yards. No mean feat. We have documentation that he has never before shot a gun. No military record. Never a hunter. In fact he supports rigid gun control laws.

"From dreams, he describes in detail a skirmish between federal lawmen and criminals in Arizona Territory in eighteen-eighty-two. He named his colleagues in crime, and this input answered questions that have baffled researchers for years."

The projector blinked and a new slide presented a frail, dark-eyed girl standing by a piano. "Nineteen-ninety, Prague. This seven year old girl awakes at night, walks to her neighbor's apartment, and flawlessly plays what would seem to be the last, unfinished concerto by Frederick Chopin. The little girl has never had a piano lesson. She was recorded on tape and witnessed by both families." Dr. Tanenbaum raised a manila folder. "I could quote dozens of similar cases." The audience was as quiet as an empty church.

"What do these people have in common other than uncanny revelations of alleged previous lives?" She touched a finger to her temple. "Dreams." She took the sides of the podium in her hands. "Dreams are, of course, another abstraction. We can quantify them only by duration, description, and our responses to them. But our research suggests that the rapid eye movement associated with dreamtime is a condition that opens the mind to an alternate conduit. Like a high frequency wave from our own genetic memory. As if the brain raises a new antenna to the radio-genes of the body, although the mechanism is enzymatic, not airwaves. Our research has brought us closer to new quantitative data."

She named two recently identified enzymes and their interactions with DNA. The talk became scientific: enzyme concentrations at peak dreaming time, longevity of chemical aggression, and the DNA "doors" unlocked by these compounds.

When the lecture ended, she opened the floor to questions and dozens of hands went up. Then followed an hour of personal stories: some specious, some intriguing. Then, at the end of the row where Ash and John sat, a tall, raven-haired woman stood up. Her eyes were so pale that it was difficult to determine what she was looking at.

"My name is Jan. Thank you for sharing your work with us." Her voice was gracious, candid. "I would like you to know that there are people who can be of help to you in your research by virtue of a gift with which they have been blessed." Jan tilted her head. "Or cursed." Everyone laughed. "There are visible proofs available to gifted eyes."

Dr. Tanenbaum nodded and smiled. "And are you one of these people, Jan?"

Jan's expression remained thoughtful, humble. "I am."

Their dialogue was a seamless exchange of curiosity and respect—a conversation between friends. Jan was quietly confident, pushing nothing. The audience listened.

"Nothing would please me more than to verify your talents," said Dr. Tanenbaum. "I would indeed welcome such an association. I must tell you, however, that we have put a score of such claimants to the test, and so far—" She smiled and turned up her palms.

"It would be difficult to test, I would think," Jan said.

"Is there any way you might shed light on your claim?" Dr. Tanenbaum asked.

Jan smiled and turned, her transparent eyes seeming to settle on Ash. "Shed light? That is a good term for it."

Ash felt as if he had gone light as air. The faint wheeze in John's breathing stopped altogether.

Jan turned back to Dr. Tanenbaum. "There is an aura in this room that I have seldom seen the match to." She offered a benevolent smile and pointed at Ash and John. "It surrounds those two young men seated there."

"Excuse me," Dr. Tanenbaum interrupted. She smiled at Ash and John. "Do you two have any objection?"

Naylor glanced at Ash, who sat mute and said nothing. "No problem," John said.

265

Dr. Tanenbaum stepped around her podium and spoke without the microphone. "Do you gentlemen know Jan? Have you ever communicated with her in any way?"

When the boys shook their heads, Tanenbaum nodded to Jan. "What do you see?"

Jan turned to face Ash. "Theirs is the most powerful aura in the room. Blue denotes a strong bond. Theirs is deeper—touched with red to make a rich purple."

Dr. Tanenbaum performed a clinical nod. "Assuming you really can see this, could they not simply be good friends? They *are* seated together." She looked to John for confirmation. "I assume you came together?"

"Yes, ma'am," John said. "We're friends."

Jan settled a pair of glasses on her nose. "The young man on the right carries a case of arrows across his back." Jan shook her head. "I've never seen so clear an image."

Inside Ash's head, Jan's voice blurred, as if he were listening from under water. He felt every eye in the room on him. After Dr. Tanenbaum spoke at length, Jan sat down, and everyone applauded. People stood and milled around, some knotting around Dr. Tanenbaum, who listened like a priest hearing confessions.

Ash's gaze fixed on Jan, who was begging off from a clutch of admirers. Cold needles of doubt pricked at him, and he started toward her, but now Dr. Tanenbaum stood before him, smiling. John stepped beside Ash, and both shook the researcher's hand.

"Thank you for sitting in the bell jar for us today. Are you boys out of school?"

"Very much so," John said.

"Well, did any of what Jan had to say have any relevance for you?" She settled her gaze on Ash, narrowed her eyes, and leaned toward him. "Are you all right?"

When Ash nodded and excused himself from the room, Dr. Tanenbaum shifted her concern to John's cast. "Well, something big must have broken that arm."

"Stopped a van," John said and smiled. "You should see the van."

"Is your friend all right?" she said. "Did we touch a nerve today?"

John considered her earnest expression. "Ma'am, you might'a touched his soul."

In front of the building, as Ash and John waited for a taxi, two different women approached them, affirming Jan's vision inside. Then a silver BMW glided to a stop before them. The passenger window lowered, and the driver leaned toward them.

"I'm sorry if I embarrassed you. I'm Jan Salvatore." She confirmed her apology with an authentic smile. "But I've never seen such a display of color."

Ash knelt to her window. "Just one question: Do you know Marin Fitzwalter?"

Jan blinked. "No. Who is she?" Her eyes slanted with empathy. "I can see I've upset you. Can I give you both a ride somewhere? It would give us time to talk."

John ushered Ash into the passenger seat. He got in back. Despite Jan's attempts at conversation, the ride into town was strained. Only when they stopped at the bus station did Ash deliberately look at her.

"Do you do this for a living? See people's auras or whatever?"

She laughed quietly. "I'm a choir director at Saint Paul's here in Athens. And I teach violin at home." She turned in her seat to address both of them. "I really don't mean to pry into your lives, but let me reassure you of something: What I see in you is good. Your bond is very pure. You should feel fortunate to have crossed paths this time around."

Ash looked out the windshield and mumbled, "You said we were purple."

Jan smiled. "I wish I had such a friend." When Ash made no reply, she added, "If you're thinking that what I've said is your burden . . . don't. This is your life—made up of your choices. You're simply living it with someone you've lived with before."

Ash swallowed. "What if it's not just us? What would you say to six or seven?"

The skin on Jan's forehead tightened. "Goodness!" she whispered.

Ash opened his door and got out. "We appreciate the ride."

"I'm glad to help," she said.

As John climbed from the back seat, Ash hovered on the sidewalk a moment, then leaned back to the window. "What's so special about purple?" he asked.

She closed her eyes and thought for a time. "Imagine mixing the blue of the sky with your own blood. When blood is in the bond, there is no higher plane."

When Ash made no reply, Jan leaned closer and lowered her voice to a whisper. "Don't give up," she said, her pale eyes intense now.

Ash frowned. "On what?"

Jan produced a helpless smile. "I don't know."

Chapter Thirty-One

"I found it," Marin said. Her voice over the line was distant but charged with purpose. "All forest lands west of the Loop Road are protected from construction. "It's in the charter, Ash, page twenty-four. I'm posting a copy to you today."

" 'Posting'?" He leaned back against the wall of Dr. Leonhardt's hallway. "You're not coming back?"

"I have so much to do here, Ash. The school's debts fall on me now."

He slid to the floor and sat. "I heard Dr. Tanenbaum." He waited, but Marin remained quiet. "There was another lady there. Jan Salvatore. Do you know her?"

The silence that followed made him regret his question. Knowing he had disappointed her, he closed his eyes and let the back of his head settle against the wall. The Atlantic Ocean seemed too great a distance to carry his apology.

"No, Ash," she said, a tone of forgiveness in the two words. Several seconds ticked by. "I left something for you at Ten Point. It's under Hubert's bed."

He imagined going there, entering that empty room and feeling her smothering absence. Over the line he heard sheep bleat in the background. Then a tiny bell rattled and a door closed.

"I have another book for you, but I can't mail it. I'll find a way to get it to you."

In the silence that followed, Ash heard a clock chime on the hour.

"I must go, Ash. The shop is closing." She exhaled a long sigh. "I know you need more explanation. I'm sorry I don't have it." She paused. "See you at dusk?"

He gripped the phone tighter. "See you at dusk." Then the line went dead.

Within the hour Alan, Cat and Tucker arrived, and all gathered around a tray of cookies and hot chocolate in Dr. Leonhardt's kitchen. They spoke of their holidays at home, though neither Ash nor John mentioned the Tanenbaum lecture. When those stories were exhausted, Ash initiated talk of their plans.

"I still see the copier as their logical source. They're not going to use the same method but they might think up something else." He turned to Dr. Leonhardt. "Will Ms. Esparza help us with that? Would she let us check her copier every day?"

"It will just take a phone call," Dr. Leonhardt said with a deep nod.

"We need someone who knows electronics," Ash said.

Cat clapped his hands once and ceremoniously swept them to Tucker, who, with a mouthful of cookie, broke into a broad smile. "That would be me," Tucker mumbled.

For ten minutes—during which time Tucker touched not another cookie—he expounded upon his expertise with machines, computers, and wiring. Because his father had been a computer repairman with a workshop in his basement, Tucker had soaked up an education in the field. When he finished, he rewarded himself with another cookie.

When the meeting broke up, Ash found Alan waiting in the hallway. "You're mighty quiet tonight," Ash said. "Or was it just Tucker's nonstop oration?"

Alan worked the buttons of his coat. "Staying in the woods tonight?"

Ash nodded.

Alan seemed curiously somber. "Elaine's out in the doc's car. She needs to talk to you. What do you say we drive you out as far as Ten Point?"

Ash nodded and got his coat.

The Buick idled in the driveway. Elaine sat in the front, her head bent forward so Ash could not see her face through the window. He got into the back and sat. Alan slipped behind the wheel and reached to Elaine and touched her shoulder. Still, she did not move. He pulled out of the drive and headed for the highway.

They drove out Seven Bridges Road and turned at the dirt lane that bumped down through the trees past the school's no trespassing signs. No one in the car had spoken a word. In front of the old lodge Alan cut the ignition, and the sound of the river drifted up to them from the valley. He reached and combed Elaine's hair from her face.

She looked up. "Can you and I talk first?" she whispered to Alan.

Ash opened his door. "I have to get something out of the cabin. I'll be back."

The room was still and cold and dark. He clicked on his flashlight and crossed the plank floor to Hubert's bed. Underneath was a long bundle of rolled-up blanket lashed with rope. On top of the mattress he unwrapped it to find Hubert's old bow, the horn, and two handmade arrows fletched with gray goose feathers. Each shaft was tipped with a broad metal point sharpened to a bright edge. All of it belonged in a museum.

Ash shook his head, certain he could never string such a stout weapon, much less draw it back. After rewrapping it, he tucked the bundle under his arm and walked outside to find Alan standing outside the car, waiting. Ash handed over the bundle.

"Store that at the doc's for me, will you?"

"Will do," Alan said and propped the package diagonally in the back seat.

When Ash sat in the driver's seat, Alan squatted next to him and looked from one to the other. "You two are the best friends I have. Remember that." He rose and shut the door, and they listened to his footsteps crunch the gravel and fade up the driveway.

Now the quiet interior of the car took on the feel of a confessional. "Just before Thanksgiving," Elaine began, "I bought a test." She looked down at her hands in her lap. A silver tear shone on her cheek. "I was flunking poli-sci. I hated my teacher." She laughed at her feeble rationalization. "That wrestler, Guy, wanted to date my roommate, so he told us he could get us the final. When he did, we really didn't know for sure it was the test. I mean, how could we? So, sure, we went over it. It had all the answers." She sighed and looked up at Ash. "It was the test, all right. I made an A."

She faced her window. "My parents had known I was flunking," she went on, her voice coming off the windowglass distant and hollow. "They wanted to take me out of school. The homecoming title was my only argument to stay, but to keep that I had to have a C average." She buried her face in her hands. "I feel like I'm part of the reason you and John got expelled. I'm so sorry."

"You don't owe me an apology, Elaine."

She turned to him with a bewildered face. "You're not angry?"

Ash chose his words with care. "Everybody makes bad decisions, Elaine." When her eyes seemed to beg for more than this, he added, "If you're worried about Alan's opinion, I think he would still love you if you single-handedly shut down the free press."

An awkward laugh burst from her, but she sobered right away. "I'm afraid some damage has already been done . . . to Alan and me, I mean."

"Well," he said, "maybe love allows mistakes . . . and expects re-pair." He listened to the sound of his own voice and knew that those were words Marin might have spoken. "Has Guy made any offers recently? About selling you any tests?"

"He told my roommate starting next week he could get her any test she wanted."

Ash nodded and watched her wipe her eyes with a tissue. "Do you remember the jock who spilled water on you in the cafeteria? Guy paid him to do that."

Her expression of atonement tightened to incredulity. "Why?"

Ash looked at his hands. "Dress code was relaxed. You had on a pretty thin top."

Two knocks sounded on the glass next to Ash, and Alan opened the door. "My noble gesture to give you privacy has just yielded to the first stage of hypothermia."

Ash stepped out, and Alan slid into the seat and started the engine.

"You have a wise friend," Elaine said to Alan.

"Young Asher of Greenwood," Alan returned. "None wiser."

Elaine leaned across Alan to squeeze Ash's hand.

"Keep each other warm," Ash said and closed the door.

Staring at Ash through the glass, Alan mouthed: *Thank you.*

The car's red taillights blinked through the black trunks of the winter trees. Then there was only the empty cabin and the cold night and the sounds of the river below. With the knowledge that Troutman was back in business, Ash started home for Beechwood.

PART SIX

The Keepers of the Wood

Ash introduced Tucker to Juanita Esparza, and the three of them looked over the copier with Tucker guiding them through the names and functions of parts. Troutman's rogue tray—that had once covertly collected tests—was missing.

"Nothing seems out of place," Tucker said. He shrugged. "Maybe he hasn't gotten to this machine yet. I'll bet rigging it will take longer than a maintenance visit."

Ash turned to Ms. Esparza. "Then he needs to get into your office after hours."

She looked at Ash with wide eyes. "Jyou mean . . . break in?"

Ash picked up a pencil from her desk. "Do you have anything I can cut with?"

She opened a drawer and handed over a new pair of scissors. Carefully, he snipped off the very tip of the eraser and plucked up the loose piece from her desk.

"Your window is pretty high to reach and very visible from the road. I doubt they'll try that way. When you leave each day, pinch this into the doorjamb." He demonstrated clamping the sliver of rubber under the hinge from the outside. "If you find it on the floor or missing, call Dr. Leonhardt."

She nodded quickly four times. "Jyes, I call heem."

*****

They were not long in waiting. The next morning when Ash stepped from the woods onto the field, John Naylor was standing by the target.

When they met, John held out a note scrawled in Dr. Leonhardt's hand. *Juan. E., eraser dropped / Mrs. Fitz. will call at 6 p.m.*. Ash looked up, his face sharp with expectation, but Naylor was studying the woods.

"Where do you stay out there? I walked around an hour following those ribbons."

"Ribbons?" Ash said.

He followed John's gaze to a pink survey tape fluttering at the edge of mid-field. Twenty yards deeper into the woods he saw another.

"It's started," Ash said.

At four thirty-five Dr. Johns drove out of the parking lot across the road from the science building. At four thirty-seven Ash and Tucker walked through Juanita Esparza's door. After proudly displaying the piece of pink eraser in her palm, she stood back as they moved the copy machine from the wall. Tucker frowned at the electrical outlet.

"There's another cord here." He opened the back panel and studied the interior.

"I have to leave by five," Ms. Esparza whispered. "I pick up my boys."

Before Ash could reply, Tucker rose up from the machine. "We should get some pictures of this," he said. "You know, document the evidence while she's here."

Ash checked the clock. "Alan's got a camera, but he's at the *Clarion.*" He picked up the phone, punched in the numbers and nodded reassuringly to Ms. Esparza. "We'll get you out of here on time, ma'am."

Alan and Cat arrived just before five. Ms. Esparza stood by the door, her purse clutched in both hands pressed against her stomach, her eyes worrying over the hardware strewn across the carpet. Alan snapped pictures to record each phase of the dismantling. Ash checked the clock on the wall: three minutes till five.

"Ms. Esparza, is there any way we could finish up without you? We'll clean up and lock up. I promise."

She frowned at the disarray on the floor. "I can be fired for this?" There was a tremor in her voice, and everyone stopped working to acknowledge her fear.

"Okay, guys," Ash said. "We're leaving. Right now. Leave everything where it is." He faced his three friends. "I'm going to need your belts."

After buckling the belts together to make a ten foot length, Ash walked to the window, unlocked it, and cranked open the glass. "We'll leave before you, Ms. Esparza. So you won't have to worry." He slipped the end buckle over the crank handle and lowered the chain of belts outside the building. Ms. Esparza's frightened eyes cut from Ash to the window. "Next time you see this room, it'll look like it did an hour ago."

With her face pinched with worry, Juanita Esparza followed them into the hall. After locking her office she led the way out the front door, which locked automatically behind them. Without looking back, Ms. Esparza crossed the street to the parking lot.

Within seconds, Ash had shimmied up the wall through the window. Shortly afterward, the outside door opened, and the waiting trio poured in like a pack of thieves.

After five minutes of following the new wire inside the copier, Tucker held his flashlight beam on a gray plastic box. "Aha!" When he ducked out from the machine, he fixed his gaze on Ash. "It's a flash drive unit!"

"A what?"

"It's the new computer storage device that's gonna replace the floppy disc. It captures everything the machine scans and stores it."

Ash knelt down to see the box. "How many pages could it store?"

"Oh, maybe ten thousand," Tucker quipped. "All he has to do is pop out the little plug-in and stick a new one back in. It would take less than ten seconds."

"It's getting dark," Cat said. "We shouldn't keep this light on much longer."

Ash looked at the clock and froze. It was five fifty. Marin would call at six.

"I've got to get to Dr. Leonhardt's house. Can you guys finish up?"

Alan tossed Ash a ring of keys. "Take the doc's car. It's in the lot."

Ash sprinted to the old blue Buick and fired it up. When he was on the uphill leg of Academy Drive, a security car rushed past him going south. It barely slowed at the stop sign and whined up the hill, stopping in front of the science building with its lights flashing. Ash braked and felt his stomach go weightless.

Craning his head out the window, he saw the campus police hurry out of their car. On impulse Ash U-turned the Buick, roared to the stop sign and braked. Up the hill he watched a man usher a tall figure to the car. The next man brought two shorter silhouettes, one rounded and the other lean. Slapping the steering wheel with both hands, Ash carved a turn in the intersection and drove toward town.

Twenty minutes late for the call, Ash found the house empty. Two calls showed on the phone's memory pad, both with an international coding. No messages were left. He tried calling the number, and the ringing went on for a full minute before he hung up.

It was three in the morning when Dr. Leonhardt returned from the campus security office. Weary and pale, he sat with Ash and John at the kitchen table.

"Your friends are still answering questions," Leonhardt began, "but I think the school will not press criminal charges. It will be handled by the disciplinary board, not the sheriff. Naturally, Dr. Johns interprets this as an attempt to steal tests off the secretary's computer." He passed a folded paper to Ash. "Alan gave me this for you."

Ash read it aloud. " 'We got the copier back together. No questions asked about it. I had the bright idea to look on Ms. E's computer to see if there was anything there that could be stolen. Computers must be tapped to security. Stay in the woods. Meet Sunday night at the doc's."

Naylor shook his head. "We're hurting on the scoreboard." He flicked fingers as he counted. "We've wrecked a van. Totaled the dean's car. Three of us booted out of school. Three more prob'ly 'bout to join us." John's intelligent brown eyes looked as hard as smooth stones lifted from a creek. "Hate losing a home game."

Dr. Leonhardt reached across the table, one hand clasping John's forearm and the other Ash's. "This is three more reasons for us to succeed. Be grateful for such friends."

*****

On Sunday night, amongst the crowd in Dr. Leonhardt's study, Ash sat with a large brown envelope in his lap. He watched Tucker on the sofa as he related to Anne Metter and Elaine the story of their interrogation by security and then their fast-track expulsion by the board. Alan, Cat and Dr. Leonhardt spoke quietly at the doc's armchair. The mood in the room was funereal.

John Naylor returned from the kitchen with a tray of cheese, crackers, and sliced apples. Everyone stopped talking when John set the tray on the table. Not even Tucker made a move for the food. Ash took the moment to begin.

"We're going to take this to a new level." He spread his hands to include all of them. "We're eight strong." He nodded to Anne and Elaine. "And you two—because you're still students—can go where we can't."

"What do we do now?" whined Tucker. "My parents expect me home." Looking sick he filled his cheeks with air and exhaled. "But I don't look forward to seeing them."

Ash sat forward in his chair. "Think of this as an opportunity. What *we* have is time on our hands. We've got no classes, no homework, no sports."

"No money, no cafeteria, no place to live," Tucker said, taking up Ash's rhythm.

Ash took his time establishing eye contact with Cat, John, Alan, and, finally, Tucker. "You can all live with me."

Elaine sat up straighter. "You mean in the forest? In winter?"

Ash nodded. "Think of it as a long camping trip." When Elaine laid her head on Alan's shoulder, Ash added. "Dr. Leonhardt has agreed to talk to your parents."

"How long will we stay out there?" Tucker asked.

"Long as it takes," Ash said. "Look, Guisburn and Troutman have a new system in place, and we know how it works. We'll catch them at it and call in the campus cops."

"Couldn't we just stay here . . . or at Mrs. Fitz's cabin?" Tucker asked.

Ash shook his head. "We've got to be close to the construction site."

"So which are you doing?" Elaine asked. "Exposing the scam or saving a forest?"

"Both," Ash said and opened the envelope. "This is a copy of the school charter that Mrs. Fitzwalter sent. It's clear. All of the forest west of the Loop Road is protected."

"Well, if we stay out there with you, what do we eat?" Tucker complained.

Dr. Leonhardt tossed a vinyl checkbook on the table. "Food's taken care of."

Ash opened the cover and read the printed name on the top check. "Fitzwalter, Limited?"

"She sent it with the charter," Dr. Leonhardt said. "I am trustee of the funds."

Alan frowned at the newly printed checks. "What about her money problem?"

Dr. Leonhardt laid a stack of twenties on the table. "I checked with the bank. There's plenty of money. I can do the shopping and drive it out to the hunting lodge."

The room was quiet as each person came to terms with what had to be done.

"We can do this," Ash said and stood. "Who's in?"

John gathered his long legs beneath him and stood his full six-foot-five. "Me," he said and glanced at Dr. Leonhardt. "Thanks, but I'm done sleeping with the snakes."

"I'm in," Cat said and stood beside Naylor. They made a matched set with their injured arms slung against their torsos.

Staring at Cat, Tucker was like a puppy in a pet store window. "Well," he said, pushing up from the sofa. "If you're sure there'll be enough food . . . I'm in, too."

Slapping his hands to his knees, Alan rose. "Young Asher, you have your scribe."

Elaine stood. "I'll help any way I can." Alan kissed the top of her head.

Anne laughed as she got to her feet. "Well, I'm glad you don't have to be thrown out of school to be in this club. But I'm definitely in."

Ash settled back in his chair and nodded once. "Okay," he breathed.

Alan cleared his throat. "Isn't this where we say, 'One for all . . . all for one?' "

They laughed, and then the room began to buzz with conversations. Alan and Elaine marveled at the snake dream John Naylor related. Cat and Anne watched Tucker arrange crackers on the table to diagram the break-in at the science building. Dr. Leonhardt read from the charter. Ash watched them all—their animation and optimism. A combined energy filled the room. He touched his fingers to the postmark stamped on the envelope. *Nottinghamshire,* it read in black ink. He closed his eyes and imagined Marin alone in a room of quarried stone as she pored over files and records by candlelight.

You're the only one missing, he thought. Then a chill rippled down his spine like ice water as he wondered, for the first time, if he would ever see her again.

Chapter Thirty-Three

They worked well as a team on the new forest abodes that were spaced around the hill from Beechwood. Digging out floor plans, sawing log supports, and hauling out dirt, six labored on the dwellings, while one always stood vigil at the edge of the west field.

Elaine proved to be a tireless worker. She had never before done manual work, but now the boys vied for her help—each wanting her shovel ringing at his personal home site. Anne, at first, showed an aversion to dirt, spending much time at the river trying to wash stains from her clothing as soon as they appeared. When Cat loaned her his woodworking coveralls, she was a changed woman. Like Elaine, she was a dynamo.

When the shelters were completed, the banished five settled into variations of their former lives as Academy students. Cat maintained a workout regimen that furthered the rehabilitation of his shoulder and brought his body back to a wrestler's fitness. One-arm pull-ups on tree limbs eventually graduated to two arms. He ran the trails by daylight and at night logged grueling sets of wind sprints in the archery field.

Tucker embraced his exile like an inductee into the Order of St. Francis. He spent long hours reading his Bible in the sunny spots by the river, where between recitations he attempted to befriend chipmunks and wrens—talking to them as though they were liaisons who would report directly to God concerning his spiritual progress.

Alan began the writing of their story that, he promised, would one day be published. At night he played his guitar inside his hovel, expanding the *Ballad of Young Asher of Greenwood* to include new characters: brother heroes laying claim to their places in the legend. His penchant for hyperbole was no longer necessary now that he had taken a front row seat in a real adventure. The truth was enough.

John cut away his cast and began the slow recovery of atrophied muscle. During this time he discovered the latent watchman in his soul. He loved to roam the fringes of the forest, observing, always on guard for the return of the surveyors. He carried his vigil into darkness, realizing his ebony skin was allied with the night for just such a purpose.

Friendships blossomed, especially between John and the others. He called Cat "Red." They shared the common language of athletics and physical discipline. John's singing voice found a fan in Alan, who wrote harmonies just for that bottomless bass.

With Tucker, whom John called "Big Tuck," Naylor whiled away whole nights in discussions of religions, especially those that embraced reincarnation. He told Tucker about the Tanenbaum lecture and the lady named Jan. Awed by this story, Tucker asked daily if anyone could see any purple air gathering around him.

On a cold morning at the end of February, Ash climbed to Ten Point for the supplies Dr. Leonhardt was due to drop off. On the cooler was an envelope from Ash's mother. Opening it he found a letter, a fifty-dollar bill, and a black and white photograph.

In the photo his mother sat by a creek. She appeared to be in her late-twenties. Her hair was long, rippling over the turned-up collar of a belted overcoat as she looked out at something beyond the frame. A sunburst of light reflected off the water—a halo backlighting her and blurring the trees. Ash opened the letter and read.

Your father never mastered the camera, but here is one we liked. Our favorite place in England. An enchanting forest and its woods nymph . . . me!

Ash looked long and hard at his mother's image and at the shapes behind her. He flipped over the photo and there was his father's faded handwriting. *Every sailor's dream—March 19, 1983—Sherwood Forest.* He flipped back to the photo. Identifying the trees was challenging if not impossible, but one drew him. At the edge of the stream gnarled roots spread from the smooth bole of a gigantic tree perched on a rise. Its ghostly trunk faded into the white frame of the photo. It looked like a beech . . . an old one.

After crossing the river back to Beechwood, Ash heard the growl of heavy equipment in the west field. He lay down the cooler and ran toward the sound. Even before he could see the field, the scent of freshly churned earth and pine sap assaulted his senses. He slowed, crept forward, and watched a bulldozer belch black smoke as it uprooted an oak. Tracks checkered across the sod in front of his target. On the far side of the field a new opening had been gashed through the pines. A dump truck and trailer were parked on the Loop Road.

Ten yards into the forest, trees lay butchered inside a forty-foot wide swath. A man in blue coveralls clamped a cigar stub in his mouth and drove the dozer's blade into a big sourwood. Ash watched it topple and crash. Another man cranked a chainsaw and began the limbing. The dozer backed up, sloshing through a pool of water where a spring had been exposed. A rainbow of oil filmed its surface. Ash ran for Naughton.

When he burst into Dr. Leonhardt's house, the old man stared at him, a coffee cup poised before his mouth. "They're cutting a road into the forest," Ash reported.

"A road!" Leonhardt stood and stormed down the hall. Ash watched him jab at numbers on the telephone. "Put Candler Reeve on. This is Dr. Leonhardt . . . what? . . . Leonhardt at Greenwood Downs Academy . . . well, I know I am, but I still want to talk to him . . . well, then tell him I have a copy of the original school charter . . . tell him the construction stops now!" He slammed the phone down and punched numbers again.

"Put me through, Sara . . . I don't care about that, and he won't ei- ther." He stiffened an arm against the wall and leaned. "Richard, get someone out to west campus to put a stop to the construction . . . well, that's what they say, but we know better, don't we? . . . That's my chapel money, Richard."

He marched past Ash into the kitchen. "He's sending someone from security." Sitting at the table he pushed away his coffee cup. "These damn lawyers. If they've doctored up that charter—" He looked up. "Where are you going?" But Ash was out the door.

At the field Ash found a security car parked at the curb. The truck was gone. The dozer sat idle in the field. A campus cop stood next to it writing something, while another man stretched yellow crime-scene tape across the new opening in the pines.

Ash skirted the field, watching the two men, until a voice came out of nowhere. "I emptied my water bottle into the gas tank." John Naylor rose up from a depression in the ground, leaves raining down from him. "Driver was getting cigars from his truck." John glared at the dozer. "It'll hold a while, but—" He shook his head.

Ash exhaled a long sigh. "I'd hug you if I thought I could reach around you."

Naylor gave him a doubtful look. "I'll settle for lunch. The doc send any milk?"

For the rest of the day the five foresters took turns keeping watch over the dozer from the shadows. It was almost dark when Dr. Johns and a heavy man dressed in a black overcoat walked under the yellow tape at the breach in the pines. The bigger man carried a long roll of paper, while his other hand tried to protect his silver hair from the wind. Stopping at the churned up mud in the field, he pointed into the woods and swept his hand like a surrogate dozer blade. Princeton Johns made deep assenting nods.

Ash worked his way around the field to the Loop perimeter and found a black Lexus parked at the curb. Peering through the dark-tinted glass he could see nothing. He walked to the back of the car. The license tag read *Reeve 1*.

*****

The next day while Naylor and Ash did laundry in the "snake pit" of Dr. Leonhardt's basement, the door flung open, and Cat rushed in breathing hard. "They're back! The dozer is up and running, and trees are going down!"

Ash pounded the top of the dryer with his fist, the sound like a big bass drum. "Better to kill the dozer than the dryer," Naylor suggested with a straight face.

Cat was still catching his breath. "How're we gonna stop 'em this time?"

"Don't know, but we'd better get out there," Naylor said and tossed a warm, clean sweatshirt to Ash, who squirmed into it without delay. When his head popped through he was face to face with one of the cages. A thick-bodied water snake was coiled on a bed of sawdust. The cage next to it contained a hefty hog nose snake.

"John," Ash said. "Find a couple of pillowcases."

The middle of the field was churned to mush. A dozen felled trees had been limbed, dragged out, and stacked on a trailer. A dozer and chainsaw growled from the woods.

"I'm going to get these workmen out on the street," Ash explained. "When I do, John, you empty your snake on the floor of the dozer. Cat, yours goes next to the big mud puddle. Then get out of there. I'll handle the rest."

"What are you gonna do?" Naylor asked.

Ash watched the dozer topple another tree. "Perpetuate a myth," he said.

In a few minutes Ash entered the field from the Loop Road, waving his arms and yelling at the workmen. The dozer operator caught sight of him and craned his neck forward. Ash cupped his hands around his mouth to yell, then pointed toward the road. The man shut off the engine and stood up in the dozer. His partner shut down the chainsaw and set it down on the ground.

"Son," the driver hollered, "you ain't s'posed to be out here!"

Ash pointed to the street again. "That trailer out there rolled a little downhill."

The man fixed a hard stare on the wide gap in the pines and then turned around and yelled to his partner. "Carlton! Did you chock the trailer?"

" 'Course I did!" the sawyer barked.

Ash walked with both men across the scarred field, telling them about seeing the trailer roll a few feet. When they reached the street, the two men scowled at the wheels.

"Somebody's took off with our damn chocks, Lloyd," Carlton declared.

"Well," Lloyd said, rubbing his chin whiskers. "I guess people would steal your socks if you didn't lace up your boots. Let's see can't we find us some rocks."

Ash was the first back on the field. Scanning the far edge of the woods, he saw no trace of John or Cat. But he could sense them out there, watching.

"Son!" Lloyd yelled to Ash's back. "You *still* ain't s'posed to be out here!"

"I know where some big rocks are," Ash called back and hurried toward the pool of water that had formed in the mud.

Now Carlton was yelling at him, explaining that Ash had to leave the work site. Then Carlton turned to a yelp from Lloyd, who cursed loudly and back-pedaled from the dozer. Sloshing into a slick area, his feet went out from under him, and he sat down hard.

"There's a damn snake big as my arm a-settin' on my floorboard!" he declared.

As Carlton edged toward the dozer for a look, Ash squatted by the puddle and then rose up holding the water snake. "You must have opened up a nest of moccasins!" he called with the snake dangling from his hand. "There's a bunch over here!"

The workmen started backing away, their heads turning in quick jerks as they inspected the ground around them. Carrying his snake, Ash moved to the dozer.

"This one's even bigger!" he yelled, his voice full of awe. He climbed up into the dozer. With provident timing, the hog-nose snake opened its mouth and hissed. Ash recoiled and followed with a dramatic grab. "I got it! But another one just crawled behind your panel! Probably drawn to the heat!" Both creatures were sluggish in the cold, but Ash made them appear to writhe in his grip.

The mud-caked driver stared wild-eyed. "I gotta damn axe out in my truck," he suggested, but he made no move to get it. Both men seemed hypnotized by the snakes.

"Sometimes a hundred den up together," Ash said. "Okay if I keep these?"

"Put 'em in a damn casserole if you want to," Carlton said and picked up his saw.

The two men picked their way carefully across the muddy field toward the new opening in the pines. When his boot made a sucking sound in the mud, Carlton made a sudden sideways jump, causing Lloyd to trip and fall on his side in a puddle.

"Dammit, Carlton!"

Carlton helped him up, and they fast-walked off the field together.

Chapter Thirty-Four

On Friday night the basketball game filled the gymnasium parking lot. Late-comer cars had spilled over onto the surrounding grass. By game-time the temperature had dropped into the twenties. A light dusting of snow had fallen and blown away. Behind the car farthest from the gym, Ash huddled in a blanket inside a cluster of holly bushes. From there he had a view across the street to the science building.

Cat and Tucker were at the art building. Alan was stationed inside the English building. John, Anne, and Elaine were on the top floor of the math building with a view of the roads in the valley.

The basketball game erupted with frequent cheers and blasts of air horns. There was no movement on the streets. A cold hour crept by as Ash flexed his muscles against the cold and blew into his hands.

A little before ten o'clock a vehicle turned into the gym lot and inched along the rows of cars. Ash ducked when the headlights swept his way and then passed over him. The car stopped and backed up. Then the lights blinked off, and the engine died.

With his cheek to the earth, Ash slowed his breathing and listened to gasoline slosh in the tank. "Hey, you still alive?" It was John Naylor's deep voice.

Ash approached and crouched next to Dr. Leonhardt's Buick. "What's wrong?"

"Nothing. Get in. Too cold to sit out there." Ash slid into the warmth of the car and pulled the door gently to catch. "Hot chocolate in the backseat," Naylor offered.

Ash turned for the thermos and saw the blanket tied up with Hubert's bow. As he starting unwrapping it for an extra layer, John's big hand pulled him down.

"That them?" Naylor whispered. "Over there by the science building?"

Ash eased his head up and saw two dark shapes move at the window of Dr. Johns's office—the same window that Ash had once crawled out. "Are they going in or coming out?" he wondered aloud. When he cranked down the car window, cold air poured in like water. He heard a metallic *pop!* At the building, a blink of light flashed off the glass as the window pivoted. There were scuffling sounds and grunts, and then all was quiet. The same blink of light flashed as the window closed.

"Here we go," Ash said and dug into his pocket for his flashlight. "I'm gonna signal Anne and Elaine." When he was halfway out the door the flashlight banged against the doorframe and hit the hard ground. He picked it up and tried the switch. It was dead. He slapped the light against his palm, flipped the switch repeatedly, and looked at Naylor.

"Gave my light to Big Tuck," John said.

"Turn the car to face the math building," Ash said. "Use the headlights."

John fired up the Buick and backed it over a rise until, like a piece of artillery, it was strategically aimed high across the valley. He worked the lights and waited.

"Keep trying," Ash prompted. "I'm going across the street."

He reached Ms. Esparza's window in time to see a faint glow of light disappear behind something placed against the glass from inside. The hushed sound of voices came from inside the room. Across the street the Buick's lights blinked its repetitive message.

A metallic *clang* broke the silence. Ash recognized the buckling of the copier's panel as it was pulled free. He knew they were inside the machine. All that was left was to collect the flash drive and insert a new one. In half a minute Troutman would have everything back in place.

Ash ran to the far side of the building where the trespassers had entered. The window was closed tight. Then it occurred to him that they had no need to leave by the way they had entered. They could exit the building through any door they chose. Now the prospect of detaining them seemed out of his reach. He took a step toward John and cupped his hands around his mouth, but before he could yell, just a few yards to his right, the building's front door opened.

Backing into the shrubs, Ash watched the door swing wider, and Troutman came out onto the walkway, followed by Guisburn, who turned and eased the door shut. Troutman started toward Ash and stopped with a sudden start. Guy almost stumbled on top of him before he saw Ash. They stood in a triangle of uncertainty, as a roar from the gymnasium added an eerie soundtrack to the standoff.

"What do you want?" Troutman challenged.

"What you stole from me," Ash answered in a flat tone.

Guy cinched up a small pack on his back and walked up to Ash until their breaths comingled into a single cloud. "What is it you think you're gonna do here, Chief?"

Ash spoke in a calm, direct manner. "You've been caught."

Guy laughed. "So *you* say." He slipped off the pack and tossed it to Troutman. "The chief's stepped into a bucket load, Trout." Even before Troutman could respond, the attack came. Ash barely got his hands up to cushion the blow. Guy's arms were clamped around Ash, driving forward like a train. Ash back-pedaled, scrambling to keep his feet under him. Then one of Guisburn's powerful legs hooked behind Ash's calf, and they slammed to the cold earth. A pain ripped through Ash from his tailbone to his skull.

Guy immediately jockeyed for pinning position, and in that split second unlocked his grip to affect a new one. Ash took this opportunity to roll away. Guy made a grab for him and was surprised to feel his wrist clamped in the archer's grip. Ash lurched over Guy's back, forcing the arm to go with him and Guisburn grimaced and cursed and kicked himself free. He stood rubbing his shoulder, but it was a ploy. In a flash he took Ash down again.

The impact was numbing. Ash felt as if his bones had come unglued.

Guisburn lay belly down on Ash's back, the wrestler's legs splayed wide for leverage and his arms tightened around Ash's chest. They were reversed in direction so that their bodies formed two Y's joined at their stems. The cold grit of the earth pressed into Ash's face. Above him Guisburn's lungs heaved in and out like an enraged bear. His weight was suffocating. Spikes of grass pricked at Ash's eyes, but still he could see Troutman's smirk.

Then something shut down in Guy. His arms slackened, and the stifling weight lifted from Ash. Guy gasped an unintelligible word—high-pitched, almost feminine—and cold air washed over Ash's back. He turned to see Guisburn hovering in the air above him, somehow floating, his arms and legs flailing, his face contorted, and his teeth bared.

John Naylor stood tall as he held Guisburn's body four feet off the ground. His left fist clasped the thick mass of Guy's curly hair, arching the neck to a cruel angle. The other hand maintained a viselike grip on Guy's crotch. In a desperate surge to free himself the squealing wrestler spat and tried to land blows on his tormenter, but he quickly stiffened with pain as Naylor lowered him—belly to the earth—and planted a knee in Guy's back, punishing the arch of his spine.

"*Don't!*" Guisburn's scream tore from his throat, uninhibited and pleading.

John raised Guy into the air again, paused for a moment, and slammed him back to the ground like a sack of cement. Air wheezed out of Guisburn in a rush, and he lay still, moaning, his eyes shut.

When Ash stood he could see that Troutman was considering his escape routes. Naylor glided sideways with three cat-like steps, effectively blocking one passage.

"We didn't do nothing to you," Troutman snarled.

"Yeah," Ash replied, "you did." He wiped his lip with the back of his hand and it came away with a smear of blood. "You stole something more than tests."

Troutman hissed through his teeth, and then something changed in his face as if an amusing thought had occurred to him. "Hell, you could be the ones stealing here tonight." He looked at the pack in his hand and laughed. "Maybe it's us who's catching you." He took a step sideways, and Ash mirrored the movement.

"You're not leaving here," Ash said.

"You talk big with that big black ape backing you."

John Naylor laughed—just a whisper through his nose. "This big black ape is not your problem," he said and nodded toward Ash. "He is."

Guy turned on his side and gingerly pushed himself up on hands and knees so that he could glare at Naylor. "You chicken-shit sonovabitch, blindsiding me, grabbing my nuts like that!" Red-faced and livid, Guisburn stood and puffed out his chest. "Let's see how you do face to face, football star."

John smiled. "Wasn't easy to find those little chickpeas of yours."

Crouching, Guisburn squared off with Naylor. "I'm gonna ruin your black ass."

Footsteps could be heard from the road, and Cat jogged into the light of the building's security lamp. "This is my dance, John," Cat said, keeping his eyes on Guisburn. When Cat stepped between them, Guy charged like a bull, lunging with arms outstretched. Grabbing fingers on each of Guy's hands, Cat backpedaled, going with Guy's momentum, and then dropped to the ground with a violent jerk, pulling Guy down. Before Guisburn could crash on top of him, Cat scooted through Guy's legs, his hold on the fingers like a vise. Guisburn hit the ground without the cushion of his arms, and his face plowed into the cold earth. Then Cat was on Guy's back, wrenching Guy's heel into his buttock with his right arm. With his left Cat locked Guy's arm behind his back.

Cat was like a spider wrapping up its prey. Guy roared and arched his back in an upward surge that momentarily jacked both bodies off the ground. But the move allowed Cat to tighten his hold, and everyone heard a wet sucking *pop*. Guy's face paled, and a hoarse scream tore from his throat. His eyes clamped down so tightly that his face appeared to shrink.

Orange lights strobed against the building, and a car skidded to a stop with its headlights lancing across the impromptu arena. Troutman started for the corner of the building, swinging the pack at Ash as he came. Ash raised an arm to shield himself from the blow, and in the tangle he snagged one of the pack's straps. Troutman lashed out with a kick, but Ash caught his ankle and drove him back, hopping on one leg into the bushes.

Troutman kicked with his free foot, catching Ash under the chin, and both boys hit the hard ground on their backs. As they stood, Troutman dug into the pack, cocked back his arm, and hurled something that glanced off Ash's head and clattered against the building. Then Troutman was running east, the pack swinging at his side.

"Everybody stay put!" a voice commanded. Two men stepped out of the car. Ash squinted into the bright light and recognized the barrel-chested black officer—Dawson.

The other officer, Purley, approached Guy's prone body. "What's the matter with him?" Guy's mouth opened and closed but made no sound. Wanting an answer, Purley turned and winced at the gash in Ash's chin. "Hey, you're bleeding pretty bad!"

"Mr. Dawson!" Ash called out. "Remember the 'red-neck, cracker' repairman?" Ash pointed. "He's getting away with stolen tests."

Pulling a flashlight from his belt, Dawson took off at a run. As soon as his foot-steps had faded, Ash heard an engine out on the Loop, turning over, trying to start.

Ash turned to Purley. "Call the front gate. We can't let that vehicle leave."

In the distance, the engine caught and fired, revved once, and stalled. Purley looked across the street at the cars starting to file out of the gym parking lot.

"We can't be closing the gate! The game is letting out!"

The engine fired again and Ash pointed due east. "He's getting away!"

Purley frowned. "The Loop's been closed over there for weeks. The bridge is under repair. He'll have to go around the long way."

Ash pointed south up the hill. "Then use your car to block the road up there!"

Purley frowned at Guy, who lay moaning on the cold earth. "I need to call in an ambulance."

Out on the Loop Road Ash heard Troutman engage a gear. After a jerking squeal from the tires, the engine stalled again.

After a quick glance at John, Ash bolted past the guard across Academy Drive toward the gym parking lot.

"Hey!" Purley yelled. "Get back here!"

Tucker jogged under the streetlight, his arms pumping and his chest heaving. Then Alan was there with Anne and Elaine, all breathing plumes of gray into the cold air.

"Hey!" Tucker yelled to Ash. "Where are you going? Are you bleeding?"

Ash threw open the driver's door of the Buick. When he saw no key in the ignition, he searched the dash, above the visor, and below the mat. When he glanced at the back seat, he saw the blanket that held Hubert's bow and arrows. Unwrapping the blanket, he grabbed the antique equipment and started sprinting up the hill.

"Now just hold it right there!" Purley shouted after him. But Ash was gone.

Troutman was not in sight, but Ash heard the vehicle winding out its gears along the Loop. Then a pair of headlights hove into view. The sound of the engine was like that of a charging beast. Ash anchored Hubert's bow against his foot and leaned into the stringing. Blood from his chin dolloped onto the bow, and for a bizarre moment Jan Salvatore's voice spoke to him about the blue of the sky darkened to purple by blood. The powerful bow bent and the string loop snapped into its groove with a *ping!*

Another car roared up Academy and braked at the stop sign, its headlights spearing across the Loop Road. It was Dr. Leonhardt's Buick. When Anne Metter rolled down the passenger window, Ash saw Elaine at the wheel.

"Don't try to block the road!" Ash yelled. "He's coming too fast!"

The Buick's high beams flashed on, illuminating a section of the Loop like a movie screen in a dark theater. Ash nocked one of the metal-tipped arrows and took his stance. In an unexpected gift, a second bright beam doubled the visibility of the road as the security car braked next to the Buick at the intersection.

A gray van tore into this light, its engine screaming. Ash drew the mighty bow, followed the tire with his arrow, and then pulled his aim forward to lead it. The van's lights reflected off the triangular point of the arrow like a beacon, and Ash released.

To all who witnessed it, the sound of impact was lost in the growl of the engine, but following that came the splintering of the arrow and a jet of spewing air. The sound of the ruptured tire gave the van a dull, grinding sound on the pavement.

"Put down that weapon!" Purley ordered from his car.

Ash had the second arrow loaded, drew again, and pivoted, firing at the rear tire as it moved away from him. Like its mate, the arrow sank into rubber and snapped immediately. But the razor point had done its work. Both tires were deflated, and the van listed, pulling right, until it straddled the curb, spraying a burst of sparks from the undercarriage.

Grinding to a halt the van dropped into a ditch, listed right, and tipped against the low bank. Troutman gunned the engine, but both left tires were four feet off the ground. The right rear wheel whined, and a cloud of black smoke filled the air with the stench of burning rubber.

On the Loop Road, Officer Dawson came running from the dark into the double set of headlight beams. When he reached Ash he stared at the van toppled against the bank. Then he looked at the bow.

"Be damned," he said between heaving breaths.

The driver's door of the lopsided van opened on top like a hatch. When it fell back, Troutman cursed. Ash laid down the bow, ran to the van, and climbed onto the side panel next to the door.

"Are you hurt?" he asked through the windowglass.

"Get the hell off my van!" Troutman screamed and pushed the door open as he rose to see the security officer approaching on foot. "You saw that! This guy tried to kill me!" Troutman stepped on the steering wheel and took a swing at Ash but missed as he lost footing and dropped back into the van. Ash caught the door and held it open. When Troutman climbed back up again, he held the blue pack in one hand and glowered at Ash. "You damned—"

Ash snatched the pack with one hand and let go of the door with the other. Gravity took the heavy door until it *banged* the crown of Troutman's head with a hollow ring. Troutman disappeared into the van. Ash tossed the pack down to Dawson.

"That should be our evidence," Ash said.

Naylor unfolded from the security car and approached, bending at his knees to examine Ash's chin. "That's gonna need stitches," John said and straightened. "But we voted you MVP tonight. Nice shooting."

They turned at a vocal outburst back at the intersection. Guisburn—his face wrung out with pain—stood between the cars yelling at Purley. Elaine got out of the Buick and stepped in front of Guy. After unscrewing the cap of the hot chocolate thermos, she tugged at Guy's waistband and emptied the steaming contents into his sweatpants. Guy howled and danced in place as he plucked at the wet material.

Dawson had Troutman sitting on the grass, checking him for injuries. Troutman ignored him and gently probed the swelling on the top of his head. He spat blood into the grass between his shoes. When Ash and John approached, Troutman opened his mouth in a scowl of undiluted loathing. A dark gash showed across his swollen tongue.

"Yo thunuvabith!" he lisped and pointed to the van. "Yo gonna pay fo' thad!"

John Naylor gave Ash a dead-pan expression. "Maybe we need an interpreter." When Ash made no reply, Naylor leaned down to inspect Ash's chin again. "We need to get you to the hospital."

Chapter Thirty-Five

Sheriff Seabolt motioned Ash to take the chair across from his desk. The man's kind blue eyes roved over Ash's face—the stitched chin, cracked lip, and scrape marks on his cheek. The sheriff reached into the pocket of his sweater vest and pulled out two foil-wrapped chocolate mints. He leaned over the desk, set one mint before Ash, and began unwrapping the other.

"I hear you been practicing your archery after hours." The sheriff popped the mint into his mouth and sucked in his cheeks, and Ash thought he saw something like amusement flicker in the man's eyes. "Did you shoot at anyone tonight, son?"

Ash hesitated for only a moment. "No, sir."

"What did you shoot at?"

"Two tires."

"And what did you hit?"

"Two tires."

The sheriff nodded thoughtfully. "How many times did you shoot?"

"Twice."

One side of the sheriff's white mustache twitched, and the blue of his eyes seemed to lighten a shade. "Two for two. And moving targets." He leaned back in his chair and clasped his hands behind his head. "Wanna tell me what happened out there?"

Ash told it all, starting with the firing of Dr. Leonhardt and his own dismissal. He described in detail the modifications made on the copy machines, their first failed attempt to catch Troutman, and finally the long cold vigils that culminated in this night's work.

"Sir, I think you should keep Guisburn and Troutman from talking to each other."

The sheriff smiled. "Well, Troutman's tongue isn't workin' too good right now."

"But his ears are fine," Ash reminded.

The sheriff rolled the mint foil into a ball and dropped it in his trash basket. Leaning forward he punched in a number on his phone. Ash picked up his mint and opened it.

"Ellis," the sheriff said into the phone, "get on the radio and get hold of Harold at the hospital. Tell him those two we brought in from the Academy are not to talk to each other." He hung up, stood, and stretched at the window. "Cold night. How long were you boys out there a-waitin'?"

"Since before the basketball game," Ash said. "Just after dark."

"And these two showed up . . . what . . . little before ten?"

Ash nodded. "That would be about right. The game hadn't let out."

The sheriff looked out at the lights of Naughton. "Can't get my deputies to stay out that long on a night like this." He stepped back to his desk and picked up a folder. "I think you'll agree we can't let *you* boys get together either." He flashed an apologetic smile. "The two at the hospital will stay there for the night. Your friend Tucker will stay with the Oberleighs. The redheaded one, Scathlock, he'll be a guest of his woodshop teacher. Naylor will stay with Dr. Leonhardt." He closed the folder and dropped it in a drawer. "You'll come out to our house. How's that sound?"

Ash bit into the mint and nodded. "Sounds good, Sheriff."

*****

On Saturday morning, filled with a generous breakfast, Ash sighted down his arrow at the big target on wheels. The stretched canvas popped a smart report when the arrow struck.

"Looks like Papaw's arrows work with your bow," Bobby Seabolt said and squinted up at Ash. "Do you ever miss?"

"Sure," Ash replied. "Everybody misses sometimes."

Bobby's face wrinkled. "When do *you* miss?"

Ash shrugged. "When I'm not concentrating . . . or concentrating too hard."

Bobby's puzzled eyes bore into Ash's. "I heard Papaw say you shot at a car."

Ash propped the tip of Hubert's bow on his foot and gazed out on the fallow field beyond the fence. "I got blamed for something I didn't do," he explained. "Me and some friends of mine. We've been trying to prove we're innocent, Bobby, and last night we got our chance. If that van had gotten away, we'd have lost our proof."

Bobby's eyes ran up and down the antique longbow until Ash motioned for him to shoot. The boy loaded and stared at the target. Deep lines set in his face as he drew.

"Now remember," Ash reminded. "You're still pushing and pulling, just not moving. When you release, let your arms finish what they started. Just let them go naturally where they're trying to go."

Bobby's arrow sailed into the bull's eye, and his eyes widened. "Like that?"

"Like that," Ash said and laughed, and together they walked to the target.

"I'll bet you concentrated just right last night."

Ash began pulling the arrows. "Guess I had to."

"Papaw said you might catch the dickens for it, but it was about all you could do with that jackass school cop standin' 'round doin' nothin'.

Papaw said both them boys got what they deserved and were gonna git a lot more."

They walked back down the drive toward the place from which they had shot. "Papaw never brung nobody here from the jail before. But for one time. That was my Uncle Dill. He used to drink a lot." The boy pointed. "Sometimes I shoot from that hickory down yonder, but I cain't hardly ever hit the target from there."

When they reached the hickory, the front door slammed. Sheriff Seabolt stood on the porch drinking from a coffee mug.

"Papaw!" Bobby yelled and pointed to the target. "Bank robbers, gettin' away!"

The sheriff lowered his cup and stepped to the rail. "Shoot their tires out, Bobby."

As Bobby loaded, Ash and the sheriff stared at one another across the yard—something intangible passing between them. Bobby's arrow flew and skipped off the gravel into the grass. Ash knelt and extended his arm toward the target.

"Distance like this tries to intimidate you. It tries to change your form."

"What's 'intimatate'?"

" 'Intimidate'. It means 'to bully.' Just shoot like you do when you're up close. The only thing that changes is how high you aim. Think of everything else as a constant."

Bobby's face compressed and wrinkled. " 'A constant' *what*?"

Ash smiled. "It means everything else stays the same."

Bobby cocked his head to one side. "How'd you learn stuff like that?"

Ash ran his fingers along the smooth curve of the bow. "I had a good teacher."

"Was he as good as you?"

Ash laughed at his answer even before delivering it. "I never saw him shoot."

Bobby frowned but only for an instant. "Okay, you shoot." He turned and yelled to the house. "Papaw! Watch Ash shoot!"

Sheriff Seabolt set his mug on the porch railing and leaned on his arms. Ash took his stance, and the details of the ambient world slipped from his senses. His eye narrowed to the shallow arc that his arrow would follow. He drew and shot.

"Whoa-a-a!" Bobby breathed. Then he yelled, "Papaw! He hit it! Dead center!"

The sheriff straightened, raised his cup in a toast, took a sip, and flung the dregs to the lawn. "We'll be headin' out b'fore long," he announced and walked inside.

When Ash offered his hand, Bobby stared at it and then placed his hand into the seal of their new friendship. They shook once and started down the drive side by side.

"Will you come back and shoot with me s'more?"

Ash laid Hubert's bow in the back of the sheriff's car, and then he stood before the boy. "Soon as I get all this sorted out with your grandfather. Until then, you work on that shot from the hickory. When I come back, we'll shoot the tires out together."

When the cruiser pulled out onto the road, Bobby was taking his shooting stance by the hickory tree. The set of his jaw was hard, and his eyes shone jewel-like.

Sheriff Seabolt chuckled as he looked in the mirror. "Reckon we won't be able to get 'im in for a meal for a day or two."

They rode past the farms, the woodlands, and winter-gray fields. With the sun just over the trees the morning was bright and clear, the morning dew shining like diamonds. When they pulled into the courthouse parking lot the sheriff shut down the engine and stared at the building.

"The district attorney'll take depositions from you boys. Whatever you say will have to stand, so tell it all and tell it straight and true." After a few seconds of quiet, he turned to Ash.

" 'Straight and true,' " Ash said.

Dr. Leonhardt got up from the kitchen table and answered the phone. He stayed in the hall a long time. By the time he had returned, Ash and John had finished their dinner.

"Well, that was the sheriff," Leonhardt reported. He sat and snapped his napkin into his lap. "The wrestler's and the repairman's stories matched. They claim you boys had gotten into the building. They confronted you, but you out-numbered them and got the best of it. The repairman says he grabbed *your* pack and went for help." Leonhardt nodded to Ash. "That's when you went after him . . . and, as he says . . . tried to kill him."

When neither John nor Ash commented, the doc continued. "The D.A. wants to put this in the school's lap. We meet with the board tomorrow at ten. If the board refuses it, it goes to criminal court."

Ash took his plate to the sink, washed it, and stood staring out the window. "If I'd just held onto Troutman's leg—" He shook his head and started on a saucepan.

Naylor snorted. "Purley would'a thought you were practicing for the prom."

Ash opened a drawer and then another. "John, where's that drying towel?"

Naylor took the folded towel from under the meat platter and rolled it tight. "Here you go," he said, cocking back his arm as if to deliver a free throw.

Ash held the pot level before him, his chest as the backboard. When John tossed the towel, it opened in mid-arc and flew past Ash, brushing his head and triggering a memory. In his mind's eye he saw Troutman throwing something at him . . . something taken from the small backpack. Setting down the sauce pan, he made for the hallway to call the sheriff.

Chapter Thirty-Six

Ash and his coterie of outcasts filed into the conference room, each dressed in the green GDA sweats that had become their habitual woods-wear. Though all their clothing was freshly laundered, the five foresters smelled of woodsmoke. Behind the wood railing, the board members stared curiously at these boys so long ago dismissed. Like revenants come to revisit the battlefield of their demise, they entered without talking and took their seats in the front row.

District Attorney Gatto sat at one end of the long table, Princeton Johns at the other. In familiar order, Mrs. Alles and the male board members filled the spaces in between. Dean Oberleigh, Dr. Leonhardt, Sheriff Seabolt, and Mr. Dawson, the security man, quietly conferred just outside the rail. Juanita Esparza sat alone in the back of the room.

In the third row of chairs a man with meticulously manicured silver hair read privately from a folder. Ash recalled him stepping daintily through the churned up mud in the archery field with Princeton Johns. And his car tag: *Reeve 1*. In front of him sat Guisburn, his arm in a sling and a constellation of small bandages peppering his face. Neatly dressed in school blazer and clean-shaven, he looked the model Greenwood student-athlete and very much a victim.

Next to Guy a curly-haired man in a tweed sport coat bounced one leg piston-like off the ball of his foot. Beneath his middle-aged spread was the same battering-ram physique of his wrestler-son. To Guy's left, Troutman sulked in an ill-fitting coat and tie.

Troutman met Ash's eyes and his mouth tightened to a smug smile. He made a slash with his thumb beneath his chin, mocking Ash's row of crusted stitches. When the chairman called the room to order, the sheriff and the others sidled into the fourth row.

When asked, Dawson took the floor and outlined the known facts about the science building break-in. In policeman's terms he reported what he had seen of the fight in front of the science building, the wreck of the van on the Loop Road, and the medical reports from the hospital. When he finished, he yielded the floor to the district attorney.

Gatto remained seated and extended a hand toward Harland Seabolt. "The sheriff and I are here because aspects of this case fall into the county jurisdiction—but only if the school presses charges." He went on to describe the depositions given by each person involved. For ten minutes the board members listened attentively.

When he finished, Gatto leaned his elbows on the table and opened his empty hands before him. "As you see, we have two conflicting stories. Today we must decide, if possible, which one is true . . . and if the county should become involved. I personally think it inevitable, since both scenarios purport crimes committed by non-students on school property. But, ultimately, the Academy decides."

First called, Guy stood and made a show of shifting his injured arm and wincing with pain. "Well, these guys—" he began and pointed at Naylor. "They got kicked out for cheating. So when I saw 'em Friday night, I figured they were up to no good. Me and Trout were at the game, but I left early 'cause I had some studying to do." He pointed to Ash. "I see him and Naylor go through a window in the science building, so I go back to the gym to get a security cop but can't find one. So, I go get Trout to be a witness."

Guy had found his rhythm in the story and seemed to enjoy the telling. "We get to the building and that one—" He pointed at Ash. "The one who almost killed Trout with those hunting arrows. He comes walking out the front door carrying this backpack. I figure the pack is full of tests. So, I tell 'im he's caught and he's not going anywhere."

"So, he starts to run away, and me and Trout stop him. That's when Naylor blindsides me with a chokehold." With a stoic grimace, Guy repositioned his arm. "I guess I blacked out then. So Trout . . . he wrestles the pack away from 'em and—"

"Now wait," Mrs. Alles said. "You blacked out. Let's hear from Mr. Trout."

Indignant, Troutman stood. "It's 'Twoutman'!" He hooked his thumbs in his trouser pockets and cocked his head. "I done wha' he sthaid. I gwabbed the pack off that'n." He stretched his chin toward Ash. "He had it wapped on his awm, so I popped him good and he leggo. I god to my van to go fo' he'p, and he stawts twyin' ta kill me." Troutman glared at Ash. "Made me w'eck my cousin's van, which he gonna pay fo'."

The DA nodded. "All right, that's one side." He looked to the far end of the front row. "You are Mr. Tucker, I believe?"

Tucker stood and knitted his eyebrows. "Sirs . . . madam." He made a little bow. "My story is the same as the story of all my friends. Of all of us, Ash can tell it best. I give my time to him." He sat down.

Alan unfolded his long legs and stood. "Likewise," he said and sat.

The DA laced his fingers on the polished tabletop. "Sensing solidarity, shall I save us time?" Skipping Cat and John, he gave Ash a crooked smile. "It would seem your friends are content to place their fate in your hands, Mr. Asherwood."

Ash checked the faces of his friends, and when they all nodded, he stood. He talked for twenty minutes, beginning with the day Mick Millerson had flashed the test in his face. The board had heard it before, but no one interrupted. Now the narrative fascinated them. The prosaic story of one or two students cheating had grown to the higher drama of fist-fights, arrows flying in the night, car crashes, and an alliance of forest-dwellers living secretly on the fringes of the campus.

Once Ash had described the details involving the copy machine duplications, he steered the story back to the day construction had begun at the west field. He unfolded Marin's copy of the charter and began reading the pertinent excerpt.

At a look from Dr. Johns, the silver-haired lawyer, Candler Reeve, stood. "If the board please, I can see no relevance here. May we stick to our agenda?"

Ash was unfazed. "I would say that this construction in the woods is our most pressing topic when you consider the school charter has been altered for personal gain."

Reeve cut his eyes to Princeton Johns. It was only a glance—a reflex—but Mrs. Alles caught it, and she turned her attention to the new biology department head.

"Nonsense!" Johns snapped. "Can we get back to—?"

"Nonsense?" Dr. Leonhardt broke in. "When the school's founding legal document has been manipulated?" He pushed himself up by his walking cane.

Princeton Johns laughed. "This . . . from our grand manipulator of tests."

The chairman raised both hands in a placating gesture, but it was Mrs. Alles who quieted the room. "I believe Robert has the floor, gentlemen."

Ash turned the paper around for them to see. "This copy of the charter—"

"Mr. Chairman," Reeve interrupted, tempering his objection with saintly patience. He stepped into the aisle as if taking center stage. "I suspect this is a scheme meant to derail the intent of this hearing." He performed an elegant shrug. "I for one would like to know which of these young men has tarnished the good name of the school by stealing and selling tests."

"And I," Leonhardt said, stabbing his cane into the floor, "I would like to know what arrogant dissimulator is orchestrating the alteration of our school charter."

The standoff held the room in check until Sheriff Seabolt stood. "Folks, I got a right busy day ahead o' me, as I'm sure Mr. Gatto does. I'd like to get back to Friday night. I brought along a little evidence you might wanna see." He held up a brown paper sack and walked it to the front of the room. "Thought I'd save it a while . . . let everybody have his say. I believe in giving a man a chance to set hisself straight." The sheriff grinned and pulled at his earlobe. "And I'll admit to a little curiosity about the performance we might get out o' the ones spinnin' yarns here today." He raised the paper bag again. "How 'bout it?" He turned to Ash as if asking permission.

When Ash nodded and sat, Harland Seabolt turned to face Troutman. "Jarvis, you've run up a right long record in the county files."

Troutman crossed his arms and rested his chin on his tie as his sullen eyes smoldered. "Least I ain't twied to kill nobody." He jerked his head in Ash's direction. "Thad one wecked my damn van and pwactically cud off my tongue."

"Apparently not enough of it," John Naylor mumbled.

Troutman turned. "You black thunuvabith, you can—"

"Here now!" the chairman ordered, slapping the table with his palm. Reeve put a hand on Troutman's arm, but Troutman jerked away and started for the aisle. The sheriff stepped in his path and clamped his hand above Troutman's elbow.

"We're not done here, Jarvis. Go an' take your seat."

Troutman jerked his arm free, stumbled backward, and toppled the lawyer into his seat. Then Guy was on his feet, standing behind Troutman, his good arm wrapped around Troutman's chest, trying to contain the Office Doctor's wrath.

"All you damn wich people! You make the wules fo' evwybody elth!" Shaking all over, Troutman strained against Guisburn's arm, his face darkening to red. Guy's hold on him now seemed less a restraint than an awkward embrace.

As Guisburn coaxed Troutman back into his seat, Sheriff Seabolt eased a hand into his pants pocket. "I'd like a few private minutes with Troutman and Asherwood," he announced and looked at the chairman. "Can you give me that?"

The chairman bent forward over the table, checking the faces of his colleagues. "I suppose a recess for everyone might be—"

"No," the sheriff said in his quiet, firm way. "This shouldn' take too long. We'll just step in the next room, if that'll be all right." He turned to Troutman. "Let's go, son."

"I ain't your sthon!" Troutman shot back.

The sheriff's kind smile did not falter. "No, but you're in my custody, Jarvis, and I'd rather not have a tussle here in front of these folks."

The lawyer leaned to Troutman and whispered in his ear. Troutman sneered, but he stood. Sheriff Seabolt glanced at Ash, and the three of them left the room.

The floor was empty in the adjoining room with folding chairs stacked against the walls. The sheriff positioned three chairs in the center of the room, and they settled into a mute triangle. For a full minute the old man stared at Troutman, whose jaw remained locked like a sprung trap.

"I know you did it, Jarvis."

Troutman looked too quickly at the sheriff and tried to cover the reaction by worming his neck up through his shirt collar. "You don' know nothin'. If you did, you—"

313

"You did it," the sheriff said evenly. But first we're gonna talk about something else." Watching Troutman the sheriff remained very still, as if he had settled into his chair for the day. "I knew your daddy, son. I know you didn't have things any too easy."

Troutman looked away, the hard edges of his face as angular as stone.

"You're about to do some hard time on the county work farm, son." The sheriff pointed a thumb over his shoulder at the hearing room. "Your friend out there prob'ly won't serve a day. I can't take him to jail until the school tells me I can." The calm in the sheriff's voice seemed to imply an unassailable truth. "More'n likely he'll get kicked out, go home, and his daddy'll make it hard for me to get him back here."

Troutman stared back at him. "If you had sthom'thin', you'da sthaid it out there."

Harland Seabolt's steady blue eyes stayed on Troutman for so long that the boy began to fidget. "You think being tough is havin' power. Maybe it was when you were a young'n and it was workin' against you." He shook his head. "You're about to lose that illusion, son. On the farm, tough gets you cleaning a twenty-foot urinal and ten commodes three times a day. It gets you enemies who will make your life miserable."

Troutman kneaded the calluses of one hand with the thumb of the other. "Why ith he here listhnin' to thith?" He jerked his head toward Ash.

"Because he's part o' this," the sheriff explained. "You made him part o' it." He leaned to get into Troutman's line of vision. "You'll come out of the farm worse off than you went in, which means you'll likely be returning to it. I've seen it too many times."

Troutman would not look at him, but his eyes turned cautious.

The sheriff leaned forward with his hands on his knees. "I'm going to give you one chance, Jarvis. Right now. Before I go back in there and pull at that thread o' truth till ever'thing unravels."

Troutman sniffed and tried to look bored. "Whad kind o' chanth?"

The sheriff waited, letting the new tone in Troutman's voice hang in the air. "Because of you, this young man here was disgraced, expelled, and had his senior credits took away. He lived in a hole in the ground out in the woods and stayed here at the school to prove he was innocent. He didn't fold. You know what that takes?"

Troutman sat back, hooked his arm over the chair back, and glared at the floor.

"Here's the best I can do for you, Jarvis. You apologize to Asherwood right here, right now, then go out there and tell those people how all this went down with you and the Guisburn boy. You do that, and I'll see you get a decent shake at the farm . . . maybe get you highway detail to keep you out o' that Godforsaken hole. I'll talk to Gatto."

Troutman squinted at the sheriff, an unasked question on his face.

"You're wantin' to know why," the sheriff guessed. "Well, here it is: Any man hell-bent on ruining his life oughta get at least one chance to turn it around. 'Specially if he got dealt a raw hand early on. I'm giving you that chance right now."

Troutman made a faint snort. He stood and scuffed the floor all the way to the door. With one hand on the brass knob, he turned to them, the light from the window reflecting wetly off his eyes. In that moment Ash could see a little boy hiding inside a dark closet, peering out at a world stacked against him. Troutman raised the middle finger of his right hand, flexed his arm stiffly in place, and walked out.

The sheriff and Ash exchanged glances, but there was nothing to say. Together they stood and left the three chairs like a memorial to a failed parley.

Everyone watched them re-enter the room and tried to read their faces for a clue as to what had happened. Sheriff Seabolt walked to the rail and resumed talking as if there had been no break in the proceedings.

"Jarvis, you stated in your deposition you broke away from Asherwood to get help. That you threw something from the backpack at him. What was it?"

Troutman shrugged. "I justh gwabbed sthomething and thwew it."

The sheriff reached into a paper bag and extracted a clear plastic bag containing broken pieces of black plastic and a coiled electric cord. "What is this, Jarvis?"

Troutman narrowed his eyes. "It's hawd to thay. Is thad whad I thwew at 'im?"

Seabolt dangled the bag for all to see. "What we have here is a computer memory unit that takes a USB flash drive. It's not standard equipment on a copy machine. It can capture and store everything printed on the machine. Had my dispatcher look it over. She's pretty good with computers. She says even before it was broken in the fight, this one was defective. I figure that's why it was removed from the copier. But the flash drive itself . . . it was intact. It had lots of information on it but it was jumbled." Setting the evidence on the table, he added, "Tell these folks your line of work, Jarvis?"

Troutman glowered at the board. "Electwonics. I fix stuff when it's bwoken."

"Computers, copiers, and such," Seabolt translated and turned to Troutman. "You work for The Office Doctor, but you don't recognize this?"

"It's all bwoke up."

Seabolt nodded at the bag. "We dusted it for fingerprints. Jarvis Troutman's prints are all over it. No one else's."

"Sheriff, if I may?" Candler Reeve stood again and spread his hands. "Mr. Troutman's fingerprints would certainly show on the unit if he threw it at someone. That his prints alone are on it suggests that others wore gloves when handling it." He smiled, ever happy to enlighten.

"Yes," Sheriff Seabolt said congenially, "but what about the other units?"

"Thath's a lie!" Troutman erupted.

Reeve placed a hand on Troutman's shoulder. "If indeed there were other units in the backpack, Sheriff, isn't it reasonable that he might have grabbed any number of them searching for an object to hurl?"

"It just might. But the thing is . . . there were no more units in the pack. I'm talkin' 'bout the ones installed around the school." He paused to watch Troutman's face. "We dusted those for prints, too." Harland Seabolt nodded to the board. "Your security man, Dawson, rounded them up for me." He smiled. ". . . Wearin' gloves."

All eyes fixed on Dawson and the bag he raised. It was filled with black plastic boxes and wires. Troutman started to object, but Reeve was quick to continue.

"Sheriff, is it not reasonable that a maintenance man for copy machines might have his prints everywhere on one of those machines?" He let his eyebrows float up.

The sheriff smiled at the floor. "Seems like you got a answer for 'bout ever'thing." He leveled his eyes on Troutman. "But that one ain't gonna float. His prints on 'em tells us he knows 'bout 'em. He's the one with access, means, and know-how. It's him and young Guisburn there who were stealing the tests."

Guy's father was on his feet. "*His* fingerprints do not implicate my son!"

Troutman's eyes locked on Guy. "You ain't hangin' me out to dwy, Gith-burn."

Guy's charade of composure snapped. "Will you shut up!" When Guy turned to the sound of the door opening, his mouth closed and his eyes widened.

Anne and Elaine walked in. Behind them came Jeep dressed in his school blazer.

The chairman rapped his knuckles on the table. "What is the meaning of—?"

"I got something to say," Jeep announced.

When the females stopped, Jeep proceeded alone down the aisle. Standing at the rail, he stuffed his hands into his trouser pockets and looked around at the faces gathered before him. Then he cleared his throat and shifted his weight from leg to leg.

"We get the tests from the copy machines and sell them. We know this grad student down in Atlanta. We pay him for the answers and include them with the tests."

"And who are you?" Mrs. Alles asked.

Jeep cleared his throat again. "Gilbert White. But I won't give any other names."

"You won't name your accomplices?" Mrs. Alles said.

"No, ma'am. I can't do that."

She leaned forward on her forearms. "Then can you at least tell us who your accomplices were not?"

Jeep remained in his rigid pose for several seconds before pointing at the five ex-students dressed in sweat clothes. "I don't even know them—except by sight."

The room was silent. Guisburn appeared not to be breathing.

"Do you know Mr. Guisburn and Mr. Troutman?" Mrs. Alles asked.

"Yes, ma'am, I know 'em."

"And you are saying you had access to tests through the copy machines?"

"Yes, ma'am," Jeep said.

Mrs. Alles cocked her head to one side. "Are you skilled with elec-tronics?"

Jeep huffed a laugh. "I can type on a computer with two fingers . . . and make a copy on a copier. I guess that's about it."

Mrs. Alles cocked her head the other way. "Then how could you know how to attach this flash drive box to a copy machine?"

Jeep shrugged. "I couldn'."

The chairman cleared his throat. "How long have you been doing this?"

"We started last year," Jeep admitted.

The chairman sighed. "But you won't give us their names?"

Jeep was still shaking his head, when Elaine spoke up from the aisle. "I will!"

Mrs. Alles sat back and crossed her arms. "And who are *you*?"

Elaine held out her arms as though displaying herself as evidence. "I am Greenwood's homecoming queen," she announced, her shy voice tinged with sarcasm. "Elaine Perrin." She pointed to Guy. "Guy Guis-burn brought tests to our dorm a few times. Several of the girls on my floor bought them."

Guy's father stood and pointed at Elaine. "That's her word against my son's!"

Elaine's reply was calm and credible. "You can ask anybody on my dorm floor."

"Did *you* buy any tests?" Mrs. Alles asked Elaine.

"No, ma'am, but I looked at them."

The chairman pointed at Troutman. "What about the repairman? Was he in on it?"

Elaine nodded and pointed at Troutman. "He came with Guy to the dorm one time when they brought the tests. I remember he smoked and the girls made him put out his cigarette so they wouldn't get into trouble with the matron."

Sheriff Seabolt checked his pocket watch and put it away. "Folks," he began, extending an arm toward Ash and his friends. "Far as these five boys are concerned, I reckon this 'bout wraps it up, don't you agree?"

"Not quite!" Dr. Leonhardt announced and made his way to the aisle with his cane. He took his time making eye contact with each of the board members. "Last fall I told you we had a problem—one threatening the reputation of the Academy. You chose to kill the messenger, and you damn well nearly succeeded." He patted the left side of his chest twice. "I went after the problem before you canned me, and these boys finished the job." He pointed his cane to Ash. Then he showed the board the contemptuous glare he had perfected in his classroom. "Now you owe us. If you do not make right by me . . . and these five boys—" He pursed his lips and shook his head. ". . . These five men," he amended and smiled as he watched Alan taking notes. "You will read the most devastating newspaper story to hit the Academy in all its history."

The room reached a new level of quiet. Even Dr. Johns did not move.

Leonhardt leaned on his cane. "I want these five young men on a special scholarship to finish their senior year by the end of the summer. They are to receive their diplomas with their classmates in June." Even as the words fell from his mouth, the terms seemed final, without recourse.

"As for myself, I will be reinstated as department head to teach for one more year starting immediately and including this summer to help my young friends here finish up." He looked at Ash for a moment before continuing. "In truth, I am ready to retire right now, but I don't want to end my career on this sour note." He inhaled quickly and stood straighter. "I want all my health benefits reinstated retroactively—to cover the medical expenses I incurred at a time when I needed them most—a time when you stripped them from me. When I retire in a year I will expect my full pension."

Ash watched Dean Oberleigh close his eyes and exhale a long sigh.

"I also advise you to turn your exacting scrutiny upon yourselves as a board. There has been a lot of hanky-panky going on among some of you in pushing through this new housing at the west end of campus. That money came from my chapel funds."

Dr. Johns was on his feet. "The construction has already begun. A lot of money has been paid out and more committed."

"Well, Dr. Johns," Leonhardt replied, "you and your colleagues will have to decide among yourselves who will pay for that. And you *will* pay! That money was mine to use on the chapel. You have conspired with a lawyer to rewrite the school charter, which, as Mr. Asherwood has explained, adamantly prohibits any alterations of the forested land on campus. You will also restore any damaged property by planting trees and seeding the field."

Reeve lost his smile. "Now just one moment. Our firm has been with—"

"Your firm," Leonhardt said with numbing force, "under the guise of a restoration of the historic charter, has been deleting provisions from the original to benefit yourselves through the construction company to which you are a silent partner with your brother-in-law. We have a copy of a letter sent from Princeton Johns confirming all this."

"Nonsense!" Johns protested. "You could not possibly have such a letter."

Reeve bristled. "Our firm has handled legalities for Greenwood for decades. If anyone knows that charter point for point, it is Reeve and Bishop."

Dr. Leonhardt waited a beat and said, "And Esparza!"

When Reeve's face lined with confusion, Dr. Leonhardt extended his hand toward the seats in back.

"My secretary," he said. "Juanita Esparza." She raised a paper, displaying it to all in the room.

The chairman cleared his throat. "I think this is neither the time nor—"

"Well, *I* want to hear it," Mrs. Alles announced, raising her voice. She smiled at Juanita Esparza and nodded. "Please enlighten us, madam."

Juanita walked up the aisle, stopped, and stared solemnly at the letter. "This ees dated two days ago. It ees written in Dr. Johns's hand along with a map he drew on the same page. It says: 'Dear Meester Reeve, the amen'ments to the charter look good. Congratulations. The only correction I suggest ees not limiting ourselves to a small part of the forest. We may want to expand again in future years (see my sketch). As before I enclose a copy of my revisions on a separate page. I trust jyou will exercise prudence by destroying this missive after you have perused it. When the reworking of the charter ees complete, get it back to the school so that I may convince the board of the soundness of the plan. The chairman ees with us. (I am sending him a copy of this letter.) I have no doubt the rest of the board shall willingly wash their hands of Leonhardt's frivolous chapel and recognize the need for faculty housing. Sincerely, Princeton Johns. P.S. Tell your brother-in-law that the sooner he establishes the foundations, the better.' "

Johns scraped back his chair and marched to the aisle. "Let me see that!" He snatched the paper from her. "Anyone could have forged this! Where did you get it?"

Juanita seemed to shrink next to Johns. "From the flash drive," she said.

Johns spun at the sound of Leonhardt's cane tapping the rail. The cane leveled out, pointing at the plastic bag on the table.

"I asked Ms. Esparza to have a look at this storage unit," Sheriff Seabolt explained, his eyes on Mrs. Alles. "So she could verify for us that what my dispatcher found on it actually were the stolen tests. It was Miss Esparza who found the letter." He nodded toward the chairman. "Lucky for us Dr. Johns made that copy for you." Then the sheriff eyed Guisburn and Troutman. "And that you two made it available to us."

Princeton Johns started for the door, but stopped abruptly when Mrs. Alles called his name. "We'll be wanting you to stay a little longer, Dr. Johns," she said and nodded to Dawson, who strode up the aisle to escort Johns back to the rail. Then Mrs. Alles leaned forward over the table to better see the chairman. "You stay, too, Jack."

Sheriff Seabolt and Mr. Gatto herded the Guisburns and Troutman to the back of the room and stood in conference with Dean Oberleigh. The board members drew together at their table, Mrs. Alles now taking over to direct them.

Dr. Leonhardt worked his way to the end of the row where the green-clad foresters ceased talking and looked up at him. "You boys will move your things into my house. You'll all be staying with me now." He shut his eyes and held up a palm. "No arguments!"

All five ex-students were speechless as they stared up at him.

Leonhardt laughed, leaned in closer, and lowered his voice. "Time to fill up those holes you've been living in. We can't give these damned lawyers something to fight back with, can we?" When Tucker started to ask a question, Dr. Leonhardt arched both eyebrows and whispered. "No construction out in the woods, remember?"

Chapter Thirty-Seven

Ash awoke to Alan's laugh. He had not heard that kind of joy in months. Then Tucker's high-pitched giggle floated down to him from upstairs. He just made out the quick whispers of females. Then, when the smell of food registered, Ash pushed himself up from his bed.

After dressing by the red glow of the reptile cages he climbed the stairs. Standing in the hall he listened to Alan and Cat trying to complete sentences between fits of laughter. When John Naylor's big bass voice joined the chorus, Ash stepped into the kitchen doorway and leaned on the frame, his arms folded across his chest. Anne and Elaine saw him first, and elbows nudged around the room, bringing eventual quiet.

"What's so funny?"

Tucker removed a warm plate from the stove and set it on the table. "Soft-boiled egg, lightly buttered English muffin, and tea," Tucker said. "Very British. Thought you'd like that." Cat pushed out a chair with his foot. When Ash sat, Naylor laid a newspaper on the table before him. The headline fairly jumped off the page: *GDA Teacher and Students Reinstated After Wrongful Expulsion—Board Members and Attorneys Under Review in Alleged Charter Forgery.*

"Eat up," Alan said jingling a ring of keys. "We're going on a little field trip."

In the old Buick they cruised north of town. Giving up on getting any answers from anyone, Ash settled for gazing out the window. They were in the old millworkers section of town where one abode had looked like any other until the neighborhood had undergone renovations and lured in the upper middle class.

As Alan drove, he kept up a running commentary on all that had happened in the last months. "Young Asher, do you realize how long the *Ballad* will have to be now? Young Asher the sylvan hermit, the cat burglar, the wrestler, the van-slayer—"

Ash kept gazing out the window. "Guisburn was the *wrestler*. I think I was the *wrestlee*."

"Until John got hold of him," Alan reminded.

"And don't forget Cat," Tucker added.

Alan laughed, "Right, there will be a verse about John finding those elusive chickpeas . . . and Cat plowing the school grounds with Guisburn's face."

John chuckled. "And don't forget Elaine serving hot drinks on a cold night."

Tucker leaned forward. "What about me figuring out the flash drive?"

Alan reached back and patted Tucker's round fuzzy head. "You'll have your stanza, Tuck."

They slowed at a white clapboard house, distinguished from neighboring houses only by a chain-link fence enclosing the yard. As they turned the corner and braked in front, a telling silence gelled inside the car.

"Guess who lives here," Alan said.

Ash studied the house and grounds, but his eyes kept returning to the fence. Its diamond pattern was festooned with dozens of rubber snakes woven through the wire.

"Welcome to the humble estate of Princeton Johns," John Naylor said in his best impersonation of the man.

Ash began to nod. "So this was your night out on the town."

Alan pointed toward the front door. "Look above the porch steps."

A wood plaque hung over the portico. Mounted on it, a huge snake glistened in the sunlight. Coiled and fangs bared, it was a frozen caricature of reptilian terror.

"It's a rattlesnake," Tucker said. "The taxidermist didn't have a water moccasin."

Ash squinted. "What's that yellow thing it's coiled around?"

"I sprung for that," Alan said. "It's a toy bulldozer. It was a steal at a dollar forty."

Ash watched his friends laugh with one another and talk about their parts in the prank. There was a sense of completeness inside the car . . . so many new friendships . . . all bound by a common ordeal. Ash closed his eyes, and a warmth spread through him. He would never have thought himself connected so intimately to so many. It had been a long journey to get where they were now. But, Ash knew, there was one more journey yet to go.

PART SEVEN

England

It was late September, and the morning mist hung thickly among the lindens and plane trees along the dirt lane. The shoulder-high stone wall running beside the lane might have contained a history of the land entire. Ash imagined each stratum of rock marking a century . . . or the reign of a different king or queen. Throughout his summer term at Greenwood Downs he had devoured a steady stream of books from the library—all of them about England.

It surprised Ash that having high school behind him contained a bittersweet closure. But the beginning laid out before him was exciting—as promising as the morning air. He felt renewed and autonomous under the weight of his backpack. His boots padded the earth lightly as he took in the rural terrain. He carried Hubert's longbow openly now, having discarded the awkward cardboard tube that had protected it on the airplane and bus.

After walking north from Edwinstowe, he chose a vibrant green field at the noon hour. There he rested and ate the sandwich that had been wrapped for him by a friendly waiter at a tavern. Across the way a cottage was set back from the road, where he heard the repetitive whisks of a broom drifting to him on the still morning air.

The home and outbuildings were old but imbued with a certain charm that he could only name as "English." It was the flip side of Appalachia. Here every piece of the landscape touched by men's hands seemed an effort not to exploit then ignore but to improve—as if they had learned the lesson of neglect and then turned to nurturing the land with uncommon devotion.

Once he had gained the Clipstone Fork his route was visibly less traveled but still well marked overhead. He had only to follow the last of the telephone wires that stretched northwest into the sylvan remoteness. Where the lane narrowed to a single track, just as Cat had drawn on his map, the lone wire swooped earthward to a cluster of shake-shingled buildings, finally terminating at a weaver's shop.

Breaking the steady rhythm to which he had marched, he approached the shop and made a tunnel of his hands against the glass. Skeins of colored yarn hung on spools along the walls. Bolts of cloth were stacked high on a cutting table. Great wooden looms and pedal-driven wheels divided the main room into its work areas. From the rafters hung a fringe of dried plants, presumably for dyes. As he studied the interior, four notes chimed from inside. Then four more. It was the clock he had heard once before over the phone line. On the counter he spotted the telephone, and he knew that Marin had stood there, holding that very phone to her ear.

Walking to the corner of the house, he spied a holding pen of sheep. All the shaggy animals reclined belly to the earth, their dun coats curled like desiccated moss.

After crossing an arched wooden bridge, he crested a hill where he could see the narrowed trail snake through a long grassy valley ahead. A broad creek sparkled with bright blinks of light from the low slant of the sun. Far up the valley, the stream poured from the shadows of a quiet and contemplative forest. This would be Sherwood, he knew.

There were no homes to be seen, but survey ribbons fluttered in an orderly grid as far as he could see. Corralled on a plateau above the floodplain were three bulldozers, two dump trucks, and a front-end loader—all idle. It was Sunday.

As he walked the path, unfamiliar birds flushed from the hedge, reminding him that he was a visitor. Yet as he moved against the flow of the creek toward its headwaters he experienced an unsettling sense of homing in on a place of familiarity.

The school had to be close. Scanning the open vistas to either side, he imagined Alan playing his guitar here or Cat emerging from a stand of trees there, a trimmed-out bow stave balanced on his shoulder. And Tucker sitting by the water, turning a page in his theology book as he unwrapped his lunch.

Soon after entering the cool of the forest he beheld the spectacle of Fitzwalter Hall, afloat on its unkempt grounds like a great ship abandoned in the dark privacy of the woods. It was an old building, its great quarried stones pieced together with a look of permanence. Black-green ivy dug its roots into the mortar, and tentacles of moss spread blindly across the walls in verdant archipelagos.

The cylindrical tower with its crenelated top gave the immediate impression of a castle, but the lyrical architecture and detail of stonework convinced the eye that here was more than a military defense. Here was a monument to loftier pursuits.

Steady hammering rang out, tapered off, and then started again. Turning from the heavy iron door knocker at front, Ash walked around the building and followed the sound. A white truck was parked next to a side door. *Arkwright Brothers, Ltd. of Nottingham*, read the lettering on the panel. A power drill whirred. When it shut off, Ash leaned in through the open doorway.

"Hello!?"

The silence inside was broken by shoes scuffing across a wooden floor. A man clad in white coveralls emerged from a dark hallway. The dark bushy mustache that covered his mouth suggested he would be sparing with words. With a cordless drill hanging by his side the man stopped and stared at Ash.

"I'm looking for Mrs. Fitzwalter," Ash said and laid down the bow and backpack.

"You and about a dozen others, lad." The man's thickly accented words tumbled out with hardly a movement of his jaw. He nodded to the bow. " 'At yours?"

"Yes, sir. Are you saying nobody knows where she is?"

"Must be a Fitzwalter student, eh? Well, you're flat out o' luck is w'at you are. She's in debt up to 'ere." He leveled a hand before his neck.

Ash said nothing to that. He scanned the ceiling, taking in the size of the building.

The man chuckled. "Just wait till you're older. You'll ring up some o' your own debts. A lot easier to sink than float these days. And that's just w'at she done is sink. Mrs. Cathcart, the real estate lady, says the Mr. and Mrs. 'ere were in the red for years."

He jerked his head toward the interior of the building. "Mortgage, second mortgage, credit, credit on credit, loans from the Commonwealth Exchange. Some holes you dig are so bloody deep you may as well just stay down in them and hide." He pushed his chin toward the road Ash had just traveled. "Oh, she's out there some'ere, all right. Probably had some strings pulled and started over with a new line of credit."

"Do you work for her?" Ash asked.

The man made a face as if he'd smelled something rotten. "Not me, mate. I get 'ard cash for my services. I'm working for Mr. Rosenthal at the bank—the new owner you might say—at least until Mrs. Cathcart makes the sale, and she will, mind you."

"Do you know Mrs. Fitzwalter?"

The man shook his head. "Never 'ad the pleasure." His eyes returned to Ash's bow. "And w'at is it you do with *that* thing?"

"I've got to find Mrs. Fitzwalter, sir."

"Take a ticket and stand in line, chum," he said, still admiring the bow. " 'Ow old is that beast? I may be daft but it looks like the one in the picture. Come inside and see for yourself." He turned and waved Ash in. "Watch your step now. I'm shoring up the walls a bit. The place is quite solid, but there's a little warp to some of the beams and that worries Mr. Rosenthal."

The hallway was cool. Ash followed and let his eyes adjust, admiring the high arch of ceiling. The workman prattled on, his vocal energy seemingly endless.

The room they entered was suffused with a dusky gray light from high, narrow windows. In the corner of the room a battery light illuminated a wall where a new post had been bolted to another from floor to rafter. Footprints crisscrossed through the sawdust scattered over a blue drop cloth.

"She left me a book," Ash explained. "Do you know where I might look for it?"

The man coughed up a laugh and posed with an expression of incredulity. "A book, you say!" He chuckled and waggled his finger. " 'Ere now, you just follow me."

In the second room a fireplace gaped in one wall, the cavity large enough to park a small car. Surrounding it were shelves of books on every wall. It was like a library—the books in the thousands. Ash touched one. The cloth spine was as soft as spun cotton.

"See what I mean, chum. You can look around, but I can't be lettin' you rummage through things, much less walk off with something."

"Aren't there any lights?"

"No electricity back 'ere in this part of the shire. Oil lamps and candles were the ticket 'ere. But Mr. Rosenthal says no open flames or generators. Fumes, you know. I have to use a battery torch just to see my bloody nose." He put one hand on his hip and pointed to a handsaw pinched at an angle in a four-by-four post. "I'm back to medieval times, as you can see." He picked up the light and motioned Ash to follow.

In the next room he set the lantern on a central table, where it threw a ring of light on another fireplace, this one even larger. More books covered the walls and above the mantle hung a huge painting of the building in which they stood.

"Come 'ere now and take a look," the man said walking to the hearth. " 'Ere you go. Tell me 'at doesn't look like 'at bow o' yours."

Ash stepped around the man to see a framed photograph on the mantle. Captured in black and white, a man with a clamp-jawed smile and a hollow-eyed little girl looked into the camera lens. Bisecting their bodies at the man's thighs and the girl's chest was the very bow that he'd left by the door. In anyone else's hands the bow would have dominated the picture, but this man—around forty years old—radiated an energy that pulsed off the photo. His shoulders were rounded with muscle. His ridged arms formed a strong V where he clasped the bow in both fists at the handle.

In sharp contrast, the young girl's dreamy introspection bordered on melancholy. She too held a bow, but in a quieter manner. It pressed vertically into the folds of her dress, and her fingers lightly touched the string as if she were about to pluck a soft note.

Ash recognized the hands first then returned to the face. A young Marin. Perhaps nine or ten years old. A leather strap angled across her child-torso and attached to something at her side. It was the mouthpiece of the old hollow horn.

"My God," Ash whispered.

"I told you, eh? Got me an eye for details, I do." The man tapped the glass over Marin's face. "One of 'is students, I suppose. Don't think the old bloke had any children. They say he was a champion of some sort. Mrs. Cathcart brings a client out 'ere, you should 'ear her braggin' on the old boy—like she bloody well knew 'im. And she goes on and on about the property backing up to Sherwood Forest—what's left of it, anyway."

Ash pulled himself away from the photograph. "I've got to find Mrs. Fitzwalter. Do you know anyone who can help me do that?"

The man's smile was one of hopelessness, and Ash looked away. That was when he saw the glove—the familiar rig of supple leather that had been shaped by his own string-fingers over the years. Lost at Hubert's grave, now it lay here on a thin book atop a table in this faraway place. Stepping closer he saw a flat copper leaf protruding from the press of pages. A beech leaf. Just like the one he had used as a bookmark in Marin's journal. The book's faded cover showed no words.

A car horn echoed through the halls and the man looked anxiously toward the door. "Come on now. And be quick about it. You're not supposed to be in 'ere." Holding the light before him he led the way back at a faster pace, looking over his shoulder every few steps. "Come'n now! Snap to it!"

In the yard a car door slammed. "Arkwright!" The workman stopped and listened intently as footsteps scraped in the foyer. He leaned to Ash.

"No arguments now," he whispered. "Get back in there and be quiet!"

"Arkwright!" the voice repeated.

"Right 'ere, sir!" He hurried off, and Ash backed into the dark room. Their voices carried from the foyer. "And what brings you out on a Sunday, Mr. Rosenthal?"

"Are you still working on the beams?" This voice was curt and impatient.

"It's slow going without the power tools, Mr. Rosenthal." Ash heard the carpenter slide something across the floor. A sawhorse, maybe.

Arkwright was, no doubt, trying to look busy. The quiet that followed seemed awkward even from two rooms away.

"You know I don't want anything removed from the building."

"Sir?"

"That archery equipment by the door. What is it doing there?"

"Oh, belongs to a lad on the grounds. Looking for Mrs. Fitzwalter, he was."

"Well, he won't find her here. I don't want anyone on the grounds, Arkwright."

"Yes, sir. 'E's just out walking around some'eres. I'll tell 'im."

"Now I want to show you what's to be done with the front hall. Bring your torch."

When the voices faded, Ash stood until his eyes adjusted, and then he moved back to the great room of books. He picked up his glove and stuffed it into his pocket. Then he carried the book with him as he followed the faint trail of light that delivered him to the outside. There he loaded up his gear and made off toward the woods.

A footpath bled off the back lawn and wound through a grove of ash and oak bedded in thick mosses and shoulder-high stands of bracken. The trail was bordered with nettles and dock. Outcrops of lichen-crusted boulders slanted from the rich black earth like leviathans turned to stone as they surfaced from a dark sea. At one of these stout stones he laid off his gear and sat with his back to the rock.

Opening the book he found an aggressive slant of lines handwritten in sharp order across unruled paper. He knew it was the work of a man. How he knew it to be Hubert's he couldn't say.

The content was all geography: directions and landmarks described in great detail. He thumbed through it and found on its final pages a sketch of trails and creeks and scores of individual features of the land marked by tiny icons labeled "cliff" and "standing stone," "spring" and "hollow" and such. By the placement of Fitzwalter Hall in the drawing, he knew exactly where he was among these boulders. He studied the map in full, gravitating to the place most heavily marked with details—a place where a creek made a hard turn and the word "Beechwood" was printed on the bank. It was all he needed.

After a mile the trail rose then descended into a new watershed—a shallow bowl of land where he met with a wide creek of dark tea-colored water. At the occasional small shoal the water plunged into a pool that foamed then darkened to black-green under the thick foliage. This stream pulled him, and the trail that followed alongside it seemed to share its current, keeping his feet in motion. He could no more stop his forward progress than he could expect this water to cease its flow. He moved quietly, and the forest opened to him as all forests had.

The sun was low on the horizon when a bend in the creek stole his momentum. A shoal whispered upstream in the distance. On the outside of the turn a magnificent beech tree stood on a level table of land, its massive trunk flexing like a ghostly muscle, its wide mesh of talon-roots clutching earth and stone and moss and stretching to the water.

He consulted the map and then folded it away and studied the place. He had seen it before in a photograph—his mother's hair lifting in the wind like dark pennants. He put a hand on the smooth gray bark of the tree. It was like stone. Two decades had barely thickened its trunk. He looked down at his feet and wondered how many others of this world had ever sought out the very place of their conception.

There by the stream he set the bow against the tree and slipped out of his pack. The birds sang to the end of day, and the damp air of twilight sharpened the scents of the forest until he thought he could taste this England. He knelt and from his pack took out the old burnished horn. Standing, he looked around as if giving notice to the trees.

Raising the horn to his lips, he closed his eyes and filled his chest with the sweet forest air. With the full force of his lungs he blew, and the note poured out lucid and effortless, first rising then falling, but scattering in every direction to herald his coming to this place.

He pulled the mouthpiece an inch from his tingling lips and listened to the wake of the call echoing through the valley. Then there was only the sound of water below and his breathing within. He lowered the horn to his side and stood very still, listening. What he expected to hear, he did not know. He only knew to expect.

And so he waited.

The Tale First Told

As the Saxon legend tells it, a renowned bowman named Robert Fitz-hugh or Fitzooth came to the aid of Much, the miller's son, who had slain one of the King's deer. Through this misadventure, Robert was outlawed and burned out of his estate at Huntingdon, forcing him to flee to the forests to live by his wits in the greenwood. In time, others of similar plight joined him to form a band of compatriots resisting the tyranny invoked by Prince John in the absence of King Richard the Lionheart, who was abroad fighting in the crusades. Prince John's cat's paw was the cruel Sir Guy of Gisborne, who vowed to rid the land of these outlaws.

Among these outcasts were: John Naylor, commonly called "Little John;" Will Scathlock, who took the alias of "Scarlet;" Alan a Dale, the minstrel who chronicled the outlaws' deeds; and Friar Tuck, a man of the cloth and boundless appetite. Many folktales developed about these men as they wreaked havoc upon the Sheriff's forces at Nottingham castle. But the oppressed common folk, Saxon and Norman alike, applauded the deeds of Robert o' Sherwood and his comrades. Even the landed gentry still loyal to Richard secretly allied with these rebels. Men like Sir Richard of the Lea recognized in Robert the honor and generosity befitting their mother England, for it was Robert who rescued Sir Richard from an unfair debt.

It was said that Marian Fitzwalter, the fairest maiden who lived inside the walls of Nottingham, loved a woodsman named Robyn and trysted with him at the forest's edge. No one knew this man by sight, for he was always cloaked in hooded cowl. When she disappeared, the town folk believed she had eloped with her Robyn, traveling to a distant land.

The Lionheart returned and defeated the corrupt prince with the help of the loyal Englishmen who had awaited him. Among these legendary archers were Robert, or Robyn, all his true companions of the greenwood, and his Marian.

Much of the story is not true. But as with all legends it began with more than a seed of truth. And there were many other heroes whose names we shall never know, their deeds heaped into the melting pot of folklore surrounding Robert o' Sherwood. But they did live, made of flesh, blood, and bone. And they lived by a code of loyalty forged in the shadows of Sherwood. So strong was this code that, it was said, so long as there be the need for such a man, there will always live in the greenwood a Robyn of the Hood.

About the Author

Mark Warren lives in the Appalachian Mountains of north Georgia, where he teaches archery and the survival skills of the Cherokee at his wilderness school, Medicine Bow. In 1999 he won the World Longbow Championship.

Coming 2023!

AWARD-WINNING AUTHOR
MARK WARREN

MOON OF THE WHITE TEARS

This modern-day, comic farce follows the convoluted paths of an ensemble cast of characters, who coincidentally converge on a small mountain town in north Georgia. There, in historic Lumpkin County, where gold was discovered more than a century and a half ago, a part-Cherokee curmudgeon named Hoke Limberlost has undertaken a mission to right the wrongs of the white man's blight on the once pristine land.

After a series of bold vandalisms in midnight forays, the old warrior enlists the unlikely help of a restaurant waitress, an aspiring barroom bouncer and his nonpareil mentor, an equestrian teacher, and a clairvoyant. As the reader follows the entwining lives of each player in the story, the past history of the characters are revealed in flashbacks to show the origins of their flaws and ambitions, which are destined to dictate their adult personalities....

**For more information
visit: www.SpeakingVolumes.us**

Coming 2023!

AWARD-WINNING AUTHOR
MARK WARREN

INDIGO HEAVEN

After the blood and gore of the War Between the States, young Clayton Jane journeys from Georgia to the Wyoming Territory to trade his battle-hardened soul for a measure of grace. Working his way to ranch foreman for an English cattle baron, Clayt believes he may have found redemption in his relationship with the land and with the crew that works beside him.

When a Pinkerton detective arrives in the Laramie Plain to probe into a conspiracy with roots that trace back to the war, Clayt's life begins to unravel. The people of Laramie had learned to trust him, but now their loyalties prove to be fickle.

Could this ex-confederate cowhand be plotting to assassinate President Grant during the general's whistle-stop campaign tour? Can a man truly change from the ruthless killer he had been?

**For more information
visit:** www.SpeakingVolumes.us

Now Available!

AWARD WINNING AUTHOR
MARK WARREN

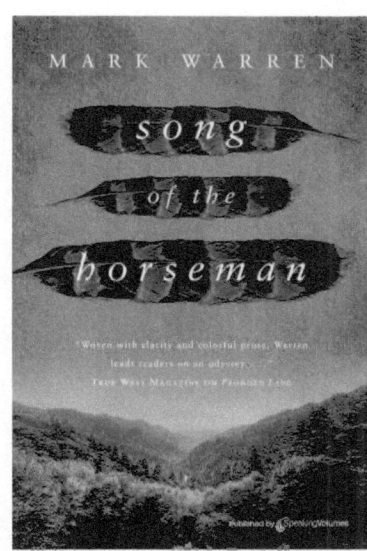 

For more information
visit: www.SpeakingVolumes.us

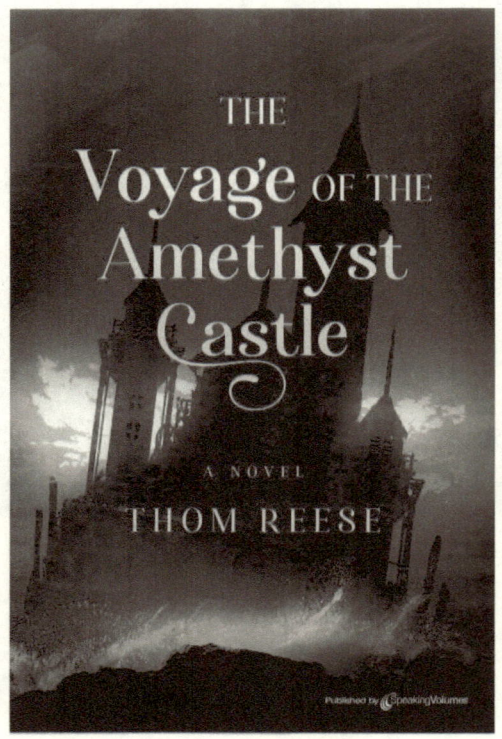

www.ingramcontent.com/pod-product-compliance
Lightning Source LLC
Chambersburg PA
CBHW020551120726
47903CB00001B/221

* 9 7 8 1 6 4 5 4 0 8 3 6 9 *